THE TOR TRILOGY

THE TOR TRILOGY

The KING SWORD

MICAH I. COOLEY

TATE PUBLISHING
AND ENTERPRISES, LLC

The Tor Trilogy
Copyright © 2014 by Micah I. Cooley. All rights reserved.

No part of this publication may be reproduced, stored in a retrieval system or transmitted in any way by any means, electronic, mechanical, photocopy, recording or otherwise without the prior permission of the author except as provided by USA copyright law.

The opinions expressed by the author are not necessarily those of Tate Publishing, LLC.

This novel is a work of fiction. Names, descriptions, entities, and incidents included in the story are products of the author's imagination. Any resemblance to actual persons, events, and entities is entirely coincidental.

Published by Tate Publishing & Enterprises, LLC
127 E. Trade Center Terrace | Mustang, Oklahoma 73064 USA
1.888.361.9473 | www.tatepublishing.com

Tate Publishing is committed to excellence in the publishing industry. The company reflects the philosophy established by the founders, based on Psalm 68:11,
"The Lord gave the word and great was the company of those who published it."

Book design copyright © 2014 by Tate Publishing, LLC. All rights reserved.
Cover design by Rtor Maghuyop
Interior design by Manolito Bastasa

Published in the United States of America
ISBN: 978-1-63122-786-8
1. Fiction / Fantasy / General
2. Fiction / Fantasy / Epic
14.03.24

To you, Mom,
for your unending encouragement, patience, and sacrifice
in this book and in my life.
I am eternally grateful to the Highest King for you!

Acknowledgments

Prologue

A somber quiet held the moonlit kingdom in a heavy embrace. Small huts and farms speckled the countryside, resting silent and dark. Only a few windows still glowed from the warm hearths within. The starry hosts blinked down on them in an amazing display, illuminating a silvery white through the scattered black clouds, with the crescent moon to govern them.

A lone figure stood on the high parapet, leaning with both hands on the stone rails, gazing across the land that had always been his home. The coolness of the night air was reviving, and he welcomed the gentle breeze against his face with a deep sigh. Lifting his eyes to the vast heavens, he whispered softly, "Father, the time is at hand. I pray you have found my life faithful to you. I have done that which I believed to be right."

He paused and dropped his head, holding back a sudden surge of agony that welled up inside him. "Whatever happens tonight, protect my family, Lord." He was overcome and dropped his face into the consoling of his right hand.

Then a gentle voice spoke behind him; one he knew well. "Sire, it has begun."

The king stood erect and turned to face the man. He could see the outline of the newcomer's robes and dark form, but his features were hidden in the shadows.

"You must go now before it is too late. Protect them, my friend; get them far away from here," the king said.

"I will leave at once," came the quieted reply, and the man began to turn.

King Valdithin's eyes went to the floor for a brief moment before glancing back up. "I hope to see you again one day."

The other stopped, glanced back around, and strode toward the king. "We will see each other again, Valdithin. That is a certain thing, for there is a better life that awaits us should our earthly path end. And it will be the greatest adventure of all." He halted before Valdithin and extended a hand. "Farewell, dear friend."

Valdithin gripped the forearm of his longtime comrade. "Good-bye, brother."

The older man turned to go, bowing slightly before another who was just entering, "My lady, we must go. We can linger here no longer."

King Valdithin saw the woman and grew stern. "Riona. What are you doing here? You must leave at once." His wife brushed past the older man and strode swiftly toward him, leaving the shadows of the arched doorway. The moonlight hit her face. Her features were fair and her skin was pale. Her hair was dark as the night itself and rested in delicate tresses on her slender shoulders. She wore a long green gown that matched her deep-green eyes.

Reaching the king, she gripped him by the arms and spoke softly, "You must come with us."

"My love, you know I cannot." He returned, putting a gentle hand to her cheek.

"Then I will stay with you. You cannot make me leave."

"You must not stay, Riona. Go with the children. Teach them to follow the Highest of Kings. Tell them of me if I do not find you."

"You will die here." Her voice broke, and she buried her face in his shoulder, allowing silent sobs to shake her shoulders.

"That is not for us to decide. It may turn out all right in the end." He spoke to encourage her, but his voice showed little conviction. Riona said nothing, and Valdithin embraced her and kissed her lightly on the forehead.

"Farewell, Riona."

She regained her former composure and looked him in the eyes. The king thought his heart would burst within him. He felt his strength waning. How he wanted to go with them. There was nothing in the world he wanted more. His wife took a step back, still holding his gaze. *Was it all worth it,* he wondered?

Just then Riona gave him a smile, however weak it was. He suddenly felt courage flow back into him. He tried to return a smile, succeeding for the most part. She continued to back up until reaching the door. The older man took her arm to hurry her along.

"Farewell, my love." Her words embraced him as their eyes held for the last time.

The king watched them disappear and then looked once more at the dark countryside.

A gentle gust of familiar wind brushed through his blond hair. The aroma it bore was one that brought him back to his childhood. He hadn't any cares then. He recalled how he had wanted to grow, to be able to do things he couldn't do yet. His father had told him, "Enjoy these short days while they last, son. For the life of a king is not so free as you imagine. A king serves the people, not the other way around. A king will give his life for his people."

He inhaled deeply and closed his eyes, remembering that day. But now the time had come. Valdithin took up his sword from the richly embroidered chest and strapped it to his hip. It was beautifully crafted. The King Sword was what it was called, and it was used as the symbol of authority and kingship in Arinon. The blade was forged in the north from an unknown metal not found in Arinon. Its color was more white than silver.

Leaving his chambers, he descended a staircase that spiraled down. Reaching the bottom, he paused before the door to the great hall. Beyond that door he could hear the din of raised voices. His heart grew heavy in his chest, resounding in his ears as a war drum.

Micah I. Cooley

A familiar verse ran through his head: "At the changing of times and seasons, with kings removed and kings set up." Were the words of the ancient prophecy to come about tonight?

"God give me strength," he murmured as he pulled the door open. The sound of hundreds of voices hit against him like a wave as he stepped into the great hall. At his appearing, the noisy clamor only increased in volume.

The king gave little heed to the angry shouts as he ascended the steps leading up to the dais where the nobles were all assembled. The first one met him with an expression of gravity. Valdithin knew the situation was very bad.

He clapped a fist to his chest and said, "I stand with you, my king." The man had to speak in a raised voice so that he could be heard.

King Valdithin's lips allowed a smile, but his eyes did not share in it. He set a hand on the shoulder of his nobleman and friend. Lord Ao-idh inclined his head. Valdithin glanced at the other lords and saw Percel. He was surveying the crowd with a guise of satisfaction. Then his eyes found the king's. Was it mockery in his gaze? Valdithin returned the gaze firmly before turning to face the crowd of people. After a brief scan of the faces there was one that stood out from the rest: a black-haired man possessing rather pale skin. An ugly scar traced a jagged line from the corner of his mouth down to his thin jaw. It deformed and manipulated the man's wicked grin. Valdithin knew who he was and why he was here. This man was the cause, the reason this moment had come.

"You have not won yet." Valdithin whispered under his breath, though the other man's eyes were full of victorious gloating.

Their gaze held.

At that moment, Lord Taromar stepped forth and silenced the crowd by raising his hands. "You all know why we are gathered here," he stated. "And now, behold, the evidence that was promised!"

Valdithin watched his friend betray him in silence. Taromar had played a convincing lie of loyalty. The nobleman pulled out the old leather manuscript on which was written Valdithin's ruin. A ruckus erupted from the crowd once more.

The king glanced to where Percel stood smiling with malicious satisfaction. In that moment, Valdithin strode forward, gripping the handle of the King Sword. He had the object that would wipe away all of their lies and false claims.

The noise faded as all eyes turned to the tall, fair-haired king. Valdithin unsheathed the King Sword and held it high above his head. The blade burned in the torchlight as though it held an inner flame.

Suddenly Valdithin felt his shoulder jerk back as something slammed into him. The dark shaft of an arrow protruded halfway out of his right shoulder, and his arm instantly lost all strength. The huge, vaulted room flew into panic and chaos as he felt himself being pulled back by strong hands.

One

The dulled clang of steel on wood echoed once in the glen and then died as the knife dropped to the leafy ground. The visible look of frustration on the boy's face, which had been mounting with every miss, let out in an aggravated cry.

"That was the seventh throw without a stick, Ao-idh!" Myran yelled angrily. "I did everything you said and still it falls!"

Ao-idh laughed to himself as he arose from the log he always sat on to write or watch his two young students practice their newfound skills. He walked the short dirt path to the training glen where the two lads waited, casting a slow glance about him. The familiar trees bore young leaves, green from the spring rains and glowing brightly in the afternoon sun above them.

The three of them lived deep in the forest of Durn, or Durnwood, where no folk usually ventured. The layout of their camp consisted of two clearings connected by a short path. One was larger, the training glen, and the other was quite small with a fire ring and two small structures. One hut was built for storing supplies and another for sleeping in when it rained or snowed. In the warm days of summer they would sleep under the stars by the fire.

A lazy stream ran along the edge of their camp and was deep enough to support some well-sized fish. It flowed for a short distance away from the camp and eventually fell over a rocky ledge in a long, cascading plummet. From where it first came out of the trees into the glen, and all surrounding their site, grew brush that was so thick with thorny briars it was almost impenetrable. This provided an excellent defensive shield for them.

Ao-idh had spent almost twenty years in the greenwood, and he was the only living resistance left against Gurn and his troops. Since the mysterious death of king Valdithin, the kingdom had plunged into despair. The king's heir had vanished and was said to be dead.

The throne fell into Gurn's hands, though many believed it was obtained by treachery. Most of the counsel of nobles swore allegiance to him, and those who did not were branded as traitors. Many of them were murdered. Ao-idh and his good friend Ethrian, nobles of Arinon, did what was in their power to stop Gurn's evil deeds through political means. But that ended when Gurn's new militia, called the Merdi, killed Ethrian in an ambush and left Ao-idh for dead. The Merdi were no more than thugs given the power to do what they wanted around the kingdom.

They had been passing through the back streets of the town of Lundel when it happened. Ao-idh and Ethrian were surrounded in a small alleyway and cut down. Ao-idh received several minor injuries and was knocked unconscious. The Merdi left, thinking him dead.

Ao-idh was driven to the forest in hiding. He did what little he could to stop the pillaging of the Merdi and defend the good people of Arinon, but he was only one man.

One hot summer night he came upon a band of Merdi encamped in the western side of Durnwood. They had pillaged a merchant's home that Ao-idh knew well. He was a good man and was away in the neighboring kingdom of Caledon for the summer.

He created a plan to send them running in a frightened panic. Using his trained knowledge of woodland vegetation, he gathered and ground up a mixture of plants and fungus that were highly flammable. Ao-idh mixed them and tied them in a small pouch to the end of an arrow. Firing it into the Merdi fire created an explosion of smoke, flame, and sparks as the concoction met the blaze. Then, with a ram's horn, he filled the woods with unearthly screams and blasts. The plan worked well and the Merdi fled into the night.

He pursued the band westward into the old forest, a place very few had the courage to enter. It was the subject of many haunting and frightful stories. The Merdi, disoriented in the darkness of the night, obviously had no idea where they had ventured. Deep and foreboding, its dark, drooping trees were blanketed by thick, heavy moss. Most places were so dense that the sun had not touched them for centuries. This forest pressed against the shore of the western sea.

However, it was not the enemy that Ao-idh found that day, but of all things, a child. He stumbled upon the toddler at the base of a black, twisted tree. The small boy lay face down upon a bed of dirty moss and did not stir. Forgetting the Merdi, Ao-idh gently turned the child over to get a better look and to see if he was alive.

The boy's face was filthy and his clothes torn. A bloodstain of deep crimson marked his left forearm, but he was still breathing. Ao-idh scooped him up and made haste for his hideout.

He named the boy Myran and, since no one in the nearby villages or farms knew anything about him, raised him there in the forest.

Myran was a good lad and a willing learner. He excelled in his weaponry lessons, but there was no mistaking he had a natural talent for the sword. He was tall and stocky in build, and his dark-blond hair accented his uniquely colored eyes. Ao-idh would never forget when the lad first opened them. They were brown but more of a gold brown; a dull amber color similar to bronze.

Ao-idh had always appreciated his good nature. Myran did what was required of him and did it well. When a mistake was made, Ao-idh could tell that it bothered the lad a good deal. There were times, perhaps too often, when it caused him great frustration. As Ao-idh strode into the training glen, he knew this was one of those times.

He stuck his thumbs behind his belt as he approached Myran who was speaking to Ao-idh's other student, Caed. Caed was laughing at Myran, trying to irritate him. He was a sharp learner as well. Nearly as tall as Myran, he was lanky and darker featured. He loved to tease and was indulging in it now.

Caed was the son of an impoverished noble who had lost everything—lands, title, and castle—in a duel. He had been mortally wounded in the fight and did not live long afterward. Just before this happened, as a boy of eight summers, he also lost his mother to a swift and mysterious illness. Caed was forced to fend for himself and survive on his own. He was close to starvation when Ao-idh found him half frozen in the streets of Lundel. Ao-idh took pity on the lad and brought Caed to the greenwood to live with him.

A summer and winter had passed, and Caed and Myran became fast friends. The two boys were roughly the same age, as far as Ao-idh could tell, for he did not know for sure how old Myran was.

Caed and Myran turned to their teacher as he approached. Myran was the first to speak, while Caed only laughed. "I have been standing in the same spot and throwing with the same speed and draw every time. What can I possibly be doing wrong?"

"Throw once more and let me see." Ao-idh's reply was unsympathetic. He stood off to the side and crossed his arms.

Myran found his distance mark and positioned himself as he was taught. He slowly pulled back his blade and hesitated only a moment before sending it toward the stump. The familiar reverberation of a wrong hit filled their ears. Myran turned to

Ao-idh with an expression of utter defeat. Ao-idh remained still for several moments before speaking, looking toward the dead tree stump.

Caed stood grinning at Myran who would not look back to further his revelry. The rustle of the wind in the leaves and the cry of a distant crow was the only sound for a moment as Ao-idh watched the target.

"If someone has a mark or a goal they want to achieve, they must walk the path to get them there." Ao-idh finally cracked the silence of the glen. "But if they are going to arrive at that goal and complete it with satisfaction, they not only must walk the path but walk it straight. Even a slight swerve can cause them to lose it. The deception is great indeed, and few are they who can see their way through it."

He drew his knife and slowly wiped the polished blade with his fingertips. He looked up at the two in front of him. It was clear that they did not see what he was getting at.

"When pulling your knife back"—he began to reveal the answer to the riddle—"the blade must be kept straight, and in the follow-through as well so that the blade can cut the air. If allowed to tilt"—he twisted his knife back and forth for emphasis—"the wind would take it easier off course."

With that he suddenly pulled his knife back behind his broad shoulder and sent it swiftly toward the target. The silver blade sang as it spun, masterfully cutting through the air. Its razor tip sank deep into the center, acknowledged by a hollow thump that was completely different than that of Myran's hit.

"Remember to point your arm instead of bringing it all the way down, and have confidence when you throw."

Ao-idh watched as Myran retrieved his knife and made ready for another throw. He followed directions perfectly, and the dagger stuck fast in the wood. The exuberant look on the lad's face was clearly visible to Ao-idh as he laughed and thumped Myran on the back with a strong hand.

"Now practice this until you both can stick ten without missing."

The two remained at their task for the remainder of the afternoon.

The seasons flew past as Myran and Caed practiced and began to master everything they were taught. Ao-idh showed them how to track game and read the signs of the forest that were invisible to the untrained eye. He taught them how to recognize and age a trail, and also decipher its traveler. Caed and Myran learned which forest plants were edible, which herbs were beneficial for healing, and those to stay away from. They were shown how to walk the woods silently and how to disappear from sight.

Soon they were old enough and had gained enough skill to embark upon a raid with Ao-idh against the Merdi. Their first fight was one that Myran would always remember.

The three had slowly surrounded a band of eleven or so through the forest brush unseen. The Merdi were looking over the plunder they had taken from a nearby farmstead, laughing loudly. Myran and Caed waited for Ao-idh's command. Myran saw him emerge slowly from the cover of a cropping of close trees. He moved so silently toward the group of unwary men, a sword in his left hand and a staff in the other.

"Greetings. By whose authority do you take what is not yours from those who cannot afford to lose them?" His voice shocked the band of thieves, and they instantaneously drew their swords and axes.

A gruff man, overly large in size, with a blackened left eye spoke for the rest. "These things belong to us by right of law!" His voice was boisterous and defiant. "Leave now before we declare you an enemy of his majesty, King Gurn!"

Ao-idh responded tersely, "The law of which you speak is a law of thieves and cowards. And I am an enemy to all who are against the Greatest King. Now"—he pointed the tip of his sword at the big man—"leave these things you have stolen as well as Gurn's services."

The men burst out in laughter. The big man snorted, "Fool! Now you must face the penalty for crossing the Merdi!" He let loose a battle whoop and, with sword raised, rushed at Ao-idh. The rest of the band followed.

Ao-idh swiftly lofted his stave and let it fly. The sturdy shaft struck the closest Merdi in the chest with a crack and bounced off. The man fell with a breathless grunt.

"Now!" Ao-idh yelled.

Myran and Caed, adrenaline pumping, rushed out from their positions and charged the rear of the enemy. The Merdi were startled at this and several turned to engage them as Ao-idh fell into heavy combat with the rest.

Myran ducked below the first swing and brought the pommel of his sword up into his enemy's ribs. The next foeman met him with a chop to the side, but Myran averted the blade and kicked the man's chest. Another Merdi engaged him making several quick jabs and slices. The flat part of the blade struck Myran on the left side of his forehead.

Myran backed up swiftly as a quick rage surfaced. His assailant pressed forward, certain of victory. Myran parried two more cuts. His counterstrike was blocked and he received a blow to the face, losing his sword.

Now standing weaponless against his opponent, Myran paused. He jumped back twice, avoiding two quick slices, and then ducked beneath a swing intended for his head. Without hesitating, he dove into the torso of the man. Myran was on top of him and delivered two quick punches to the face. Then he rolled off and snatched up his sword once more.

Ao-idh moved through his assailants quickly and masterfully. His arm was quick and his mind quicker still. The blade in his hand seemed weightless in his powerful grip. As one man sliced down over his head, Ao-idh parried and then, moving quickly forward, elbowed him in the jaw. The unfortunate sprawled backward with a yelp.

Caed took on two attackers with skill and accuracy as well. He was quick and dodged in and out around his opponents. When once he was at the right of his foe, the very next moment he was on the left. One Merdi attempted a mad and desperate swing to catch this quick young man. Throwing all his strength into it, with a cry of frustration, he struck air and the momentum spun him about. Caed was at his back in a flash and cut the straps that held up the man's trousers.

As they slid down around his ankles, Caed put his boot on the man's backside and gave him a sturdy shove. The man hit the dirty forest floor on his face. The next opponent flew at Caed with abandon, but Caed hopped back, and the man tripped over Caed's firmly planted leg.

The agitated man rose and lashed out repeatedly. At last he was successful in breaking Caed's defense. His balled fist struck Caed's cheek. He then brought up his foot and kicked Caed against a tree.

He thrust with his sword, and Caed barely knocked it aside. Caed's fist connected with his opponent's nose and the man fell away.

The fight was soon ended. The Merdi, beaten and humiliated, ran from the forest like the cowards they were. The large man with the blackened left eye knelt before Ao-idh. He had been wounded when Ao-idh's blade had grazed his shoulder.

Ao-idh stood over him and charged strictly, "You will go back to your master, Gurn, and tell him of what has happened today. I advise you to leave his services for good, for the next time we meet in combat"—Ao-idh leaned closer with a lower tone—"you may not escape with your life."

Two

They brought the stolen goods back to the farmer who, thinking them to be Merdi, met them with angry threats from his door. But when they drew near, he realized they had come to return what had been taken from him. He was a strong man of average height, with flat features and a hoarse voice. His name was Aethelbeorn, but all who knew him called him Beorn.

His wife, Rhia, was a small but strong and hardy woman. Her brown hair had faded mostly to gray, and her face was freckled. She chastised her husband for his rudeness and welcomed them to stay for a meal.

"You were the one who told me to run 'em off the place when they was comin' up the road," the farmer defended himself. She was silent then but delivered him an unpleasant look.

Rhia cooked up a pot of beef stew and warm, brown bread. As they ate, Beorn told them of the Merdi raid on their house.

"I was out attendin' to the cattle when I noticed 'em stridin' in tord the house. I knew right off they was Merdi." Beorn's raspy voice cracked slightly as he unfolded his tale. He itched his gray stubble chin as he continued. "I knew they was up to nothin' good so I ran as fast as I could to the house, havin' no weapon but mi'staff. When I reached the front door, they was already rummagin' through the place, takin' whatever they fancied and breakin' most everything they didn't." He paused and glanced at his wife.

"Rhia had delivered a nice blow to a big fella, who then ordered her tied to a post in the other room. I ran in and yelled at 'em to get out, but they laughed and shoved me aside. That's when I began beatin' 'em with mi'staff. I am not a man quick to anger, milord, but I have a right to defend my property and family."

"Of course," Ao-idh spoke up as he lifted his mug toward his lips. "I would have been surprised had you not fought back."

"Well fight I did, and I'll say they received some well-placed bruises. However, nine are far too many for me to take on, so I was overpowered, and that's how I got this here crack on mi'skull. I woke after they was long gone." He raised his pewter mug to his lips and took a gulp, all the while frowning in disgust at his story.

"Things have grown dim these past years," Ao-idh remarked.

"Aye they have, milord," Beorn agreed. His manner seemed to become a bit more reserved.

They talked for some time over stew and ale. Ao-idh finally rose and said, "We must be off. Thank you, Mrs. Rhia, for that very delightful meal and for your hospitality in allowing us to dine in your home." He bowed formally at the waist.

"It is I who should be thankin' ye, milord Ao-idh, for returning our things. Ye will always be most welcome here," she returned in a gracious tone, much impressed by Ao-idh's polite compliments and manners. "And both of ye as well." She addressed Myran and Caed with a kind smile. "We very much appreciate what ye have done."

"Aye, ye've done a great service this day," her husband concurred. "If I can ever repay it just say the word." Beorn stood and shook each hand firmly. When he reached Ao-idh, his tone suddenly changed and he said in a sober voice, "I was never for it. Ye must understand, milord. I didn't want it to happen."

Myran and Caed looked at him quizzically, but Ao-idh said, "I do not believe you were, Beorn. You are a good man…one of the few."

An expression of relief came over Beorn's face. He smiled and shook Ao-idh's hand more firmly.

As the three left the farmstead, all were in good spirits. They walked lightly in the direction of the forest. The sun was nearly touching the western horizon and cast a golden wash over the green country. A warm wind swept through the grass at their feet and rustled their clothes.

"Why would they address you as milord, Ao-idh?" Myran wondered out loud. The matter had puzzled him since hearing it.

Ao-idh walked in silence for several more strides and half squinted in the light of the dying sun. "I was a lord. When Valdithin was king I was one of his nobles. I governed this region and lived in Erindril Keep."

Myran had never heard this before. They continued in quiet once again.

Soon Caed could not contain himself any longer and said, "We have done a very good deed today. Tonight I will rest with the satisfaction of knowing what I have done."

Ao-idh looked straight ahead without a word for some time. Myran knew that something about what Caed said bothered him.

Soon Ao-idh spoke with a serious voice, "The glory of this victory does not belong to us, Caed. To claim a victory belonging to another is not right."

Caed gave him a look of confusion. "But we are the ones who defeated the Merdi and delivered what was stolen. How is the success not ours?"

"Yes, we won against the Merdi band and returned what they took, but without the guiding hand of the Highest King, we might have been the ones defeated. We must give the credit to where it is due, and it belongs to him…always."

"Of course." Caed conceded almost angrily, his head downcast.

Ao-idh looked at the sullen young man, smiling encouragingly. He clapped a hand to Caed's shoulder. "Rejoice in the victory, but give the glory to he who gave it."

Caed smiled forcibly and remained silent the rest of the way. Myran too was quiet and pondered his teacher's words thoughtfully.

They reached their humble woodland dwelling when the moon shone bright in mid-sky, and the stars blinked and reflected its glow to brighten the night.

That evening, as they were resting about a crackling fire, Ao-idh recounted to them the tale of The Seven. It was the story of seven friends, as close as brothers, who saved the kingdom of Lloches Ynry from a terrible beast. Lloches Ynry was a hidden realm long ago in a forgotten land across the sea. The seven fought in a line, and by aiding each other side-by-side, they could not be overcome. They were heroes of highest renown. Of all the old tales, this was Myran and Caed's favorite.

When they let the fire burn down for the night, sleep evaded Myran for some time. He lay awake watching the branching arms of the trees waving gently in the night breeze. He had done the same as Caed in his heart.

While staring up into the unfathomable depths of the heavens, he spoke in his heart, *Forgive me, Lord. You do deserve the glory for this victory. May I never become so deceived and think otherwise.* He felt peacefulness then and closed his eyes and slept.

The three made many friends among the townsfolk and farmers as they continued on through the summer, fighting the Merdi thugs wherever they found them. Myran and Caed learned many things, most importantly lessons in honor and justice. They were taught to love the truth of the Highest King. His truth, Ao-idh told them, would guard them from falling into the snare of deception.

Ao-idh saw that Myran took to heart all that he was taught. Caed always listened, although slightly disinterested. He pursued his fighting skills with more dedication than anything else.

The night was silent indeed. Far out across the landscape, small lights flickered inside huts and farms. There were not nearly as many as when Valdithin ruled. Folk were happier then. But now he was king. Yet the control that he inflicted upon the people of Arinon seemed to be diminishing. Gurn knew that with Ao-idh facing up to his Merdi and humiliating them as he did, the people would begin to have hope and entertain thoughts of rebellion.

He stood gazing out from his dark quarters, a chilling breeze blowing in through the open window. *Something must be done about Ao-idh*, Gurn thought to himself. When Valdithin was alive, Gurn and Ao-idh were fellow nobles. But Gurn had never liked Ao-idh and was always jealous of his close fellowship to the king.

Then there came a window of opportunity for him. Gurn recalled the night of King Valdithin's death. He was surprised at how easily things fell into place for him. It had not been difficult to get the majority of people to ally themselves to him and set him on the throne. The people were easily persuaded with gifts and the promise of more in the future.

Now, discovering the kind of ruler that Gurn was, they were becoming unsettled and resistant. The good life promised them was never realized, but there was nothing they could do. Their weapons had been confiscated long ago, and the Merdi could not be stopped.

Gurn fancied himself a more adept ruler than Valdithin ever was and ruled with a heavy hand. After all, the people were always going to be unsettled, and there was only one way to deal with it. To force obedience, you must use strict and unrelenting discipline.

A handful of nobles had not accepted him as the next king. They had done all in their power to keep him from the throne. Even Gurn's brother, his own flesh and blood, had been against him. But Gurn found effective ways of silencing them. It was easily done and Gurn had replaced the empty nobles' seats, including his brother's, with men who were undoubtedly loyal to him. Only Ao-idh now remained to resist his authority, and try as he might, Gurn was unsuccessful in disposing of him.

Learning that Ao-idh was training young warriors to fight against him was a thought that he didn't like to entertain. Soon Ao-idh could have a sizeable force and, since he had been Valdithin's most skilled knight, they would become much more than a thorn in his side.

The news Gundoc, the leader of his Merdi, brought of the attack in the forest enraged him greatly. Ao-idh was becoming an arrogant windbag. He must die, along with his little warriors who followed him. It now seemed to Gurn that his Merdi were becoming incompetent and losing their fear factor.

"There were only three of them?" Gurn had raged at the man. "And yet you fools let them make a mockery of you!"

Gundoc remained silent. Gurn was seething. "Do you not understand that I am the one mocked when my men are treated so? If you value your life you will not allow this humiliation again!"

The door of Gurn's room creaked open, bringing him back to the present, and the humbled voice of one of his pages drifted to him. "My lord." It sounded weak and afraid, something he relished hearing from his subjects. "He is here, my lord."

A faint smile parted Gurn's lips. Now at last he had his tool to uproot any last vestiges of opposition. Once this was done, there would be nothing to resist his power.

Three

A bright summer sun beamed down upon Arinon's green realm. Large clouds swelled like the sails of a huge ship; they drifted lazily on the wind's current toward the eastern horizon. In the western sky the clouds darkened in a slow-approaching thunderstorm.

It was a warm afternoon and the forest granted welcome shade to travelers. In the high-up branches of oak, hornbeam, and chestnut, a happy chorus of birds lightened the day with their song.

Two figures rested amidst the mossy roots of an ancient oak that coiled up from the soft earth in entangled knots and loops. The older of the two lay still, eyes closed as though asleep, while the other stared up through the waving branches of the forest that shaded them so perfectly from the heat of the afternoon sun. A sigh of contentment escaped his lungs and the older one stirred.

"Caed hasn't returned?" Ao-idh opened his rested eyes and looked Myran's way.

"He's been gone all afternoon; I expect he will be back soon." Myran did not take his gaze off the pieces of bright-blue sky that danced and moved with the tree branches. How he loved that place. The peaceful solitude of the deep forest, away from the bustle of large towns and crowds, was something that Myran told himself he would never give up. He would live here his whole life with his two friends and not grow tired of it.

"I have been meaning to talk to you about Caed." Ao-idh sat up and brushed the dirt from his green shirt. "I fear for him, Myran."

Myran looked over at Ao-idh. "You don't think he was ambushed, do you? He has been gone a long while. Perhaps we should look for him."

"No, it is not physical danger of which I speak, Myran. Caed has grown arrogant and does not take my lessons of truth to heart. You spend more time with him than I. Have you noticed it?"

"He is a little arrogant," Myran admitted with a shrug. "But that's just Caed. He has always been that way." He snapped off a twig from a low-hanging branch and tossed it toward another tree several strides away.

Ao-idh's hard eyes glanced down at the leaf he was twisting in his fingers as he gathered his thoughts. "With arrogance is self-love, and this leads to blindness. I fear he will not hold out against the deception when it comes. The bitterness of losing his father and mother still has a strong hold on his heart. Caed hides his anger well, but I have seen him when he thinks he is alone." Ao-idh looked sadly at Myran. "The root of bitterness is like poison. I pray Caed is not consumed by it. Maybe you can speak to him."

Myran nodded and looked down at the forest floor. An earthworm was just disappearing into the rich, damp soil, and a wolf spider darted from cover to cover. The larks' song rose high, and the scent of the woodland plants filled the air with its intoxicating aroma.

"The deception is great in this land." Ao-idh sighed as he leaned back again, looking up at the swaying treetops. His aged but sharp eyes searched the oak boughs as though they could see the fearful shadow of deception creeping up on them. "And I fear it is only getting darker. There are few who can see through its subtle ways now, no matter how blatant things have become. Even those touted as wise can fall prey if they do not have the foundation." He looked at Myran; the young man returned his gaze.

"Always remember that only the light of truth can penetrate the dark lies of the Deceiver, Myran. There is no amount of earthly wisdom that can save you from it. I can only tell you of this weapon against deception, but it is up to you, as it is to every man, to make it your own. You must love the truth…or the darkness will crush you."

The sound of rustling leaves drew away Ao-idh's gaze as Myran stared in contemplation of his words. Caed came through the bushes and took the ash wood bow from his back. He didn't say a word as he walked past them.

Myran looked his way. Caed unstrung the bow and set his quiver down.

"I see the mighty stag has eluded you once again." Myran laughed, but his jest was dulled by what Ao-idh had spoken.

"The stag has escaped, yes, but I have found something bigger. A band of Merdi has just entered the forest with spoils from their most recent theft. They were making camp in the ash grove." Caed strapped his sword to his belt and picked up a short spear.

"What did they steal this time?" Ao-idh began to rise.

"I saw several sacs, I don't know what they contained, and some valuables I recognized from Beorn's house. There could be no more than ten of them."

"Let us go then." Ao-idh retrieved his sword, as did Myran, and they darted from the glen.

The ash grove was a fair distance for those who didn't know the forest, but they could be there in half the time. They knew all the hidden pathways as well as they knew their own names and could get anywhere long before an outsider could.

They moved quickly along a thin path that skirted the side of a steep, mossy hillside and then led into an entangled mess of briars. But the path led on, carving its way through the brambles, coiling and snaking through the trees and into thinner brush.

Soon they could see the ash trees ahead and they slowed their pace, replacing their speed with stealth.

The Merdi band was cooking meat over a healthy blaze and rummaging through the stolen items. Ao-idh, with a series of short, practiced hand motions, told Myran and Caed to surround the camp in the procedure they had practiced so many times before. Myran moved off, crawling on the soft dirt and making sure not to snap a twig or crunch any leaves under his weight.

Large ferns surrounded the clearing that was in the middle of the ash grove. They were tall enough to reach Myran's midsection. He moved easily through them, well hidden from the eyes of the enemy. There were but a handful of them, and Myran had confidence that this fight would be like all the others. The Merdi would receive a good beating and return to Gurn with their tails between their legs.

He finally found the right spot and then looked to see if Caed or Ao-idh were visible from his position. If he could see them, then the enemy might as well. Ao-idh had taught them to watch out for their companions when in battle. They were nowhere in sight, so he eased back on his heels to await Ao-idh's signal.

As he crouched waiting, something caught his attention. He had glanced back behind him when the sun glinted off a silver object, but the flash was only visible for a brief moment. Perhaps it was something the Merdi had dropped on the way in, a stolen trinket of some sort. Whatever it might have been, Myran discarded it and turned his attention back to the Merdi. Still it nagged at him. He couldn't shake the feeling that it was important in some way. But after a short time of running it over in his mind, he forced it aside and looked to see Ao-idh stepping from the underbrush. He addressed the men to offer a chance for mercy before attacking.

Ao-idh did this knowing that nine times out of ten they were not going to accept it. Once or twice before, they did surrender, avoiding another chance to be humiliated as they usually were, and went away leaving the things that they had taken. But today it was not to be so.

A shout rose up from the Merdi and they began to rush at Ao-idh. Myran jumped from cover and charged the rear of the howling group. He dropped one man bearing a rusty sword and a cracked buckler by slapping the back of his knees with the flat of his sword. Caed then followed, dashing in from the right. It proved to be a tough fight. The thugs seemed confident of victory and showed no intentions of retreating.

Caed met one who wielded two short swords, and he lost ground as the man struck quickly and furiously, without relenting. He missed a stroke and was grazed on his upper left arm. He stumbled back two steps holding the spot, but his attacker came at him again swinging high toward his head. Caed parried the strike downward and the man's momentum bent him forward. In a flash, Caed stepped aside and shoved him face first into the trunk of a tree.

Ao-idh had most of them after him but moved about swiftly, keeping them at bay. Many received broken noses and sore lumps and bruises.

Myran fought a man who lunged too far and too hard. He kneed the Merdi in the stomach, grabbed the back collar of the man's shirt and pulled it over his head. Desperately the man fumbled to remove it from his face. Myran stepped aside, and with a mighty swing spanked the struggling man with the flat of his blade.

Then, from behind the fight, a company of fresh Merdi troops charged into the fray. As the first one broke into the grove, Myran saw his shining helmet and suddenly realized this was what he had seen while he was hiding. His heart fell as he realized the grave mistake he had made. It was a trap. Myran felt a rock settle in his stomach.

Ao-idh instantly recognized what was happening and yelled to Myran and Caed, "Fall back!"

They would retreat to the safety of their hideout. It was in a part of the forest where the trees and plants grew too thick to get through, mostly consisting of thorny briars and thick brambles. Only one path led through the entangled mess of underbrush, vines, and trees, and only Ao-idh and his young friends knew it. In fact, Ao-idh was the one who cut it out before he found Myran and after Ethrian had been killed.

The three broke from the attack and ran for the trail on which they had come. Ao-idh brought up the rear and Caed led the way. It seemed as though they would escape with little trouble. The pursuing Merdi were advancing with much difficulty. They were no woodsmen, and the brush and undergrowth was clawing at them and slowing their pace. Myran could hear their curses and angry cries as they fell farther behind. He breathed an easy sigh of relief.

That was when they ran into another company of enemy warriors. This time instead of Merdi they were a part of Gurn's regular army. They were well-armed, fully armored warriors and came swarming out of the surrounding brush.

Caed narrowly escaped losing his head to a foeman's weapon by ducking an instant before the blade carved the air above. He sliced his attacker across the upper leg, and the man hit the ground. Myran rushed up to give aid to his friend and stopped a cut aimed for Caed's ribs. He spun and elbowed his enemy in the nose.

Ao-idh reached them and they fell away, disappearing into the cover of the forest underbrush.

The day had clouded over and the wind carried the scent of impending rain. The treetops began to wave more violently, losing leaves. Although it was much cooler now, sweat poured down Myran's face and stung his eyes. His shirt was soaked and his arms and legs were burning. He ran on behind Ao-idh as they put good distance between them and the enemy.

Then Myran saw a familiar tree marking that they were very near their forest home. At last they had made it. He glanced back but saw nothing of the enemy and relaxed his stride, jogging more easily. He could see the trees thicken up ahead where their hideout entrance was.

They reached the hidden path and paused. The entrance was in the thickness of the scrub brush and was concealed by a large, healthy gooseberry. But before they could enter, the enemy warriors broke from the trees behind them. They were on the three in an instant and the fight ensued once again.

Ao-idh recognized that the main force of the army was against him, and he used it to draw them away so that Caed and Myran could escape. He gave ground step by step, and the way cleared for the younger two.

Caed reached the entrance first. In the confusion of the battle, he ducked in and out of sight, unnoticed by the raging enemy. Myran ran to assist Ao-idh, but Ao-idh stopped him.

"Folach!" Ao-idh yelled as he pressed into the enemy warriors. Myran halted. That word was what they used as a hidden signal meaning 'get away.'

Ao-idh took down three of them, knocking aside their weapons enough to ram into them, and they all, including Ao-idh, toppled to the ground. Myran feinted once from a heavy swing and rammed his sword hilt into his assailant's abdomen. The Merdi fell to his knee and Myran swung his fist into the man's temple.

As the man fell, Myran took his opportunity and rolled into the brush and on to the path. He crawled down the way and then halted, waiting to see if the enemy warriors would discover where he went in. Satisfied they had not, Myran crawled farther down the path and then stopped again to wait for Ao-idh.

Moments went by and the clash of steel suddenly ended. He could hear shouts from the Merdi but could not tell whether they were in triumph or anger. All he knew was that Ao-idh had not come through the entrance yet. Myran gripped his sword firmly and crawled slowly back. His heart was beating like a drum inside his ears and his breathing came heavily.

He hesitated before the entrance, gathering his courage, and then made to lunge back out but was caught in mid motion. Whoever it was who had grabbed him began to drag him for some way before letting go. Myran turned to see Ao-idh's grim face, and he saw right away a large, crimson blood stain on his left shoulder.

Ao-idh was good in the woods, and Myran knew he could move quickly with little noise. He had found some other way onto the hidden path, losing the enemy in the process.

Ao-idh's voice was tired and drawn when he spoke. "We must get to camp."

As they went down the path, they put up brush walls prepared for such a time—to confuse any enemy who came in after them should they have found the way.

A clap of distant thunder reverberated across the land, issuing in the first few droplets of rain. They fell to the earth and landed with tiny, hushed explosions.

It was some time before they reached the end of the tunnel and came out to the clearing. The rain was like a mist now and the thunder was louder and its echo lasted longer.

The forest was void of the activity that had earlier been so prominent; not a bird sang nor did any animal rummage through the under brush and leaves. Ao-idh and Myran stumbled into the clearing wearily and were met by Caed. He was waiting not five paces from the path.

"That was close." His voice carried a shaky edge. "I guess old Beorn won't be getting his things back this time."

Ao-idh was silent and slowly walked away from the two, stopping to squint up at the gray sky and gaze around the place they called home. Myran looked after him and said encouragingly, "Perhaps we will get another chance at it. If we discover where they bring Beorn's things, we can…"

"No," Ao-idh said slowly, almost sadly. "We have to leave this place," he said without turning to them. "The brush walls will slow them down, but it is only a matter of time before they are here."

Ao-idh looked at Caed and said nothing. If his eyes had voices they would have cried out in bitter mourning at the look. Myran thought there was a sorrowful inquiry in Ao-idh's expression. Caed shifted uneasily under Ao-idh's gaze and looked away.

Before any more could be said, they heard heavy footfall and the sound of clinking armor coming up the path. He heard the shouts from the advancing enemy and the sound of sword hacking through the underbrush.

Myran drew his sword again and turned to face the direction they came from. Caed joined him as Ao-idh walked up behind them, clutching his sword with his good hand. Crimson blood mixed with sweat and rainwater rolled down the fingers of his other hand that hung limply at his side.

Myran could not believe the Merdi had found the way in. Never before had they done so. Now that they did, where could he and his friends run? They were trapped.

He heard Ao-idh's low voice behind him. "This fight is different, lads. This time we must fight to kill."

Myran's face was hard. He had never killed a man, nor did he want to. But this fight was different from all the rest. It was their very lives they were defending now.

The first of the enemy broke from the trail and Myran was the first to engage him. He was a big man with a two-handed sword. Myran recognized him instantly as Gundoc, the Merdi leader they had encountered before.

Gundoc parried Myran's attack and knocked him to the ground with a powerful sweep of his left arm. Myran's vision darkened after a bright flash of light, and he hit the wet, muddy earth.

Caed rushed to the fight and Ao-idh drew his knife and threw it into Gundoc's side. The big man bellowed and ripped out the small blade. Rage filled his features as he hurled it back at Ao-idh but with too much force. It flew too far to the right. Gundoc ran at Ao-idh swinging his huge sword about his head in a circle.

Myran recovered and picked himself up. Caed was pushed away from them and cornered against an old oak. Seeing his friend trapped, Myran fought to reach and aid him. Ao-idh was kept at bay by Gundoc's ferocious blows and seemed to be tiring fast because of his wound.

It was then that one of Caed's attackers found an open spot and cut a long gash across his ribs. Caed cried out and stumbled to his knee, a look of shock spreading over his features. Myran yelled and pressed forth with all the strength he could muster. Another Merdi struck Caed in the face with the butt of his ax and Caed fell.

Myran cried out in anger and desperation. He knocked aside an opponent's sword with his own and then cut back across the chest. His enemy fell with a dying cry and Myran moved back. He sprinted to join Ao-idh.

He and Gundoc had battled up the trail from the training glen to where the hut stood. Suddenly Ao-idh's knee buckled and he stumbled beneath Gundoc's heavy strikes. The big man took a step back, a hand pressed to his wounded side. Ao-idh now knelt with his back to the brute as though in defeat. His shoulders lifted up and down as he was struggling for breath.

Myran threw all his strength into running, but he knew he wasn't going to reach him on time. Suddenly Gundoc dropped his sword with a loud cry.

Myran saw Ao-idh's sword protruding from Gundoc's barreled abdomen. Ao-idh still gripped the handle and was facing away from him. He jerked it out, and Gundoc fell and was silent.

Myran reached his friend and collapsed to his knees. He helped Ao-idh to his feet and Ao-idh placed a hand on Myran's shoulder. He saw that Caed was not with them.

"He is..." Myran's voice broke. Ao-idh looked at him and nodded somberly, knowing what he meant.

They stood side by side as two more Merdi began to charge up the path from the training glen. The rain was thundering down and frequent lightning flares lit up the trees.

One man was farther ahead than the other, and Myran clashed swords with him. As their weapons connected, a whistle sang in Myran's ears and a thud came from behind. The sound was followed by a breathless grunt. He spun around to find what he feared. Ao-idh took a halting step backward, a crossbow bolt lodged deep in his chest. Myran was stunned and froze.

The Merdi grabbed him from behind around the neck, lifting up his sword to drive into Myran's skull. But Myran, acting in a blinding rage, elbowed the man in the face and forced his sword backward into his enemy, then shoving him off.

The second one flew at him with a scream. Myran drew out his knife swiftly and blocked his assailant's swing. He brought his sword forward into the man's unprotected chest.

Then Myran grasped Ao-idh and hauled him away. He went into the hut and through a hidden back door. This would buy him some time away from the enemy warriors. Then they struggled to the edge of the glen where the stream ran its course. The flow was swelled and ran swifter.

Ao-idh grabbed his arm and spoke in a choked voice, "You must flee; follow the stream." He lifted a weak finger toward it.

"No!" Myran nearly choked himself as hot tears ran down his cheeks. "I will fight to the end!"

"Go, Myran! If you die here too, there will be no one left to fight for the freedom of Arinon. You must find king Valdithin's heir. Find him..." Ao-idh coughed.

"No! I won't leave you!" Myran tried to stand, but Ao-idh pulled him close with surprising strength and spoke in a commanding but weak voice, "Obey!" He winced and clenched his teeth. His voice softened. "May the Highest King overshadow you...and keep you from the Deceiver." Ao-idh's grip loosened and he lay still, staring upward with cold eyes as the rain beat down upon his face.

Myran lowered his head onto his friend's lifeless chest in bitter grief, but the enemy warriors had made it through the hut and saw him again. He turned and ran as best he could down the cold stream, just evading another deadly crossbow bolt.

The rain was thick now, and the trees' bark had darkened. Several smaller streams had formed, running down the banks and spilling into the larger torrent of the brook.

The Merdi pursued and loosed their crossbow bolts after him. Myran could hear the wicked bolts as they whistled past. But in his misery and anger, he didn't care if one should strike him and take his life. With his only friends dead, life did not matter to him anymore.

Myran reached the falls and stood at the edge not knowing what to do. Another bolt whizzed past and he looked back. Their figures, dim through the rain, were drawing very close, and he had nowhere to go but down. It was a high cascade, but he knew the pool at the bottom to be a deep one with no rocks, for he had swam there many times with Caed.

He drew a deep breath to jump, and something slammed into the back of his leg inflicting a searing pain. His knee buckled and he plummeted over the falls' edge.

Four

It was a brilliant sun that broke forth from below the horizon, spilling glorious light over the waking landscape. A golden haze now fogged the country. An amazing chorus of songbirds welcomed the pure light, each with the song given it. The dew from the preceding night gleamed like glass as the lustrous rays pierced the liquid beads.

Theadrin stirred as the intense light shone through the window and pressed upon his face. He put up his hand to shield his blinking eyes. This morning's ritual he had grown accustomed to. Where he lay, nearly every sunrise would wake him in this fashion.

The sound of footsteps on the wood planking sounded from the hall outside his room, and an instant later it swung wide revealing the familiar face of his younger sister. Her eyes scanned the room in one quick sweep and came to rest on him.

"You haven't gotten out of bed yet?" She was both shocked and aggravated at the same time. Taking a step into the room she put a hand on her hip. "You can't have forgotten what today is, Theadrin."

"Enlighten me." He rubbed his eyes and slumped back on his pillow, showing no intention of getting up yet.

He loved to tease his sister, and it was such an easy thing to do. Since childhood he had reveled in every chance to do just that. But then there were many times he wished he had not. Lianna was a flame not to be toyed with because it could quickly turn into a raging wildfire. He would not forget the time when he had merely joked about her slightly overcooked venison roast when she almost upended the table on him. He never said anything negative about her cooking again.

As much as she was a good cook, she was an even better gardener. Lianna spent every free minute in the garden beside the country house. Theadrin knew no other who could coax a flower from the earth so beautifully as his sister.

Being the older of the two, Theadrin protected and watched over her. There was no one in the world he cared for more.

She was shorter than him by several inches. Her long dark hair fell past her shoulders and her eyes were of the deepest green. These same dark eyes now spoke a warning to Theadrin.

"You are doing it again. If you don't get ready, we will leave you behind." Her tone was threatening and one Theadrin knew all too well. The wildfire had been kindled.

"I have been working hard. Don't I deserve to sleep in a little?" He acted as though he still didn't know what she was talking about, although in truth he knew well. This was his new tactic to irritate her.

"Stop it! We are leaving for the fair now. You can come or stay as you please, but we aren't waiting for you any longer." She stormed out.

Theadrin laughed and threw aside the covers but remained abed. The Spring Fair of Caledon was a huge event that was held once a year for a length of seven days. He had been busy the past few weeks, planting the fields before the rainy season, but no task could make him forget about the fair. It was the biggest, most-looked-forward-to happening of the two kingdoms Caledon and Arinon.

He and Lianna lived with a huntsman and his wife near the town of Faranor but worked on the neighboring farm in the spring to earn extra money.

The previous day he had pushed to get his work finished, and had done so only by working into the late hours of darkness, but the task was done nonetheless. Now the festival and the rest of the summer lay before him.

Hearing the horse-drawn cart being brought to the front of the farmhouse brought Theadrin out of bed with a leap. He was dressed in seconds and running down the stairs.

With the magnificent Aegris mountain range tipped fiery gold and walling the western horizon behind them, they left the farm. The old shire horse walked along at a lagging pace, bobbing its head in rhythm with the beat of its hooves. Theadrin drummed the side of the cart impatiently with his fingers as they ambled along the cobblestone road. He had missed breakfast, and his stomach groaned in anticipation of the delicious foods and goodies that awaited him. He had to put away the image of a large slab of pork, smoked and seasoned to perfection, from his mind.

There was an endless list of things to do. There were games, performances, and shops selling everything from clothing, which he usually skipped, to weapons and armor that lined the dirt streets. There were booths where one could throw knives, axes and spears, even shoot arrows, for prizes.

His personal favorite was the tournaments. Knights and lords from across the kingdom, and often from neighboring Arinon, came to joust and fight in the melee battles. Lianna detested these events. She told Theadrin she didn't see the thrill in watching men beat each other senseless with sticks.

Oh, but it was not just that, Theadrin would argue back. There was skill and strategy involved.

"I guess you would have to be a boy to appreciate such barbaric sport," she retorted when he had attempted to explain it to her.

After a seemingly long and tedious trip, the fair grounds came in sight. The road had become rather busy. People and carts crowded them on every side. The fair was located in the countryside where an arrangement of buildings and arenas had been permanently set up for it. The plain surrounding it was now completely covered by tents and pavilions housing the fair attendees.

It was a sight to see mounting the hill that overlooked the entire scene. Waving banners of many colors crowned the pavilions where knights and noblemen camped. The grounds sprawled across the plains below them as far as the eye could see.

Upon reaching the place, Theadrin and Lianna were paid for the completion of their spring hire, and they bade the farmer and his wife farewell. Then began their excursion of the fair. Theadrin right away bought a square of buttered cornmeal and devoured it before buying a leg of mutton and a cup of fresh milk. The day was warm and sunny without a cloud in the sky. The two continued to browse through the booths until early afternoon when the first tournaments were to be held.

The stands and everywhere surrounding the arena were crammed full with people. The activity for that day was melee fighting. The participants were folk not well-known, most of them there to earn the reward of one hundred silver coins. The winner would be the last one standing. Any who had fallen to the ground were eliminated.

Theadrin found the best seat he could which was several rows from the bottom. Lianna had gone to some quilt-judging competition—something of no interest to him.

As he waited, Theadrin fingered the medallion about his neck. It was something he had all his life, and the only thing he had that used to be his father's. Although Theadrin was too young to remember the time it was given to him, Roryn, the hunter he and Lianna lived with, told him it was so.

The medallion was crafted in the shape of a beautiful sword. It was bound around his neck by a leather string and hung above his chest. It pointed downward in the outline of a cross.

A trumpet announced the tournament beginning, and thirty eager men ran out onto the field. Most were shirtless; others had sleeveless shirts, and all carried a blunted sword made of ash wood. The crowd roared as they clashed together.

Many bets were placed in these tournaments. Men of all positions partook in them against friends or rivals. Theadrin, never taking part in the bets, liked to pick one of the contestants to root for. He did this every year but never was able to pick the one who ended up winning.

"I'll wager the big fella' on the far right." A close voice startled him. There were lots of noisy people about, but this voice was shouted practically in his ear. He turned to see a burly, slightly overweight man with a chubby face. His hair was short and brown and his arms were hairy.

"The big un with the eye patch. On the right." He came again. "Which un do you choose?"

"I'm not making any bets, sorry." Theadrin looked back to the field, but he couldn't shake the man off that easily.

"I didn't say I was makin' a bet, boy. I was just a' telling you which one was gonna win. B'sides, I already got one goin'." He took a mouthful of day-old mutton and said, "Which un are you guessin'?"

Suddenly his man went down. "Aw, come on!" He shouted, spewing bits of mutton, and putting up his hand in disgust. "He looked to be a sure winner. Now you see why I am not making a bet with ya, lad?"

Theadrin scanned over the fight and saw a young man, who must have been no older than Theadrin himself, fighting a bigger man with a fuzzy beard. He watched him a moment and said, "I going with him"—he gestured—"the young one. But I am not taking any bets."

The man beside him peered into the frenzy and nodded. "Aye, he looks to be a good un'. Got to have some real gumption going up against Hectur right away. But I don't think he'll last very long." He dug into his mutton leg once again.

"Hectur?" Theadrin puzzled.

"Yup. He won last year's melee. A tough un' that un', and also my friend. We are neighbors just near the border. I may as well root for 'im."

Hectur's skill was well honed, but his blows were heavy and his swings a bit too wide. Theadrin saw the young man take advantage of this and strike the other side after an overextended thrust, knocking him to the ground with a rap to the back of the head.

"A real champion, this Hectur." Theadrin looked at the man beside him who was yelling.

"Hectur! Aah! Yer better 'in that, man! Come on! I had a bet placed on ya an' ever'thing!"

The young fighter moved through his opponents with speed and accuracy. This was a strange sight; the youngest of the group was putting the rest to shame. As he engaged a tall thinner man, another ran up behind and nailed him in the right knee. He stumbled backward.

"Aha! Ya see he's gonna fall. I was right, was I not?" The burly man next to Theadrin had been watching the young man with growing interest. There was almost a hint of disappointment in his voice.

Before Theadrin could answer, he was drawn back to the young man who was able to regain sure footing while fended off several attacks from the one who hit him. A moment later he knocked his opponent to the dirt and moved on to the next.

"Hoo hoo! Now there's a fighter fer ya!" Theadrin heard the man at his side yell.

The number of contestants quickly diminished until only five remained. The young man engaged one while the other three were in a hot battle a ways off. It was then Theadrin noticed that two of the three were working together. They dropped the third man and ran to where the young man had just defeated his opponent.

He swiftly turned to meet them as they split and attacked from either side. Parrying the first few strikes the young man backed up. The crowds were going wild at this point, and most were cheering for the young man.

The attacks were quick and furious from the two, and the young man began to falter, favoring his right leg. Theadrin had to stand to see because everyone else had done so. His muscles tensed as he watched the heated fight. The burly man beside him was yelling, waving his arms and punching the air.

The young man was losing ground fast, nearly trapped against the palisade wall that rimmed the field. Suddenly the two both struck at once, one swinging low and the other at the lad's head. It would be impossible for him to block these two blows. But to the crowd's amazement and sheer delight, he leapt up over the low cut and parried the higher one. Spinning in the same motion, he then hit the one who had swiped low in the side of the head.

The other attacker stepped back, visibly shocked at the skill of his young opponent. It was just the two left now, and they engaged each other with quick, hard cuts. The younger man swung to the side, but his opponent blocked it with his arm and then struck him in the side of the head. The crowd gasped in one breath as the younger one stumbled and nearly fell, losing the grip on his sword.

Weaponless, he faced his opponent. The other man raised his sword to finish it. The crowd raged at what he was about to do, most of all the hairy man next to Theadrin. He was shouting his displeasure at the turn of events.

"Ya cowardly, belligering…buffoon! How dare ya! Ya better…" His voice was lost in the roar of the crowd as the man swung his weapon at the young man's head. At the last possible moment, the young man ducked. As the weapon slowed, he took firm hold of it and yanked his older opponent forward. He laid a backhand punch to the man's face and sent a sharp knee into his stomach. Then, wrenching his weapon away, the young man held it ready to strike.

"Finish the dirt bag!" Theadrin heard the burly man again. The young man did not move. Theadrin held his breath and didn't blink. He saw the young man's lips move as he spoke to his opponent. The other man responded by raising his hand in the sign of surrender. The onlookers burst into a thunderous cheer as the young man cast the sword away. Theadrin sat back as the tension lifted. The new winner walked off the field with the roaring acclamation of the crowd still resounding over the arena.

The burly man sat as well with a throaty sigh, tinted with slight dissatisfaction. He looked over at Theadrin and said, "I'da clobbered that man good—but all the more credit to the youngster for doin' what he did." He glanced at the field and shook his head. Then he looked back at Theadrin. "You comin' to the tournament tomorrow? Man, you sure can pick a winner."

"I might be." Theadrin started standing to take his leave.

"Well if ya are, you can tell me which un' will win, and I can make a bet to get back my losses." The man looked up with hopeful eyes.

"This is the first one I've ever picked that's won," Theadrin replied.

"Well that's more'n I c'n say. I'll try an' find ya."

Theadrin shrugged and started to go. He did not intend on seeing the man again.

"The name's Yan. What's yers?" The other man quickly stood.

"Theadrin."

"Well, hopefully see ya tomorrow, Thaydrim." Yan smiled.

"It's Theadrin."

"Ah, right…Theadrin." Yan looked a little embarrassed.

Theadrin couldn't help feeling a small liking for the comical fellow.

At the next tournament, he did not see Yan, nor for the rest of the melee fights. It was now the fourth day when Theadrin and Lianna decided they had had their fill of the fair. They would leave on the morrow after the joust.

Five

That afternoon Theadrin stood looking over a variety of swords and axes. They lay in order on a table covered in a blue cloth that was trimmed with gold tassel. The blades were beautifully polished and expertly crafted.

"May I help you, my lad?" The owner of the weapons booth addressed Theadrin with a well-seasoned sales smile.

"No, thank you. I'm just admiring your stock." Theadrin placed his right hand on the naked blade of a broad sword and ran his fingers to the point. The metal was cool and sang under his touch.

"That is an interesting medallion you wear. I can tell you like swords." The merchant grinned. "But what young man does not, eh? You look like a lad of strong build. A farmer?"

"I work for one during the spring, but I'm brought up as a huntsman," Theadrin answered

"Your father must be a good man to raise such a fine young gentleman." The merchant's smile was tireless.

"Actually my father is dead. Both my parents died when I was too little to remember."

"Oh? I'm sorry to hear that. Was your father a hunter as well then?"

"I never knew him." Theadrin began to step away from the table. This man was asking too many questions too fast and Theadrin didn't like it. His smile was infectious and Theadrin was certain that if he stayed longer he would be wrapped up into a deal. "I have to go."

"It was nice to meet you, ah…" The booth owner looked at him for an answer.

"Theadrin."

"Theadrin." The man said, nodding slight approval. "I like that name. Take care, Theadrin." The man gave another pleasant smile and turned to a different customer.

Theadrin moved off in the direction of the arena. The main tournament would begin soon. This was where the knights and lords would compete in jousting contests. He found an open seat with a good view and watched as the contestants were introduced.

There were many familiar participants from previous years, and several new. Halfway through this, a familiar voice brought him around. His sight met the scruffy face of Yan adorned with a broad smile.

"So here at last I've found ya. These past tournaments have nearly run me dry." Yan felt his pockets and gave a dry cough.

"How are you, Yan?" Theadrin gave a squinting smile against the sun.

"Oh, not so bad now that I found ya." He took the empty seat beside Theadrin. "Hectur! Over here, man!" Yan waved his bearded friend over who was standing and looking through the faces of the crowd. Hearing the voice of his friend, he quickly moved to join them.

Yan turned his attention back to his new young friend, getting right down to business. "So, have ya been searchin' out the contestants fer a winner?"

"I am sorry. I can't tell you which one will win."

"Oh c'mon. With the luck ya had the first time? If ya tell me which un' ya think I can make a bet with some fella' an' get back some money lost. Maybe even make a profit."

"Sorry." Theadrin ended it.

Yan's smile fell and he leaned back in his chair with a grimace. Hectur came up and took his place beside Yan. "Hectur, this is Thedim. He's the one…"

"Theadrin." Theadrin corrected his name.

"Right. Sorry boy. Anyway, he's the one I told ya 'bout." Yan informed his friend. Hectur merely lifted his chin a bit and looked at Theadrin. His hair nearly touched his shoulders and his beard grew up and connected into his sideburns. His countenance was lofty and his eyes were round. His nose was long and thin, but his nostrils were wide.

Theadrin nodded in greeting and turned back to the tournament. He didn't want these two to distract him from the biggest tournament of the fair. For now, however, they seemed content to speak to him, mostly Yan. Theadrin found that Hectur wasn't much for words. He was soon able to figure out that Hectur's pride and honor had been hurt in the losing of the melee.

Meanwhile, Lianna had gone to get a lunch and brought it to the edge of the fair grounds to eat. Very few people were out that way, most being at the tournament. She sat in the cool shade of an abandoned booth. The distant throng of the crowds played in the back of her mind as she ate.

Almost immediately after the first bite, she heard someone approaching. Then two scruffy men appeared around the back of the booth. They were dressed in muddy, torn clothes and their intensions were clear from the mischievous looks in their eyes.

They were out to make trouble and must have been following her. They saw her sitting alone, and the one in the front released a yellow grin. His hair was unkempt and his mustache was sparse. They were both young, probably in their mid twenties.

"Here is a prize for us, Arin," the leader said through his disgusting grin. The other, Arin, looked younger than the first and had rusty-colored hair. He did not smile and his eyes spoke worry.

"Let's make this quick," he said. His eyes swept their surroundings.

"There'll be no one to bother us." The leader flicked his hand and took a step further. "The big tournament's drawn them all away."

Lianna was on her feet and running as he quickened his pace and caught her arm. She spun and struck him below the eye, but his grip remained strong.

He pushed her against the side of an empty building and grabbed her around the neck. She retaliated by striking out and gouging his jaw with her fingernails. She called out.

"Help!"

The yellow smile on the robber's face disappeared for a moment, and he pulled a knife from his belt and rested the point at her stomach.

"Don't scream or I'll be forced to use this," he threatened.

Lianna froze and the man grabbed her purse and tossed it to Arin who turned and began to rummage through it. Then the other put his face up close to hers, his sickening breath overwhelming her senses.

"Let me go!" She started to struggle again.

He laughed and started to speak but was suddenly jerked backward. Another man had him by the shoulder and spun him about, laying a punch to his face and sending him sprawling to the ground. Arin spun about and froze. His eyes were wide with fright.

Before them stood a young man in stained and weathered clothes, mostly made of dark leather. A sword was strapped to his back and its handle protruded over his right shoulder. He was tall, had dark blond hair, and broad shoulders.

The one on the ground sat up with a curse and ordered, "Take care of him, Arin."

Arin drew a knife and slowly advanced. The newcomer stood and watched the approaching man with no concern. Arin drew within arm's length and stopped, brandishing his blade. They stared at each other for a time, not flinching, and Arin gave a slight frown of confusion. The voice of the other thief cracked the silence.

"Get 'im, Arin! Attack, you coward!"

Arin was brought from his daze and suddenly struck out with his small blade. But the defender acted with incredible speed. He grabbed Arin's arm and twisted it sharply. Arin shrieked and dropped the knife. The newcomer snatched away the purse and shoved him back, kicking the knife behind him.

Arin stood rubbing his wrist and looking in shock at his opponent. The other thug was on his feet and, agitated with Arin, ordered him to attack again. But Arin slowly backed up, still watching the other man. Then he turned altogether and ran away, disappearing amidst the vacant booths and tents. The young man then turned his attention to the other robber, whose lips were cracked and bleeding. The thief's eyes were filled with a hateful rage.

"I'm gonna kill you," he breathed through clenched teeth.

"Have at it then," came the cool reply.

With that the angry thief rushed at the newcomer, who stood his own, and, just before the mugger reached him, leaned to the side leaving his left leg firmly planted in place. The man toppled head over heels and landed on his face in the dirt. He rolled over and held up his right hand, but his knife was gone. It lay at the feet of his adversary, who kicked it back.

The thug lifted himself again from the ground and took up his dagger. His face was smeared with blood and dirt. The newcomer stuffed the purse in his belt to free up both hands, and the thief charged him again. He slashed at the young man's head but struck only air as the defender ducked beneath the strike.

As he brought the dagger back around, the young man caught his arm and put force against the back of his elbow. The cruel sound of cracking bone resulted. The mugger screamed in pain, but it was stifled as his opponent made a swift chop of the hand to his throat and then kicked his legs out from under him.

Lianna had stayed against the wall watching and holding her throat. When the mugger was lying on the ground and not attempting to get up again, she breathed a sigh of relief. The young man stood motionless a moment, watching the fallen thief, and then retrieved her purse from his belt.

"Thank you," she said. Her eyes were cast down as he handed it back to her.

"It isn't safe to be out here alone. There are some who would do worse than these two," the young man replied, scanning the area.

"I know that now." Her eyes flitted to the man lying in the dirt.

"Follow me." The young man started off, and she followed, studying him. He was always very alert, watching all sides, but was not jerking in his movements as one who is nervous. He was calm and his movements were fluid. He walked with a small limp in his right leg.

They weaved through the tents and came to the busy streets of the fair. He stopped, studying the people going by, and said, "Stay where there is a good amount of people from now on, and you'll be all right." With that he turned to go.

"Wait!" She put out a hand and stopped him. He halted and looked back at her. Suddenly she forgot what it was she was going to say. This was the first time she had seen his eyes, and she caught herself. Never had she seen eyes of that color. They carried something inside them, but she wasn't sure what.

They looked at each other until she realized he was waiting for her to speak.

"I meant to thank you," she recovered.

"It was no trouble," he replied. "They were inexperienced thieves up to no good."

"Well, I would be without my purse right now had you not showed up. You have my gratitude." He nodded and made to leave again.

"What is your name?" Lianna asked.

He stopped and hesitated, half facing her and looking down. "Myran."

"I am Lianna." She returned, brushing a strand of hair behind her ear. "Perhaps we will run into each other again?"

Myran didn't answer. The corner of his mouth lifted, and he turned and disappeared amidst the crowd before another word could be said.

⌛

Theadrin still sat at the tournament where there was only four contestants remaining. Yan had attempted guessing the winner on his own but had been wrong three times already. He now sat back with disgust and disappointment. Hectur had remained mostly silent. From what Theadrin had observed of the two men, they were completely opposite from one another. Yan was content to watch the games and place bets, whereas Hectur would rather be a part of the sparing.

On the opposite side of the jousting field the king of Caledon sat with family and retinue. There was a large colored sheet of canvas that shielded him and his party from the midday sun. The arena was not as wide as it was long, and Theadrin could see him fairly well. He sat smiling as the two riders each took a side of the field, with his chin slightly supported by his fingers.

King Brudwyn was known as a good king who was wise with age. He ruled Caledon, the neighboring kingdom to the east of Arinon, as a part of the line of Caledovi kings. The Caledovi had come from the far north, long before, with the Arnoni tribe. Through wars with hostile inhabitants and allying with others, each had become prosperous and built a kingdom.

Brudwyn's hair was turning gray but the flaming red was still there. He had a long mustache that grew down past the corners of his mouth to his chin, and he wore a green-and-black checkered cloak and a light-blue, long-sleeved shirt over dark-brown trousers.

His son, prince Ruadhan, looked much like his father. He was a clean-shaven man with the same red hair as the king. He stood off to the right at the end of the king's banister, arms folded. Theadrin thought this odd, for it was the prince's place to sit to the right of the king. But the prince stood apart and watched the field with hard eyes.

The two riders in the next round were Sir Dathin of the Antion region and Lord Balthir. The crowd cheered as king Brudwyn rose to start the joust. He dropped a small bright-red cloth, and the riders took off toward each other. Theadrin could hear the heavy steps of the large chargers pounding on the hard packed dirt. The sound of an army must have been something to hear. A thousand strong in full gallop over the battle plain would be like the echo of thunder.

Sir Dathin unseated Lord Balthir after several runs and so went on to the final round. Then it was Lord Thur from Naradrin against the knight from Arinon—Theadrin did not know his name. Lord Thur was knocked off on the second pass and thus eliminated. The final round was an exciting one. Neither could unseat the other until both fell. They drew their swords and rushed each other.

They had amazing skill. They attacked and parried with quick precision. Theadrin had practiced sword fighting before, playing battles with other boys his age when he was younger but had only used sticks.

He was much better in archery, for he had been brought up hunting. Yet he had always dreamed of being a knight. Every boy did. Still he knew that there was very little chance of it happening.

The fight had turned to Sir Dathin's favor, but the knight from Arinon quickly executed a move that left Dathin's right side wide open. The knight hit Dathin in the knee and he went down. The standing knight lowered his blade to the other's neck, and Dathin put his hands up in surrender.

The tournament was over. A seneschal rode to the middle of the field along with the winning knight's standard-bearer. His crest bore a black dragon on a dark-green background. The dragon's forefeet gripped a black spear in a strong grasp.

"Another tournament gone by an' no win'ins," sighed Yan. "Well, Hectur, there is no point in stayin' at this blasted fair another day. What will ya do now, young friend?" Yan asked Theadrin.

"I am leaving as well," Theadrin answered. "I have had my fill of the fair until next year."

They left the arena together, squeezing their way through the press of the crowd. Hectur fell behind and disappeared. Outside on the street they stood watching the people pass by for a moment until Hectur could rejoin them. As they waited, an angry shout caught their attention. A big man with a deep brow was coming toward them. Seeing him, Yan turned and made to run but the crowd was too thick. The big man grabbed him by the shoulder and whirled him about.

"My due!" growled the stranger.

"A minute please." Yan struggled.

"Pay me now or I'll…"

"I haven't got anything left!" Yan bawled.

"If you can't pay, I will take it another way." The man lifted a balled fist.

"Excuse me." Theadrin stepped between them. "How much does he owe you?"

"Ten silver coins," barked the man in a gruff voice.

"And you have nothing?" Theadrin questioned the bewildered Yan.

"Nay, least ways not enough…" he stammered.

"Give him what you have."

"But he won't be satisfied with anythin' less," Yan wailed pathetically.

"Give him what you have." Theadrin restated. Yan reluctantly pulled three silver coins and gave it to the huge man.

"Three?" The big man was incredulous. "This won't do!" He started at Yan, who cringed, but Theadrin remained in front of him.

"Out of my way!" He growled.

"Here is the remaining seven." Theadrin took his own coins out, and the big man started to count them. "Go now." Theadrin said.

The man left with a satisfied grunt. Yan released a nervous sigh. "Thank you, kindly friend."

"I've a mind to make you pay me that last seven. You shouldn't be gambling money you don't have."

"I thought it was a sure win. It was the second melee and…"

"Save the story. That was my last seven coins." Theadrin was visibly agitated.

"Well surely I'll pay it back when I get it," Yan assured.

"Forget it." Theadrin softened his tone. "I suggest you stop your gambling from here on, or I may make you pay it."

"Oh, thank ya, my friend. Be assured I'll stop. I niver won anyways."

"I wish I could be," Theadrin stated flatly.

"Ya doubt the word a Yan? There are some things I might be, but a liar aint one of 'em."

"Then I suggest you leave the fair and remove the temptation," Theadrin said.

"Oh, aye, I said I was leavin', did I not?"

"I have to go meet my sister." Theadrin looked out across the crowded grounds.

"Then it is good-bye." Yan stood, scratching his stubble-covered jowl. "If ever yer near the western border, come an' visit. You've made a friend in ol' Yan."

"I may do that, if only for the reason to collect my seven coins if I catch you gambling again."

"Oh no! Not Yan. Ya can have faith 'n me."

Theadrin smiled. "Good-bye, Yan." He looked to Hectur who had just come through the swell of people. Despite his first impressions of the two characters, he had come to like them. "It was good to meet you both."

Six

The journey home was slow and wet. Although it never poured, the drizzle was constant and the wind was strong. Vapors of rain blew sideways through the valleys on the sturdy gusts.

They finally arrived, well past dark, at the humble country cottage. The huntsman, whose name was Roryn, and his wife greeted them warmly, and they shared a meal of venison stew and freshly baked bread. They slathered the warm bread with homemade butter and dipped it into the steaming soup, allowing it to soak in the flavorsome broth.

Roryn was a quiet man, serious most of the time. His hair was dark and his build was strong. He made a steady income from selling meat to the butcher shops and to the nearest castles and keeps year round.

Theadrin and Lianna told of how the planting and work on the farm went, and of the spring fair, for Roryn and his wife had not been able to attend. When Lianna told of the incident with the bandits, Theadrin was in as much surprise as were the other two.

"How is it you never told me?" He nearly jumped out of his chair, a deep frown crowning his features. "I'm your older brother!"

"I'm sorry, but there was nothing you could have done. And besides, you were wasting your time watching those hackfests. I hope you enjoyed them while not giving a care to my safety," she chided him.

"So now I am responsible for it? I told you to stay at the shopping booths. How was I to know that you were going to disobey?" Theadrin's irritation was mounting.

Roryn put up a halting hand. He looked at Theadrin, who shook his head a couple times in disgust but said no more. To Lianna, Roryn asked, "You said you were *almost* robbed. How did you get away?"

"I was getting to that before Theadrin suddenly got angry," she replied innocently. Theadrin huffed at this and took another mouthful of stew.

Lianna continued, "They already had my purse when another man came and helped me. He fought and beat them both and returned my purse." She paused. "He was young; I would say Theadrin's age."

"Then what?" Roryn asked.

"He seemed in a hurry to leave. But not before I got his name." She acted as though she had a hard time remembering. "Myran, I believe it was."

"Well, your safety is what's important," Roryn said.

"Thanks to my ever-protecting elder brother," she said playfully.

"Had to get that last bit out," Theadrin muttered.

⌛

Gurn sat comfortably in his luxurious chair before the fireplace in the great hall. The small table to his right was covered with his untouched evening meal of chicken and an assortment of side dishes. A goblet of red wine also occupied the round table and had only been sipped once.

He stared into the flickering tongues of flame, devoid of movement. For several nights now he had gone without sleep. The news the messenger brought had stirred him to the core. The account was strange in and of itself. Gurn was returning from Lord Percel's estates several months before.

The day had been wet and cold. He was soaked and miserable, cursing the inclement weather, when a rider approached from the opposite direction.

The man was cloaked and hooded. He halted in the center of the path so that Gurn could not pass. Gurn, thinking him only a peasant, ordered him to move. Receiving no response from him enraged Gurn, and he threatened to have him run through. But the man remained calm and said, "My master sends his greeting and a message of gravity. The heir of the late king is still alive."

Gurn did not believe him. "How dare you speak lies to your king! I have had men killed for much less."

"King you may be, but you're only a pawn in the hands of someone greater."

"Who is your master?" Gurn was not sure what to think of this man's tale.

The mysterious rider, his face hidden beneath his black hood, said, "You do not know him, but he knows you. You would do well to heed his words."

"Where is he?" Gurn began to worry in spite of himself.

The man ignored his question and added, "The heir is living in the kingdom of Caledon. Find him and kill him." With that the rider turned and left, leaving Gurn alone and silent in the saddle.

It was not possible. Lord Percel's warriors rode them down as they escaped and burned them alive inside the coach. There were no survivors. Still, Gurn decided he could not dismiss the stranger's warnings any longer. He could not afford to disbelieve them. If a son of Valdithin was alive, it was only a small matter of time before he appeared to claim his throne. What would anyone have to benefit from lying about something like that?

So he sent out spies all over Caledon to search for the location of Valdithin's son. All had returned empty handed. Then the Spring Fair of Caledon had come. It was the biggest yearly event that took place, and every young man in Caledon would be there. Gurn knew that he could be no more than twenty-five summers.

The sound of the creaking door brought Gurn from his troubled thoughts. His chamberlain entered the hall and announced, "My lord, the weapons merchant has returned."

"Send him in immediately," Gurn ordered. This was what he was waiting for. He had hired a weapons merchant from the city to go and keep his eyes open for the lad. What young man would resist a booth of swords, axes, spears, and the like? Yes, if he was at the fair, he would more than likely be at the weapons booth.

The man entered and spoke in a grand voice. "Lord Gurn, how has life been treating you since we last met?"

"I do not wish to carry on a conversation with you, merchant. Tell me what I want to know and get out!" Gurn snarled, his mood dark and unforgiving.

"Yes, yes," the man replied coolly. "But first..." he rubbed his fingers together.

Gurn's answer was low and menacing. "You will get nothing unless you speak. I will decide if your information is worthy of pay."

"Oh, you will find that it is," countered the merchant.

"Then spit it out! Or shall I have it tortured out?" Gurn raged with irritation.

"I have found him," the man conceded, smiling slyly. "He lives with a hunter near the town of Faranor."

"I am not convinced."

"But my lord, Gurn..."

"What proof do you offer? I need proof of his identity!" Gurn glared impatiently at him.

The weapons merchant smiled and lifted a finger. "I know it was him, there can be no doubt." He chuckled at his own cleverness, which only served to increase Gurn's impatience. The king tapped his armchair loudly to show it.

The merchant continued, "He wears a medallion in the shape of a sword."

"What proof is that?"

The hands of the merchant went up and he chuckled again. "You do remember the King Sword, do you not? Well, I, being a purveyor of fine swords, know my weaponry and..."

"Just give me your proof!" Gurn snapped.

"The medallion the boy wears is an exact replica of the King Sword. No one in all the realm of Caledon would wear such a treasure than the one you seek. As I said before, he lives outside the town of Faranor in the hovel of a huntsman."

Gurn scowled at the fireplace as he contemplated this. Soon his eyebrows lifted as he realized this boy had to be the one. His eyes snapped back to the merchant.

"Well done." He tossed a small coin bag and said, "Now leave me."

The merchant quickly counted the contents and grinned with satisfaction. He spun on his heel and left.

Silence followed as Gurn contemplated how best to take care of Valdithin's heir. The chamberlain stood motionless, watching his lord with expressionless eyes. He had grown accustomed to Gurn's moods. They could fluctuate like the weather. One moment he might be content, and the very next he could be livid with rage. The chamberlain knew when it was best to hold his tongue and when to speak, and most often what to say.

When Gurn stood, the man asked, "What is it you want done, my lord?"

"I will go to my chambers. When I have a plan I will call for you," was his lord's reply.

Gurn snatched up his goblet and guzzled down its contents in one huge gulp as the chamberlain bowed and left in a hurry. Then he wiped his mouth and left the great hall. There were several ways he could dispose of the lad, but of which way he was uncertain. To send soldiers over the border would be sure to arouse suspicions from King Brudwyn. The alliance already hung on a thread between the two kingdoms. No, the job must be done as quietly as possible.

Gurn stood in his room pouring another cup of wine. As the first drops touched his tongue, a sudden chill went through his spine. The hair stood straight on the nape of his neck and on his arms. He could hear a steady, gruff breathing from behind. Turning slowly, he looked across the room. The window was open and the cool night air leaned against the curtains. Although he saw no one, his heart thumped a quicker beat. Some papers on a table turned up at the corners against the gentle breeze. Then a shadow moved. There, on the right side of the room, stood a tall black figure. Gurn's heart nearly leapt from his chest and he lost his grip on his cup.

SEVEN

It was an overcast day; the sun was masked but its light was not altogether concealed. The leaves had long since turned color and fallen; the land was bared and ready for the impending arrival of winter.

Theadrin sat amidst the deepening shadows of the forest, leaning on his elbow at the pool's mossy edge. He watched his hollow wooden bobber sitting motionless on the surface of the water that mirrored the surrounding poplar trees and overcast sky. A leaf drifted past him on the breeze and alighted softly on the face of the mere, creating tiny ripples that drifted off in all directions.

The forest grew over the rocky foothills of the Aegris mountains like a carpet. The mountains formed a broken spine that divided the two great kingdoms of Arinon and Caledon.

Summer had come and gone quickly, passing as it always had. The harvest had come in and the fall feasts had been held only days before. The wind was becoming colder, and it now nipped at his ears. It carried the familiar scent of the dead leaves that blanketed the ground around him.

He had been there all morning, catching a fish now and again, but none sizable enough to keep. It had been a long wait since the last bite, and he yawned, settling himself deeper into the thick moss and crispy, red leaves. He glanced up at the sky as a crow flitted just overhead. It cackled a couple of times, and Theadrin saw a smaller blue bird in close pursuit.

It was then he felt the pole jerk in his hands and he looked to see the bobber had been pulled under. The fish gave a heroic fight, swerving and diving to escape, but it was a losing battle; the hook pierced deep for an unbreakable hold. Theadrin hauled it above the pond surface and onto dry land.

It was a sizable catfish and would be enough to serve as his lunch. He removed the hook and placed the squirming fish in a pouch, leaving the pool.

The forest underbrush was thin, mostly red elder and fern; the trees were a mixture of oak, hornbeam, maple, and chestnut. Deer paths and game runs were abundant, and he chose one that took him to a small glen where a fire ring had been made of round, gray stones.

Theadrin stacked wood and tinder inside the ring and lit a fire. As the tongues climbed up the pile, he cut up the fish. Soon hungry flames licked at the dripping fillet. It had started to mist, and the brown leaves began to darken from the light rain. He turned the juicy meat on the spit and inhaled the delicious aroma.

It had grown quiet in the forest as the drizzle began. Theadrin was running his fingers through his damp hair and wiping the mist away from his eyes when a voice suddenly called out, "You're surrounded! Surrender that fish or I'll take it by force!" The voice was mature and one he knew well.

"Would you steal the humble meal of a poor peasant? That wouldn't be very chivalrous for a warrior of the king," Theadrin called back. He fed the small fire with the wood he had gathered, now dampening from the misting rain.

The answer was not long in coming. "Oh, come now, you probably stole the thing anyway. As a King's warrior I am duty bound to uphold the law."

Theadrin didn't answer but jabbed at the succulent meat, causing more juice to spill out on the fire and sizzle temptingly. There passed a period of thoughtful silence from the person in the wood, and then, "At least share a morsel with a weary and starving traveler."

"Oh, a traveler is it now? Come on out, Peran, and have some. It's almost done."

"A warrior could be a traveler as well." Peran stepped out from behind a tall oak with a broad grin. "They are often sent on missions by the king you know."

Theadrin had grown up with Peran, and they had been best friends as long as either remembered. They shared many interests and had grown up playing knights, defeating countless imagined enemies in the very woods they were in now. With other friends from the village, they had most often recounted the tale of The Seven in their play: an old story of seven friends who had defeated a terrible beast by standing as a strong line of warriors. As children, Theadrin and Peran fought many such beasts that were ravaging the kingdom in their vast imaginations.

Peran was shorter than Theadrin and not quite as old, but had the same adventurous spirit. He was a joker and could always provide a good laugh. His hair was a rusty red, like his father's, and his face was freckled.

"So the king is so short of food he sends out his finest warriors to take from his even hungrier subjects?" Theadrin taunted his friend.

Peran's smile grew wider. He sat down opposite of Theadrin and inhaled the mouthwatering fragrance. A refreshing wind fought against the flames and turned the smoke into his face. Peran blew stiffly out of his nose and moved to the side, wrinkling his brow. Putting his hands near the flames he allowed the warmth to soak in. Then, looking up at Theadrin, he continued on the subject of warriors.

"Ah, if only I was a knight in the king's court. We aren't so bad at sword fighting, Theadrin. We've been practicing for years now." His eyes were on Theadrin but they seemed to be focused on a distant object. "I wonder how one of common birth does become a knight. Is it possible, do you think?"

Theadrin answered, "Well, sometimes the parents will take their child to the castle to become a knight. He starts as a page, then rising to become a squire. After that is knighthood."

"I am way too old to become a page," Peran said in disappointment. Every boy around had dreams to be a knight, but none surpassed Peran in his hope and desire.

When they were young lads, they would play soldiers from dawn until dusk. Peran was always the most serious in it and had not outgrown the deep desire for obtaining knighthood when most of the others had. All were young men now and worked at jobs.

Peran's father was a fisherman and owned a shop on the lake Aldwin. Peran spent more days looking after it, now that he was older and had become an excellent fisherman himself. But the life of a fisherman and shop owner was not for him.

"I have heard stories, however," Theadrin went on, "that if one accomplished a great feat of heroism then the king might knight him. So all you have to do is win a heroic battle or slay some monstrous beast." He said this nonchalantly as he lifted the sizzling meat from over the fire.

"Oh, sure, nothing too difficult. There aren't any monsters around here anyway." Peran watched Theadrin handle the hot fish.

Theadrin laughed and handed his friend half of the meat. "And if there were, you would be the first to have at it, I wouldn't doubt."

Peran received the catfish and nodded his agreement with the wide grin that was his trademark. Theadrin leaned back against a log and took a bite, savoring the flavor. The warm sun that pierced like spears through the thinning clouds felt good on his face. He breathed a contented sigh before asking, "What brings you out here, Peran?"

His friend looked down trying to remember, and then his eyes brightened. "Oh yes, I remember. Something interesting happened. It was last night. My father and I had closed up the shop and were riding out to my uncle's house. He is a hunter like Roryn." Theadrin nodded that he knew, and Peran continued.

"While eating supper there, my aunt cried out, and we were all startled to see a figure just outside the window watching us. No one could make out who it was since it was so dark. It was gone as soon as we saw it."

"A traveler, perhaps? Passing through?" Theadrin didn't take much interest in the tale.

Peran stopped eating. "Travelers do not stand outside someone's window and watch them as they eat, Theadrin."

"Why not? If he was hungry he might."

"If he was wanting food he would have been knocking on the door." Peran returned. Theadrin realized he was right. Perhaps it didn't make much sense.

They talked on into the afternoon and the shadows lengthened. The rain had ceased long since and the day had brightened with what light remained before the sun disappeared. Peran left, having work to finish before the day's end, and Theadrin doused the fire and went home.

Eight

A pallid moon clung to the inky black sky that blinked with a never-ending quantity of twinkling eyes. The country lay in a passive slumber, every home lit with a warm fire beneath its hearth. Nights had grown cold. The winds were stronger and brought the chill of a fast-approaching winter.

The small fire began to dwindle before another pile of sticks was carefully placed on it. It lit the surrounding brush and trees and cast dancing shadows upon the young man's face. His dark eyes stared back at the bright tongues that licked the cold night air as he shifted to stoke the burning pile. Glowing, fiery sparks escaped and drifted upward before fading to nothing in the black air.

Myran leaned back and pulled the folds of his cloak about his shoulders. He stretched his leg out slowly and rested it on a rock. His injury reclaimed its fury after the melee fight at the spring fair.

His thoughts had scarcely left the happenings of the fair ever since he had left. He had been walking the abandoned paths alone when he heard the cry for help. The girl, Lianna, had looked to be his own age. Although he knew it unlikely they would see each other again, his thoughts could not escape her. She was different from any other he had seen, and Myran found that thinking about her and their brief meeting helped pass time.

He kept his sword loose within its scabbard and at a place where he could reach it quickly. The night was quiet, and he was wary of danger. It was unfamiliar territory he was in, in southwest Caledon.

A cricket started up behind him somewhere, indicating that the temperature had not dropped too quickly yet. Then, slowly but steadily, more joined the first. The crickets were now in full song, getting in their last performances before it grew too cold for them. Suddenly they stopped. The quiet came abruptly, and Myran's eyes darted to the surrounding wood.

There was something there, and its presence brought an icy silence to the night. Myran's hand found the handle of his sword and he waited, listening. For a long time everything remained the same. But then the crickets began once more. They started on his right and built slowly toward his left.

By this he knew that whatever had been out there had moved off in the direction of his left.

Something had been watching him from beyond reach of the firelight, but whatever or whomever it was had now passed and gone away. His hair prickled at the thought of being watched by something that made no sound. But something had definitely been there, just watching him.

Living alone in the forest, Myran had grown accustomed to hearing the sounds of night. But whatever was out there that night was something he had never experienced before.

He found little sleep after that. So long as the crickets sang their tune he felt safe, but he slept lightly. By midnight they were quiet again, but only because the temperature had taken a dive. Myran built up the fire to a healthy blaze before dozing off once more.

The next morning he was up and moving as the sun broke free and spilled over the land in a golden flood. The wind was colder than the previous day, Myran noticed as he walked the grassy hills. The rays of morning had done little to bring warmth to the air. He traveled north, and was glad to leave that place behind.

His path took him through the village of Roradrin, a fair-sized town that was big in wheat trade. Entering the marketplace, he bought some provisions with some of the money he earned from the tournaments. Next he went to the stables. He had gone far too long on foot, never being able to afford a horse until now.

The man who was working there greeted him with a powerful handshake. He was wiry, mature in years, and his chin and jaw were covered in grayed stubble. He wore a faded blue wool shirt, and a torn scarf was wrapped loosely about his shoulders. They bartered until a deal was finally struck. Myran bought a middle-aged roan from the man for twenty silver pieces.

"Headin' far?" the man asked as he stored the money away.

"Eventually. I hope to head north of Arinon before the snow flies," he replied as he loaded his things onto his new steed.

"Ah, that may be sooner than ya think." The livery owner implied the cold weather with a sweep of his hand. "How far north would you be thinking of goin'?"

"I am not sure yet. As far as I can."

"You would go into the lands of terrible legend and myth?" Myran did not reply to this. "That is wild country up there, and vast too."

"So I'm told." Myran continued to secure items and look the horse over.

"There is a reason why our ancestors left that place behind and never looked back. Great mystery enshrouds that land. There are stories of monsters and giants." The livery owner watched him carefully.

"I have heard them." Myran finished his work and turned to the older man. "The horse looks good."

The man nodded. "He'll get you places."

As he left and mounted the horse for the first time, the stable master called after him. "I'm curious"—he stepped away from the table he had been behind—"what would lead one as young as you to a place such as that?"

"There is nothing left for me here." Myran trotted away without looking back. He left the village and continued on his way.

It was much easier traveling now that he owned a good horse, and safer as well. A horse can tell much better than you when danger is present and can make a faster getaway if you have to escape in a hurry.

The late morning at last brought some warmth, though the wind still owned a sharp edge. The steady, rhythmic drumming of the roan's hooves was relaxing and Myran eased back in the saddle.

The question that the livery owner had asked kept coming back to plague his thoughts. He had no home and wandered the countryside alone.

It had been nearly two years since the death of Ao-idh and Caed, though it seemed a lifetime. Yet their memory had not faded in his mind. He could still see their faces clearly and could hear their laughter and voices.

Now he was alone. Most people were content to shun him, barely sparing an acknowledging nod as he passed by. There was only one person in the entire world whom he counted a friend: an old hermit. The kindly man dwelt in the forest north of the village of Faranor that was not far from the western border. Myran met him when he had first come into Caledon.

It was at a time when Myran was struggling, and the old hermit had been very kind. He was a very peaceful man, his hair was white with age, and most of the time a bright smile gleamed from behind his long beard. Caithal was his name, and he had strengthened Myran when he was ready to give in. Myran planned to stop at his forest dwelling and stay for the night.

As he rode, an image flashed in his mind. He had seen it countless times before. It came back to him now and again. It was as if he had dreamed it once, or perhaps seen it long ago. This and a scar on his left forearm were always there to remind him that his whole life was a mystery, for he knew nothing of his life before Ao-idh found him. The image consisted of two pictures, one of the seas, churning and roaring in a raging tempest, and a face; but the features were blurry.

He wasn't sure if he would ever find out the answer to that mystery. All he had ever known was his life in the woods with Ao-idh, and then after his death, the life of a lonely wanderer.

Myran had come to know much of the forest, and of snaring and hunting. All his life he had slept in the woods or atop hills, wandering the far countrysides of two kingdoms, and fighting to stay alive. That fight had proven harder than he could have imagined. His experiences had torn and battered him, and had transformed him into a hardened man.

But in all his wanderings he had not entered the forest where he and his friends lived, and he had been about his task ever since. Ao-idh told him that the true heir of Valdithin was alive, the true line of Arnoni kings was not broken, and Myran was to find him. So, since waking up that wet morning after the ambush, he had left that place behind, not daring to look back.

He had not begun his task right off. In truth, it was far from his mind as he fled Arinon. Instead, his aim was to avenge his friends by killing Gurn. But after meeting the old hermit, something had reset inside of him. The hermit was a servant of the Highest King, and Myran felt much restored after his long stay with him. Still, the memory of what had happened to his friends would not let him go completely.

Myran had searched Caledon for one and a half years for Valdithin's heir. It was an arduous and difficult task, for he knew not what the person looked like or how old he might be. Caithal, the hermit, assured Myran that the Highest King would reveal Valdithin's heir at the right time. But Myran had grown impatient; his faith in accomplishing the task died, and he had become set on traveling north of Arinon, hoping to find a new life there.

Micah I. Cooley

The country he was traveling in became hilly with a lone oak here or there, and every so often a large rock formation rose from the tall, golden grass. Often they would be immense enough to dwarf a farmhouse, resting in large heaps. The sky clouded over, and with the imprisonment of the sun, the day became colder than ever. Now and again the clouds released a soft, icy drizzle.

His water skins were empty and he hadn't had a drink all day. On the near horizon he saw the outline of a forest and spurred his steed on at a quicker pace toward it. The trees would provide a better defense against the cutting wind.

He let his horse have its reins and wander after he entered the wood, knowing that a horse can find water much faster than a man. The forest was still and silent, and to Myran it seemed as though there was a menacing air about the place. The roan followed a deer path, eventually opening up into a meadow. It stopped, putting its nose into the crispy red and brown leaves.

Myran gazed through the clearing as the tiny white flakes started to appear. They fluttered wildly on the slight clean breeze wafting toward him. As he sat watching, a red fox darted from the brush across the glen, stopped at seeing him, and fled to the left into the bushes.

For the cunning and elusive fox, this behavior was unheard of. It would have known of his presence as he entered the glen and stayed well away, and certainly would not have come out of cover toward him.

His horse started walking again. It turned right, to the western edge of the meadow, and went down a small incline. A stone toss further, the roan stopped by a fast running brook that ran along the bottom of the gap.

Myran dismounted and allowed the horse to drink as he stooped to refill his water pouches, all the while remaining wary of his surroundings. The brook was cold as ice on his fingers and had a smooth, sandy bottom. As he held the water skins under, he noticed the clarity of the water suddenly darken. He brought the skin out quickly as a dirt cloud floated past. Something had stepped into the water farther up the creek, disturbing the bottom.

Had the incident with the fox not happened, he would have thought it a deer or raccoon, or some other forest creature, but none of these things were enough to frighten a fox.

Myran tied the reins of his mount to a low-hanging branch and crept off upstream. Since the night before, there had been too many strange occurrences taking place. Something, or someone, was trailing him. He wanted to discover the source, whatever it may be.

The snowflakes had increased in size and began to fall more rapidly, and already the frozen ground was beginning to turn white. The only sound was the current of the stream trickling swiftly onward.

A little farther along, the hardwoods gave way to a wall of dead pine. Although lifeless, the branches were clustered thickly together, still clinging to long dead needles, hanging gray and limp on the rotting branches. Moss hung like spiderwebs from their limbs, moving slightly on a soft breeze.

He stopped and glanced warily about. The dark pine before him gave him a sense of foreboding. In the old tales it was places such as these in which evil would dwell, where hideous beasts lurked, waiting and watching.

On the ground before the dark wood, he noticed several broken pine needles. Lowering himself to one knee, Myran examined the spot closely. There was a slight depression in the soft bed of dead needles. Although it was hard to tell, they looked to be freshly broken along the edge of the track.

He rose and took a step further, listening, hearing only the enticing whisper of a gentle wind through the tangled pine branches. The floor of the pine forest was heavily blanketed with brown and gray needles, muting all sound of footfall. The stories he had heard as a child began to come back to him, of monsters too terrible and ugly to imagine.

Micah I. Cooley

A long moment passed before he drew his sword and pushed into the entangled mess. The limbs did not thin as he entered, making the going incredibly arduous. The wispy moss brushed past his face and clung like grasping fingers to his clothes. Past the first several trees, the dead wood became as black as night and was weighed upon by a heavy silence.

Becoming too thick to continue standing, he crouched and put a hand to the soft ground. His palm landed on a cold, hard object half buried in the soft dirt. As his fingers closed over it, his eye caught a flicker of movement ahead of him.

Nine

Theadrin strode steadily down the white trail of the barren forest, his thoughts straying. The snow fell in heavy, wet flakes, clinging to tree, shrub, and earth. The sky was dull gray and the air was chilling to the skin. All was still in the forest.

He rounded a tall rock formation and met Lianna. She came around the bend holding a basket covered by a plain gray cloth and walking at a brisk pace. A dark-blue shawl hung over her head like a hood with the end tossed over her right shoulder.

"How did it go?" Theadrin asked, stepping beside her as they started down the path leading home. She had been to town and Theadrin had come to meet her.

"Fine," she said, leaving it at that.

"Was it very busy today?" Theadrin was just making conversation.

"No." Her mind seemed to be dwelling on something else.

Theadrin said nothing more as they walked down the path. The snow crunched beneath their feet, sticking to their shoes. Daylight had faded and gave way to evening's luminous glow.

Theadrin gazed around at the trees and falling flakes. The first snow was always a beautiful thing to him. The large, sticky flakes clung to every stalk and twig in the forest.

Glancing behind them for a moment, his eye caught movement. Something had crossed the trail behind them and he saw the last of it as it moved into the cover of the trees. He assumed it to be a deer and kept walking, but he began to feel uneasy. The feeling surprised him, for he had seen countless animals here before and felt he had walked every path in that forest.

Farther along, it struck him that although the sight had been only a glimpse, it had appeared to be walking upright. His apprehension grew when a stick snapped off through the trees. Then he began to catch other glimpses, shadows that moved from tree to tree. This, he told himself, must be the deceiving twilight and his own imagination. A raven took flight up the path and cackled off into the night.

Straining through the poor light to the area where it had been, he stopped short. His heart leapt in his chest. He thought he could make out an erect figure on the edge of the path under a thick oak facing toward him.

"What's the matter?" Lianna paused and looked back.

Theadrin blinked and looked again but saw nothing this time. The poor light and falling snow had played a convincing trick on his eyes. "Nothing. I just thought…" He paused and shrugged. "Nothing." He started walking again. Lianna gave him a perplexed look but did not pursue the matter further.

After passing the large oak and seeing nothing, he began to relax. The ground started to slope upward to a tall ridge; beyond it was the hunter's cottage. The snowfall was beginning to thin and the night deepened.

The trail had grown slick and they were forced to slow their pace and pick their footing with greater care so not to fall.

Halfway up the rise, however, a rock was dislodged under his foot, and he fell. The cold snow stung his bare hands. Instantly following, a sound reached his ears of a dulled thud, and he heard Lianna let out a startled scream. Theadrin was on his feet in an instant and saw Lianna pointing behind him. Stuck fast in a dead ash tree was a dagger of black metal. It had obviously been intended for him but his fall had saved him.

He spun around knowing that it had come from the opposite side of the trail. No sooner had he looked than a dark mass dropped from a high tree limb. It landed silently and took off toward them, running upright. Theadrin heard the ring of cold steel from a blade that was drawn.

He grabbed Lianna's arm. "Come on!" They both began to run. Lianna slipped once but Theadrin hauled her up again.

Whoever was after them displayed incredible speed and broke onto the trail before they had gotten five paces.

Theadrin stopped and drew his hunting knife. "Keep on, Lianna!" he shouted. His adrenaline was running wild. Two paces before it reached him, he saw it more clearly.

Dressed all in black, with its face shadowed by a dark hood, it swung at Theadrin's head with a short black sword. Theadrin ducked beneath it but received a kick to his face.

He landed on his back as the attacker lifted his sword to strike again. Theadrin's right hand, holding his knife, was up above his head. He flipped the handle up, caught the blade, and cast it at his enemy. His attacker had not been prepared for this and tried to move aside, but they were too close and the knifepoint pierced deep into its lower abdomen. The man, for man it must have been, grunted in pain. He took a backward step and slipped on the snowy incline.

Theadrin rolled over and got up, looking up the trail for his sister. Seeing her nowhere he felt a sudden panic. He ran several steps up the trail and found her footprints leading into the forest, and another larger pair followed them.

Fear mounting and heart pounding in his chest, Theadrin plunged into the woods as fast as his legs would carry him. The tracks led a good way into the forest. Eyeing a stout-looking limb ahead of him, he snatched it up as he ran past. He tested its strength on a passing tree. It was sturdy oak and would serve as a useful weapon.

The prints led on until they suddenly vanished in a jumbled mess of tracks. From the signs it looked as though there was a struggle.

He looked desperately for his sister, but she was nowhere in sight. Then there came a sound like rushing wind, and something struck him in the back. He fell on his face and the cold stung his skin. Rolling quickly to the side, he scrambled to his feet.

There was another man, much like the first in appearance, who thrust swiftly toward Theadrin's chest. Theadrin knocked it aside with his oak limb. He parried several more strikes until his club was cleaved in two. He was struck in the face by a quick fist and narrowly avoided a slice to the ribs. Ducking beneath one more swing, Theadrin rammed into the chest of his enemy and they both sprawled down the snowy, forested incline.

Their fall was stopped hard by a tree, Theadrin's assailant taking the brunt of the collision. Theadrin recovered and laid several angry punches to his enemy's face, which was coated in a black substance like dried clay. The man's eyes were nearly black as well.

Then higher up on the ridge another appeared. Theadrin dove for the sword that was in the snow only a body's length away.

He no longer noticed the icy sting of the cold night, although his fingers were bright red. He gripped the black leather handle and stood. The attacker halted and the one that had been stabbed by Theadrin's knife emerged from the other side. They came slowly for their prey. Theadrin's blood ran hot with anger for the thought of these men harming his sister.

The one on the ground drew another sword from its cloak and he saw yet another stalk slowly from the cover of the trees. His hood was off, revealing only one tail of hair on the top of his head.

It was now four to one, and all confidence he had began to drain quickly. Theadrin knew he could not take them all on. They started to move in from all sides. He squeezed the handle tight and darted for the one with the knife injury.

The blow was parried, and he punched Theadrin in the stomach, and the others encircled him. Theadrin attacked once again with several quick thrusts and cuts, but all were parried with easy skill. And then all at once the four went in for the kill.

At that moment a bright light flashed. Theadrin made to parry, but the attack didn't come. The four moved back. Another flare came and the four darted away as if in panic, leaving Theadrin standing alone.

⧗

Myran crouched in silence, barely daring to breath. Whatever he had seen move had vanished into the shadows. A chill trickled down his spine as he felt the menacing sense of eyes upon him. He lifted the small, metal object he had found and tucked it into his belt before cautiously backing out of the dead pines.

When he was out at last, the foreboding sense eased somewhat. Myran took a deep breath and returned to his horse. Mounted once more, he spurred his steed and left the stream.

Myran could not shake the sense that he was being watched. It felt like the eyes of a wolf. He had known the feeling before when a hungry pack had hunted him last winter. At night, when he couldn't see their eyes glinting in the firelight, he could feel them watching him from the shadows.

He turned in his saddle and glanced behind. His blood went instantly cold. There, standing between two green firs, stood a tall, black-clad figure. Its terrible red eyes studied Myran intently with a face painted black.

Myran did not take his eyes away and sat poised in the saddle. The man backed into the shadows of the trees and disappeared without a sound. Although he had never seen one before, Myran knew what it was. Only in legends had he heard of them, but the description fit the dark figure all too well.

As he rode away and evening drew on, he remained vigilant, keeping his sword loose in the scabbard. Rounding a large rock ledge, he noticed his horse's ears come up. The roan shook his head and nickered. A moment later he saw, distant through the trees, a white light flash twice.

⌛

Theadrin looked about for the source of the light and saw a dark figure move from behind an oak several trees away. It beckoned him frantically. Cautiously, he moved toward the figure, sword ready but sensing no danger. This person was not anything like the four black figures that had attacked him.

Reaching the spot, he found it was an old man. He wore a long cloak of dark brown and had a gray beard with a hood that covered his head.

"Come with me." The voice was well aged but contained strength. He was nimble, considering how old he looked, and Theadrin found himself following along behind.

They hurried on throughout the trees and snow, at last cresting the top where several boulders lay crowned in white. The old man halted in front of one and called out softly.

"It's all right. Come on out."

Theadrin watched as a slender form appeared in sight from behind the boulder. His heart sighed with relief at seeing the face of his sister. She saw him also and ran to him.

"Are you all right?" Theadrin put a hand on her shoulder and looked her up and down.

"I'm fine. What about you? Your chin is bleeding." She touched his jaw lightly and examined it.

"How did you get away?" Theadrin did not notice the warm trickle of blood or the soreness of his jaw.

"I am safe thanks to our new friend." She looked at the man who was leaning on one of the rocks, watching them from under his hood.

"Thank you, sir. We are deeply indebted to you," Lianna said gratefully.

"The least I could do," the man replied with a slow nod. His eyes gleamed beneath the brim of his hood as he studied them.

Theadrin looked to where the trees and ground fell away several long strides in front of them, and he could see their cottage in the valley below. "We best get home, Lianna." Theadrin said and Lianna turned to the old man. "We would be pleased if you joined us for a meal tonight. It is the least we can do to repay you," she said.

"You can't go back now."

Theadrin's head whipped around and Lianna stared at him in stunned silence. The cold white flakes no longer fell, and the snow illuminated a soft pallor from the moon that shone through the thinning clouds.

"What do you mean? Our home is just there." Theadrin lifted a cold finger to the silent house. "We can make it back."

"It is no longer safe for you," the man replied, unmoved.

"We are safer there than we are here," Theadrin argued.

"You don't understand," the old bearded man started to explain.

"I'm afraid my friend speaks the truth." The voice came from the forest behind. All looked to the place to see a tall figure stepping from the forest edge.

Once out of the shadows, they could see clearly the features of a young man. He wore dark clothes and a cloak that reached his ankles. The handle of a long sword protruded from behind his right shoulder.

The old man was the first to speak. "Greetings, Myran."

Lianna heard the name and squinted through the poor light at the young man. The shadows did much to hide his face, but there was no mistaking him.

Myran returned the man's greeting. "Hello, Caithal. It is long since we last saw each other."

"Long for you, perhaps, young man. But when you get to be my age it seems as only a day," Caithal said with a spark of humor.

"And I believe you." Myran chuckled. "Who are your friends?"

"I have only just met them. My lady here is Lianna." He introduced the girl first.

At the name, Myran's eyes darted to the dark-haired young woman. Their eyes met and they recognized each other instantly.

"Hello again, Myran." Lianna smiled lightly without removing her eyes from his. Myran nodded his greeting since he did not trust his suddenly weak voice. Then he glanced quickly to Caithal once again.

"You have already met then?" Caithal's eyebrows rose.

"We met briefly at the Spring Fair," Lianna explained.

"And this must be your brother." Caithal looked at Theadrin.

"I am Theadrin, and I am grateful that you helped us. But the danger is past, isn't it?" His mood was not in the pleasantries.

Myran looked at him. "The four will come again and keep on coming until they succeed in killing you. You have no choice but to leave."

"How do you know this?" Theadrin inquired with a frown, for in his mind they were no more than a band of thieves.

"Assassins will not give up after an encounter like this."

"Assassins?" Lianna's eyes widened in horror. She knew the implications of what that meant. "Someone wants us…dead?" Her voice faltered.

"I'm afraid so."

"But who?" Theadrin couldn't believe it. "We are nobody, just common folk. Perhaps there is a mistake."

"Your death is in someone's interest." Caithal told him. "They make no mistake about their target."

"What can we do?" Lianna's voice betrayed her fear.

"I will take you to my house. At least for tonight you will be safe there." Caithal said, looking at Myran.

"Can we at least go back and get some things? To say goodbye?" Lianna glanced down at the cottage in the valley.

"You can bet that they are watching your house for your return. They are not going to give up because they failed once. No, you must come now. I will explain things once we are out of harm's way." The old man started away. "My house is this way," he said, walking past Myran and into the forest.

Theadrin stood and watched the cottage, the place he had always known as home. The moon was vivid and the fresh fallen snow illuminated its light. The windows of the house glowed red-gold from the fire beneath the hearth. Roryn and his wife were enjoying its warmth, still expecting them to return at any moment. Theadrin wished he could let them know that they were all right, but there was nothing he could do.

"Roryn will come looking for us if we do not return; the assassins would kill him if he is not warned," Theadrin called after Caithal.

Myran looked at him. "Your family is only in danger if you are near them. Leaving now is the only chance they have of not being hurt or killed." He glanced once at Lianna and then turned to follow Caithal.

Theadrin knew Caithal and Myran were right. They could not go back. For himself he was not afraid, but now he had to do what he knew would keep Roryn and his wife safe, as well as his sister. With a silent sigh, Theadrin turned away. He took Lianna by the arm and they left the ridgetop.

Ten

Caithal's hut was built deep in the wooded foothills of the Aegris mountains. The hovel was roughly squared and made from head-sized stones stacked atop one another with mud packed around them. Its roof was sod and it was built against a gray rock face that sided a ridge. A bench, hand-crafted from a fallen log and deerskin, rested outside the front door.

Along the southern wall was evidence of where a garden was kept during the warmer months. Wisps of smoke wafted from a stone chimney atop the hut. A fire was already lit within.

Inside was completely different from what one would expect after looking at the outer appearance. The wall to the far right as they came in was covered in shelves that were clustered with books and scrolls of various sizes. The far wall was of a solid stone mass and had a deer hide hanging in the middle. The left wall had a fireplace with a mantle also piled on with old manuscripts and books. A large chair cushioned by green fabric sat before the hearth.

A table that appeared to be used as a study desk took up the center space of the room. It was rectangular in shape, and its four legs were carved with intertwining lines. Four simple, wooden chairs sat around it, one on each side. The table held a lampstand with four candleholders and several maps. Beneath was spread a large rug of bearskin.

All in all it was small and a little cramped, but it was quaint and warm. The four entered and Caithal beckoned them to sit. A kettle was heating over the dying fire and he went to retrieve it, first stoking the embers back to life. To Lianna he said, "Fetch those mugs on the shelf if you please, my lady."

"My whole life I have explored this forest and still I never knew anyone lived out here." Theadrin sat and continued to scan the small room.

Lianna brought over four pewter mugs and Caithal filled them with the contents of the kettle, steam rising in tiny, white curls as he poured. Myran entered the hut after seeing to his horse and wiped the snow from his boots that were thickly wrapped with strips of cloth. He rubbed his stiff fingers and sat across from Theadrin at the table.

When each had a warm mug in hand and were seated comfortably, Caithal said, "The assassins will not come here tonight, so you all can rest easy. Tomorrow, however…" he smirked with a wink. There was a twinkle in his eye and Theadrin laughed. His spirit began to lift for the first time after the sudden twist his life had taken.

He took a sip of the hot liquid. It was sweet, and thawed the chill still left in his bones. "It is good," he said, sipping it again. "I have never tasted it before."

"It is a northern drink. I learned to make it years ago and have been trying to perfect it ever since." Caithal took a hearty sip of his own, and added, "But I haven't quite done so yet."

Silence followed save the cracks and pops of the oak wood on the fire. Myran picked up an old, scarred leather map and studied it, now and again taking a swallow from the pewter mug.

Lianna sat back in her chair and gripped her cup in both hands, sipping at it sparingly. Her green eyes were cast down at the mess of books and scrolls across the table, but every now and again would glance up to study their new acquaintances.

Theadrin began to think back on the whole matter from its beginning. After Lianna had disappeared and the four assassins were closing in on him, he recalled the flashes of light.

"How is it you came to find us?" he finally asked and looked at Caithal. "Your hearth was lit and the kettle was already boiling when we arrived here, so you can't have been away very long."

Caithal answered. "I have learned to hear, and not only to hear, but to heed."

Theadrin did not understand, and said as much. Caithal set down his cup for an instant. "I serve a God who is omnipresent. He is everywhere and sees and knows everything."

"The Highest King?" Theadrin asked.

"He is the King of kings, and that is what most people know him as. But he is much more than that."

"And what were the flashes of light? They were of your doing, weren't they?"

"Ah that." Caithal's hand left his cup and went toward his side. "Yes. That was something simple. The thing that servants of darkness fear most is light." He retrieved two rocks from his robes and placed them on the table. "Strike these together and the result will be what you saw, a brilliant flare of white light."

Theadrin took and examined them. "They don't look to be of ordinary stone. And they are not flint." One of the rocks was pale, milky white, and the other had a bluish hue.

"The white rock is called illmal, and the blue is minaw. They are invaluable and cannot be found around these parts," Caithal informed them. "I have had them a long time."

Theadrin shook his head and replaced the stones. "I still cannot imagine who would want us dead." He noticed Caithal glance quickly at Myran.

"They may have been sent by Gurn." Caithal hid the glance by lifting his cup to his lips. Myran's eyes snapped up when he said this.

"Gurn." Theadrin frowned. "The king of Arinon? How could he know that I even exist, let alone have any interest in a commoner of another kingdom?"

"He did not until recently, or the assassins would have come long ago."

Theadrin stared in confusion at the old hermit. "What are you saying?"

Caithal eyed him with a sudden air of mysterious gravity. "He wants you dead because you present a threat to his rule."

Myran's bronze eyes turned toward Theadrin. He slowly lowered the old map to the tabletop.

Caithal continued, "Years ago the throne of Arinon was held by King Valdithin; Gurn was only a minor lord. But the king was killed, murdered. There was fighting among the lords and nobles and somehow Gurn gained the throne—through treacherous ways, there is no doubt. However, before the king died, he sent his wife and two children, a son and daughter, away to safety under the guidance of his advisor and friend."

Caithal fixed his gaze on Theadrin. "You, Theadrin, are that son, and Lianna the daughter."

Theadrin found that words failed him. He disbelieved it instantly, there was no way it was possible. But as he thought, it explained several things. Roryn had always seemed like he was holding something back. Theadrin had always thought it odd when he would add in something strange to a conversation and then suddenly drop it or change the subject.

Lianna was the first to speak. She asked, "If our mother went with us when we fled, why is she not here now?" Theadrin looked astounded at his sister. Only an evening had they known this fellow and she appeared to believe every word that Caithal had told them.

The old hermit took on a saddened countenance. "We were pursued. The night was dark, and enemy horsemen were close on our heels. A flaming arrow hit the coach, setting it on fire. I threw myself over you and your mother to shield you from another volley of arrows. I was hit in the shoulder. When I reached to pull the shaft out..." Caithal paused and stared into his steaming cup, "I saw that the queen was dead." He did not continue for a moment. Caithal's eyes gleamed unshed tears at the memory of that dark night.

"The flames were climbing higher on the coach. I took the two of you in my arms and jumped out. In the darkness and confusion, our enemy did not see us as we rolled into the trees. They pursued the burning coach and passed us by."

"I took you to Caledon and to the hunter, Roryn. I had no way of caring for you, but I knew Roryn to be a good man, a faithful servant of the Highest King. I went into hiding myself, but never far away. Now, you are here and we are once more together."

The room fell silent. The fire crackled and the muted sound of the wind moaned outside. Once a barred owl called out from a tree, its voice barely audible in the night.

Theadrin pondered what Caithal had said. The implications of what it all meant suddenly struck him. He was the heir of King Valdithin, and that meant he was supposed to be king!

"And now Gurn knows we are alive and has sent assassins so he can remain king." Theadrin thought out loud. "How did he find me?"

Caithal turned his eyes back on Theadrin. "You had something of your father's, a medallion. Do you still have it?"

"The sword medallion? Yes. I always have it on." Theadrin's hand went to his throat but found the object missing. Surprised and a bit alarmed, he padded his shirt where it should have been hidden and then ran his fingers along the back of his neck. "It's gone! I must have lost it in the struggle."

"But you were wearing it? Then it is certainly what Gurn used to identify you." Caithal confirmed.

He went on. "It was made to look like the King Sword—the sword your father held, like every other king before him in the true line of Arnoni kings, as the symbol of his authority and kingship. He gave it to you the night we fled so that when you would return to take your place someday, there would be no question as to who you are."

Theadrin groaned, "And I have gone and lost it."

The hermit was quick to reassure him. "Do not fret over its loss. It must be in the great plan of the Highest King for this to happen. We must trust his plans are for the better in the end."

"What of the real King Sword? Does Gurn have it?" Theadrin asked.

"No. The sword disappeared after the night of your father's murder. Though he yearns for it greatly, Gurn has never held it." Caithal told them before taking another drink.

"The blade of the King Sword was forged of ember iron, the most rare metal in all the world. The story is told that at the creation of the world, the Highest King made one deposit of ember iron in all the earth. He created it for the special purpose of the ordination of kings. For this reason, the metal is also called 'crowning metal' in many of the older texts."

He thought for a moment and then added, "The King Sword would prove that the throne belongs to you. The line of the kings of Arinon is recorded on the King Sword, the true kings of Arnoni blood, starting with Penred. Your father's name was inscribed on it as the true king. You are his son and, before his death, he had your name inscribed upon it."

The Arnoni were the tribe that came from the north. They had allied with some of the people already dwelling in the land. After years of warring and fighting between them and others, the kingdom of Arinon was born. Penred, chieftain of the Arnoni tribe, was named king, and his line held the throne until the murder of Valdithin. Gurn was not of Arnoni blood but of the people who were allied with them.

"That evidence is gone too." Theadrin shook his head, lamenting the disappearance of the object that bore his name as the succession of the Arnoni line of kings.

Caithal looked intently at Theadrin. "That inscription is not the only proof, however. There is a prophecy that was spoken of old when the King Sword was forged in the ancient kingdom of Lloches Ynry. You know about that ancient kingdom, it is there that the tale of The Seven took place. It is now enveloped in the shroud of legend, but there remains the prophecy that was spoken at the making of the sword. It is this:

> At the changing of times and seasons,
> Where kings are removed and kings set up,
> Let wisdom be given to the wise
> And knowledge imparted to those of understanding.
> Deep and hidden things shall be revealed;
> In the hand of the chosen dwells kingly light.

"But it remains incomplete," Caithal added at the end. "In the early struggles of the Arnoni under Penred's grandson, many things were lost. One of the larger aggressive tribes that lived here warred against our fathers and stole many invaluable treasures. Historical documents were burned. The manuscript with the written prophecy was damaged so that all that could be read was what I told to you just now. It is said a copy was made of the prophesy by a scribe and smuggled out but that is little more than a fading hope."

Caithal grew contemplative and silence followed. The fire popped behind them and painted their shadows on the opposite wall.

"It is lost forever then," Theadrin finally stated sullenly. What did they have? The King Sword was gone, his medallion, and perhaps the most important piece of the prophecy. Caithal did not answer but buried his sudden gray mood inside his mug.

"What are we going to do now?" wondered Lianna. The news of not being able to return home still stuck in her mind. "Where can we go if Gurn is hunting us?"

"We will talk in the morning. But now you must get some rest." Caithal stood. He looked at Lianna and said, "There is a bed in the other room. I hope it will offer you some comfort."

Lianna made to protest but Caithal quickly added, "It is my pleasure to serve you in any way that I can, my lady." Caithal insisted. "As I did for your dear mother, I would be honored to do for you."

With a nice smile and crimsoned cheeks she accepted.

Myran drew Caithal aside. "Caithal, is it really true? Is Theadrin the heir of Valdithin?"

"Without a doubt," the hermit affirmed.

Myran looked down. "I was on my way north, but if they are who you say…"

Caithal patted Myran's shoulder with a confident smile. "They are, Myran." The old man left the conversation as it stood and began to douse the candles about the room.

"But why didn't you tell me, Caithal?" Myran followed, keeping his voice low so Theadrin and Lianna would not overhear. He was agitated with Caithal for keeping this from him. "I have wasted so much time trying to find them, and all along you knew where they were."

"It wasn't the right time. You weren't ready, and neither were they." Caithal answered simply and would say no more.

The following morning was gray and blustery. It had snowed again during the night and left a fresh coat over every rock, tree, and bush. When Theadrin woke, Caithal was sitting in the chair by the fire, reading a red leather book. Lianna emerged from behind the deer hide on the rock wall that served as a door to another room. Myran was gone.

Theadrin stood, stretched, and then went to look out the small round window to the right of the door. The wind caught the snow like dust and carried it in swift billowing currents across the ground. Caithal's hut proved to be sturdy, and kept the heat in well.

He heard the old hermit's voice behind greeting his sister. "There is bread on the table and some raspberry jam." Caithal didn't rise but set down his book momentarily. Directing his attention at Theadrin, he said. "How was your night's rest?"

"Fitful." Theadrin confessed, turning and going to the table.

That is to be expected." Caithal smiled. "I can't imagine any young man at your age finding out they are the successor to a kingship and then sleep very well."

"It wasn't because I was excited about it." Theadrin said. He didn't want to tell the truth at first, but quickly relented. "After thinking on it, I… I do not want be king."

Caithal did not answer, and so he continued. "I don't have the wisdom or experience to lead a kingdom." He looked down. "I don't want to become king," he said again.

Caithal looked long at him, as if weighing what he said to be true or false.

The door opened allowing snow to blow in and Myran entered. Latching it shut again, he stepped into the room brushing the powdery snow from his clothes.

"How did it go, lad?" Caithal inquired.

"The forest seems quiet enough. I saw but one traveler on the road. It is too cold for people to be moving about much." Myran answered. "The Cruthene hide themselves very well."

"Cruthene?" Theadrin did not know the word.

"They are the ones hunting you." Myran told him.

"Then we must be off soon." Caithal placed his palms on the arms of his chair and stood slowly.

"Where are we going?" Theadrin asked.

"We must leave this place." Caithal stated. "We will go north."

"But that will take us to the border, and closer to Gurn," Theadrin warned.

"But that is something he will not expect." Caithal said. "To keep on top of the enemy, we must do the unexpected."

Theadrin looked down at the table. An old map lay unrolled before him. It was brown with age, and the edges were tattered and stained. Myran had been studying it the night before while they all sat talking. He picked it up gently and examined the drawings. It showed a large landmass that was mostly forested. There were mountains as well. Set apart from them, however, was an odd-looking mass. It was circled and had some words that he could not read next to it.

"Where is this, Caithal?" Theadrin asked.

Caithal came to stand at the table. "This is the land of the far north," he said, glancing at Theadrin.

Theadrin had heard many bizarre and fantastic stories of that place. No one alive was known to have been there. "What is this?" He put his finger on the circled portion.

"That is the Tor. It is there that our fathers lived before leaving to establish the southern kingdoms. The stories vary of why they left. There are many strange tales of the seven tribes that originally lived there, but only two exist today. One, Caledovi, founded Caledon; the other, Arnoni, founded Arinon under King Penred. The rest have passed into legend. All historical documents perished at the same time as the missing piece of the prophecy, and so our reason for leaving the Tor is not remembered."

Theadrin had heard that history before but never imagined he was a part of the Arnoni bloodline, let alone the line of kings. Roryn was neither Arnoni nor Caledovi, so Theadrin assumed the same of himself. He wondered what became of the other five tribes. Perhaps they were still there, hidden away in the farthest reaches of the north.

"Your father was always interested in the mystery of why they left." Caithal recalled. "He believed there was some connection to the lost kingdom of Lloches Ynry, where the tale of The Seven originates. He may have been right, but I just don't know."

Theadrin looked at the map. The stories had always intrigued him as well. He would learn the answer to the mystery one day. He felt, somehow, he had to know.

They packed some things they would need and set out. Caithal had a pony that he rode. Myran offered his saddle to Lianna, and she accepted only after Myran insisted he wouldn't ride anyway.

They left the forest and kept a slow but steady course northward, stopping little. At nightfall they made camp by one of the many tall rock formations scattered about this part of the country. The boulder blocked most of the wind, and a sheltering oak that still carried most of its leaves spread its bows above them.

When a fire was lit and carried a healthy blaze, Myran left the camp to scout about the area. Theadrin fed the fire and watched Myran's tall, lean form slowly melting into the darkness of the night. Lianna sat on a spread-out deer hide and wrapped her cloak tightly about her shoulders.

"Who is he, Caithal?" Theadrin asked of Myran after he was gone.

Caithal looked at the fire for a long time, his dark, hazel eyes catching the glint of the flames. "Myran is a man who has nothing left to lose. I first met him when he was very young. He lived in Arinon with a good friend of mine who was one of your father's loyal nobles. Myran was full of life then. There was a fire in him that burned brighter than daylight." Caithal's eyes gleamed at remembering.

"Two summers ago he showed up near my hovel. He did not remember me, for he was very young when I first met him. But the change that had taken place in him was drastic.

"Myran was bone weary and carried a heavy burden. He was not the same person as the high-spirited boy I met earlier. The light in his eyes was gone." Caithal stared into the flames and sighed before continuing.

"And whether that light will be restored again is not for me to say."

"What happened to make him so?" Lianna asked. The fire's red glow played upon her saddened face.

"That is not for me to tell." Caithal looked slowly at her and managed a smile.

A moment later Myran returned.

"We are safe for tonight." He said, settling himself by the fire.

Lianna looked at him. The first time she saw him, at the fair, she had seen something in his bronze eyes she could not place. Now she knew. Caithal was accurate in his description; the light was not there. Or at least, Lianna allowed, it was greatly diminished.

"Who are the Cruthene?" She asked him as he unsheathed his knife and began to sharpen it.

He glanced up at her. "Cruthene is the old word for shadow. In old tales and legends they were said to be of the very shadows themselves, hence their name. Earlier tales say that they were a tribe of barbarians in the farthest reaches of the north that would kill for the sport of it. They would make a game out of killing without being seen or heard. Some accounts tell how they are not men at all but wicked creatures that come from the cavernous depths of the earth. The last account of them was long ago. I don't know how Gurn could have found them."

Myran looked to Caithal for affirmation, but the old man remained silent and stared into the flames as if he had not heard what was said.

After this they fell into silence. From a distant patch of pine echoed the call of a whippoorwill. Caithal's eyes located the spot.

"I recall an old legend." He ended the quiet between them. "There was once a race of forest dwellers who were very short; none known to be taller than the height of my waist.

"They were an elusive people and preferred not to be bothered by us taller folk. They have not been seen for centuries. Some folk entertain that they are still around; only we can never detect them because they have such a skill in hiding. It is said they dwell in the most remote parts of the forests, in hidden hollows of trees where they can watch us without being seen."

He leaned forward. "Some even believe the many sounds we hear at night, like the whippoorwill, are the forest folk talking to one another. Have you ever tried looking for a whippoorwill when it is calling? You will never find it."

"Do you believe those stories?" Theadrin asked.

The hermit shrugged as though he didn't care, but said after thinking a moment, "In my life I have seen many strange things and many wonderful things." He looked about at the others as the firelight portrayed in his eyes a look of hidden mischief. "There are hidden things no man has yet discovered. Our Great King is infinite, and he has created untold mysteries waiting to be uncovered; and I, for one, want to discover them. For I know that with each discovery I will learn something new about the Infinite One."

Theadrin looked at the fire. "That makes me think of the prophecy 'Deep and hidden things will be revealed.' What can it all mean, Caithal?"

"The two first lines I believe have come to pass, or are in the process. With the death of your father, *kings removed and kings set up*, the times and seasons are changing in Arinon. A new king has been set up, Gurn, but he will not be the last before this is over."

Theadrin's head was spinning trying to understand it all.

Caithal shrugged. "One can never know the meaning of a prophecy until it actually happens."

They talked longer until one by one they drifted off to sleep. Myran remained awake, still uneasy. He had told them it was safe, and for the most part he really believed they were. But he was not familiar with the way the Cruthene worked. Would they strike night after night relentlessly or wait longer periods? He was unsure of what to expect.

He sat with his back to the fire, so that his eyes would be adjusted to the dark, and watched the surrounding land. They were on somewhat of a hill and so had a good view of the outlying area. It was a starry night and the moon glistened off the fresh snow, brightening the countryside.

Again the whippoorwill called out its mysterious-sounding song. Myran, living alone in the forests and countrysides for two years, heard sounds from sources he knew not. Thinking of this, he was reminded of something.

He reached into his pouch and brought out a small object. He had found it in the dead pine forest before meeting Theadrin and Lianna and just before glimpsing the Cruthene assassin. It was a curious thing—the length of his middle finger and made of engraved metal. There were images of horses and warriors intertwined about its length, and it appeared as though it had a part broken off at one point. But Myran could not make out what it was.

When the fire dwindled, he turned and refueled it and then lay back. An unimaginable number of stars blinked down at him. He knew a couple of the many constellations, but apart from that, the heavens were a glorious mystery. What kept them on their courses and burning so brightly? What a great God was the Highest King.

He watched the stars until his eyelids grew too heavy to hold open any longer and sleep overcame him.

Eleven

They continued north at a brisk pace and reached the border of the two kingdoms before midday. A wide stream, not yet frozen over, curved in front of them. It ran from a small forest to the west, with various-sized white-capped rocks rising from the black running surface.

Halting before its edge, they discussed the course from thereon. Theadrin looked across the stream and saw a rider crest a hill a bowshot from them. He stopped and seemed to be scanning the lower country, then moved out of sight once more.

They were not unaccustomed to seeing other travelers and Theadrin thought nothing of the sighting. He turned and looked at the others.

"...to cross over to Arinon or stay in Caledon," Caithal was saying. "Here we must decide."

No one spoke so Caithal continued. "We are eluding the enemy for now, but we don't have any other plan of action. We can't hide forever."

It was then that a low, eerie howl escaped the bounds of the forest and found them. It was clumsy sounding and was similar to, but not altogether the same as, that of a wolf. Caithal glanced at the wood and then spurred his pony, saying, "Quick! Across the stream!"

They splashed across just as the first beast leapt from the forest line on the far side. It was massive and covered in matted brown hair. It had the shape of a wolf but was three times the size of any Theadrin had seen before. It had a grizzled hump on its shoulders, and foaming slobber dripped from its yellow fangs. Its tail was unlike a regular wolf, being long with a tuft of hair at the end.

It loped over the snow and was joined by five others. They moved quickly and were across the stream before the four had made it to the hill. Myran halted and drew the sword from his back, ready to face them. Theadrin stopped when he saw Myran standing alone and shouted to Caithal.

"Get my sister to safety!"

"Wait!" Caithal's call stopped him. He grabbed a long bundled item from his pony and unwrapped it revealing a sword. It was not an extraordinary sword in appearance, but was sharp and sturdy.

"I have been saving this for you." Caithal said as he tossed it to Theadrin.

Theadrin drew it out swiftly and started back to where Myran was bracing himself for the first attack. The huge, dark animal leapt up toward his face, snarling ferociously. Myran dropped and rolled as the beast flew over him.

Theadrin reached it as it landed and swung his sword level. It had little reaction time and Theadrin's blade caught the side of its face. He brought his sword up again and finished it with a chop to the back of the neck.

⧖

Lianna and Caithal had crested the hill and saw an old country house. It had at one time boasted skilled craftsmanship, but it was clear that its current owner cared little for maintaining it. The doorposts were sun dried and split, its wooden tiled roof needing desperate repair.

They pounded on the door and were answered by a slightly overweight man with unkempt hair and a bristled double chin.

"What do you want?" he demanded, scratching his belly beneath a worn brown shirt.

"We need help, please! My brother…" Lianna frantically tried to explain but could not spit the right words out.

"We were attacked by wolves down the hill," Caithal helped. "Two of our friends are still down there."

Another man, tall and bearded, who carried a noble bearing, appeared behind the man in the doorway. His large eyes scanned over the two but he said nothing.

"They need help, please," Lianna begged.

The bearded man placed a quick hand on the shorter man's shoulder and whispered in his ear, at the same time reaching for something out of sight behind the door jamb. Lianna suddenly became wary. What if these men were no better than the ones she had encountered at the Spring Fair? Her heart leapt when the man with the beard pulled two short spears from behind the doorjamb. He immediately brushed past them and through the doorway. "Don't ya be a frettin, maam," said the heavyset man to Lianna. "We'll soon send them howlin' brutes ta runnin'!"

⌛

Back down the hill the fight ensued. Myran swung at one of the wolves with his sword, but it suddenly pulled back then leapt on him. Its ugly teeth lashed out for his throat, but he brought his dagger up and punctured its neck as they fell to the ground.

He quickly got back up and swerved to the side just in time to avoid the deadly jaws of another. Theadrin stood facing two of them on either side. One made to lunge but feinted from Theadrin's blade at the last minute as the second beast leapt to the kill.

Theadrin, half expecting this, was ready and spun on the oncoming animal. It hit into him with forceful impact, and he landed on his back.

The giant beast had Theadrin's sword blade in the grip of its teeth and began to shake its head viciously. Theadrin could not maintain his hold on the sword and it spun away, far out of reach. The beast looked down at its victim with bloodlust in its eyes. It drew its head back to make the fatal bite when it jerked violently and toppled to the side, a spear shaft protruding from its grizzled hump.

A man came running down the hill and pinned the second beast to the snow with another spear. He charged past Theadrin, letting loose a battle whoop. The man was very tall, with a beard and long brown hair. Theadrin thought there was something very familiar about him, that he knew him from somewhere.

The man ran up to Myran and they together brought down another of the ravenous animals. Only one remained. He was a massive beast with a thick, black hide that was knotted horribly. Until now it had been waiting, watching the other wolves, like a cunning war chief observes his warriors while they execute his well-devised battle plans.

It came for Theadrin first, boring headlong into the bearded man and knocking him to the snowy ground. Its gait reminded him much of a lion.

He had seen one once, in a show at the Spring Fair. They were known to populate the Ambered Hills to the far south of Caledon. This beast, although unmistakably wolflike, had such shaggy hair around its head that it appeared to have a mane. And its tail was more lionlike as well.

When it was still ten paces from Theadrin, it leapt high and came down fast. It attacked with such incredible speed Theadrin barely had time to react. He mimicked Myran's move earlier and dropped to the ground and rolled. Hot searing pain erupted as the animal grazed the back of his left shoulder blade and landed behind him.

He ignored the fiery pain in his shoulder and swung at the lunging beast. His sword caught its front legs and it fell flopping in the crimson-stained snow trying desperately to recover itself.

Myran came up as Theadrin ended the creature's thrashing with a final thrust. The bearded man came slower. He limped to one of the beasts and yanked his spear out. Theadrin knelt, still gripping his sword tightly and catching his breath. His shoulder had gone numb, but he felt any movement would bring an eruption of pain.

"Odd beasts." Theadrin recognized the voice of the bearded man and turned to see the same lofty bearing and long proud face of one unexpected.

"Hectur?" Theadrin supported himself with his sword.

Hectur inclined his head to Theadrin, showing little surprise at seeing him. "How did you…."? Theadrin didn't know what to say.

Hectur smiled. "A young woman and an older man almost pounded my door in. Said their friends needed help. They said it was wolves but…" He looked down at the carcass of matted brown fur, "I have never seen wolves like these."

"Nor I," Myran said, prodding one of the dead beasts with the tip of his sword.

"Is my sister safe?" Theadrin began to rise.

"They are at the house," Hectur informed him. At that moment a second man came puffing up, spear in hand. He stopped, out of breath as sweat poured over his red round face.

"Yan!" Theadrin erected himself and winced as the fire leapt back in his shoulder.

"You're hurt?" Myran asked.

"Just a scratch."

"It must have caught you with its claws when you ducked," Myran observed. "We will have Caithal examine it. He has some knowledge of healing."

As they turned up the hill, Theadrin glanced back to the wood where the beasts had come from. The snow was bright and he was forced to squint. But something caught his eye, a flicker of movement, a tall dark shape melting into the forest.

Yan was ecstatic to meet Theadrin again. He had lost his house and property in his gambling at the Spring Fair, and Hectur had agreed to house him for the winter, under the promise that Yan would find an honest job and buy a new house when summer came.

They talked much and shared a meal together.

"We saw the fam'ly resemblance in yer sister," Yan was saying over a greedy mouthful of venison. "A course we would'a helped ya anyways, even if we hadn't."

"I have no doubt," Theadrin laughed.

Hectur and Myran recognized each other from the melee fight that spring, and Hectur immediately became resentful toward him, remembering how he had been bested and his pride hurt. Hectur was a man who put great store in honor, and that incident had done much to harm it in his eyes.

Myran sensed his sudden mood change and said, "I have never seen such skill with the spear. The power and precision behind each thrust was amazing. And that first throw—that is the skill of a veteran warrior."

Hectur's countenance softened. Myran continued, "Had you been allowed to use a spear in the melee, no doubt you would have won outright. You fight like a bear and stand strong as a wall. Hereon I will call you Mathwin." Hectur's cheeks colored a dull crimson. He was proud of the high praise given, and all dislike for Myran was instantly shattered and replaced with the opposite. That day Myran won a loyal friend to his side.

Caithal cleaned Theadrin's wound well and put a salve on it that he had in a box in his pocket. Then he bandaged it saying, "This salve will protect the wound from any poison or bacteria that may have been on the animal's claws."

Soon twilight leaked into the sky and the sun submerged under the fiery gold waves of the western hills.

"Ya'll be stayin' the night, won't ya?" Yan watched Theadrin hopefully. "Hectur wouldn't mind a couple more guests. Would ya, man?"

At this Hectur grunted. "Indeed. Such company would be welcome after putting up with you."

Theadrin looked around at his companions. Myran looked at Caithal who nodded his assent.

"We will gladly stay. But we are indebted to you already for helping us," Theadrin said.

"Nonsense! The least we kin do, aye, Hectur?" Yan beamed and wiped juice from his double chin; he was very obviously proud of the honor Theadrin was giving him.

"Your kindness to us has far surpassed what I did for you," Theadrin said.

"Niver say it!" Yan protested. They fell back into easy conversation and laughed much.

Caithal sat quietly watching them. He couldn't help but smile. Theadrin may not have noticed it, but he was already producing qualities of leadership to be found in a king. Small as it may be, he had gained the loyalty and admiration of the two men as easily as speech flowed from his mouth. "Much like your father," he said under his breath.

That night when all slept peacefully, the Cruthene struck again.

Twelve

Theadrin awoke with a start to heavy silence. His dream, though its memory had slipped away as his eyes opened, had been a dark one. His heartbeat was quick and he forced himself to breath slower, wiping the sweat from his eyes.

It was dark in the room with only a shaft of dim moonlight coming through a high window. The old house, its ancient wooden support beams cracked and dried out, creaked and popped against the breeze. Outside the night was bitter cold. Aside from the frequent wind gusts, nothing stirred.

Rising to his elbows Theadrin looked about and could barely see the dark humps across the floor of the other sleepers. He wasn't at all tired and began to sit up straight when a strong grip on his arm prevented him.

Myran was still lying on his back, but his eyes were open and alert. He looked up at Theadrin with a warning written across his features. At that moment the pale beam of moonlight flickered. Myran glanced at it, and then pulled Theadrin close and whispered in his ear, "Your sword."

Theadrin loosened the blade in its scabbard and quietly rolled to his stomach. He rose slowly and crept to the door of the room that Lianna slept in. His heart began to beat rapidly and his muscles tensed. He reached the door and lifted the latch.

As he crossed over to where she slept, a chilly wind brushed past him. A shiver shot through his spine and he stopped. The window on the far side of the room was open to the pallid night outside. The gray curtains moved softly from an invisible breeze.

His sword was out in a flash as the shadow came at him. He could see no discernible shape but swung at the figure that was rushing toward him. The Cruthene swerved to the side avoiding his blade and became one with the darkness in the corner of the room.

"Lianna!" Theadrin shouted to warn his sister as the shadow moved again. Lianna was up and on her feet. She saw Theadrin attacking the shadows and heard him cry out in pain. As he extended his arm, the wound from the wolf attack suddenly reclaimed its fiery anger and he faltered. The shadow sprang forward and knocked him against the bedpost. Myran darted in from the other room and hurled a piece of furniture at the figure. It struck home and they heard the sound of a body hitting against the wall. Lianna's eyes had somewhat adjusted and she caught a faint glimpse of the Cruthene as he regained his footing.

The assassin moved toward the man who had kept it from its prey. Myran shoved a small side table, but the assassin leapt over it with ease knocking him to the floor. As the Cruthene raised its blade ready to strike, Theadrin rose up on one knee and cut into its side. A loud shriek sounded, and the dark figure darted across the room and out the window. Caithal, Hectur, and Yan entered then bearing lights and weapons. Blood ran down the length of Myran's sword blade.

"Is everyone all right?" Caithal asked, putting a hand on Lianna's shoulder. "You're not hurt, are you?" Lianna shook her head. She couldn't speak.

"What in blue blazes was it?" Yan cast a nervous glance at the window. Myran ran over and looked out.

"It's gone," he said after a careful inspection and returned.

"Let's get the fire started." Caithal put an arm around Lianna's shoulders and led the way out to the other room.

When a healthy blaze burned beneath the old hearth, Theadrin began to tell Yan and Hectur of their real reason for being there.

He described the first attack of the Cruthene and how they met Caithal and Myran. He explained to them why he and Lianna could not return home.

"Then yesterday, the wolf pack attacked us. The rest of the story, you know." Theadrin finished.

"And I still say they are the oddest wolves I have ever seen." Hectur added his input.

"Wolves they were not." Caithal informed them. "They were trained, like hunting dogs. They are called Ustvil." He was silent for a short time. The name was faintly familiar to Theadrin, but he could not place it.

Caithal continued, "The Ustvildu are a beast that inhabits legend and myth. If you look into many of the older tales, you will find mention of them. These Ustvildu were like the Cruthene, not from here nor anywhere near here. They are from the northern lands."

"What are you saying?" Theadrin asked with a frown, trying to make sense of things.

Caithal explained, "Something doesn't add up. How is Gurn attaining these things to send after us—things only remembered in our oldest tales and legends?"

"How kin we find that out?" Yan wondered.

"We may not be able to. Unless"—he leaned back as a thought came into his head—"unless we were to go into Arinon and find out; to Avross, into the wolf Gurn's very den."

Avross was the capital city of the realm of Arinon. To go there was to beg capture and probable death. Caithal was not at all surprised that they looked at him with stunned expressions. Perhaps they began to wonder at his sanity, that maybe more than the color of his hair had faded with age.

He smiled reassuringly and said, "Gurn and his men would not know you by sight, Theadrin. Without your father's medallion they cannot identify you. And it is unlikely Gurn would be looking for you in Avross of all places."

After a moment of running it over in his head, Theadrin agreed. "I see what you mean. We will go to Avross then, and see if we cannot study Gurn a bit—see what the people really think of how their king has ruled these past many years."

"We must leave before daybreak and cover our back trail to avoid being followed again," Myran put in.

Yan looked at Theadrin and said, "Whether Theadrin's a king's heir er not, I'd still gladly help 'im 'n this quest. A'course"—he added quickly—"Bein' that he is, it does make it all the better." He stood in front of Theadrin and then went down on one knee. "I'll follow ya wherever ya go and give my all to help ya gain back the throne a yer father."

Theadrin was shocked at this unexpected and sudden action. "Yan, I..." He looked over at Caithal, who looked on with a smile. "I accept your services, Yan." He quickly stood the awkwardly kneeling man back up. "I am honored to have you."

As Myran watched the scene, Ao-idh's words came back into his head: *You must find king Valdithin's heir. Find him...*

Now that he had done this, what was next? There was nothing for him anymore...nothing but this.

With Ao-idh's words ringing clear and fresh in his head, Myran went and stood before Theadrin. He drew his sword and held it point down, hilt against his chest, while placing his right hand on Theadrin's right shoulder. This was the way warriors would pledge fealty to their lord in older times.

"I offer you my sword in reclaiming the land of Arinon. I vow to protect you with my life against the danger that will face us in the paths ahead."

Theadrin put his hand on Myran's shoulder and looked him in the eye. "I accept it, Myran Cai, though I am not worthy of it." He wasn't sure why he had added *Cai* onto Myran's name. It was perhaps more surprising to him than any other in the room, but Myran seemed not to mind.

Hectur was quick to follow Myran's example. Theadrin was filled with an overflowing mix of emotions. He felt proud, but humble and undeserving; he felt like crying out in joy, but also somber. He felt a strong friendship begin to knit between them—one that would grow and strengthen with every trial and battle they would face together.

Before the gold morning light seeped warmth into the white land, the small band left the old house and traveled west. They crossed the border and were well into Arinon by midday. The people there were content to study them from a distance. Some watched them with cold stares while others were expressionless.

They arrived in the town of Lundel and stopped at the Inn. It was still a half day's ride to Avross. Housing there for the night, they started out the next morning after breaking fast on sausages and muffins freshly made in the inn's kitchen.

Avross was indeed a city for a king. At first sight, Theadrin had to catch his breath.

Its walls were high and its gates beautifully crafted. It was built on three hills, in the shape of a triangle, and the main gate was facing south. The western hill was where the king's palace was, with the great hall inside. Atop the hill on the eastern side sat the Barracks and armory. A large cathedral crowned the center hill. This was for a purpose, and Caithal explained it to the rest of them.

"King Penred, who built the great city, erected it before any other building. He put it there because he wanted the rest of the city to be built around it. This showed that he wanted the worship of the Highest King to be the center and foundation of all in the kingdom," he told them.

They entered through the center gate and stopped to behold the great building which, since the time it was constructed, had been enlarged to a much greater scale as the city grew.

But as they admired it, Caithal's forehead creased in a frown. "Something is wrong."

"What is it?" Theadrin asked.

"I can't place it"—Caithal answered as he squinted up at the cathedral—"but something about this building is greatly altered."

As if to confirm Caithal's words, the beautiful doors opened and a procession of richly robed men emerged. They strode elegantly in two rows led by a single man who wore different clothing from the rest. His robes were deep blue with golden hemming and red designs across the chest.

The procession moved slowly down the first flight of steps to a paved plateau and halted, soaking in the attention they were attracting from the people. After a brief time the lead man stepped forward and raised his hands.

"Is that Gurn?" Theadrin asked Caithal.

"No. That man is much too old. I have never seen him before."

The man looked about at the people gathering and proclaimed, "The new moon begins tonight. Let all prepare themselves, for tonight the sacrifices will begin!"

With that, one of the men behind raised a horn to his lips and blew a long blast. The robed men turned and walked back into the building. Caithal watched with disgust and finally spoke, "So that is it."

The rest waited in silence for him to continue. "This building is no longer the house of the Highest King, but a temple to a pagan god."

"Sacrifices?" Theadrin looked at the closing door of the temple. "What kind was he talking about, Caithal?"

"I don't know. We've got a lot to find out." Caithal glared back at the temple.

⌛

Myran and Hectur entered one of the taverns and stood by the door, studying the people around the room. Most looked to be of the rowdy sort—thugs. There was also a table of off-duty soldiers. One man sat apart from the rest of the crowd and looked, by his clothing, a farmer.

Myran said, "There, Mathwin, the man seated alone. He should tell us what we want to know." They walked to the table where the man sipped at a pewter jar of ale and took a seat. The man lifted his eyes to them but remained silent.

"Greetings, friend," Myran said agreeably. He received a curt nod but nothing more.

"We are travelers from Caledon." Myran explained. "We couldn't help but overhear about the sacrifices."

"Aye. The sacrifices." The man's eye narrowed and he took a larger draught of his ale. It appeared he was trying to flush away the reminder of the sacrifices.

"What kind do these priests perform?" Myran inquired.

"Why would you like to know? If y'aren't from here, they wouldn't be concern'n you now, would they?" Myran perceived something in his tone and manner. This man had no taste for what was going to take place. "Ya waste your time askin'. I haven't the heart to talk of it," the farmer muttered. "Now leave me be."

Myran saw that pressing the matter further would only serve to lessen their chance of learning. He accepted the man's words with a nod and a shrug and, leaning back in his chair, glanced about the room. Mathwin looked at the man, who was taking another gulp of ale, and then at Myran.

The room was dark, and the pipes that many of the men were smoking created a gray haze. On the far side of the room, the group of soldiers burst into obnoxious laughter after one had told some crude joke.

Myran returned Mathwin's look and lifted his eyebrows. "What god is served in that temple?" He asked the sullen farmer. "The last time I was in Arinon, the Highest King was still worshiped here, and no sacrifices took place."

The man looked up at him. "Now *there* is a name not heard in this place for a long time. Few, if any, still profess to serve the Highest of Kings. Arinon is given over to the worship of Amlek." The name was almost a curse on his tongue. Even if they had not received the reason for coming, they had learned one important thing, and it was the people were unhappy.

The palace of the king was a massive structure with many beautiful domes and arched doorways. A small stonewall surrounded its perimeter and the tops of the leafless trees could be seen growing from the gardens within. The two-door gate that was the main entrance began to creak open.

Theadrin, Yan, Caithal, and Lianna stood across the street when the gate doors parted. Several riders appeared at a slow pace in the direction of the temple. They trotted along in rich apparel and with a pompous air. The foremost wore a thin crown of gold and Theadrin knew him without having to ask: Gurn.

He rode with his head high in arrogance, making a show for all the people to see. He was a small man, but for what he lacked in build and height, he more than made up for in pomp and wealth.

As Theadrin stood watching them ride past, he heard a faint cry from the opposite side of the riders. Peering through the entanglement of horses' legs, he made out an old beggar sitting against the cold stonewall holding out his hand. Most ignored him. One laughed and yelled something that Theadrin could not make out.

None of the others with Theadrin seemed to notice the beggar. Theadrin continued to watch the old man as the riders passed on and people began to move in the street again. Caithal was explaining different things about the palace, but Theadrin was hearing none of it.

The beggar would plead to the people close to him for food but all shunned the poor man. Some even spit on him or kicked at him. One foot caught the side of his face, knocking him to the ground.

Theadrin was unable to bear it any longer and started away from the rest. He ran to the man lying in the cold snow, placed a gentle hand on his shoulder and helped him back up to his sitting position. He then brushed the snow away that stuck to the man's clothes and skin. "Food, sir. Please." The man's voice cracked. Theadrin saw that he was blind.

"Easy, friend. I have some for you." At the sound of his voice the beggar turned his head in Theadrin's direction. Caithal, Lianna, and Yan came up behind as Theadrin gave a small cake of bread to the man and wiped the spittle from his face with the edge of his cloak. He then lifted the water skin to the man's cracked lips.

"When did you last eat, friend?" Theadrin's voice was soft and showed the compassion he felt.

"Your voice," the blind man's words were a hoarse whisper that cracked. "It is very familiar to me."

"I cannot say I have seen you before," Theadrin confessed.

Suddenly, after Theadrin said these last words, the beggar reached out toward him. "My king!" he said. "My lord, am I dead?" Unshed tears formed in his eyes.

Theadrin gripped his arm and said, "You mistake me for another."

But the man seemed all the more certain when Theadrin spoke. "My king." He began to sob. "King Valdithin."

Thirteen

"That's gotta be them." The knock at the door sounded again and Yan opened it wide. Myran and Mathwin entered the room in the Red Leaf Inn grim faced.

"What have you learned?" Theadrin met them, still pondering his brush with the blind beggar.

"Caithal was right." Myran sighed. "The Highest King has been thrown aside for some pagan god."

Caithal sat in a rounded chair and asked, "What do they call this god?"

"It is a name I have never heard." Mathwin spoke up.

"Amlek," Myran answered.

"Amlek," Caithal repeated. "Of all names..." his voice trailed off.

"What of the sacrifices?" Theadrin asked.

"The farmer we talked to would tell us nothing, so we asked a soldier. He already had had several cups of ale and did not suspect us for anything, so he told us." Myran's face suddenly went cold.

Theadrin saw and pressed. "What is it, Myran?"

"There are three sacrifices that will take place; one every night for the next three nights. The first, tonight, will be a ram. Tomorrow night it will be a bull." He stopped and glanced at Lianna.

"Tell me," Theadrin insisted.

"The last sacrifice requires a child, Theadrin." The room fell silent as Myran looked back at him.

"They wouldn't," Theadrin whispered as a hot rage leapt inside of him.

"Have the people of Arinon become so deceived that they would allow such a thing?" Caithal wondered aloud.

"It hasn't happened before," Myran told them. "I learned that this is to be the first. Also most of the kingdom does not know about it yet."

"We've got to stop them." Theadrin looked down, already attempting to form a plan.

"How would you do that?" Caithal brought the question that had to be asked.

"We have to do something if we can," Lianna said.

"We will." Theadrin set his jaw. He was determined, and nothing else would rest in his mind until the child was saved.

They stayed in the Red Leaf Inn that night, and the next morning Theadrin had devised the beginnings of a plan. He and Myran went out to get the lay of the city. Yan and Hectur went in search for the safest and quickest way of escape, should one be needed.

Meanwhile, Caithal and Lianna went to the temple itself to find out what they could about the child. They entered through the main door into a large room. Rows and rows of benches were laid out all the way up to the front. Lianna followed as Caithal walked to the right side of the room and into another smaller room. She noticed how he seemed to know every turn.

They went through another door that led them down a hallway and back outside. A pathway, swept clean of the snow, led up an incline and to a round structure. A stone altar was set in the center of a polished marble platform. Several priests bustled around it, cleaning from the sacrifice of the ram the night prior and making preparations for the next.

When Caithal and Lianna approached, one of the priests met them. "You are not allowed to be in this area," he told them with an annoyed voice.

"We come to inquire of the sacrifices," Caithal said.

"What is it you would inquire? Out with it and be gone that I may get back to business." The priest was irritated with them for bothering him and could not stand still. He shifted positions constantly. He had a long, pointy face and sharp, squinty eyes.

"What time will the final sacrifice take place tomorrow?" Caithal asked.

"You should know." The priest wasn't paying much attention. He looked to the others moving quickly around and past them, surveying their work.

"Forgive me, but we are newly arrived here," Caithal explained.

"When the sun has set and the moon shines forth," the priest said distractedly. "Will there be anything else? I am very busy."

"I think that is it. Ah, has the child been chosen yet?" Caithal subtly inquired. "Yes, yes of course. She has been selected. Go now and excuse me." He nearly sprinted off, calling out a correction to one of the priests.

"A girl." Lianna looked horrified at Caithal. "They're going to kill a little girl."

Caithal did not speak but drew a breath, and they turned to go.

That evening, as the sun set behind a dim horizon, Theadrin and Myran leaned against the wall of the cathedral and watched the second sacrifice begin. There were torches all about the outside yard that cast dancing shadows over the grim faces in the crowd. Away to the left of the altar, around a corner of the temple, a low bellow from the ox pen sounded. Two priests appeared a moment later leading the choice bull toward the altar platform.

The high priest stood beside the heavy stone altar holding the sacrifice knife. Gurn stood on one end of the platform with an escort of guards placed about him. On the other side the nobles of Arinon stood. Theadrin could tell from their number that several were missing. There was a small flight of steps from the platform to the court below where the people of Avross watched in silence.

Theadrin scanned the back of the yard where there were two doors, one open and the other closed. The open door was where the people entered the yard, he and Myran included, but the other door was for the priests.

Theadrin tapped Myran's shoulder and indicated the closed door. "I bet that is where the priests will enter with the girl tomorrow night."

Myran nodded, thinking it likely.

Theadrin looked about to make sure that they were not being watched by anyone. "Let's slip inside and have a look."

As the bull mounted the platform behind the two priests, Myran and Theadrin crept unnoticed back inside the temple. There was a short hallway lit by torches tucked in elaborately carved sconces. They walked quickly and into the main room where they paused to look about.

The cathedral was a beautifully made structure. Candlelight skipped and played on the smooth walls of stone, and curtain folds hung from the ceiling to the floor, evenly placed around the perimeter of the great room. There were many rows of benches that led up to the front where there was an open area vacant of furniture. It had not been used for the purpose it was built for in nearly a decade. Although the Highest King was no longer worshiped there, Theadrin thought he could feel a small remnant of the peace that used to dwell there. If ever he did become king, he vowed the peace would return.

"Theadrin." Myran's voice brought him back from this thought. "Look here."

They found two wooden doors side by side. Dim light flickered through the bottom of the left and the other was dark. Theadrin tried the handle on the right door and found it was not locked. It creaked slightly in the silence of the building until Theadrin stopped and peered inside. It was a storage room. There were chairs, tables, and various other pieces of furniture stacked and piled inside. From the dust that covered them it looked as though they had not been used since the time Valdithin had ruled.

Theadrin stepped inside while Myran kept watch in case someone came by. The room was very dark and Theadrin nearly tripped on a short stool of some sort. He held out his hands and moved to the wall that was in between that room and the one to which the other door led. It was made of wood planking. Moving his fingers along it, he touched an object that stuck out just enough to feel the edge. It was small and round—a knot in the wood.

With a sudden inspiration, he drew his knife and loosened it. It came loose after working it for a short while and he peered through. The elongated room on the other side was lit by candles and was easy to identify as the preparation chamber for the priests. This would serve useful later on. Theadrin stuck the knot back in its hole and left the dark storage room. He informed Myran of his find and they went back out to the yard.

The bull had just been killed when they came through the door. The high priest was drawing the knife away. Theadrin looked over at Myran. His friend's eyes were on Gurn in a firm gaze.

"Come on, Myran," he whispered.

They withdrew from the temple and returned to the inn where the others waited. Theadrin gathered them about the table and set down a map on the surface. It was a rough sketch he had made earlier that day of the city's layout surrounding the temple.

"Here is the plan." He began.

Fourteen

By the following evening everything was set. Theadrin gave one final rundown before they all moved off to their positions. At Penred's Cathedral the people gathered. The high priest stood beside the altar and watched them assemble. Most were grim faced and held a somber countenance.

Gurn arrived and stood off on one side of the platform as he did on the other nights. He was dressed well for the occasion but his face showed that he had little time for things like this. His arms were crossed and his foot tapped swiftly on the pavement.

The sun had just begun to touch the western hills. From the temple mount, one could get a wide view of the country around. The land rested in the dying light of evening, coloring the snow with an amber hue. Many places were already consumed by the lengthening shadows. The moon hung in the sky growing brighter as the sun diminished.

Inside the temple, two figures moved silently across the polished floor. Myran lay hold of the latch and opened to a dark room. They moved in without making a sound and closed the door.

Theadrin removed the loose knot from the wood board and peered through. The room was full of priests preparing to make their entrance. He caught a glimpse of golden hair and then his eye landed on the small figure. The child was sitting on a bench against the wall. Theadrin backed away and replaced the knot.

"They are almost ready. We must act now." Theadrin said to Myran with a nod of his head. Myran followed the signal and left the room. He went and pounded on the door to the chambers. One of the priests answered with a deep scowl.

"What do you want? Away from here."

"I must speak to him." Myran pointed a finger toward the long-faced priest who would lead the procession to the altar.

"We have no time for this." The priest made to shut the door.

"It is most urgent."

"Go away."

As the door closed Myran stopped it with his hand.

"You don't understand." Myran saw that he had gotten the lead priest's attention.

"What is going on over here?" The other priest placed a small blade, used for the sacrifices, on a side table and walked up. "I will deal with this." He told the one at the door.

"It is very important," Myran said. He slipped his foot unnoticed inside the doorway.

The first priest backed away as the other approached. "We have no time for any intrusions. Be gone with you!"

Before the words were out of his mouth, Myran was leaping into the room and shoving past the man. In a flash his fist closed over the knife handle and he turned to run. The lead priest made to block him, but Myran propelled into his chest, shoulder first, sending him backward into another priest. Then he was out of the room again.

"Get that knife!" Screamed the priest as he regained his breath.

The rest darted out in desperate pursuit. Myran ran at a slower pace so that the priests would follow more vigorously.

When they were halfway across the room, Theadrin made his move and slipped into the chamber. He saw the girl sitting wide eyed on the bench and darted for her.

"Who are you?" The priest, who was still bent over in pain, shrieked. "Stop!"

Theadrin grabbed the girl by the arm and turned to the door. The priest took hold of him but Theadrin's quick fist folded his nose. He scooped the trembling girl into his arms and exited the room. They were soon at the doors of the temple. Theadrin paused, set the girl down, and quickly knelt to look her in the eyes.

"Don't be afraid. I am going to get you to safety." He spoke kindly and glanced down to Yan and Hectur's position.

Realizing they were not there sent a rush of panic through him. Where were they? Fighting back the feeling of dread, he stood once more. Down the first flight of steps they went through the cold winter evening.

Halfway down Theadrin halted once again. A large band of riders approached the bottom and began dismounting. From up at the temple the enraged voice of the priest shrieked, "Stop them!"

The knights saw Theadrin and the girl and started after them. Theadrin went down on one knee and spoke quickly to the young child. "Listen to me. You must run and let no one catch you. Run to the city gate and you will see a woman and an old man. They will help you."

Her eyes were full of fear and she couldn't move. Theadrin stepped in front of her and drew his sword. His heart was thumping heavily in his chest.

"Run!" He ordered the child while clashing steel with the first soldier. She took a step backward but froze again.

Theadrin deflected the blade of the soldier and hit him in the face with his sword hilt. Still the girl did not move and one of the soldiers grabbed for her. But Theadrin's sword was quicker and the man drew his arm back gripping the wound he had been given.

Finally, the girl began to run but it was too late. One of the knights grabbed her and began hauling her, struggling and screaming, up the stairs. Theadrin was instantly surrounded. There was nothing he could do but lower his blade as ten sword points guarded him. The nobleman walked up and observed Theadrin with haughty eyes. The priest came running up holding a bloody rag over his nose.

"Kill him!" he shrieked angrily. "Kill him, Lord Percel!"

"He will be dealt with later," Lord Percel answered. "Hold him here until the ceremony is finished." Four men remained to guard him while the rest left for the ceremony.

Reluctantly, Theadrin sat against a pillar. He could not imagine what had happened to Yan and Hectur. The priests, who had finally retrieved their knife, came past and entered the temple.

The sun now only showed a sliver over the horizon. It was only a short time now until the sacrifice would begin. A star glimmered in the east where the night was gathering. Theadrin watched it along with the growing darkness. A realization struck him that a darkness was growing in the hearts of the people of Arinon.

Something had to be done. Someone had to put a stop to it.

Then Theadrin's mind began to race. How could he recover from the shattered plan? The disappearing of Yan and Hectur and late arrival of the Lord had thrown everything off.

"Highest King, help us," Theadrin whispered.

Just then three figures approached the bottom of the steps. The men guarding Theadrin watched them suspiciously as they drew near. When they were only several strides away, one of the guards called out, "What is your business?"

"Late for the sacrifice, sir." Theadrin's heart leapt, for the voice he knew well.

"Then you best hurry. It is about to begin." The guard's interest diminished.

Suddenly, the one who spoke struck out hitting the guard in the jaw. Myran drew his sword from under his cloak and engaged the next man. Hectur and Yan took on the last two. Theadrin leapt up and retrieved his sword from where the guards had placed it and ran to help Yan, who was the least of a fighter among them. The four guards, seeing how they were suddenly outmanned, quickly surrendered. When it was over they stood catching their breath.

"You came just in time, my friends. The sacrifice is beginning," said Theadrin.

"But our plan has failed." Yan pronounced through his heavy draws of breath. "I'm sorry, Theadrin. Hectur an' I woulda bin 'ere, but…"

"We were detained by some guards and questioned," Hectur explained briefly. "By the time we got here you had just surrendered."

"It's all over now." Yan shook his head in hopelessness.

"Yet we can still do this." Theadrin spoke in a tone that ushered out courage to his friends.

"And what of these men?" Myran wondered, still guarding them with the point of his sword.

⌛

Back inside, the high priest raised his staff high and called out to the people gathered. "The final sacrifice begins. May Amlek the powerful be pleased with our final offering this night. Behold! The sun disappears to give way to the moon! Bring forth the child!"

Doors from the temple opened and a procession of priests came forth with the child walking in the midst of them. Only a girl of five summers, her gold hair glinted in the firelight from the torches. She wore a simple white gown that flowed gently as she walked. Her head was down as she strode barefoot toward the altar. There was grumbling from some in the crowd, though none made to protest.

They mounted the platform where the altar rested and the priests parted and went to their allotted places to stand. The girl stood before the stone structure. Tears were streaming down her face and her shoulders trembled. Two priests took her and laid her on her back across the flat surface. The high priest moved forward, speaking in a tongue indiscernible, and didn't notice the growing bellow of cows. He held the knife in both hands. Then raising it, his voice still droning on, he stopped beside the altar.

"Look out!" one of the guards behind Gurn cried out.

The high priest froze; the knifepoint had not begun its fatal plummet. He spun around to see the bulls barreling through Gurn's warriors. The people began to panic.

"Get those beasts under control!" Gurn shouted.

In the confusion Theadrin and his companions, dressed in garb of Percel's guard, gained the altar plateau. As the stampede moved away down the hill behind the altar, Gurn's startled scream drew everyone's attention. All looked to see the king standing rigid against one of the pillars, a sword blade at his throat. His warriors moved back up the incline to his aid but halted at Theadrin's warning command.

"Another step and your lord dies." Myran held the sword as Theadrin made his way to the altar.

"Throw away the knife," he commanded the high priest.

"How dare you interrupt this affair!" the priest raged. "You will die for this!"

"Do as he says, priest," Gurn shouted.

"My lord..." He started to argue but was silenced.

"I command you!" Gurn yelled as Myran applied a little force behind the sword.

The high priest glowered at Theadrin and cast the knife angrily to the floor. He backed away as Theadrin approached, sword point toward his throat.

"People of Arinon, listen to me!" Theadrin said so that the whole congregation could hear. "Who has bewitched you that you stand and watch the murder of your own children?" His accusation penetrated deep into the hearts of the crowd.

"Hear him!" A voice suddenly called out from somewhere. Theadrin was surprised at the voice and looked to the crowd.

It continued, "Hear the voice of your king!" This caused a wave of concerned murmur through the assembly. Theadrin, too, became alarmed at these words.

Caithal emerged from the crowd, Lianna following in his wake, and came up to the platform. Lianna went quickly over and took the petrified girl off the cruel stone altar. She drew her away and held her tight, doing her best to soothe her crying.

"What is this?" someone in the crowd yelled. "What's going on?"

"This is your rightful king, the son of Valdithin." Caithal stated confidently.

"What lie is this!" Gurn shouted, shocked and outraged at this sudden claim. "Valdithin's son died long ago. You are lying!"

"Quiet!" Myran threatened.

"Good people of Arinon!" Caithal held out his hands to silence them. "I am Caithal. Does that name mean anything to you?"

A pause followed until a new voice said, "Caithal was Valdithin's advisor." One of Arinon's lords stepped forward. He was young and tall with dark-brown hair and a long mustache. "My father was his friend, and I knew him well as a lad."

"Lord Anromir, you remember well. Yes, I was advisor and friend to King Valdithin. I can attest that his son did not die. I took him into Caledon myself, to a huntsman. There he has grown into a man—the man who stands before you now."

A murmur rose from within the crowd again. Gurn's face was hot with rage, but Myran held him back. Hectur and Yan stood ready, weapons in hand. They had not expected Caithal to come like this. The plan had changed and they waited uncertainly to see where it would go.

Theadrin had not expected this either. There was nothing he could do now but trust that his friend knew what he was doing.

All the lords began talking among themselves.

"All lies!" spat Gurn. "Get out of here, you vagabonds! No one here will stand for your outrageous... uh!" He choked as Myran put pressure at his throat.

"Look at him yourself. You who do not believe?" Caithal persisted. "Does he not have the likeness of his father?" For those who had seen Valdithin, they could not deny the incredibly strong resemblance. In the torchlight Theadrin's blond hair shimmered and his face held firm countenance. His eyes showed strength and confidence the same way his father's always had.

"This is a grave matter you have brought forth. It must be decided elsewhere." One of the lords stepped forth. It was Percel. He was a tournament champion and, although his girth had widened considerably since his last fight, few dared insult him for fear of a challenge. "Such things take time to decide. I call for a counsel to be held."

Another one of the lords, Taromar by name, moved to second it and was followed by the rest. Gurn was forced to relent and it was determined a counsel was to be held in three days' time.

The high priest retrieved his knife. "We must finish the sacrifice."

Lianna bent in front of the girl to shield her. "You will not touch her!"

Theadrin stepped quickly in front of the priest. "We are taking the girl with us."

"You cannot! My lord, Gurn…"

"Gurn is in no position to prevent us." Theadrin took a step toward the high priest and then turned to the people. "No more will such wickedness take place in Arinon."

"How dare you say that!" The high priest watched him with murderous eyes. "Amlek will not take this lightly."

Percel put out his hands and said to the crowd, "Go to your homes. This matter will be solved in three days' time."

So the lords and people began to leave, all talking excitedly of what had taken place and what was going to happen.

"By what authority do you do this?" the high priest raged at Theadrin.

Theadrin turned on him. "Under authority of the Highest King!"

The rage dwindled on the priest's face. His eyes narrowed. "Oh. And who is this Highest King that you speak of? How is it he has authority higher than the great and powerful Amlek?"

Theadrin stepped toward him and opened his mouth to speak but suddenly realized he had no answer. A cruel smirk curled the lips of the high priest.

"Just as I thought. This 'king' of yours is false."

Anger leapt up inside Theadrin. The high priest looked at him and laughed. He turned to leave, but his mocking laughter stung Theadrin's ears until he was gone.

Yan and Hectur relaxed and came to stand by Theadrin, who stared after the high priest. Myran still held Gurn at sword point. Theadrin sighed and turned away. He went and placed a hand on Myran's shoulder.

"He can go, Myran."

But Myran did not flinch. The entire time he had not taken his fiery eyes from Gurn. He held his sword firmly at the man's throat, a dark anger kindled in his eyes. "Let me go!" Gurn shoved at him. Myran grabbed Gurn roughly by the shirt, his eyes flashing. For a moment it looked as though he would run Gurn through.

"Myran." Theadrin spoke calmly but adamantly. Finally Myran backed away. Gurn tugged the wrinkles out of his shirt and stomped quickly off.

"I must say, my lords..." It was Lord Anromir who spoke. All the other nobles had gone and he alone remained. "Had you been a moment later in your coming you would have been to late. I was about to act myself. My hand was already on my sword when you appeared."

Theadrin faced him and allowed a friendly smile.

Anromir walked forward in a sturdy gait and clapped a tight fist to his chest, bowing slightly at the waist. "I am Anromir of Caulguard. And I hope you are not planning on staying here in Avross while you wait for the counsel. For I must warn you that if you house in this city your lives will be in danger." He indicated the direction Gurn had left in case any further explanation was needed to understand what he meant.

"I thank you for your concern, my lord, but we have nowhere else to go." Theadrin answered. "We have a room at the inn."

"That will not do," Anromir stated. "Please. You are welcome to stay with me. My keep is not far from here, and I would be highly honored to have all of you as my guests."

Caithal came up to Theadrin and said, "I think it would be wise not to turn down the generous offer of Lord Anromir."

Theadrin nodded in concurrence and said to Anromir, "Your kindness is appreciated."

Fifteen

Gurn flew down the hallway in a hot rage. "Percel!" he roared.

The nobleman turned coolly on his heel to face the livid king. Gurn's eyes were murderous. "Are you against me? Why did you call for a counsel? We could have had those liars silenced then and there!"

Percel remained passive. "I was acting in your best interest, my king."

"Just explain how that is!" Gurn was not settled.

"To silence them then and there would not rest well with the people."

Gurn quickly countered. "No fool would believe such a claim as they made!"

Percel put up a steady hand to calm Gurn. "Let me explain myself."

"You had better!"

"To silence them right now would speak loudly to Arinon that you consider them a threat. In turn they will begin to wonder if the accusation is true. By granting a counsel you will prove your confidence and, may I say, fairness. The people will deem you as just in granting Caithal's claim a chance."

"Am I indeed, Percel?" Gurn glowered. "I am the rightful king of Arinon! The people themselves chose me!"

"Of course, my lord, of course," Percel soothed. "And I will stand beside you always. I hope you have not forgotten my part in helping you gain the throne. Caithal cannot win at the counsel. And in the end you will have an even stronger hold on the kingdom by proving them false."

"You are certain we cannot lose?"

"Beyond any doubt, my king. The nobles of Arinon are loyal to you."

Gurn looked about and, leaning closer to Percel, whispered his fears, "Could they have the sword?"

"Impossible!" Percel assured, "The King Sword is gone forever."

Gurn nodded and was forced to agree that Percel was right. Before leaving, he warned, "If you are wrong, Percel, you will deeply regret it."

The noble gave a crafty smile, though his heart burned with anger at the threat. He bowed at the waist before leaving Gurn.

⌛

The following three days before the counsel were busy for all in Arinon. The whole kingdom seemed set to bursting from excitement. There was talk of nothing else. Each of the nobles took counsel with advisors to learn what decisions they would best profit from.

Anromir's keep, Caulguard, was built south of Avross across the river. It was a well-maintained estate surrounded by a clean, well-kept village. The keep itself was cylindrical in shape with ramparts at the top, and another taller but thinner tower fused to the side. A tall stonewall surrounded the grounds with a wooden gate reinforced with strong iron bands.

The golden-haired girl came to stay with them, since she had no family. She spoke very little to anyone but Lianna, who took it upon herself to care for the girl. She was very slender and her movements were graceful as though she were always dancing. Her name was Cadi.

Lord Anromir was an excellent host. He kept his guests well fed and gave them the most comfortable rooms in his keep. His wife, Ellia, was more than pleased to have them stay in her home. She was small, petite, and had large dark eyes. She and Lianna became fast friends in those three days. They talked often, always sitting together when at the dinner table. In fact, it was rare to see them apart.

Myran remained mostly to himself during the wait. It was true he was quiet before, but he became even more withdrawn since that night. Often he would ride out alone to roam the surrounding hills.

Theadrin was downcast as well. The argument with the high priest had started him thinking. He had grown up hearing and learning of the Highest King, but now he realized he did not know the Highest King. This troubled him greatly.

Finally he could not bear the weight of it any longer and he brought his dilemma to Caithal, who listened carefully to all Theadrin told him. He sat in his chair and rubbed his gray beard, eyes glimmering as he listened.

He was quick to discern what needed to be done. "You must make it your own," he said simply. "You have heard with your ears, but you have not seen with your eyes. Our sovereign Lord is not some isolated object demanding our service. He is a person longing for his children to come to him and share sweet fellowship."

"What must I do?" Theadrin's anguish did not surprise the old man.

Caithal's answer was confident. "You must search. Search with all you have in you and you will find. That is certain. You *will* find, Theadrin."

Theadrin was somewhat put at ease, and he made it his goal to search. Even though he was not exactly sure how, he would search with all that he had to know the Highest King. He would make it his own.

They stood on the ramparts on top of the keep, staring out over the bustle in the town below. They watched the horse-drawn carts and various people either on horseback or walking to the small market. Booths were full of various assortments of meats such as chicken, ham, and venison.

"You had this planned all along, didn't you?" Theadrin spoke at last. Caithal looked at him as though he didn't understand.

Theadrin explained. "Ever since that first night we met, you knew we would come here. You acted otherwise, but you had it all planned out."

Caithal stared back. "I knew that our road would lead here. You are Valdithin's son, and the throne is yours by right; of course we would have to come here."

"Yes, I know, but why did you tell everyone who I am?"

"You did not know it, but Percel sent men to await for your departure. You would not have made it out of the temple alive." Caithal turned his eyes back to the grounds below. "I had to step up and tell them who you were, for that was the only way to ensure your safety. Gurn cannot touch you now until the counsel is over."

He went on. "In any case, the people were ready to hear it. Remember when I told you that Gurn rules with an iron fist?" Theadrin nodded in recollection.

"In consequence of this," Caithal went on, "the people regret ever giving him the throne. They gave away the liberty they once had under your father's rule. With your appearance they have a new hope. The counsel of nobles is only the first step. Even if we should not be accepted by them, the final decision rests with the people, and the people are ready."

"Do you think we can win the counsel?"

"If we had the King Sword victory would be sure, but alas we must fight without it."

On the second day, as Theadrin was standing on the breastwork of the wall, he saw Myran riding out of the keep and decided to follow. He saddled his horse and trailed him west, climbing several hills and passing through a number of smaller forests. Snow particles drifted in the myriads, sparkling like a mist of diamonds in the clear afternoon sun.

Mounting one of the hills, Theadrin stopped to look about. Myran's horse stood on the next ridge, its nose digging in the snow for grass.

When Theadrin arrived at the spot he found Myran sitting on a rock jutting out from the white hillside, looking west. He got down from his horse, wrapped the reigns around a low tree branch, and sat down beside his friend.

Neither said a word for some time but stared out over the open land. Myran acknowledged his presence with a slow glance and didn't seem at all surprised to see him.

Below the hill, the country flattened out all the way to a large forest. Theadrin could see the white frosted treetops glittering on the near horizon. He saw a glimmering river snake across the open ground and continue on to the cover of its den, the forest. Several farms and houses dotted the sparkling white country, their thatched rooftops blanketed from the last snowfall.

A field mouse peeped out from a hole in the snow where an oak sapling grew to observe his unexpected guests. He didn't like what he saw and disappeared once again. The sun was warm on their faces though the cold breeze stung the skin.

"It was my home." Myran said at length, watching the horizon. "The forest."

"How long has it been"—Theadrin looked at the frosted treetops—"since you left?"

"This is the third winter, though it seems much longer."

They fell silent again. Myran picked one of the long brown grass stems that were still visible and fingered it. A whispering wind rustled their hair and tugged at their clothing. One of the horses behind them blew from its nostrils and took a crunching step in the snow.

"Do you know the Most High King, Myran?" Theadrin asked at last.

Myran thought for a long time, and Theadrin began to think he would not answer. "No, to be truthful. I don't know him. I did… well, I thought I did, years ago, but now I know that I don't."

Theadrin sighed. "I also thought that I knew him, but faced with the question I had no answer." Theadrin's voice was full of remorse.

He sighed again. "How are we to stand against the deception when it comes, Myran? How will we know the lie for what it is?"

Myran stared off at the distant forest, seeing a memory of long ago. "A very dear friend once told me that only the light of truth will guard us against the darkness of deception." He looked at Theadrin. "Everyone has their own opinions of what is right and wrong. What is truth?"

Theadrin thought for some time. "I guess I don't know that either." They lapsed into silence again, both deep in thought. The sobering realization of how much they didn't know was disheartening.

"I wanted to kill him," Myran spoke again.

"Gurn?" Theadrin remembered the night of the sacrifice.

Myran nodded. "For a moment I believed I could and it would be all right. I have killed before, but always in battle and self-defense—always when I had no other choice. Some people can kill and think nothing of it. But we are all made in the image of the Great King, and killing is"—he sighed deeply—"It weighs heavily on you."

He looked westward again and added. "I believe there will be more of it before this is over…much more, I fear."

Theadrin accepted this without a word. He too had thought of it. "I would have you with me in the counsel, Myran Cai."

"You need not ask. I will gladly help," Myran said without hesitation.

Sixteen

The counsel was held in a large room adjacent to the great hall of the palace. The room was circular and covered by a massive dome. White marble pillars enclosed the circle with a seat in between, one for each of Arinon's twelve nobles, and above all of these hung the banner of the lord that held the seat. All the nobles had with them at least two advisors who stood behind their lord's chair.

Behind Lord Percel stood a tall man wearing a black cloak and a dark-green tunic that bore the emblem of a black dragon gripping a spear on the left shoulder. He also wore a helm that concealed his face. Theadrin recognized him by his crest as the knight who won the tournaments in Caledon that spring.

Although it was difficult to tell because of the helm, Theadrin thought that the knight was carefully observing him, for he was turned in Theadrin's direction.

When all were assembled, Gurn stood and announced, "We are here to settle the grave matter which has arisen three nights ago—that of the appearance of the claimed son of King Valdithin. It is our goal here to discover the truth. If this man is whom he claims, then I will be the first to give my allegiance. However, if he is not, then we will know them for the liars they are.

"Let us begin by hearing Caithal's story." Gurn's speech was smooth and he held calm countenance. He did not seem the least bit worried of what might happen that day, and even appeared to show fairness by letting Caithal speak first. Theadrin felt a pit settle in his stomach wondering what scheme he had laid out.

Caithal came to stand in the middle of the room. "I was the advisor to King Valdithin when he sat on the throne. As you all know, our king was killed. By whom it is not known, but the wound in his back was made from a dagger." He was looking at Gurn.

"The same night, before it happened, he instructed me to lead his wife, the gracious queen Riona, and their two children to safety. We both knew that the events of the night might unfold against him and his family, that he and his family were in danger. On our journey away from Avross we were attacked. I managed to get the king's children to safety. As for Queen Riona, she was sorrowfully killed in the ambush." His eyes grew sad at the retelling.

"So I took the two children to a hunter in Caledon where they could be brought up safely, hidden away from enemy eyes. For if their whereabouts were known by the one who was in charge of the ambush, he would once again attempt to murder them. I lived in the forest near where Theadrin and Lianna grew up. One day, the day of this year's first snow, assassins attacked them. That is how they ended up with me. We came here and now he is revealed to you."

Caithal stepped away and the room was filled with the noise of people whispering back and forth.

Lord Percel stood. His tone of voice was elegant and it dripped with arrogance. "I have several questions concerning Caithal's story." Gurn allowed him to continue, and Percel addressed the old man. "You mentioned that 'assassins' attacked Theadrin and his sister. Are you indeed certain they were such? People are attacked by bandits every day."

"There was no mistaking them," Caithal declared. "They were Cruthene."

"Cruthene?" Percel's tone was a mockery. "Everyone knows the Cruthene race died out hundreds of years ago. They have passed into legend. What could possibly make you believe that they were Cruthene?"

"I am a witness." Myran stepped forward. "They were as he said."

"Oh?" Percel lifted his eyebrows in derision. "Have you seen one before this to know what they look like?"

Taromar chuckled, encouraging several other nobles to do so. But Myran was not put down.

"They fit the descriptions of every written record," he stated boldly. "They were painted black and their eyes were red."

Gurn stood, composed, and put up a hand. "I think it would be wise to establish a couple of facts. We can argue this assassin matter afterward and perhaps then in a better light. The first is did Valdithin indeed have children? Who among you remembers?"

Most of the lords voiced their affirmation. Gurn continued, "It is rather well known then. Let us ask the second: Is this man who he claims to be? Is he Caithal?"

Lord Anromir stood and said, "As I have said before, Lord Gurn, both I and my father knew him well. There is no mistaking him."

"We have one who says yes. Are there any others?" Gurn looked about the room.

No one else did anything but remained seated. Gurn waited a moment longer before continuing, "I see. Not very many seem to recognize him. This leads us to say that he may still be, and yet he may not be. Therefore, we cannot deem his story as true quite yet."

Lord Anromir looked about at the other lords incredulously. "Most of you were lords when King Valdithin still ruled. You all should have seen Caithal many times. Taromar, Haltrenn, all of you would recognize him. And you, Belrant, open your eyes!"

"This man may have similar qualities," Haltrenn allowed, "but hardly can we say for sure whether he is Caithal or not."

"Rhyd, surely you remember." Anromir looked at the other lord. Rhyd was among the younger nobles. He was fair haired and blue eyed, and had been good friends with Anromir as a child. With a look of consternation he studied Caithal's face.

"Haltrenn is right," he conceded. "I just never knew him well enough to recognize him now. I am sorry, Anromir."

"He has not changed so much! A blind man could see who he is!" Anromir's voice rose in heated disbelief.

"If you please, Lord Anromir." Gurn stopped him. Anromir sat, still glaring at the other lords.

At this point Caithal stepped forward and stated, "I admit that I have changed. Twenty summers does a lot to age a man. But"—he held out his right hand—"I still wear the ring given to me by King Valdithin."

Percel wiped his trimmed beard and pursed his lips. There was no mistaking Caithal's identity now. "So you are who you say you are. What of it?" he said. "We are here to decide the identity of this boy who claims to be Valdithin's son."

"My story is true," Caithal proclaimed. "This is Theadrin, son of Valdithin, of the bloodline of Arnoni kings, true heir to Arinon's throne."

Theadrin saw the first hint of fear in Gurn's eyes. He looked like he was about to say something but closed his mouth and glanced at Percel.

The crafty nobleman did not appear worried in the least. Looking right at Theadrin, he stated, "You do resemble Valdithin quite closely." Percel put up a hand to stop Gurn. At this Gurn's eyes widened, and Theadrin saw the gleam of perspiration on his forehead. "But everyone knows of the three nobles who murdered Valdithin and his family." Percel continued, "Indeed it is true. That night, an unseen assassin shot Valdithin. The room was thrown into panic and chaos. Two lords, Balthor and Dolemar, carried the king to another room while we sent soldiers after the archer. When we returned, we found Valdithin dead and Balthor and Dolemar's weapons drawn.

"The archer assassin was caught. He wore the crest of Lord Falkar. The three were arrested for murder, but before there could be a fair trial, they killed themselves. That, in the end, proved them guilty, and the matter was resolved."

Theadrin listened to the account painfully. He wished he had been older at the time so that he could have known his father and stood at his side in that dark hour. He longed for that relationship that was lost at the fatal plunge of a knife.

Percel added, "As for those who killed the king's family, well, that remains a mystery. The coach was found burned to a pile of ash."

Gurn swallowed hard.

"So"—Percel gazed at Theadrin—"I am willing to accept that you could be who you claim."

Gurn appeared as though he was in a fire. He shot out of his chair and froze, staring at Percel. The nobleman smiled slyly and turned to face Taromar.

"Lord Taromar, I believe you have a document in your possession."

Taromar got up and drew an old leather manuscript from his belt. "If we think back to the night King Valdithin died, we will remember the reason we were gathered. It was because of this." He unrolled the parchment and held it high. "It is well known that King Valdithin's brother, Seldivar, was killed in a hunting accident long ago. This is the deathbed confession of Begron, royal huntsman of Valdithin's father, King Seldavin. He admitted he witnessed younger Prince Valdithin murder his brother and heir to the throne, Prince Seldivar, during their hunting trip, and upon promise of death was sworn to silence."

"That's a lie!" Caithal interrupted.

Gurn backed up slowly and took his seat again. Taromar went on. "It is stated in the law that if the throne is gained through treason or murder, it can never be true kingship."

Caithal shot from his seat then and yelled, "Anyone who knew King Valdithin would never believe such lies!"

"The one who takes the throne in such a way"—a smirk played on Taromar's lips—"must be dethroned, and his line abolished. Theadrin, being Valdithin's son, can never be king!"

Caithal's eyes burned against Taromar. "The King Sword proves that allegation false, for the true line of kings has been faithfully recorded upon its blade. And only in the hand of the true king will it shine its true light!"

"The King Sword is lost, and any proof it may have contained is gone. The document, however, we have with us." Percel looked smugly at Caithal. "If Theadrin is Valdithin's son, he can never sit upon the throne."

"The King Sword is out there somewhere," Caithal assured the counsel. "It was stolen the night of the king's death, and it will be returned to the hand of the true king!"

Percel faced Gurn and said, "Now, as is fitting, the counsel must take a vote on the final decision. Is Theadrin the rightful king? Or do we stay with Gurn."

All who would support Gurn cast a blue cloth into a silver bowl that was passed around. Those who were in support of Theadrin threw in a red cloth. As expected, Gurn came out the victor with only one vote for Theadrin, which was Anromir's.

In a show of fake humility, Gurn stood and addressed the counsel with arms upraised. "So be it. I bow to the decision of this honorable counsel." He looked Theadrin's way. "You and your followers will leave this city and never return on penalty of death!"

The ride back to Caulguard was a sullen one. The day was cold and the wind was biting. No one said a word the entire journey, aside from Caithal when they first started out. "Theadrin, do not for a moment believe what they said of your father. Valdithin loved no man more than his brother, and no man was hurt more by his death," he said and looked down sadly. His mind turned to the outcome of the counsel, and Theadrin heard him mutter, "I should have expected this."

By nightfall they arrived to be met by Anromir's young wife, Ellia, and Lianna, standing on the steps leading to the main door. They didn't need to ask of the results from the grim faces of the men.

When all were inside and seated around the fire with hot drinks and food, they began to talk of what happened.

"Percel is a cunning snake, and the entire counsel was easily persuaded by his twisted words." Anromir summarized the counsel for the women. "I just can't believe them. Most I have known all my life, men I shared supper with, called my friends."

"That is the sum of it," Caithal said. "They are blind men, given over to deception. I should have seen it," he said again.

"You are not to blame, Caithal," said Theadrin. "We could not have foreseen this. What do you advise us to do now?"

Caithal looked at him. "Even though Gurn believes he has won, and despite what Taromar has said, the kingship resides with the people, not with the lords. We must find a way to win the hearts of the people. But even with that, it may all be for nothing in the end if the King Sword is not reclaimed."

Theadrin accepted this and asked, "Is this true about the three lords who killed themselves rather than face a trial?"

"The opposite is true," Caithal answered in remorse. "They were the loyal ones, framed for the death of your father. They did not kill themselves. Although I have no proof, I believe it was Gurn who had them murdered." He looked down at his cup and added, "That was a dark night, and most everything you hear about it now are lies."

Theadrin sat with his fingers wrapped around the warm mug. There was more to this mystery than he imagined. Caithal had told him that night in his hut that the line of Arnoni kings was recorded on the blade. He looked up at Caithal and wondered aloud, "You told me the line of kingship was written on the King Sword's blade." Caithal nodded once and Theadrin went on. "How can it be known that a false name was not inscribed? You say the sword will prove my father's innocence, but how?"

Caithal leaned forward. "Because of the light, Theadrin. Part of the prophecy says that 'in the hand of the chosen dwells kingly light.' It has been the test of true kingship for ages. For the one who is rightfully king, the sword's ember iron blade dances with light. This the sword did when Valdithin held it. And when you hold it someday, it will once more dance with light like embers."

Theadrin took this in with an air of wonder. Would he one day hold the sword of true kingship and see its light? But what if it didn't shine? Theadrin did not think of himself as worthy. He turned to Anromir. "I thank you for standing with us, Anromir. You have become a good friend in these few days," he said.

"I am only acting for the good of the kingdom. Gurn and his pawns have run it long enough in tyranny." Anromir looked thoughtfully at him, "Caithal's words may be easily achieved. The people do not like Gurn. Only by his military might and power has he held on so long. The people will not like the decision of the counsel, I am sure." He took a sip of his drink.

"And we have something else on Gurn," Theadrin said. "I've had time to think on the way back." He sat forward on his seat. "Living in Caledon my whole life, I have learned one important fact: King Brudwyn has no liking of Gurn."

He allowed the rest time to understand what he was proposing. Caithal looked at Theadrin but said nothing; there was something hidden in his glance. Anromir was quick to perceive things and answered, "Of course! If we could gain King Brudwyn's trust, he would be a powerful ally."

"Exactly," Theadrin said, inching further forward. He could barely contain his growing excitement. "With the people's support and Caledon to back us, Gurn will not be able to keep the throne. What do you say, Caithal?"

Caithal's mysterious manner suddenly changed and he said, "You would be wise to approach the matter carefully. Depending on how you come to the king of Caledon will greatly determine whether he will accept you or not. It would be near impossible to get him to trust you for what you appear right now, a simple hunter."

"Your counsel is wise. How would you suggest we go about it?" Theadrin asked.

"First you will need to look like someone who has strong bearing and influence, one who can support his claim to the throne," Caithal answered.

"Leave that part to me." Anromir smiled.

Caithal added, "And you would also be wise to bring something to offer in return for his aid."

So they talked and planned on into the night until Caithal rose from his chair and said, "Come, we must rest. Things usually look different in the light of morning. Perhaps our plans would be more solid if made on fresh minds."

They all left, and Myran walked alone down the hallway to his room. The ceiling along the passage was arched and there were torch sconces lining either side, most with their flame long died out. As he made the corner he stopped short. Lianna was coming around the other way. She had left the conversation earlier to make sure Cadi, the golden-haired girl, had gotten to sleep all right.

"My lady." Myran made a slight bow of his head and stepped to the side so she could pass.

Lianna smiled and laughed lightly. "Your courtesy is flattering."

Myran's cheeks colored. "Your father was a king and your brother will be king. The least I can do is show you the courtesy of a princess."

Her smile widened and she chuckled again. Myran's eyes brightened and he laughed. She saw, for the first time, a light come into his eyes that was unmistakable.

Her eyes searched his face and she said, "Have they decided on what to do?"

"We are going to Caledon," Myran informed her.

"Back to Caledon?"

"Theadrin wants to acquire the support of King Brudwyn."

She nodded; her eyes lowered to the floor and then looked back up at him for a short moment. "Thank you for helping my brother. He could place his trust in no better man."

Myran's mood became suddenly serious. The spark in his eyes went out as though smothered. "Such praise is too high for me," he said.

"I think it not high enough." She studied Myran's eyes with an inquisitive gaze.

"I would keep you no longer, my lady," he said, still bearing a grim face.

Lianna accepted this and stepped lightly past, but then turned toward him once more. "I much rather prefer to be called by my own name," she chastised him lightly. Her eyes were bright and gleamed as the light of the flickering torches danced within them.

Myran consented to a smile. "Then goodnight, Lianna."

A delicate smile parted her own lips and she returned, "Goodnight, Myran." Her voice fell on his ears like a gentle silver rain, and he stood soaking in the fading memory of it as she moved away down the hall.

Seventeen

Gurn strode down the darkened corridor and through a doorway that opened up to a winding stairs. He clutched a torch in his right hand and held it forward to light the black passage. The soft light danced over the stone as he climbed the steps at a slow pace. Fresh night air met his approach at the top of the tower.

Dark clouds blocked the light of the moon and stars. It was a black night, black and cold. So were all the other nights, he thought to himself, when the visitor came.

As Gurn waited on the top of the tower, he heard the swoop of giant wings. Behind the visitor alighted on the chest high wall. Gurn turned to face the black, winged beast. It watched him with venomous yellow eyes, daring him to make a move. Gurn stood rooted to the spot.

Presently its rider slipped off its back and the winged beast took flight once again; its black form instantly disappearing into the shadows of the night.

The rider stepped into the torchlight, removing the black hood from his head to reveal a young face. He flashed a cunning smile. "Greetings."

"Hello, Vithimere." Gurn replied, not returning the smile.

"Make your report."

"I make no report, Vithimere!" Gurn's temper suddenly flared. "Your master is not my master! I am king of Arinon, not him!" Gurn raged.

"Make your report." Vithimere told him flatly, not needing to say more.

Gurn despised the man before him. Ever since the first meeting, on the road from Percel's cantref, Gurn did not like him. He was arrogant and treated Gurn as an inferior. The fact that Vithimere was much younger than Gurn only served to increase his irritation.

Vithimere acted as his master's voice and often talked as though he were the same person. It was evident that he relished his position of power and ability to degrade Gurn at every turn.

There was something in his face as well. Gurn thought there was an air of familiarity, although he was certain he had not seen him before the meeting on the road. Vithimere was dark haired and could be no older than twenty-five summers. Whatever it was, Gurn did not like that feeling of familiarity. It made him uneasy.

"Tell your master that the counsel went according to our plans. It's over for the little brat." Gurn said this in smug victory.

"Do not be so easily deceived, Gurn. The battle is far from over."

"There is nothing he can do. He has lost," Gurn said again. "If he were to start a rebellion he could not win. He has no soldiers except perhaps those of Lord Anromir, the impudent traitor. My men far outnumber his."

Vithimere thought of this. "No matter how you see it, Theadrin's existence will always present a threat to the throne. He must be dealt with."

"How would you suggest we do this? Would you send the Cruthene and Ustvildu again? Your assassins and hounds have failed so miserably it is embarrassing."

Vithimere glowered at Gurn. "My assassins, as you put it, were sent to you; under your command. If they failed, it was only because of your inept planning. It is the same with the hounds. I thought you would have been capable of so easy a task."

Gurn's face was red with anger, but he did not speak.

"We must wait for him to make the next move." Vithimere looked at Gurn with strict, commanding eyes." Gurn relented with a sullen nod. Vithimere held a small object to his lips and blew into it. It was a strange call, mournful and eerie. Immediately from the darkness swooped the winged beast. It circled once and then perched on the rampart. "Watch him. Make no hasty decisions. Such blunders will not be tolerated again." With that said, he mounted the beast and was gone in a heartbeat.

Anromir gave his finest clothes to Theadrin. The two were similar in height and build, and the clothes fit him well, if not comfortably.

The rest of Theadrin's companions were also given new clothing. Yan shaved and had a haircut and wore finer clothes than he had ever laid hands on. Mathwin's beard was trimmed and his hair brushed and he was also arrayed in fine linens. In the end, they looked every bit the convoy of a king-to-be.

Anromir and his wife accompanied them, to speak on behalf of the people and show that they had military support. Indeed, Anromir did have a good amount of men. He took fifty mounted warriors with them for escort and a small show of arms.

It wasn't until after a day and a half of preparation that they left.

They crossed the border and went southward. Theadrin wanted to stop at the hunter's cottage to ask for Roryn to come with them. Roryn was a witness to Caithal's story, and it would be useful to have him when appearing before the king.

To say the hunter and his wife were happy to see the two again would be an understatement. They greeted Theadrin and Lianna with tears of joy. For since the day of the first Cruthene attack, they had been thought dead. Roryn went to search for them and found blood in the snow where the attack had happened. Returning with the terrible news, all their friends mourned.

"I also found this." Roryn pulled something from his pocket.

"My medallion!" Theadrin gasped. "How I have regretted losing that." He accepted it from the hand of the hunter. The small object was well crafted. The tiny blade shone beautifully in the sunlight streaming in through the open window.

The company camped around the humble cottage and Theadrin and Lianna told of everything that happened. They told of the attacks of the Cruthene and the wolflike beasts. These seemed to Theadrin just as they had happened yesterday, but at the same time distanced by a great void of blurred time.

Roryn and his wife were introduced to all of their new friends. They knew Caithal already from years before. The rest they met happily.

They sat with Theadrin, Lianna, Myran, Anromir and his wife, and Caithal. The sun was low and the last of its light poured into the windows of the country house. A fire was lit beneath the hearth, the sound of laughter filling the room.

Then Theadrin told of why they had come. He explained their plan of going to King Brudwyn and why they needed Roryn to come with them.

"It is not a bad plan." Roryn rubbed his jaw with his fingers. He looked at Caithal and the corners of his mouth rose so slightly it went unnoticed. Then he looked up at Theadrin. "Have you taken into account the situation with Brudwyn's son?"

Theadrin frowned. "What has happened?"

"Prince Ruadhan has left the palace and taken to the woods. It is said there was some dispute. Whatever it was, the prince has left. Some would say he is starting a rebellion."

Everyone in the room was silent. Theadrin's frown deepened as he slumped back in his chair. This could bring down the whole plan. If the king had an ill disposition, he would hear their plan less heartily, that was true, but if he had a rebellion on his hands he could not afford to fight Gurn besides.

"There's nothing we can do but to try anyway," Theadrin decided.

Roryn agreed to go with them and they left a day later. Traveling at a leisurely pace, enduring the cold weather with hopeful spirits, they journeyed through the snowy land. As the day wore on, snow started to fall in big, heavy flakes. The wind was almost nonexistent; when it did blow it was only in light gusts.

Theadrin went up and down the line, speaking with individuals and providing a laugh for those who needed it. He was born to leadership and already commanded the respect of the troops that rode with them. By that point in the journey they had taken to him as their leader and would follow his every command as if he had been their battle chief for years.

Halfway through the second day they stopped for a rest in an old forest that embraced both sides of the roadway. As lunch was being eaten, Theadrin strolled off into the woods alone to think. The wood was silent as he walked farther from the convoy and he was soon out of sight. Every tree branch and twig was heavy with the sticky snow. He stepped over a log and stood still, listening to the quiet snowfall.

The crisp afternoon chill reddened his cheeks; the wet flakes clung to his clothing and eyelashes. He blinked and they took flight again, though some melted and dripped down his cheeks.

His thoughts were on all that had taken place in the last few weeks. All that had happened was beginning a change in him. He felt older and more mature than ever before.

He sauntered down a slow decline into a small ravine and walked along the bottom a good way, bending under broken limbs and stepping over fallen trees. The snow deepened almost to the top of his boots so he stepped up on a fallen tree trunk and followed it back to the slope.

He thought on the past events and of the future. When he was king, he would put all the wrongs in the kingdom aright. The people would love him and he would rule them wisely.

He suddenly stopped. His cheeks heated and Theadrin felt ashamed. What did he know of being king? Following had always been easier and he did well in that. The realization that he did not know the Highest King proved to further defeat him.

Slowly he began to turn his way in the direction of the camp, knowing they would be off again soon. He walked back up the slope and through a close crop of birch. A chickadee peeked around one of the white trunks and chirped once at him, warning that he was drawing too near its home.

Suddenly he was face first in the snow, someone on his back. He managed to throw his assailant off and get up on his knees. Snow stuck to his face and clothes and stung his skin. He saw his attacker getting up to his right and jumped on him. They wrestled around in confusion disturbing the even blanket of fresh snow.

His opponent was hooded and had a scarf covering his face to his eyes. He was strong, but Theadrin managed to gain the upper hand and pinned him to the ground. The man squirmed but to no avail. Theadrin held him fast. The man gave in and looked up. His eyes were blue as the sky and the brim of his nose was freckled.

"Theadrin?" The voice sounded familiar but was ruffled under the scarf.

Theadrin did not let go.

"Theadrin! Get off me, man!" It was then Theadrin's heart jumped. Though the voice was still muted, the mannerisms were familiar to him. Suddenly recognition struck him and he knew beyond a doubt.

"Peran?" Theadrin released him and sat back.

"I didn't recognize you in those fancy, rich clothes, Theadrin." Peran removed the scarf from his face and grinned.

"I see you are still waylaying innocent travelers." Theadrin breathed a chuckle.

Peran's grin widened. "Theadrin, it has been too long. I thought you were dead! We all did." They both sat in the snow staring at each other, their breath coming out in steamy puffs.

"Who is your friend, Peran?" The new voice came from behind Theadrin.

Peran instantly stood. "My lord, this is Theadrin. We have known each other since childhood."

Theadrin got to his feet and looked to see a tall man, slim, with blue eyes and a hood the same as Peran's. A mustache and beard had begun to appear for the absence of a shave. He carried a strong bow in his left hand and had a sword clasped on his hip. Theadrin had seen him before, and though it had been from a distance, he recognized him now. It was Prince Ruadhan.

Eighteen

"So, you are Theadrin. Peran has told me of you. You look as though you know who I am." Ruadhan's steely eyes studied Theadrin carefully.

"You are the prince. I saw you at the spring fair, at the tournaments."

"Ah, yes. You have a good memory for faces, and it appears some skill in wrestling." His comment was more directed at Peran but his eyes never left Theadrin.

"He whopped every boy who challenged him in Faranor growing up." Peran praised him highly and clapped a strong hand to his friend's back.

"Yet I have had plenty of beatings myself." Theadrin laughed. Ruadhan chuckled.

He drew back his hood, revealing a shock of flaming red hair, and men began to appear from behind cover. They were all dressed in woodsman garb and looked more like a band of outlaws than the warriors of the prince. Theadrin had not forgotten what Roryn had told him.

"You are traveling with a wealthy company, Theadrin," the prince said.

Theadrin was unsure how to answer and so held his tongue. Ruadhan continued, "Don't worry; we were not going to attack you. But I am interested in where you are headed."

"In truth, Lord Ruadhan, we are on our way to see your father, the king," Theadrin answered. He waited to see what effect this would have on him. Ruadhan weighed this carefully before answering. His eyes remained on Theadrin but it was as if he was looking through him, to discover what secrets may lie deeper within.

"What business have you with my father?" Ruadhan watched him suspiciously. "Could you answer that?"

"That may depend, Prince Ruadhan, on where you stand," Theadrin answered rather boldly.

"Oh? How so?"

"Are you an ally of the king's?"

"I see." Ruadhan said slowly. "You have heard of our... disagreement."

"I was told that you left the palace," Theadrin admitted.

"And what do people say of it? Perhaps rumor says that I am starting a rebellion against the king?" Ruadhan watched him, and Theadrin didn't answer but looked about at the woodsmen. The prince knew what the glance meant. Why would he be raising men if not to fight?

"I can only ask you to believe what I say. I am no liar. I am ever and always an ally of my father, the king, even when he does not see it. I would do nothing to harm my father."

"I believe you, Ruadhan," Theadrin said in truth. Something in the prince's eyes showed he held no lie or deceit. Already he liked Ruadhan. He carried no air of malevolence but seemed genuine.

"Come to our camp and we can talk more," Theadrin offered. "We can explain much to each other, I think. You will be welcomed as friends."

Ruadhan was apprehensive but Peran put him at ease by saying, "You can trust Theadrin, sire. I have never known him to be dishonest."

So Ruadhan relented. "Very well. You trust what I have told you, I will trust you in return."

They were received like friends as was promised. A circular canopy was erected to shelter from the snowfall and camp chairs were brought out. As they were being set up, Myran spoke quietly to Theadrin.

"Why are you trusting Prince Ruadhan?"

Theadrin answered, "We don't know everything. He assured me he is not against his father and I believe he is telling the truth."

"Just as you said, Theadrin," Myran warned, "we do not know everything. Be reserved in what you tell him."

Theadrin took Myran's advice. He told the prince how they were on a diplomatic mission to the king; that they were against the tyrant, Gurn. Ruadhan listened to all that was told him very closely. He nodded slowly now and again, stroking his whiskers.

Theadrin left much untold, including his tie to King Valdithin, as Myran advised him. As he spoke, he studied Ruadhan's reactions. But the prince did not reveal any hidden malice. His eyes were steely and confident, showing genuine interest and care.

"I can tell you that my father and I have also been watching Gurn carefully," he affirmed. "He is not trusted nor well thought of in my father's house."

"Then d'ya think King Brudwyn'll join us?" Yan asked hopefully, standing behind Theadrin's chair. He was wearing a new blue shirt with a fine, dark leather vest and dark-green trousers. From his appearance, one would never guess he had been a poor gambler only the summer before.

Myran, standing to Theadrin's right with arms crossed, glanced at Yan in silent warning. He knew Yan had a tendency to blurt information without thinking.

Ruadhan shrugged. "I cannot say. We've been having trouble with barbarian raids on the northern border again. Their numbers have grown since their last attacks two years ago. I don't know if he could support you in a war against Gurn."

Theadrin thought for a moment. An idea popped into his head. "If we were to aid him in the north," he said slowly, "maybe then he would help us."

Ruadhan nodded as he lifted one eyebrow in response.

"Yes, that is it. Anromir"—he turned to his friend who sat near—"would you lend me troops to help the king?"

"You need not ask," Anromir said without hesitation. "The men are yours to command."

"Fifty armored horsemen will soon wash thin the barbarian lines," Theadrin said.

The snowfall had remained steady; only the wind had picked up. Caithal spoke up reminding them of the time. "If you don't mind my interrupting, the day is dwindling and we have yet to reach Monivea by nightfall."

"You are right." Theadrin glanced at Ruadhan. "Will you come with us?"

"Nay. We return to the woods." He stood, and Theadrin noted something at last in the prince's eye. Sadness? Regret? He could not tell for sure.

Ruadhan added, "But I truly hope your mission is successful."

"Thank you." Theadrin got up and they shook each other's hand. "It was a pleasure to meet you."

Peran came to stand before Theadrin. "It is all the world knowing you are alive. Just you stay that way." He gave Theadrin a playful punch on his shoulder.

"I'll try." Theadrin smiled. They stood looking at each other. Neither had seen the other as they were now—Theadrin richly dressed and Peran in outlaw garb.

"Why don't you see them off, Peran." Ruadhan had been watching them. "Ride with them for a ways."

Peran looked at the prince. "Thank you, sire. I will return before nightfall."

So Ruadhan and the rest of his men disappeared into the forest as the company moved on once more. Theadrin and Peran rode together at the head, catching up on past events. Theadrin told him about the night he and Lianna disappeared and were believed dead.

"You know," Peran thought, "the night I told you I saw someone outside the window—you remember, don't you?"

"Yes." He remembered that day in the woods last autumn.

"I bet you it was one of those assassins; a Cruthene."

"Could have been." Theadrin thought it likely.

Theadrin then told Peran how Caithal found them and the unfolding of his true identity.

"Wow." Peran shook his head, wearing the grin that was his trademark. "If we could've known who you really were when we were younger..." He looked excitedly at Theadrin. "A king. I can't get over it."

"Not yet. And it isn't as romantic as you may think," he told Peran honestly. "In fact, I much prefer a simpler life, to tell the truth."

"That's ridiculous! Why, when we were growing up back in the woods you always would say how you wanted adventure beyond the life of a hunter."

Peran was right. He had been for the most part content with his life but was hungry for more. He always felt as though he was meant for something different.

"What about you, Peran?" He looked at his freckled friend. "How did you wind up out here?"

"I, King Theadrin, am well on my way to knighthood," he answered pompously.

"A knight, huh. How do you figure to accomplish that if the prince has left the palace?" Theadrin said this hoping he could learn from Peran more of what had happened between Ruadhan and the king.

Peran did not answer right away; his mind seemed to be deciding something. "It is only temporary. What we are doing is very important. All the kingdom will know that soon."

"And what is that?"

"I can't tell you, Theadrin; at least not yet. Believe me." Peran was, for the moment, unusually serious.

"Why not?" Theadrin puzzled.

"You will just have to take my word for it. All will know in time, but I have sworn to tell no one." He smiled. "You know, a knight is sworn to honor. All I can say is the prince is not against King Brudwyn."

"All right then." Theadrin became silent. Peran looked down at his hand and said nothing for a time.

At last he looked up and made to speak but closed his mouth again, thought, and then looked Theadrin in the eye. "You don't know how much I want to go with you, Theadrin."

Theadrin returned his glance and answered. "Why don't you? I would like nothing better than to have you in my company, Peran."

"I cannot. I am sworn to follow the prince; at least until this is over." Theadrin did not reply.

"I should be on my way back." Peran said, observing the low sun blazing behind the gray veil of clouds.

"Until we meet again, brother." Theadrin clasped Peran's extended arm. "And Peran... promise me you will not reveal my identity to anyone yet."

"You have my word, Theadrin. Farewell."

Nineteen

A messenger was sent ahead to announce their coming to the king, and they were accepted into the city and given the guest chambers of the palace. They slept in comfort and broke fast the next morning on little less than a feast. King Brudwyn saw them soon after.

He was seated on a large chair below the dais with many of his advisors about him. His silvery red hair was combed back and his mustache was neatly trimmed. He welcomed them with a friendly disposition.

"Welcome, friends." His voice boomed through the hall. "I hope your stay thus far has been tolerable."

"My lord, King Brudwyn, we are in your debt for such a welcoming reception. Never have we spent a more comfortable night in another's home." Theadrin stood ahead of the others. His words pleased the king greatly and his teeth showed in a proud smile.

"What brings you here this day?" He didn't waste any more time with pleasantries. His mood was still pleasurable, but he was a busy man.

"As you know, good king, we are from Arinon. My friend, Lord Anromir"—he beckoned the man beside him—"and his wife represent the people there." Anromir took a step and bowed as his wife curtsied politely.

Theadrin went on. "I also bring before you one from your own realm—Roryn the huntsman of Faranor." Roryn came forward and bowed.

"I would also introduce Caithal, once chief advisor and good friend to my father, King Valdithin." King Brudwyn's eyebrows rose and he leaned forward, hands on knees. Theadrin saw his reaction. He went on.

"My fair sister, Lady Lianna, and my faithful friends, Myran Cai, Yan, and Hectur, also called Mathwin."

King Brudwyn stared at Theadrin. "Is it really...you and your sister..." He rose from his throne and came forward. "You are alive?"

Studying Theadrin's face, he exclaimed, "But I should have recognized you when you first entered! Alas, it has been so long!" King Brudwyn embraced the startled young man.

Then Theadrin, the king holding him at arm's length, asked, "How is that you know me, sire?"

"I would know my own brother's son! To look into your face is to see him alive again!"

"Your brother?" Theadrin was taken aback.

"My wife's brother by blood, and mine by law and bond of friendship. Did you not know?"

"My lord"—it was Caithal who spoke—"he has only this winter learned that he is the son of King Valdithin. He still knows very little." Theadrin glanced back at the old man who would not look back.

Brudwyn smiled. "Caithal, I did not recognize you behind that beard. It has been long my old friend." He turned back to Theadrin. "Forgive me, son, it seems I have some things to learn as well. You must tell me everything."

The king called to his servants. "Bring in chairs and refreshment, we may be here a while!" While they waited, Brudwyn spoke to Caithal. "But why have you never told me my nephew and niece were alive? You should have brought them here after Valdithin died."

"The enemy was still on the lookout for Theadrin and Lianna. To bring them here would be expected. They would have been found and surely killed," Caithal explained, and added, "If you knew they were alive you would have insisted they be sent here. It was for the best."

Brudwyn grunted. He did not like to admit that the two would not have been safe in his own house, but Caithal was right. The refreshments came shortly and they were each given something to drink with fresh warm bread and butter.

Theadrin told again their story. He had recited his tale so often he had grown tired of it. But each time it seemed he learned something new that added another piece to the ever-growing puzzle. He found out that King Brudwyn and the princess of Arinon, Valdithin's sister, had fallen in love and married. Sadly, after the birth of Prince Ruadhan, the queen died. The King never remarried and stayed close friends with Valdithin.

When all had been told to each other's satisfaction, Theadrin brought forth the reason for their coming. King Brudwyn listened carefully as he conveyed the events at the counsel—the treachery of the lords, the forged manuscript, and Gurn's threat.

Theadrin ended by saying, "It is well known throughout Caledon that you do not favor Gurn either."

"Yes, that fact could not be more true," the King sighed.

Theadrin told of his plan. The majority of people in Arinon wanted to be free of Gurn, and he was certain that he could gain them to his side. Anromir had warriors, but they would need the help of Caledon as well to be able to stand against Gurn's forces.

"I would grant help gladly," said the king when the story was finished. "And I mean to do just that."

"Your generosity is overwhelming, my lord," Theadrin said. It had gone far better than he could have dreamed.

"However," Brudwyn put in, "it may be some time before I can send help. You may have heard that our northern borders have been under heavy raids from marauding barbarians. When I have put them down I will do what I can to aid you."

Theadrin had been prepared for this. "That will be my part of the bargain. I have fifty mounted knights. We offer our service against these barbarians."

"I require nothing from you. You are my brother's son, and that much is enough."

Theadrin looked thoughtfully at the king. "Do you believe Gurn is responsible for my father's death?"

Brudwyn scratched his mustache in thought. "I have always believed there to be sedition involved in the death of Valdithin as do some of Arinon's nobles. I never had proof, however. What do you think, Caithal? You are the wisest man among us and you were there."

"I was gone before Valdithin was killed." Caithal, arms folded, peered at them under a bushy brow. In his eyes was the familiar and mysterious gleam of knowing. "But I think Gurn is not smart enough to have planned all of that. He is charismatic and he gained the loyalty of the people in the beginning, but there is so much that I do not think he could have done."

"I have to agree with you." Anromir put in his opinion. "No, I would say there is another."

"You have hit on the mark, Anromir." Caithal commended him. "It is something I have long suspected. There *is* another. I am certain there is one far more dangerous than Gurn, and that he is in possession of the King Sword. He is crafty and subtle, biding his time somewhere, using Gurn as a pawn." Caithal's forehead wrinkled in a frown. "I believe he is the connection to the Cruthene and even the Ustvildu. But I do not know who."

"We must keep wary then," King Brudwyn said.

Theadrin, then, told of his meeting prince Ruadhan the day prior. Brudwyn listened to the account with a hard expression.

At length he said, "My son has developed a disliking for one of my nobles, Sir Dathin of Antion." Brudwyn frowned. "He claims that Dathin is a traitor and a part of a vast plot to overthrow me."

Theadrin's eyebrows lifted. "You don't believe him?"

"Dathin is my most loyal noble and has proven himself to me time and again. He is to be married to the daughter of another one of my nobles. Ruadhan has fallen in love with the girl and will stop at nothing to see that they are not wed. That is why he wants to discredit Sir Dathin. And so, after seeing that I would not believe his claims, he left the palace," The King concluded, "But you need not be bothered with such affairs."

Theadrin didn't press his uncle and dropped the subject. They talked for a short time longer until Theadrin rose from his chair. "We have kept you from your business long enough, my lord king. I will ready the men to aid you in the north."

"You need not."

"Nevertheless, it is the least I can do for my kinsman and his people."

"Very well," King Brudwyn consented. "My general, Aedrius, will train you. When spring comes you will go with him to the northern border."

Theadrin bowed in acknowledgment. He turned and saw Yan standing with a look of apprehension. He gave Yan a smile and said, "What say you Yan? Are you ready to release the warrior inside?"

"I ain't much likin' the notion a' becomin' a warrior," he said sheepishly. "Niver was very brave."

"Yet you shall become a fine one"—Theadrin clapped him on the back as they walked out of the great hall—"with a little training."

Caithal came along side and Theadrin looked toward him. "You knew all along about the king being my uncle."

"Yes." This was all Caithal's answer consisted of and he continued to walk, his eye twinkling with mirth. This look Theadrin had grown familiar with. How many more secrets did Caithal hold from him?

Theadrin halted. "So why keep that secret from me?"

Caithal slowed and looked back. "I was testing you."

"Oh? What test was that?"

Caithal did not answer but turned and strode after the others.

General Aedrius looked like he was built of iron. His broad shoulders held thick, chiseled arms and wide-palmed hands that were streaked with battle scars. A long, black mustache that hung down to a powerful jaw accented intense russet eyes beneath a dark brow. His skin was rough and sun-worn.

So Theadrin filled the days with training. Myran, Yan, Mathwin, and the fifty warriors trained with him. The general was a man who took no nonsense. He drilled them hard and relentlessly.

As the winter drudged on and grew colder, Theadrin practiced hard every day. All his experience from before, sparring with his childhood friends, was like broken fragments that pieced together as he practiced now to form an acquired skill. His vigor surpassed the rest and before long he was among the top swordsmen. Only Myran Cai was considered to have greater skill.

Yan was least prone to the training. The first time he held a sword, it looked so out of place Theadrin had to laugh. Aedrius worked hard on Yan; harder than Theadrin thought necessary at times. Theadrin encouraged Yan and kept him going, and his skill grew.

They stayed at the palace with the king during that time. Many an eventide they filled the hall with laughter and songs. While the cold winter winds howled and raged at night they sat warm about the great hearth.

On one of these nights Theadrin had his fifty warriors dine with him in the great hall. Myran sat to Theadrin's right, who sat to the right of King Brudwyn. Supper had just been finished and he was draining the last of the contents of his cup when he heard the men begin to call for a song.

King Brudwyn spoke. "I wish to hear someone different tonight. My bards we have heard every night." He turned to Lianna at his left hand. "Would you so grace us this night, my lady? I should enjoy nothing better than to hear your voice fill my hall."

She promptly made to decline, but Theadrin was quick to act. "Go on, Lianna. Would you refuse the request of our gracious host?"

A clamor rose from among the warriors' tables to hear her sing, so she relented and stood. Myran sipped at his cup and sat back in his chair, watching as she gracefully made her way to the center of the hall. The room was suddenly hushed, and a moment later she began.

The first notes were soft and started low, then gently lifted higher. She sang an old song, forgotten now by most of the world, a hero's tale. It was of the faithful warrior, assailed by the darkness of the enemy, but who remained true to the Highest King.

> The day wanes on, evenings dying glow,
> Flowers wilt, winds caress,
> The river ceaseless flow;
> Warrior stand, Warrior fight,
> With darkness adjoins the foe of night.
> The sun is gone, in western hills afar,
> No glistening moon, the road to bless,
> No light of flaming star;
> Warrior stand, Warrior fight,
> Against the shadows, victorious is truth and light.
> Over grassy lawn, leaves rolling in the wind,
> Storm cloud mounting, thunder roar and lightning dress,
> The darkness has not thinned;
> Warrior stand, hold fast the night,
> Though deep the wound, abandon not your plight.

Myran watched rapt by the strong and steady, yet soft and delicate, voice. Time seemed to slip away and vanish as her song carried on, verse by verse. He watched as her smooth lips formed each perfect word, and he drank in every wonderful and lovely note. Her dark-green eyes were cast downward, now and then closing for silent emphasis on different parts of the song.

Then they were on Myran. He realized this with a start and felt like he was pitching backward in his seat. He gripped the table edge to steady himself. Unable to hold her eyes, Myran glanced down, but it was only for a moment before he found himself looking back. He thought he saw the corner of her mouth lift. A smile?

When the last beautiful note faded, the silence in the hall remained. Lianna looked down. In the entire room not a muscle moved nor eye blinked for the space of several heartbeats, for all were still held captive.

Brudwyn slowly rose and stated in an awed voice. "Never has a more beautiful voice sung within this hall in all my days as king."

Lianna smiled as her cheeks colored at the great compliment. She curtsied before making her exit.

Twenty

Several days after that night, one of Brudwyn's nobles arrived at the palace. His daughter, betrothed to Sir Dathin, came with him. She was beautiful indeed, with deep hazel eyes and auburn hair. She was slender and graceful but did not carry a happy countenance.

King Brudwyn welcomed them very warmly and Theadrin learned they were to stay for several days. Theadrin was still unsure of what to believe. He didn't like to think that the prince would discredit a loyal noble over a woman, but it seemed plausible.

The noble met Theadrin with the powerful handclasp of a battle veteran. "I have heard much of you already," he told Theadrin. "Your reputation is great for one still young."

"I am honored to meet you, sir," Theadrin returned respectfully.

The nobleman then introduced his daughter. "This is Merion, my daughter."

Theadrin bowed and kissed her hand as was customary. "I am very pleased to meet you, my lady."

"The pleasure is mine," she answered with a pleasant voice, though without a smile.

Theadrin straightened once more and said, "I have been told you are betrothed to Sir Dathin of Antion. My best wishes for you. I have seen him in tournament and from what I hear he is well thought of by the king."

Theadrin thought he saw her face harden. "Yes," was all she allowed.

"Come, Merion." Her father quickly ended their conversation.

With that Theadrin made a polite exit. The meeting, however, remained in his thoughts all that day while he was out in the practice yard training with the others. Afterward, he decided to walk through the gardens. Even though they were empty and covered in snow, there were still many beautiful stone carvings that he could see, and he was sure that he could be alone there.

He strolled slowly along the paths that had been swept clean of the snow and stretched his tired muscles. He didn't get as sore or stiff after training now. His body was hardening to the task it took daily.

Presently he found a white marble bench before a smooth stonewall and sat down. In the distance he could hear the sound of carts and horses moving along the cobbled streets of Monivea.

A crow fluttered overhead and landed in a barren apple tree. It cocked its head and studied Theadrin through a black beaded eye. The wind ruffled its glossy feathers and then it took off again, cackling twice. Theadrin leaned back against the wall and closed his eyes.

After some time, he thought he caught the sound of voices from somewhere nearby. He sat forward and listened. There was unmistakably someone close by, talking. It sounded like two people. After several moments of straining to catch the direction, he realized the voices were coming from behind the wall at his back.

Out of curiosity Theadrin stood up on the bench and peered over the top. Instantly he ducked low again, for on the other side of the wall was the prince himself. Ruadhan was talking to Merion in a hidden part of the garden.

Theadrin didn't wonder how Ruadhan knew that Merion had come to the city, for he probably had all of the roads watched. However, he couldn't figure out how the prince was able to get into Monivea unseen.

From where he was, Theadrin could overhear most of their conversation.

After they had both laughed lightly over something, Ruadhan whispered, "Come away with me. We will leave Caledon and go far away to lands beyond the sea."

Merion replied, "You still have a chance to..."

Ruadhan interrupted. "My father will not listen to reason, Merion. He will not see the truth."

Merion was not swayed. "Things will come together, but if we leave it all now we may regret it for the rest of our lives. Your father and the whole kingdom would believe their suspicions; that you are a jealous lover, and do not have the true heart of a prince. The heart that I see in you."

Theadrin peered over the wall again.

Ruadhan looked down, observing her hand in his.

Merion pressed. "You would be betraying your father if you left him now."

Suddenly Ruadhan stepped away from her, drew his sword, and pointed it at Theadrin who had accidentally pushed a pile of snow from the wall. For one moment the prince did not recognize him.

When he did, he called guardedly, "Are you alone, Theadrin?"

"I am," Theadrin answered.

Ruadhan's eyes darted quickly about to assess if it was true. Then he motioned with a side sweep of his head saying, "Come over here."

Theadrin cautiously pulled himself up onto the top of the wall and then dropped to the other side. "How did you get in here without being seen?" Theadrin wondered out loud, brushing snow off his shirt.

The prince did not answer, so Theadrin assured, "Don't worry, I will tell no one. Trust me, cousin." The prince looked questioningly at Theadrin, who said, "I see you have not heard of our kinship. But it is true; your mother was my father's sister. I am King Valdithin's son."

Ruadhan calculated his options quickly. His blade lowered and he said, "I know the streets and secret alley ways of my home city. It is not hard for me to enter unseen." He regarded Theadrin and then consented to sheathing his sword, saying, "I don't know why, Theadrin, but I believe you are telling the truth."

The prince glanced quickly at Merion and said to Theadrin, "Now you know why I have left the palace then."

The tension in Theadrin eased at seeing the prince put away his weapon. "Some of it," he admitted. "I still fail to understand why you believe your father is in danger. And why have you raised a small army?"

Ruadhan grimaced and looked back at him. "I have been doing so in the hopes that with my men we will be able to stop a plot to betray my father."

"What plot? Who would do this?" Theadrin asked.

"My ward, a man who is trustworthy and loyal, whom I grew up with, was on errand at Sir Dathin's keep. He overheard Dathin, one night, speaking to someone in a tower room. They were discussing what will happen when the King is 'removed.' Though I cannot know for sure, I believe he plans to have my father killed. Merion is betrothed to Dathin. He is a trusted noble and has earned the king's respect and trust over the years." Ruadhan seemed anxious to go on, "And I am only a jealous son unable to have the woman I love. You see, I was against this betrothal long before my ward's fateful errand. My father does not believe me. He does not trust my motives."

"I see." Theadrin pondered his cousin's dilemma. "And how do you think Dathin will go about his plan?"

"That is just it." Ruadhan expressed his frustration. "He doesn't have the means through strength of arms. I can't see how he will do it, but he seems confident. Merion is to be wed soon, but I fear it will be *before* he makes his move."

Theadrin paused to think. "The lady Merion is right, cousin." he finally concluded. "You would be wrong to leave Caledon now. You cannot abandon your father and lose your honor. You have a chance to save your homeland. Don't run away from it."

Ruadhan considered Theadrin's words. Merion looked at him and placed a hand on his arm. "Things will turn out, Ruadhan. If at the time of the wedding we have thought of nothing else," she said, "then I will run. I will not let it happen."

Ruadhan turned his eyes onto hers. "If it comes to that, meet me in the glen. You remember where it is." He took her hand and held it for a moment before looking back at Theadrin. "Thank you for believing me, cousin. I will not forget it."

Theadrin nodded, and the prince said, "I must take my leave now."

With a parting smile, Theadrin said, "The Highest King go with you, cousin."

⌛

By midwinter, folk in the castle became restless. The days had been uncommonly cold and the winds numbingly harsh. The streets of the city were empty, gray, and windswept.

Lianna sat before the blazing hearth with the others. Theadrin was discussing with the king and Aedrius a recent border report that had arrived involving the progress of the war. Lianna had lost interest long ago in the conversation and huddled as close to the warm fire as she could.

She longed for the long winter to end and for spring to come. When Caledon's gardens bloomed it would be a happy day for her. She yearned to dig her fingers into the rich, black soil and take in its earthy aroma and the fragrance of fresh blossoms. She had been cooped up inside long enough.

As the voices of the others began to buzz in the back of her mind, her eyes grew heavy from boredom. She pulled her warm, woolen blanket tighter about her and leaned back in her chair. The yellow tongues of flame danced and blurred together as her eyelids slowly shut.

When she awoke once more, the king's hall had darkened into night and become quiet. The others had gone. She sat forward and rubbed her shoulders. The fire had died down to glowing red embers.

Presently a side door swung open and Myran entered the hall with an armload of chopped wood. He laid it down beside the large hearthstone and began to feed the live coals.

"I didn't know how long you would be down here so I was going to stack up the fire," he said, glancing her way briefly.

She granted a light smile. "Thanks."

Myran Cai nodded and finished piling the wood. With the black iron poker he stirred up the coals and blew into them. They glowed brighter and soon a fiery tongue leapt forth. He leaned back on his heels and watched the flames climb into the stack of dry timber.

Lianna listened as the cold wood began to split and pop under the heat. Her eyes turned to Myran's face, ruddy in the firelight. His eyes seemed to catch and hold the light of the blaze as he stared into it. They looked happy, as they had that night the two of them talked in the hallway at Caulguard.

"Cadi told me today that she likes you," she said, cocking her head to one side. "But she thinks you are too serious all the time."

Myran smirked and held out his hands to the warm fire.

"She confided in me that she would like to dance with you." Lianna regarded Myran with amusement.

"I am afraid she would be quite disappointed with my level of skill," he admitted with a chuckle as a spark glimmered in his eyes.

"She would never dare tell you this herself," Lianna laughed.

Myran laughed with her. Their voices echoed dimly in the big, empty hall of the king. Then for a time they were quiet.

"Do you live in Arinon, Myran?" She asked after a moment. "I know we met in Caledon, but Caithal implied that you were from Arinon."

Myran became at once somber. Lianna feared she had said the wrong thing again, but her curiosity overcame her hesitation. Myran stared deep into the golden flames.

"I did… not anymore," he answered quietly. He squinted as though holding back a painful thought or memory. "I don't have a home now."

She wanted to press the matter further but thought better of it and remained silent. Then, when no more was said, she stood and yawned.

"I suppose it is late. Goodnight, Myran."

Myran stood. "Sleep well, Lady Lianna."

At last the day came for them to ride to war. The first rays of a new spring sun seeped warmth into the frozen country. While it would still be many days before it thawed the cold heart of the land, the war band set out.

Brudwyn had his smiths and tailors fashion new suits of armor for Theadrin and the rest of the men over the winter as a gift.

Each warrior wore a shirt of a single color; either red, green, blue or yellow, with a short-sleeved mail shirt over the top. All had a thick, hardened leather breastplate and wore spaulders, which was armor covering the shoulders. They also had on their forearms a pair of metal vambraces. For leg armor they had splinted metal greaves that reached from their ankles to their knees with an oval piece covering the kneecap.

The leggings they wore were simple cloth and were either checked or striped. Their shoes were thick leather covered on the top by layered strips of armor. They wore helms of iron and cloaks of deep red that were clasped on the right shoulder by a bronze brooch. For weapons they had a sword on their hip, an oval shield, and a spear.

They rode in two columns through the wide gate of Monivea with Aedrius at the head. He wore a white cloak and a red plumed helm, distinguishing him from the rest. Theadrin and Myran rode first in the two columns with Yan and Hectur after and twenty-five men behind each of them in turn.

The entire city came out to see them away. The people cheered and shouted blessings to the warriors as they trotted by along the main street.

Before passing through the gate, Myran glanced back to where Lianna stood by the king. They had spoken very little over the winter months. He saw her standing rigid with her hands on the shoulders of little Cadi. She was watching him. Of all the brave men and even her brother going out that day, her eyes were on him.

Twenty-One

They traveled on one of Caledon's main roads that took them north and made very good time. Winter gave one final battle against the forces of spring. The snow fell fast and furious but the battle was lost from the start. It lasted only half a day before it surrendered to the warmth of spring. Soon patches of fresh green grass were visible.

The road took them to Drefarin, a town near the northern border where they met up with a unit of Caledonian warriors.

That evening Theadrin and Myran shared supper with the general. The sun had set and the town of Drefarin grew dark and shadowy. Warriors huddled about bright burning fires in small groups.

Aedrius's quarters were small. They gathered about a table and ate with the light of the hearth dancing on their faces.

General Aedrius had talked with the captain of the garrison and learned of the barbarian placements and how the fight had gone through the winter. Now he shared with the two his plan of action. He moved a battle-scarred finger over the surface of a worn map, speaking in a low voice, the dim gold light flickering on his face.

"The Kaidri numbers grow with the passing days. The winter was harsh this season and even they were forced to lie low until the thaw. But now they have been on the move again. They travel quickly. My captain has had a challenge to keep up with them."

"Where was the last sighting, sir?" Myran asked.

"They are amassing a force in a valley not far from here. That is why this town has been garrisoned. Scouts last reported that there were five hundred encamped in the valley, and more are coming." He paused and scratched his chin. "Aside from our additional fifty, there are three hundred good warriors with us."

"Where are the rest of Caledon's armies?" Theadrin asked.

"Spread abroad all across the border. It must be that way or we could not keep up with their attacks."

Myran Cai seemed unimpressed with the Kaidri's numbers. "I have heard these barbarians hold little in the way of tactics."

Aedrius was in agreement. "Indeed. I battled them before. They rely on brute strength mostly, and that they have. But it is cunning that wins the battle. Now here is my plan. We will bring the fight directly to them. They know our numbers are less than their own and expect us to dig into the village and wait."

He shook his head. "We'll hit them hard on three sides with the footmen. Our horsemen will encircle the battle blowing horns. Our goal is to deceive the enemy into thinking we have greater numbers."

Theadrin nodded. It was quite a simple plan, and he wondered if it could be pulled off. But Aedrius seemed entirely confident. "Where do you want us?" he asked the commander.

Aedrius straightened and answered, "You and the fifty are my guard. You will join me at the front of the footmen. Now get what sleep you can; we must be in position before first light."

Theadrin and Myran saluted their commander and left to join the rest of the men outside. Despite what Aedrius said about sleep, Theadrin and his friends could not find any that night. They sat together around a red fire in companionable silence, each to his own thoughts of the coming fight.

Theadrin wondered what would become of his sister should he be among the casualties. At least she would have a home with their uncle, King Brudwyn. That much was comforting.

Commander Aedrius emerged from his quarters long before dawn. Theadrin wondered at his cool demeanor on such a day. He called the men to arms and they moved out, leaving one hundred men in Drefarin.

They moved across country in the cover of a moonless night. Before drawing too close, Aedrius sent Myran and a handful of others to check for lookouts. They slipped out of camp quietly and did not return until the first rosy light was showing in the east. There were no lookouts. The Kaidri were unafraid of an attack. With that report, Aedrius sent out fifty riders each with a battle horn to circle the encampment.

Then he formed his men around him and signaled to move out. Armor clinked and rattled as they jogged forward. Theadrin's heart began to pound; his fingers felt weak. He drew a deep breath and trotted on behind Aedrius.

All at once, the commander stopped and lifted a hand. The army halted as one in the trees. Aedrius turned about to face his men. "When we charge, I want you to give a battlecry worthy of the name. Press onward and give them no rest. Now, my brave warriors, with me!"

At these words Aedrius turned and sprinted off toward the unseen enemy. Myran was the first to follow but was ahead of the rest by only two strides. The ridge line dropped away and the Kaidri encampment lay sprawled below. To Theadrin there seemed much more than five hundred.

Aedrius drew out his sword and with a mighty yell charged downward. The rest of the army plummeted down after him, releasing a deafening cry. Theadrin saw heads look up in the enemy camp, and all at once the sound of rams' horns bellowed from the hills all around them. To Theadrin it sounded as though there were thousands. He could see a great stirring below and they were panicking.

At the head of his men Aedrius hacked into the enemy. Sword drawn, Theadrin surged on after his commander into the barbarians.

The Tor Trilogy

The Kaidri were much more imposing close up than what Theadrin saw on the hill. All were massive in build and hairy. They wore filthy skins and furs, and their hair and beards were knotted and dirty.

Their charge drove them deep into the middle of the enemy camp, and still Aedrius pressed on. The Kaidri fought wildly but were unorganized. Theadrin evaded a deadly chop of a battle-ax and drove his sword point into the enemy's chest.

Myran raised a spear he had snatched up and sent it into one barbarian's abdomen. He stayed even with Theadrin, fending off many attacks to the right.

The battle passed in a blurred memory for Theadrin. The Kaidri fled in fear and they pursued long into the day, dealing them a great blow. At one point, they ran into another large force of barbarians who had been on their way to join the encampment of the first. Outnumbered once again, the tide could have easily turned against the Caledonians.

Aedrius was prepared for such an event, however, and lifted a horn to his lips. The blast summoned the horsemen from the hills who swept into the rear of the fresh Kaidri force. All the while, the commander pressed onward against the enemy.

At last, commander Aedrius halted his men, leaving a handful of enemy warriors to return to their clan chieftains and tell of the defeat that day. The men cheered greatly and applauded their commander. Theadrin unstrapped his helmet and moved along with the rest.

But when he looked back at the aftermath of the battle, Theadrin's stomach tightened. As he looked at the bodies, lying lifeless on the black-stained ground, cold eyes staring blankly, he realized the reality of what war really was. It was not all glorious as he played as a child. His first impulse was to turn and flee the horrid scene, and he took an involuntary step backward. His stomach churned and he turned away.

Myran came up beside him and placed a steadying hand on his shoulder. "It is finished."

Theadrin drew a breath and looked at his friend, grateful for his composure and assurance. Yan and Hectur joined their side and together they followed Aedrius and the rest back to Drefarin.

Twenty-Two

Breath came from the horse's nostrils in large billows of hot steam. The battle-hardened steed pawed the ground impatiently, scraping the wet, shallow snow from the stubby grass. A heavy mist had formed obscuring everything a stone toss away from sight, and drifted on the silent currents of the fresh breeze.

The line of horsemen rimmed the hilltop like a wall, listening intently for any sound but hearing nothing save the low murmur of the wind. Then the mournful sound of a war horn rose from a distance away. The warriors waited and the horn sounded once more.

Soon the distant sounds of battle reached the hilltop. Still they waited. For a long time they sat as the far-off battle ensued. Another distant blast from a war horn resonated through the mist, different from the first. At its sounding, a rider trotted his horse along the line and stopped in the center. He drew his sword; the cold steel sang as it left the scabbard.

Swords were drawn all down the line in accordance. The lead horseman started forward and as one the line moved after him. Through the fog they rode with only the sound of the horses' hooves falling heavy on the earth and their own breaths and heartbeats.

Theadrin and his men had followed Aedrius through the summer trying to keep up with the Kaidri who, for some time, would not fight them outright. The news of their first victory kept them aloof. They would raid towns and settlements and sack farmsteads.

At last, toward summer's end, they began to press the barbarians back. They had gotten wise to the Kaidri way of fighting and could predict accurately where they would strike next. When the enemy saw that they could no longer make successful raids, they turned their full strength against Aedrius's army. It was harder when the cold of winter arrived and the battles grew few and far between.

But at last, after two smaller fights, the remainder of the barbarian army, who hadn't already fled back across the border, amassed as one. Aedrius had attacked them in the mist and drawn them to a position where their back was to Theadrin and the fifty warriors of Arinon. Aedrius had stationed them there with orders to attack when they heard the Caledonian battle horn.

As they pressed on through the vaporous fog, the barbarian army began to materialize before their eyes and the clash of battle was much louder. The force of mounted warriors hit the Kaidri hard in the flank, flooding over the first lines with ease.

Now surrounded, the barbarians fought with everything in them. Their war leader, Rhodgrim, a huge man with a yellow beard and battle-scarred face, rallied his men together. He bellowed a braying war cry over and over again that seemed to increase his warrior's moral.

Theadrin saw the barbarian war chief and fought his way toward him. The chieftain met him with a crushing strike of his war hammer. Theadrin's horse went down hurtling him forward. He hit the ground hard and lost his breath.

Rhodgrim kicked him in the face and brought his hammer downward. Theadrin narrowly avoided the death strike. It came again, and once more, each one closer than the last to crushing him.

Rhodgrim lifted it again. Theadrin, on his back, kicked hard into the barbarian's knee. It caved and Theadrin heard the loud crack. But Rhodgrim did not cry out, or even fall, but he dropped the hammer and clung tightly to the pole of his banner.

On his feet once more, Theadrin defended against two barbarians that had flown to their leader's aid. One held a chipped, two-bladed ax and the other used a falchion. Theadrin managed to bring them down in two quick moves. His adrenaline was running wild. Others came at him, but Myran Cai was at his side.

The chieftain, leaning on the standard, had his war hammer in hand once again.

Theadrin moved in on him. Avoiding another heavy swing, Theadrin thrust toward his chest. Rhodgrim dropped his hammer and grabbed Theadrin's arm. The point of Theadrin's sword had just grazed his chest and gone to the side.

Theadrin was pulled forward and head butted. The chieftain's face was twice the size of his and hard as a rock wall. Theadrin's sight blackened, but only for a moment. He was on his back and the war chief was about to impale him with the sharpened bottom of the standard pole.

But he still had a grip on his sword and hit the point of the standard aside. Up on one knee, he rammed the butt of his sword into Rhodgrim's ribs and laid a strong punch to his face. Again the contact was hard and Theadrin's knuckles cracked and bled.

At that moment Theadrin's men surrounded the spot. The barbarian war chief, guarded on all sides by spear points and swords, cast down the standard in surrender. This took the fight from the rest of the Kaidri army immediately. The war was over.

When all were lined up and guarded, Aedrius came up to where Theadrin stood before the beaten Kaidri chieftain. "Well done, Captain, well done," Aedrius commended. Three other men joined them.

"Seventy prisoners, sir," Mathwin reported. He stood holding his naked blade stained black and red. His face was filthy but his manner was composed.

"Good," Aedrius nodded and looked at the barbarian chief who knelt and glared defiantly back at the victors. "You have taken Rhodgrim alive—that is no small accomplishment."

He faced Theadrin. "You have done all I required of you and far exceeded it. I am honored to have trained you." The commander extended a muscled hand. "You may return to Monivea with your men. Give the king my report."

Theadrin saluted the commander he had come to greatly respect and then went to his men. Some were still astride horses, but most were standing about the prisoners with their weapons drawn. "Mount up. We are going home, men."

Upon their return to Monivea, they received a reception much the same scene as when they had left. King Brudwyn stood atop the flight of stone steps that led up to the great hall with those of his household. Lianna was beside him, dressed in a fine white dress with a green sash about her waist.

Cadi stood in front of Lianna with her hands clasped in front of her. Her shimmering, golden hair was braided and tied with a white band behind her neck.

The men came to a perfect stop as Theadrin lifted his hand. The king came forward and looked them over. Theadrin drew his sword and lifted it in salute.

"My lord, the king, Commander Aedrius sends this news: Caledon has been rid of the barbarians." This brought forth a cheer from the people.

"Well done!" boomed the king. "Get down off those horses and refresh yourselves." Theadrin turned about in the saddle to face his men. They remained erect, waiting for his orders.

"Dismount!"

Pages and stable hands came to take their horses, and Theadrin and Myran, along with Yan and Mathwin, entered the hall with the king. At the top of the stairs Lianna met Theadrin with a happy embrace.

"It has been so long!" she said. "Are you all well?"

"Very." Theadrin returned the hug and then knelt down so that he was face to face with Cadi who had been shyly observing them from behind the folds of Lianna's dress.

"Look how you've grown!" Theadrin smiled warmly. "I do believe you've become even more beautiful than you were before." The girl blushed crimson and gave him a hug around the neck.

Caithal appeared with a smile on his lips. "Welcome back! You have done exceedingly well. Praise to the Highest King!"

Inside the hall drinks were poured and food was laid out before them. They ate and talked heartily until they could eat no more. Stories were told of the heroic feats witnessed by comrades and how they had fared the winter.

Lianna noticed a change in her older brother. He held a more serious countenance, and his laughter was more reserved. His boyish features had hardened into maturity.

The only one who did not seem very altered from it was Myran. He was still as quiet and somber as always, content to sit back and let the rest do the storytelling, though allowing nothing to escape the sharp gaze of his bronze eyes.

But Lianna became worried for Theadrin and later brought the matter to Caithal. He was reassuring and stated, "The effects of war can be hard on men. Don't be anxious over your brother. He has experienced the horrors of battle, and it will take some time before he is himself again."

"If he ever is." Lianna fretted.

"Oh, he will, for the most part anyway. But a part of him will not go back. He has matured and that is for the better. All men come from battle changed in some way."

"Myran seems the same," she told him, shaking her head. "Always so quiet."

Caithal was thoughtful a moment and looked at Lianna as if he was deciding whether to tell a great secret or not. He brushed his gray beard with his fingertips.

She knew what he was debating in his mind. Lianna remembered the night around the fire when Caithal was telling her and Theadrin about Myran. The matter had not left her mind.

"A great mystery surrounds Myran Cai's life," he began, choosing his words slowly, "Ao-idh, a trusted friend and lord under your father, found him in the old forest on the western sea as a very young child. He was never able to find if Myran had any family or kin. So he lived and grew up in Arinon in the forest with Ao-idh and another young orphan boy named Caed. Myran and Caed were willing students of Ao-idh. Myran looked to him as a father and he taught Myran everything he knew. Back then, Gurn's personal militia, the Merdi, were given their way in the kingdom. They were thieves, doing as they pleased. The three did what they could to stop these marauders. The people called them heroes, but they were labeled outlaws by Gurn.

"One day, Gurn's men caught up with them. Caed fell first, and Ao-idh was pierced in the heart by a crossbow bolt. He commanded Myran to flee with his last breath. Although Myran was reluctant, he barely escaped with his life.

"Afterward, he traveled to Caledon and I found him near my hut. I did what I could to bring encouragement; but only the Highest of Kings can truly restore a broken life.

"So, as you see him now is how he has always been since. You know, it is interesting how Theadrin called him Cai. Cai means 'rejoice.'" Caithal chuckled and paused a moment in thought.

"I understand," Lianna answered a bit sadly. "Poor Myran." It was a sad story but Lianna had known several people growing up who had lost loved ones. Why did it affect Myran so drastically?

Caithal seemed to read her thoughts and added, "Something happened that day in the forest beyond the death of his friends. I don't know what, but it weighs like a heavy burden on Myran."

Lianna wondered what it could be. What yoke was Myran suffering under?

"The change you see in Theadrin is for the better," Caithal continued. "He has become stronger and wiser. And he has become a better leader."

Twenty-Three

When three days had passed Theadrin went before King Brudwyn. "My men are anxious to return home."

"Of course." The king replied understandingly. "They have been away from home for a long time. I and my men stand ready to aid you, just send us word when we are needed."

Theadrin bowed politely at the waist. "Thank you. We will see how things stand when we return."

"Gurn is the kind of man who would rather die than lose his power. Call on us when the fight comes," said King Brudwyn.

"We have greatly enjoyed our stay with you and are forever indebted for your hospitality."

"Nonsense! Rather, I am in your debt for your help in defending this kingdom."

They shook each other's hands firmly as kinsmen and then the king turned to Lianna who was standing behind Theadrin. "Farewell, my dear. Your gracious presence will be sorely missed in this city. I must say the palace gardens have never before flourished as they did while you tended them. You have your mother's gift."

Lianna smiled and kissed him lightly on the cheek. "Goodbye, uncle."

The journey to Caulguard was uneventful. Spring came on fast and everything was green by the time they arrived. It was a bright, clear day when they rode into the keep. Anromir met them in a jubilant mood.

"Hail, Prince Theadrin!" he called. "It's good to see you in one piece! We've heard news of your victories in the north. Most excellent!"

"My lord Anromir, these men are the heroes; Arinon's greatest warriors!" Theadrin called back while clapping a congratulating hand onto one of the soldier's shoulders.

After Theadrin dismissed the men, Anromir practically dragged them inside.

"We will hold a feast tonight!" he declared happily.

What a feast it was! The families of the knights came and the reunion was joyous. The food flowed endlessly and the celebration lasted long into the hours of the night. There was much laughter and stories. Songs were sung, filling the hall again and again with the merry tunes. The somberness that had been over the men lifted and Theadrin could not remember ever enjoying himself as much.

When time came to go to their beds, all slept sounder than they ever had. Tonight all was well.

"You can bet Gurn is anticipating your return," Anromir said the next day. "Don't look so surprised. By now the whole kingdom knows of your arrival. Word flew on the wind even as you crossed the border."

"What has Gurn been up to while we were away?" Myran asked.

"I have not heard much from the palace. Needless to say, I have not been in good standings with Gurn and the nobles since siding with you at the counsel," Anromir said but waved that matter aside.

"The people have talked of little else than you, Theadrin. It is clear that at least the majority would take up arms for you against Gurn should things come to it. There is no doubt in their minds that you are the son of Valdithin. By now they all know of King

Brudwyn's acknowledging you as such. I tell you the time is ripe!" He pounded his fist into the palm of his other hand.

"You can bet Gurn knows this too," Myran warned. "He will have a plan by now."

Anromir had to agree. "Aye. We must be ready for his retaliation."

Theadrin listened but did not say anything. He showed no enthusiasm for any of the seemingly good news. Soon he dismissed himself and left the room.

Caithal found him on a stone deck overlooking the western hills. He stood with his hands on the railing, the spring breeze waving his hair. It was cool on his face and carried the sweet aroma of new flowers. Theadrin turned when he heard footsteps and Caithal came to stand beside him.

"You do not seem at all happy with Anromir's news about the people," he said.

Theadrin answered. "No, I am. It is encouraging to hear." He fell silent and looked away.

"What troubles you?" Caithal asked after brief observation. He came to lean on the smooth, stone railing.

Theadrin searched the horizon with eyes full of despair. "You said I would find him, Caithal. This past year I have searched relentlessly. Why haven't I found him?" He turned on Caithal, a quick fire flashed in his eyes.

The old man remained calm at the sudden outburst. "I don't know," he said simply.

"I'm sorry, Caithal. My temper got the better of me."

"No need to apologize."

"I know his hand was with us in the war, but I have not had satisfaction in my search." He stared across the countryside. "I will not be king until I find him. I cannot be." He looked back at Caithal, agony framing his features. "I don't think I can even live without him."

Caithal smiled. "You keep searching, and wait patiently for him. Your search has not been in vain. You have found one thing, at least."

"What is that?"

"Just what you said. It has been revealed to you that you cannot live without him. That is a step closer." Then he smiled most reassuringly and placed a hand on the young man's shoulder. "There is no doubt in my mind, Theadrin, that what you seek is just around the bend. He surely wanted to see if you really did want him."

Something in Caithal's words brought peace to Theadrin's mind. He managed a smile, and the two went back inside. When they entered the room where the others were, Anromir was standing apart talking to one of his servants.

Anromir saw Theadrin enter and hurried over to him. "A messenger has just come from Halendin. He bears important news. Sit down and he will explain."

They took seats and listened to Anromir's servant. "My lords," he began. "I have come from the town of Halendin. I was there on business for my lord"—he indicated Anromir—"and witnessed a meeting. There was an assembly of forty men in all. The village elders met with those from other towns and villages. The entire kingdom knows of the outcome of Gurn's counsel a year ago. The elders met and..." He stopped and looked at Anromir.

"Get to the point man. What was the outcome?"

The messenger straightened and took a breath. "They are supplying the people of their towns with weapons to fight for King Valdithin's son." He looked at Theadrin. "They have heard of your return and they will take up arms. They look to you to lead them."

Anromir looked at Theadrin who asked the messenger, "You are certain?"

"There is no doubt, sire," he replied. "I expect you will receive word from them very soon."

"So it is as I said," Anromir declared. "Gurn's demise is at hand!"

The messenger's words proved to be accurate. Two days passed and there came to the keep a man sent by the village elders. He requested immediate audience with Theadrin.

"We stand ready to fight," the messenger said when all were gathered. "You are requested to attend a gathering in the town of Lundel. There everything will be put under your authority."

"When?" Theadrin asked.

"Tomorrow, sire," the man replied and added, "We do not want to give the enemy any opportunity."

"I see. Tell those who sent you I will come," Theadrin said and turned to Anromir. "Let this man have something to eat before he leaves."

"Yes, sire," Anromir said and left to arrange it.

"They will be untrained," Myran said. "Gurn's men are armored. We cannot supply armor for all of these men."

"I know," Theadrin confessed. "But I cannot deny them the right to fight for their freedom. I want to give Gurn one last chance. This will not be a counsel of war. I want to avoid that at all costs." Theadrin looked at Myran, but his eyes were seeing again the terrible aftermath of those battles. "From what I have learned fighting the Kaidri in Caledon, we do not want to settle this by losing so many more lives. If he refuses to step down, then we have no other choice. These people will never be free under Gurn."

"I couldn't agree more, Theadrin. But I cannot believe that Gurn will ever surrender," Myran added as Theadrin turned to leave.

Caithal came up beside Myran. "Your counsel is wise, Myran. Never cease to give it to Theadrin. He will need it greatly in the days ahead."

Myran smiled at his friend and looked down at an object in his hand. Caithal noticed him fingering it and inquired, "What have you there?"

"I found it in the forest," he answered, handing it to Caithal.

"This is an artifact of the Dorrani, an ancient tribe," he said after a brief examining. "I have seen similar works in my time. This was once the handle of a small knife; a chieftain's, no doubt, because of the intricacy. May I hold on to it for a while?"

"By all means. It is of no use to me."

Evening drew on and Theadrin went early to his chamber. The only window in the room faced the east where night gathered. One star glimmered bright in the blackening sky, and Theadrin watched it as he lay in his bed.

One by one other stars joined the first until the whole sky burned with them. Theadrin remained awake, his mind straying over the matters at hand, until at last weariness overtook him.

Suddenly he was awake again. He knew not how much time had transpired or even where he was at first. Something had stirred him from his slumber; a voice. Someone was calling him.

He got up and looked about intently.

The voice called again, very distant, but he knew it was calling for him. His heart began to beat wildly as he looked for the owner of the voice. He found himself on a high parapet and ran to the stone rail to look about. There was a thick fog over the land and dark clouds mantling the heavens.

For a long time he stood, searching, but the voice came no more. A great heaviness descended over him and he made up his mind to go back to bed.

"Theadrin." The voice was behind him and he turned. Immediately he was hit by a light so intense and powerful that it brought him to his knees. He could not bear to look at it. The brilliant light engulfed everything around him.

Then a voice, "Beloved." It was the most loving and tender, yet most strong and mighty voice Theadrin had ever heard. It was so beautiful Theadrin wondered that he didn't burst at its sounding.

The same word came again. "Beloved."

"Who are you, my lord?" Theadrin's voice sounded like dust blowing past on a midsummer breeze.

"I Am," came the mighty voice. "I am the Light of the Morning, the Great Light. I am the Restorer and the Redeemer, the Strong and Mighty. I hold authority over heaven and earth. I am the Higher Rock, and a Strong Tower. I am the Purifier and Refiner. I am the Maker. I am whom you have been seeking. I am the Lord your God."

Theadrin was trembling at the awesome presence before him. With each name he heard, a new revelation washed over him like an ocean wave. He was flat on his face shielding his eyes from the fierce and terrible beauty.

"Lord, I am unworthy to be in your presence," Theadrin cried after a sudden sense of lowliness and insignificance. He could see plainly now his filth for he was in the presence of a Holy King.

"Beloved," the voice came again. "You did not choose me, but I have chosen you. Even before the earth began, I chose you for this time. And My plan for you is greater and farther beyond anything that you could ever imagine."

"Why, Lord? Why have you chosen me?"

"You cannot understand. This mystery goes deeper than you know. Only believe."

"I believe, Master." Theadrin felt that if he moved an inch or opened his eyes he would die. He felt the light like a fire about him. It penetrated him and he felt cleansed and revived. He felt all the dirt and grime wash off him.

It was like living water rushing over him and Theadrin felt the love and holiness come in the light like waves of silver rain. It flowed through every corner of his being.

"Look north." The Lord spoke again. And turning his face northward Theadrin saw a great black cloud that churned and swelled. It was growing larger with every passing moment. It continued rapidly to grow until it consumed the land and burst forth toward him.

Theadrin saw it engulfing the land, swallowing towns and villages. There was no part of the kingdom, or anywhere in his sight, that was not enshrouded. But as he watched, there appeared several lights. The darkness tried to cover them once they appeared, but the lights only grew brighter. Soon they began to move, and all joined together in one marvelous light that began to push back the darkness.

The black shadow continued to snake across the face of the land and finally reached the platform where he stood. He closed his eyes and put his hands up to sheild his face as it swarmed over him. "Lord!" he shouted out. When he opened his eyes again it was gone and he was once again immersed in the pure, radiant light of the King.

Theadrin was quaking at the vision of the darkness, but the presence of his Lord immediately washed away the fear and filled him with great courage.

"What must I do, Lord?"

"Begin at my sanctuary." Theadrin was hit once again with a wave of love. "The land must be cleansed from the darkness that has been consuming it."

"How can I fight the deception, Lord?"

"I am the Truth. The truth is in you. Go, my chosen one." The voice was like a trumpet.

Theadrin was filled again with great fear. "If you do not go with me, I will not. I cannot!" Theadrin sensed the pleasure that flowed out from the Great King. It was more than he could bear.

"I am with you; I will never leave you. Go, chosen and beloved."

⌛

The following day Theadrin rode out of the keep with a small company. Myran Cai rode on his right and Anromir his left with Yan and Mathwin behind. Ten of the warriors who followed Theadrin in the war against the Kaidri brought up the rear of the group. The day was overcast and the clouds drizzled a light, cold rain.

Theadrin's mind never left the vision he had the night before. He was in his room once again and he looked out the window from where he lay. He felt perfect peace. That morning Yan had awoken him.

"Theadrin?" He looked at him apprehensively. "Are you awake, sir?"

"I am, Yan." Theadrin sat up and smiled at his friend. Yan's expression was of slight confusion. Theadrin waited for him to speak and finally asked, "What is it, Yan?"

"Oh." He blinked and came to himself. "You asked me to wake you."

"I did." Theadrin nodded and rubbed the back of his neck.

Yan studied him for a moment longer before saying, "Breakfast is ready."

Yan was not the only one to regard Theadrin strangely. When they broke fast at the table he received many interested glances. He could not imagine what it was that captured everyone's attention.

Afterward he managed to get Caithal alone before his departure. "What is so interesting about me today?"

"Why do you ask that?" Caithal wondered. Theadrin knew he was toying with him.

"Everyone seems to regard me different than before," he told him.

Caithal's answer was straightforward. "You look different today. They are trying to figure out what it is about you." He leaned back to study Theadrin. "They cannot tell, but they know something is different."

"You know, don't you?" Theadrin said flatly.

Caithal smiled. "Yes, I know."

Theadrin then told him of his vision, ending with, "I can't say I found him. I suppose it would be more correct to say that he found me…He called me."

Caithal's smile widened and he put a hand on the young man's shoulder. "Now begins the great journey, my son. Run the race with endurance."

Theadrin gripped the reins tightly as they trotted along the road to Lundel with this memory fresh in his mind. A burning desire had risen up within him to know the King. To have his presence always was what he wanted more than anything.

Before the town came in sight they spotted the smoke. Dark, black columns rose on the horizon. Lundel was burning.

Twenty-Four

The soft glow of candles lit the stuffy interior of the room below the keep. Caithal turned the broken knife handle in his wrinkled fingers. The artwork of the horses and warriors carrying spears was trademark to the Dorrani tribe. He had examined many artifacts from the destroyed clan. Myran said he had found it near where Theadrin and Lianna had first been attacked by the Cruthene, an area once under the dominion of the Dorrani.

It was the warlike Dorrani that battled against Penred's grandson, plundering the city of Avross. It was then that the manuscript with the prophecy of the King Sword had been torn and a portion disappeared. Caithal had taken every chance to study artifacts found of Dorrani origin, in case there was some clue to that time. But he had never found what he was looking for.

A sigh of disappointment escaped him as he set down the knife handle. He had been there since first light, and there was nothing unordinary about this piece of Dorrani history. Had he really expected that there would be something there?

Caithal picked the handle up once more, irritably. He had always firmly believed that he would find the missing piece, that it was the Highest King's will. Now his hopes had been dashed once again as they had so many times before.

He tapped it on the worn oak table and drew a breath hot with disappointment and anger. The time was too late now to continue to wait for a clue to the missing puzzle piece. Theadrin would have to go on without the King Sword, the only thing that could prove his right to rule.

In mounted fury, Caithal raised the small object and slammed it down hard on the table. The frail wooden legs quivered and moaned against the sudden aggression as the small pommel of the handle snapped off.

Caithal wiped a hand over his weary face and rested his bearded chin on his thumbs as he stared at the broken artifact. The silver was untarnished where it had formerly been attached. Caithal frowned. The piece that came off did not look broken but as though it had been made to come on and off at will.

As his heartbeat quickened with excitement, he snatched up the handle. It was hollow inside. He beat it against his palm and the brown edge of parchment came into view. In his excitement and intrigue, he did not notice the call of alarm raised in the keep above.

Theadrin and his men spurred into a gallop. The horses' hooves kicked up water from the muddy puddles scattered over the road as they raced on. They descended into a valley between two hills, and the smoke momentarily disappeared. It was in sight again as they mounted the slope, although the columns were larger and more ominous.

They couldn't cover ground fast enough. The billows had reached their peak and were already starting to lessen in size when the first buildings came into sight.

Theadrin's adrenaline was flowing as he beheld the daunting vapor looming high above. They passed the first building, discovering that the black smoke rose from the center of town.

Flying onward at a quick pace, they came to find its source. The inn was charred and part of it had fallen in. Although the flames had mostly died away, there was little that was left salvageable. The area was deserted.

Theadrin quickly dismounted and walked forward, picking his way over some of the blackened debris.

"Look there!" one of the warriors shouted and lifted a finger. All eyes turned to see the body of a man hunched over part of a collapsed wall. Theadrin was the first to reach the spot and gently turned the man over. Wide eyes stared back up at him in frozen horror. The man was dead, an ugly gash across his chest.

Theadrin recognized the man as the messenger sent from the village elders the day before. He put his hand on the ashen face and slowly closed the lifeless eyes.

As the others reached the spot, he looked past the crumbling wall and beheld a terrible sight. There were other bodies strewn about. All of the elders who had come to meet Theadrin were dead, and other villagers with them.

Myran walked steadily up beside Theadrin and looked about without a word. Then he went a few paces away and crouched beside one of the bodies. Mathwin came and stood behind Myran, staring downward without expression. His big arms hung limply at his sides.

Yan did not come near the bodies but sat rigid in the saddle staring in wide-eyed horror. Anromir looked down at the fallen messenger in silence, fingering the hilt of his sword. No one spoke save the dark mutterings of several of the other warriors. Myran leaned back on his heels and looked sorrowfully at the dead man before him. Parts of his clothes were burnt and he lay in a dark pool of blood. Then something caught his eye. There was a rolled-up paper tied with a leather cord lying on a block a pace away. Leaning over, he picked it up and examined it briefly.

He gently untied the string and scanned its contents. His eyes hardened and he got up and took it to Theadrin who carefully read it. It was a letter from Gurn. Anromir saw it and approached them with a dark frown on his face. Theadrin looked at him as he drew near and held out the letter.

"Gurn's own hand," Anromir stated after a glance. As his eyes scanned what was written, his frown deepened to a scowl.

Yan had gathered his courage and now came stumbling up behind. "What have you found?" he asked in a quavering voice. His face was pale.

"Gurn has issued a dire warning," Theadrin said as Anromir handed Yan the paper, and then added, "He even challenges us to try again."

"He mocks us, and relishes in the murder of his own subjects, his own countrymen," Anromir growled angrily. The hate mingled with grief was not hidden in his voice.

Yan looked up from the letter, his eyes wide. "This is a small demonstration?" He repeated one of the lines on the message.

Myran spoke for the first time, saying, "This is nothing for Gurn. Believe me when I tell you he is capable of far worse." He watched Yan and then looked away. Yan swallowed hard.

The sound of shifting rubble came from behind a pile and they caught a glimpse of someone darting back behind it.

"The people think we are Gurn's men returned," Anromir said to Theadrin. "That is why there is no one else out here."

Theadrin called out, "Don't be afraid! We are friends!" This produced no effect. "We are friends!" he said again. "I am Theadrin, son of Valdithin!"

At last the man peered out of his hiding place. It was not until after more careful observation that he emerged. Theadrin met him.

"What happened here, friend?" he asked gently, his eyes and voice showing compassion.

"Gurn's soldiers," the man muttered. "They came on us without warning." He looked about to assure himself he was no longer in danger.

"They have gone," Theadrin reassured him. "It is over."

Then others began to appear from where they had been fearfully watching. The trickle grew to flowing as more people came.

"They killed many and set fire to the inn." The man looked into Theadrin's eyes. "That was where they were assembling; to meet you." He knelt down and put a hand on one of the bodies of the elders.

A woman, middle aged and thin, began to weep aloud and threw herself on one of the fallen men. Theadrin went and put a gentle hand on her shoulder. "My lady, are you hurt?"

"They killed him!" the woman sobbed. Her tears fell and landed on the chest of her dead husband.

"Is there anything I can do to help you?" Theadrin asked gently. The woman did not answer but bent down and put her forehead against the breathless body. Theadrin felt helpless. He glanced around as others ran and wept over fallen loved ones, and grief gripped his heart. These were his people, the people his father had loved and given his life for.

He felt then the first pressures of kingship. Although these people were not under his authority yet and he was not king, he felt a responsibility for them. To see them murdered or gripped with such agony stirred him greatly.

"How can I provide for the children?" He heard the woman whisper, still pressed upon the lifeless man. Theadrin looked back at her. "Bring your family to Caulguard. I will see you are well looked after."

The woman slowly turned her eyes toward Theadrin, who stood and held out his hand. She looked at it for a long time, tears rolling down her stained cheeks. Then, apprehensively at first, she reached out and took hold of it and Theadrin helped her gently up.

The lifeless body of a woman caught Myran's eye. Her hair was yellow gold and even though the sun was concealed, there was no hiding the bright beauty of it. He looked away and his eyes fell on a young lad who had the same bright hair color as the woman. He was searching about the area with his wide eyes until they landed on Myran, then on the body of the woman before him.

Instant tears filled the lad's eyes and he ran to the body. A whisper escaped his lips, "No," and he knelt at the head of the woman. "Mother." Gentle sobs began to escape the lad's lungs, and Myran had to hold back a sudden surge of emotion.

He put a strong, reaffirming hand on the boy's shoulder. "Where is your father?"

At the sound of his voice the lad turned blue eyes upward into Myran's. "He is working." The boy's voice quivered. "We were going to market." He looked back down. "Suddenly there were soldiers and she told me to run." The lad began to weep again.

Myran's bronze eyes gazed softly on the boy. "What is your name, lad?"

The boy could not answer but wept at his mother's side.

"Myran!" Theadrin called him from behind. Myran patted the boy's shoulder and rose slowly before returning to Theadrin. They took brief counsel together over what had happened and what should be immediately done.

"We must march upon Avross and repay this wicked deed," were Anromir's first words. Even before he finished saying them he knew it was folly. They had not the strength of arms to besiege the city. "We must retaliate in some form at least." He subsided.

"We will." Theadrin looked at the noble. "It is war before us now. But it is Gurn who has begun it. Let that be known abroad."

"A plan of retaliation must be formed with more time," Myran counseled, and added, "We must first decide what to do about those affected by this massacre."

"We will meet the needs of the people as best we can," Theadrin said, casting another glance around them. Then he looked to Anromir. "We may need to house a few in Caulguard."

"We will find room if that is needed," Anromir returned, but put in, "However, we cannot hold all of Arinon behind Caulguard's walls, should this continue."

Theadrin nodded. "We will return to the keep and take counsel there."

After seeing to the families of the victims, they returned to the keep. A spitting rain plagued them on the road back and did much to dampen their miserable spirits. Theadrin looked up at the gray, overcast sky. He longed for a ray of warm sunlight to penetrate the thick mantle of clouds and heat his cold wet skin.

The clouds rolled as the sea, the waves falling slowly, if they fell at all, resembling a satin sheet. On the horizon they darkened, and Theadrin was reminded of his vision once more. He recalled the dark cloud that had inundated the entire land and lastly engulfed him on the tower, and his heart began to thump heavily inside his chest. The black cloud was already beginning its surge.

Contemplating what darkness and troubles lay ahead, Theadrin felt hollow in the pit of his stomach. Did he have the strength to face the coming days?

As the party mounted a rise in the terrain, Caulguard came into sight. The gates were flung wide open and armored warriors were flying through into the keep; all of them looked to be Gurn's men.

At first, panic seized Theadrin and it took all his courage to mask it. He quickly assessed the best options of action. "Weapons!" he shouted and drew his sword. The ten warriors with him brought up their spears. "With me!" He spurred his horse and began the race to Caulguard.

Theadrin tried to number the foemen. There were at least one hundred outside the walls from his best estimation, and there could be two hundred more inside as far as he could tell.

The enemy warriors were so focused on gaining the inside that they did not see the riders closing in behind. This is what Theadrin was hoping for. It was their best shot at achieving any advantage. The ten warriors leveled their spears and, at full gallop, they slammed into the enemy ranks, cutting as far as the gate.

Theadrin knew they had to keep an advance or they would easily be overwhelmed. He cut and slashed at the front of his men, pressing onward.

When the footmen realized they were being flanked, Theadrin expected them to turn in force on him and his men. But instead they flew into panic, and he quickly realized that the enemy did not know how many men Theadrin had with him, since their backs were turned. In their minds it could have been a large force.

This gave them the edge and they drove inside the keep. The enemy soldiers were everywhere pillaging the buildings that were inside the walls. But they had not gotten wind of Theadrin's attack.

Theadrin cut through them to the door of the keep itself. They dismounted in the confusion their presence had inflicted and climbed the short stairs. Theadrin led the way through the door meeting two enemy warriors.

The first turned on him, quickly swinging for his head. Theadrin ducked beneath it and came up, bringing the crossbar of his sword into his enemy's jaw. He knocked the sword of the second man downward and then swung up and cut him across the chest.

"Anromir!" he yelled to where the noble had quickly dispatched a foeman. Anromir glanced up at him. "Hold this door, we will move further in!" Anromir gave a fast nod and began to deploy the ten men in front of the door.

Myran, Yan, and Mathwin followed Theadrin into the keep. They fought through the corridor into the main hall where the major part of the fight progressed. Anromir's main body of warriors had united and was standing ground there.

Men from both sides were everywhere. Theadrin and his three friends moved quickly toward the center of the fray. They pressed on and overwhelmed the foemen. The fight ended in the hall and Theadrin led the way to where Anromir and his men had managed to close and barricade the door. Seeing all was now under control, Theadrin turned to one of the warriors.

"Brond, where is my sister? And the rest, are they safe?"

The man's breathing was heavy and sweat ran down his temples. "They are secure beyond the hall, sir. We were holding the enemy back from reaching them."

Theadrin clapped a hand to Brond's shoulder and breathed easy. "Very good. You have done well."

Anromir came up behind Theadrin. "There are many yet outside. What are your orders?"

Theadrin lifted his voice so all his men could hear him. "We will drive them back to where they came from!" The men shouted concurrence.

Before moving out, Theadrin called Yan to him. "See to my sister and the others." Yan nodded and darted off.

The door was opened and Theadrin headed the charge. He met the first man and dropped him with one mighty chop. With the men of Caulguard rallied and unified, Gurn's warriors fell apart. They had lost too many men already and had initially based their attack on surprise.

With Myran at his right hand and the army at his back, Theadrin drove the enemy from within the walls. The fight ended soon afterward when Gurn's men saw they were outmatched. They fled back across the plain with the warriors of Caulguard cheering in victory behind.

"That will teach Gurn!" shouted Anromir, lofting his sword high above his head as he let loose a victorious whoop.

Theadrin watched the retreating army, which was greatly downsized now from its original strength.

He heard his name called and turned to see Yan approaching in a run. "Theadrin! Ya gotta come quick!"

"What is it, Yan?" He slowed his friend with a steady hand. "What has happened?"

"Caithal's wounded. Ya must go ta 'im at once."

Twenty-Five

Theadrin raced back into the keep, following Yan to where Caithal lay. Lianna and Ellia were with him, and Caulguard's physician was bent to his work. As Theadrin approached, he saw the gash in Caithal's right side. It was deep.

Lianna looked at Theadrin as he entered. Their eyes held and Theadrin saw worry. He knew it was not good.

"He was injured on his way from his study," Lianna said as he drew near.

Caithal's eyes opened and went to Theadrin. Perspiration soaked the front of his shirt and ran down his face. "Theadrin! Quickly! Waste no time!"

The physician stopped his work and quickly tried to restrain his patient. "Please, lie still. You mustn't move so. Sir, your wound," he stammered.

Theadrin went quickly to his friend, going down on one knee. "Caithal, calm yourself."

Caithal gripped Theadrin's forearm tightly. Theadrin saw he was barely holding on to consciousness. "You must go—go to the Tor. There is little time left…so much has been wasted already!"

"I cannot go. War has begun."

"You must!" Caithal's grip strengthened. "It will be too late!"

"Caithal, you are injured; lie still."

"It will be too late!" he said again. "The darkness comes. You must…must find…" Caithal wavered between losing awareness.

He lifted a shaky hand and pressed a small roll of parchment into Theadrin's palm. Before falling back onto his pillow, he managed, "Deep...deep and hidden things...shall be...revealed."

The physician inspected him and said to Theadrin, "He is unconscious."

Theadrin didn't speak. He rose slowly and pocketed the small scroll absently. After lingering a moment longer he turned and left the room.

He called an immediate counsel with Anromir, Myran, Yan, and Mathwin. A plan of action was quickly agreed upon. They would send a letter to Caledon requesting the King's aid. Until Caledon's armies came, they would hold as best they could.

Theadrin stood with his palms on the table. He heard Anromir saying, "I will send a call through my lands for every able-bodied man to join us." He paused and looked at Theadrin. "What is on your mind?"

Theadrin took a breath. "Caithal."

"He is a tough one. He will make it through, I have no doubt."

Theadrin nodded and looked at the table for a moment as his mind turned something over. The rest waited on him to speak. "I have to go north...to the Tor."

"What'd ya say?" Yan wondered with a frown of bewilderment.

Theadrin shrugged. "Caithal discovered something. I think"—he hesitated—"I think he meant the King Sword is at the Tor."

"Do you realize what you are saying? Your people need you here!" Anromir shouted. "Caithal was speaking feverish nonsense!"

"The fever does not come on so quickly," Myran asserted quietly.

Theadrin looked down at the maps spread across the table without a word.

"You must make a decision, sire." Anromir straightened. "Defend your country or go chasing something blindly."

Theadrin looked at his friends. Myran was watching him thoughtfully; Yan and Mathwin seemed confused. Theadrin knew they thought it was folly to go north, and it looked that way to him as well.

How could he leave when the kingdom was about to plummet into war? The people needed a leader, and this was surely what he was called for.

"Send King Brudwyn the letter," he said and left the room.

When evening was drawing on, he went to Caithal's room. Standing in the doorway he leaned against the wooden frame and watched his friend lying silently on his bed.

"You have put me in a difficult position," Theadrin said quietly. He reached into his pocket and took out the paper that Caithal had given him, unrolling it. The words of the prophecy were written there. But something was different. It was an extra line longer.

> At the changing of times and seasons,
> With kings removed and kings set up,
> Let wisdom be given to the wise
> And knowledge imparted to those of understanding.
> Deep and hidden things shall be revealed
> In the deepest dark of the highest height,
> In the hand of the chosen dwells kingly light.

The second to last line was new. Theadrin had never heard it before, but it meant nothing to him.

The sound of footfall came from the hall behind. He looked over his shoulder and saw Lianna coming along bearing a metal tray with a bowl of broth.

"Is he awake?" she asked.

Theadrin shook his head and looked back into the room. Lianna stopped at his side and for a long time seemed to be contemplating something. "Why do you think he wanted you to go to the Tor, Theadrin?" she asked at last.

Theadrin took his time in answering, and with a frustrated sigh said, "I wish I knew."

Lianna looked down at the tray. "Are you going to go?"

"I don't see how that is possible." His voice rose and Lianna looked up at him. He caught himself and rubbed a hand over his jaw. "I have a responsibility to the people. I cannot abandon them to fend for themselves against Gurn. I must lead them."

Lianna's answer was not long in coming. "Caithal would not have told you to do something that was foolish."

"I know that." Theadrin got heated again. "But how do we know he was not delirious?"

Lianna remained cool tempered. "I was with him the whole time after he was wounded. He was hanging onto consciousness for you, Theadrin, because he knew that what he had to say was important."

"But it makes no sense! And even if I knew it to be true, I still could not leave." His sister watched him but said nothing. Theadrin knew what the look meant. "You wouldn't understand. I have no choice in this matter. I must protect the people."

"If Caithal was right, you would be protecting the people by doing what he said." Lianna pointed out.

"You are impossible," Theadrin complained, trying to explain away her logic in his mind. He could not leave Arinon in its time of need.

She stared at him in a look he had seen many times. It was the look she always gave when he was avoiding the truth. "I can't force you to a decision, but I can give you my advice. Do as Caithal says."

Theadrin looked down at her unrelenting. "I have already made the decision to send a letter to King Brudwyn. There is nothing I can do about it now. I have to lead the people."

"Let Myran take charge while you are away. He is a capable man."

"That would not do." Theadrin stiffened and looked away.

"Why? Are you afraid someone else will gain the glory you yourself want to have?" Lianna's hot words stung him.

Theadrin stood fuming in silence, but all argument failed him. "I cannot leave Arinon," he stated for the last time and stalked away angrily.

A heavy rain had begun to fall and thunder boomed loudly around the stone keep. The windows flashed with the bluish white of lightning. The wind roared in violent gusts, bending the trees and flattening the grass.

Theadrin entered his room and threw the window open wide allowing the droplets of rain to hit against his face and hands. Lianna was wrong. She just could not understand the pressure that was on his shoulders. There was no way he could just up and leave the people to Gurn and his armies.

It had nothing to do with gaining glory. That was a ridiculous and silly notion she had brought up. The people looked to him as their leader—it was not what he wanted.

White hail suddenly began to hammer against the window ledge and sting his skin. He quickly closed the shutters and slumped back on his bed, sunken in misery. After lying there for quite some time, his head began to cool and he sighed heavily. He realized then that deep down inside the desire for glory was there, however well masked it was. Since his vision, circumstances had quickly darkened. Even his attitude had dimmed. Why could this be?

He thought it would be easy once he found the Highest King. But since then, every wrong attitude had come out in force inside him. He let out another sigh of frustration and threw his head back on his pillow. Anger welled up inside him for doing nothing but failing since his encounter with the Highest King. He pounded his fist against his bed and sat up, putting his head down into his hands.

He ran his fingers slowly through his damp hair. Then, leaning with his forearms on his knees, he lowered his head until his chin was nearly touching his chest. Taking a breath, words slowly came forth from his mouth. "What am I doing wrong, Lord?

Why can't I overcome these wrong emotions and stop them from governing my actions?"

He went down on his knees and prayed for a long time.

Meanwhile, on the opposite side of the keep, Myran strolled along a thin hallway alone. His mind was on what Theadrin had told him about going to the Tor. Since hearing about Caithal's insistence, Myran had become troubled. He wished he knew more about it. What was it that seemed so pressing and important to Caithal?

He made his way through a corridor and up a winding flight of stairs to Caithal's room. Before entering, he stopped and listened for any activity inside. He didn't hear anyone. Caithal must have been asleep and the physician gone. Only the sound of the wind and rain on the window could be heard.

Satisfied that he could be alone with Caithal, he entered. It was dim inside, having only the light of three small candles on an oval table. Also on the table was a tray with a bowl of cold broth.

There was a three-legged stool at the bedside and he sat down on it. Caithal lay motionless on the bed with his eyes closed. Myran watched him with a heavy heart. He could not lose another friend.

Caithal's advice had always proven trustworthy. Myran had never known him to be wrong. If it were his decision, he would start out the next morning to go north. But there was nothing he could do. Thinking longer, he realized there was one option that had not occurred to him. In the morning he would see it out.

He remained in Caithal's room for the night, sleeping little, hoping the old hermit would awake so that he could explain everything to him.

The following day, as the honey-gold light of the morning sun dressed the countryside, he found Theadrin walking the stone ramparts of the keep alone. The morning was warm and the rich aroma of wet flowers and dirt filled the breeze, embellished with the spirited chatter of numerous songbirds.

The blue-green hills rolled on around Caulguard, each more faint and gray than the first. The distant trees were tipped silver and bent and swayed in the warm, late spring breeze.

Theadrin greeted Myran and turned to gaze across the landscape. His hands were clasped behind him as he drew in the fragrance of spring. After a moment, he stated, "The message was sent to Caledon this morning. Brudwyn will soon join us."

Myran nodded, placing his wide palm on the breastwork. "About what Caithal said," he began, getting to business without unneeded delay. Theadrin blinked slowly and half squinted, still looking out at the swelling hills. He looked as though he knew what Myran would say.

"Did Lianna ask you to talk to me?" he asked in a disappointed way. "To try and convince me that I am wrong?"

"I haven't seen her," Myran countered, and continued. "I know it is your duty to stay here. You must fight for the people and lead them to freedom." He paused and Theadrin glanced down before looking at him.

"Send me. I will gladly go north in your stead."

"I will need you at my side, Myran Cai."

"Theadrin, I believe Caithal's words to be true. One of us must go to the Tor, and you cannot leave, but I can."

Theadrin was not swayed. "I need you here," he said stubbornly and started to leave.

"Theadrin. Someone must go."

Theadrin halted. Myran stood in place saying no more. After a moment, Theadrin whirled about with a quick fire flashing in his eyes. "What would we even be looking for? I…" he began hotly but his voice died away. Myran held his gaze tightly.

The anger melted away and Theadrin spoke in a softer voice. "I will think on it. Give me some time alone."

The days passed on and Theadrin spoke little to anyone. Myran figured that Theadrin's mind had not swayed, but continued to leave him to himself. Gurn had remained quiet, as though he waited for them to make the next move. Caithal's condition did not improve, and he slept nearly all the time, waking only to eat the broth that Lianna would bring him. He was too weak to speak to anyone.

He became feverish and would thrash around reopening his wound. After some time had passed, the physician gave them the dire news—pneumonia was setting in. All were disheartened. Theadrin became even more withdrawn.

One day, an unexpected visitor arrived, requesting immediate audience with Theadrin. It was young lord Rhyd of Averby near the western sea.

He came on his knees. "My lord, Theadrin," he began in a humble manner after Theadrin had gathered his advisors. "I have made a grave mistake in siding against you at the counsel. My father was loyal to Gurn until the end of his life. I, too, believed Gurn a great man. But I do not hold this belief any longer. Some of my men were in Lundel when the massacre took place. After hearing of it, I realize the man he truly is and cannot support him. I offer you now my sword of allegiance, if you will have me." He stopped and looked extremely uncomfortable at what his next words were.

"I understand if you will not."

Theadrin, keeping his eyes on the man, leaned over to Anromir. "Do you know him? Can he be trusted?"

"I believe he can be, sire." Anromir whispered back. "He was my good friend as a child."

Theadrin stood and walked forward. His countenance was unsympathetic. "How can I know you are not lying?"

"My lord," he said meekly, prepared for this question. "I ask not for position of authority. I give my men to you to command. I myself will fight as a common soldier. I relinquish my position as lord of Averby. I am not worthy of it." The man then offered his sword to Theadrin. This showed that he was in earnest, for each region had a sword with a special emblem. The man who held the sword was lord of the region it represented. This tradition followed that of the King Sword.

Theadrin took and examined the blade thoughtfully. "Rise, Rhyd, lord of Averby. Take back your sword." He extended the handle to Lord Rhyd.

Rhyd would not accept it. "Lord Theadrin, I cannot take it back. I entreat you, put another more worthy commander in my place."

"Take it. For no doubt your men would more readily follow someone they already trust. Swear allegiance and take your place."

Rhyd stared in astonishment at the sword that Theadrin offered. He was taken back by Theadrin's mercy and trust. It was clear that he had come that day in full expectance of being stripped of his position.

Slowly he gripped the sword and looked at Theadrin in awe. There, in front of everyone, he pledged his allegiance.

It was halfway into the first fortnight that the armies of Caledon arrived at the border. The news came to Caulguard one evening at sunset that the Caledonians remained encamped there waiting to hear word from Caulguard. Theadrin assembled his friends and advisors in his quarters.

"I suggest we march on Avross," Anromir proposed forthrightly. "We now have the strength of arms with the men of Caledon alongside us."

"I agree," Mathwin said. "Let us set out at once and leave no more time for Gurn to prepare." Besieging and capturing Avross, they figured, was the quickest way to win the war.

"We must take into account that Avross is a strong city," Myran counseled. "Its walls are high and its gates thick. No enemy has yet been inside."

"No enemy but Gurn." Anromir made light of Myran's advice. "Do you have a better suggestion?"

"A siege could last into the winter and much longer. If we could draw Gurn out of the city, we would have a better chance."

"Do you really think he would fall for any tricks?" Anromir questioned.

Myran countered, "Have you taken into account the rest of Gurn's nobles? They each hold a fortress of their own with plenty of men to defend them."

"You are right." Anromir conceded, and added, "But once Avross is captured the fight may be taken out of them."

Theadrin had not spoken. Anromir noticed this and pointed it out. "You haven't said anything, my lord, yet the decision lies with you. You have heard our counsel, now we would hear your decision."

Theadrin erected himself and looked about at his friends and advisors with his jaw firmly set. His eyes were commanding and strong, and when he spoke his voice carried on these attributes.

"My friends, your loyalty and bravery are encouraging to me. After hearing your counsel with open ears, my decision is set and unwavering." He held each man's eyes for a moment in a steady gaze as he continued.

"I trust every one of you, and know you will carry out my orders. I would have you meet with King Brudwyn and move on to Avross. Meanwhile, I will journey north."

Anromir took an incredulous step forward. "What are you saying? You are abandoning Arinon?"

The words visibly stung Theadrin, but he held fast. "My decision is made, Lord Anromir. I cannot ask you to understand, only to accept it."

"But, my lord," stammered Anromir in distress. "You cannot leave. The people would take it as an act of forfeiting the throne."

"Then let it be so, Anromir. I would gladly sacrifice it, as well as my own life, to save this kingdom and its people. I will take Myran, Yan, and Mathwin with me."

Yan stared mutely at Theadrin, and Mathwin glanced from him to Myran, who watched Theadrin with steady eyes.

"Anromir, I leave you in charge. This must be done." He placed a reaffirming hand on the noble's thick shoulder. "I will return."

Anromir swallowed his utter disappointment and nodded. "Of course," he managed. "I will do as you say."

Twenty-Six

"Our plan is running beautifully," Gurn boasted gleefully. He stood wrapped warmly in his expensive, fur-lined cloak on the top of the tower. Vithimere was handling a dagger and observing its beautiful craftsmanship.

"You made sure to kill all of them?" He checked coldly, refusing to take part in the mood of victory.

"Yes, of course." Gurn smiled cruelly. "I made sure of that." A wind gust suddenly whipped through the dark banner on the stonework. Its cloth snapped and rippled.

Vithimere continued to admire the dagger; its gold pommel formed as a dragonhead, the two ends of the hilt its claws. "And you are certain that it has sparked some form of retaliation?"

Gurn nodded. "I set one of my men there disguised as a villager. He talked to Theadrin himself and overheard their declaration of war."

"Excellent." Vithimere looked up. "My master will be most pleased with your work." The young man looked at Gurn, satisfied with what he heard, and smiled.

At that instant Gurn's heart seized within his chest. In the crude light of the torches, Vithimere's expression seemed to change him. Gurn saw someone else standing there for a fleeting moment, someone who had been long dead. He blinked in sudden fear and panic at the familiar face. But looking again it was

Vithimere standing there once more, polishing the blade of his dagger with his cloak.

Gurn forced down the fearful thoughts suddenly assailing his mind and said, "Things have been quiet since then." He had not told Vithimere of his attack on Caulguard. His plan was to take the keep by surprise and lay an ambush for when Theadrin returned, ending the matter in one day. But that plan had gone miserably wrong.

"Things are falling into place," Vithimere was saying.

"No doubt they will call Caledon to join them," Gurn reminded him. "And Brudwyn will not hesitate to come."

Vithimere looked up at Gurn. "That is what we want, Gurn. Have you forgotten?"

Gurn gave a look of disgust, forgetting his scare. "I don't see why. Caledon has a strong force. I can't possibly hold out against them. Even my own subject lords are turning on me. First Anromir, now Rhyd. My army is dwindling."

"You will show Lord Rhyd the folly of his decision so others might not be tempted to do as he has." Young Vithimere spoke this as more of an order than a question, at which Gurn scowled.

"Where does your part come in?" Gurn sneered at Vithimere. "You ought to be on the front lines of the war with me."

Vithimere glared back and tilted the knifepoint in Gurn's direction. "Fret not, your part is only a ploy." Gurn stiffened, but Vithimere continued. "When Theadrin and the armies of Caledon are focused on destroying you; the jackal, they will not see the roaring lion at their back."

Gurn sulked. He hated this younger man treating him as lesser.

Vithimere tucked the gold-handled knife into his belt and said, "It would be better if you kept to the defensive. Put up a fight when needed to prod them on, but let them come to you. I will return to my master and then we will commence with our plan."

He departed in the usual way, by raising the whistle to his lips and flying off on the winged beast. Gurn watched him sullenly until the darkness took him from sight. Then he left the top of the tower, taking hold of the waiting torch from the sconce to light his way.

Vithimere must think him incompetent. *He is always telling me how to go about my own affairs*, Gurn thought to himself. *I am quite capable to fight a war in my own way.* He was fed up with Vithimere and his impudence. Someday he would put that weasel in his proper place.

Gurn's heart began to pace wildly as he remembered what he had seen in Vithimere's face.

As he walked fretfully down the hall to his room, his chamberlain, Saren, met and greeted him. "My lord." He bowed smoothly. "Out for a late night stroll?"

"Never mind." Gurn waved his hand distractedly without stopping.

"I have a report, your lordship," Saren informed him.

"I am very tired, Saren. Whatever news you have can wait until the morning."

"But, my lord, the news is dire." Saren's voice was grave. Gurn caught the severity in his voice and halted.

"Make it quick."

"The armies of Caledon are encamped on our borders and are dressed for war," the chamberlain reported.

"Already?" Gurn whispered to himself.

"My lord?"

"They have not crossed the border yet?" Gurn looked at the chamberlain, who shook his head. "I must find out which of my nobles are still loyal to me. Send out riders, Saren. I want each to meet me in counsel in two days' time." The chamberlain bowed once more and moved off to his newly assigned task.

When Gurn's noblemen arrived on the appointed day, they found their lord dressed for battle. He wore a breastplate of silver with a wolf's head engraved in gold. He had vambraces of the same making and underneath he wore a fine, midnight-blue shirt. His cloak was black and a war helm was on his head. The nobles knew something of great importance to be at hand.

After all had been seated, Gurn rose and stated, "My loyal lords and noblemen, the reason for which you are summoned to counsel this day is grave indeed. The threat of war has come to our borders." A murmur passed through them.

Gurn stood regally for several moments, allowing his words to sink deep, and then removed his helm and sat down. "This boy, Theadrin, whose claim to the throne was proven a fraud, has called upon Brudwyn, king of Caledon, and together they will march upon this great city."

"My lord, Gurn." Lord Haltrenn stood up and addressed Gurn. "There is something that has troubled me of late."

"Speak freely, my friend." Gurn told him amiably.

"I have heard rumors already that war was starting. But through sources that say it was you who started it." Gurn's eyes hardened. "They say," Haltrenn continued, "that you attacked the town of Lundel, leaving many of its innocent citizens dead in the streets. Lord Rhyd is one who has brought this matter before me."

Gurn rose from his seat to answer the subtle accusation. He was happy that Lord Haltrenn had not heard of his attack on Caulguard as well. "Haltrenn, my brother, your sources were not altogether accurate. I did indeed send men to Lundel, but, you see, war had already been secretly declared," he lied. "I got wind of their actions and moved to put a stop to it. Some of the traitors were meeting secretly in Lundel to hold a counsel of war. My men were to arrest the perpetrators but were forced to fight when opposition arose.

"I had hoped," he continued further, warming to his tale, "to put an end to things right there. But this little rebel has now amassed an army and will not be deterred. Lord Rhyd has betrayed us all and gone to join him. He believes, no doubt, that his fortunes would be better with the warmonger. And, though this betrayal grieves me, it must be met with justice."

Haltrenn seemed pleased with what Gurn told them and took his seat once more. "Now, my lords." Gurn looked about at their faces. "Here is my plan."

Twenty-Seven

Myran walked the top of the wall as the sun began to show itself in the eastern sky. He welcomed the warmth of the morning rays and the joyous melody of birdsong; the day was alive with it. The wind was rich with the sweet fragrance of the honeysuckle bushes growing in abundance below the wall.

As he strolled, he ran his hand slowly across the smooth stonework. They were to leave for the north that day. He had been up walking the walls since before the light of morning. Theadrin had made the right choice. He only hoped and prayed it was not made too late.

Myran entered a small tower built on the wall and ambled through the circular room to the other side. Opening the wood-planked door, he halted. He was surprised to see her, but it was not from a start that his heart skipped a beat.

Lianna stood on the rampart gazing across a green land tinted silvery gold by the rising sun. The wind gently rustled her dark locks and the morning light was on her face, expounding her exquisite features.

She turned and looked at him standing awkwardly in the doorway. She did not smile, nor did she appear agitated that he may have disturbed her morning peace; she simply looked at him. Her eyes alighted on his and Myran felt a quick moment of panic.

Hesitantly, he walked forward. She turned and looked back at the northern horizon without a word. Myran stepped beside her and turned to gaze over the fair land. He placed his hands on the stonework in front of him and breathed a low sigh.

He felt strong with her beside him, braver. If he had felt any apprehension of the impending journey before, the feeling was not there now.

Soon he realized she was looking at him again. He looked back and her eyes dropped. Her cheeks were colored a light crimson.

Lianna was dressed in a long blue gown that brushed the tops of her bare feet. Her dark, lustrous hair was combed neatly and cascaded effortlessly over her slender shoulders.

"Will you be gone long?" she asked, her voice soft and quiet.

"There is no way of knowing," Myran blurted, instantly regretting and hating the loud blare of his own voice. It was wholly unequal and not worthy to be heard with hers. He tried to correct it feebly. "We will be gone until we find what we seek."

"I wish I could go as well. It will be different with all of you gone," she said at length. Her tone was curiously different from what Myran had ever heard before.

"It would be too dangerous. Besides, you have little Cadi to watch over," offered Myran.

Lianna accepted this with a slow nod and sweep of the eyes. She leaned against the stonework with her hand, still looking down.

"Don't worry for Theadrin." Myran tried to bring comfort for what he thought bothered her. "I swore to protect him, and I will."

Lianna looked at him then with eyes that Myran studied but could not read. It was as if she was saying something that he should grasp and understand.

She stepped away from the stonework toward him. Their gaze held until Myran lost track of the time of day. She looked down again and smoothed the folds in her robe. She was searching for the right words.

A moment passed and she looked him in the eye so unfalteringly that it almost threw him off balance. He swayed slightly as his heart began to pound through his chest. She inched closer and placed a delicate hand on his shoulder. Her touch was gentle, and Myran savored its feeling.

Then she rose on the tip of her toes and, leaning forward, touched his cheek with her lips. The contact sent a wave of warmth through him, and the burn lingered hours afterward. Before she withdrew she whispered near his ear, "Come back to me, Myran Cai."

She turned quickly and darted away, leaving Myran standing like a mute horse staring dumbly after her.

Later, as the band mounted at the gate, the people stood about to see them off. The farewells were made and nothing remained to be said. Anromir stood silently in the front and lifted a hand in farewell. Theadrin looked encouragingly at him and returned the gesture.

Lianna stood beside Cadi on a flight of stairs. Myran looked at her, arrayed in a midnight blue dress, around her waist a sash of deep red. Her hair was decorated with many thin braids worked without.

Myran knew not the road ahead. But sitting in the saddle facing the uncertainty, he knew he would move heaven and earth if he must to return. Since Caed and Ao-idh's deaths, he had lived unconcerned for his life and safety. But now he was determined to survive. He would come back. Alas, he did not want to leave.

Keeping a direct course northward, the small band passed the time with talk. They covered a wide range of topics before coming to the errand at hand. Yan admitted he still failed to see why they were leaving Arinon.

"What're we lookin' fer?" he asked, and Theadrin hesitated to answer.

"I don't know," he admitted at length. "We will go to the Tor, and then I believe all will become clear to us." He looked ahead at the green hills patched with swaying trees.

Myran watched him thoughtfully but did not say anything. Then at length Theadrin spoke again. "Caithal gave me this parchment." He handed it to Myran. "It is the ancient prophecy but there is an extra line on it." Myran read, "In the deepest dark of the highest height."

"Whatever it means, Caithal must have understood and it was reason enough to try and get us to go to the Tor." Theadrin took back the parchment and returned it to his belt pouch. He looked down at the leather reins in his hand. "I fear I have made the decision too late."

Myran looked at him with the hint of a confident smile on his lips. "I believe there is still time. Whatever it is we must do, if it was too late we would know it."

Theadrin seemed encouraged at his friend's assurance. He lifted his head higher and set his gaze on the trail ahead.

Their path soon took them to Lord Percel's lands. The day had grown warm and humid; the sun was in mid sky. They halted the horses and studied the outlay of the land.

"We may have a heap'a trouble waitin' fer us in there," Yan groaned as he loosened his shirt about his neck. If discovered and caught by Percel, they would be instantly put to death.

"We will keep off the roads," Theadrin told them. This they did, but it was soon apparent that their presence had been discovered.

Myran saw the dust first, rising up from under the distant horses' hooves. When Mathwin saw them he muttered, "Percel must have eyes in every valley."

"Perhaps he hasn't seen us yet," Theadrin said. "Let's keep out of sight, into the woods. We will see if they pass by." Theadrin turned his horse into the tree line.

Inside the folds of the forest they dismounted and waited behind a patch of thick brush. The riders, twenty-five in all and dressed for a fight, approached and stopped at the forest edge. Theadrin saw the leader clearly—the knight with the dragon crest.

Words passed between the dragon knight and the soldiers, too quiet for them to make out. One of the men moved forward to enter the woods, but the knight stopped him with a sharp command. Theadrin wished he could hear what they were saying.

At last they turned away and Theadrin breathed a sigh of relief.

"Their leaving may be a ruse," Mathwin warned. Theadrin agreed.

"We should travel in the forest as long as we can," Myran advised.

As they traveled on through the trees, keeping their original course as best as they could, the land grew hilly. They rode in between two ridges along a dried-out creek bed. No one spoke for fear of being heard.

The horses' hooves sank deep into the pebbly and muddy bottom of the old waterway. A jay called out several times from a hidden perch, and once a flight of crows cackled overhead as they caught scent of a new source of food.

Myran suddenly put up his hand and stopped his mount. "There is something out there."

Theadrin motioned for them to fan out and advance with caution. The forest thickened and they were forced to dismount. Theadrin kept one hand on his sword handle as he walked slowly forward.

His horse grunted nervously and suddenly he came face to face with the knight of the dragon crest. He appeared out of nowhere and Theadrin's sword was drawn instantly. But it was Myran who met him first. He leapt from the bushes to the side and engaged the knight. The clear ring and resounding clash of steel echoed through the trees. Myran and the knight exchanged several fast placements before pausing to reassess each other's skill.

Theadrin had his sword drawn, ready to meet the rest of the men who followed the knight, but none came. With close observation of the fight between Myran and the knight, he noticed how similar the two fought. Each stroke that came seemed anticipated by the other.

Yan and Mathwin came running up through the brush a moment later having heard the clamor of steal. Mathwin lifted his spear over his head to hurl at the enemy champion, but the knight must have known and kept Myran in between himself and Mathwin. When he saw that he would not get a clear shot, Mathwin stuck his spear into the dirt and drew his sword.

With two against him now, the knight should have lost ground, but he didn't. He dodged, parrying and striking back. He knocked aside Mathwin's blade and shoved into Myran's chest, sending him against a tree.

Yan rushed into the fight and thrust at the knight's chest. It was easily parried and Yan received a kick to his gut and fell on his back, struggling to regain his breath. Theadrin was in the fight by this time as well. He engaged with speed and held a solid defense against his foe.

Myran was back up and Mathwin came in from the side once again. Still the knight could not be overcome. He moved in and out with catlike quickness. It seemed to Theadrin that he was actually enjoying the fight.

Myran, after blocking a side cut, dove at the knight, and they fell onto a patch of large fern. They rolled around trying to outmatch each other in strength, but once more they were equal.

Suddenly the knight began to laugh. The sound was twisted and muted by the helm covering his face. It took away his strength and Myran pinned him.

"I yield," he laughed. "Let's be done with this."

Theadrin noticed something pass over Myran's features. It was like a cloud blocking the sun for one clear instant and was gone again.

"Come on, get off, Myran," begged the knight, still chuckling. The fact that he had said Myran's name did not hit Theadrin at first.

Myran dropped his sword. He took hold of the helm, whipped it off, and cast it aside. Then he stumbled backward in clear surprise.

"It took you long enough to guess." The face was not familiar in any way to Theadrin. But he was surprised to find the dragon knight was young.

"What trick is this?" Myran frowned back at the knight.

"Can't you believe your own eyes?" The knight smiled and propped himself up on his elbows.

"Caed…can it be?"

"None other." Caed had dark hair and sharp features. He was as tall as Myran but more lanky.

"How?" Myran was at a loss for words. "I saw you…"

"I was near death, but death could not prevail."

"Caed…after all these years. Why haven't you tried to find me?"

"You act as though I knew you were alive. I only realized when you appeared with the heir to the throne at the counsel." The easy grin never left Caed's beguiling face.

"Where are the rest of your men?" Theadrin spoke to him for the first time.

"I have sent them away, do not fear. It may be difficult to believe, but I am your ally."

"Aye, that'll be kin'a hard fer sure," Yan interjected. He stood rubbing his belly with a scowl.

"Why do you serve Lord Percel?" Myran asked, remembering the circumstances.

"It was a way to get closer to Gurn. I saw that Percel was the most loyal of the lords and that Gurn trusted him. So I offered him my services as a warrior. He accepted. I began as a soldier, but my skill in weaponry helped raise me quickly through the ranks. It was not long before Percel saw my skill and made me his champion.

"So I have been waiting for the right time to repay Gurn for what he has done, but have not had the chance yet." Caed looked at the four around him. "I know you are heading north and I wish to accompany you and prove my friendship."

"What of Lord Percel? Will he not grow suspicious if you disappear?" Myran asked.

Caed shrugged. "Let him be suspicious; the circumstances have changed. I am no longer his man."

Theadrin looked at Myran, for Myran was the only one who knew Caed and could best judge whether he could be trusted.

It was Yan who was the first to voice an opinion. "I wouldn't put no faith in the man."

Caed looked at Yan but said nothing to his defense. He then looked at Myran.

"I will trust your decision, Myran." Theadrin said.

Myran Cai looked at Caed for a long time. His old friend only smiled back the same mischievous smile Myran had once known and now realized he had deeply missed. "Theadrin," Myran rose to his feet, "I would trust him with my life."

Theadrin nodded and then reached out to give Caed a hand up. "Welcome to our company, friend." Caed took his hand readily and they set out again, one man greater in company.

Caed's word proved true in that they encountered the soldiers no more, and Percel's lands were soon behind them with no more trouble.

They reached the northern border of Arinon and camped there late that night. After leaving the kingdom, they moved with all caution. The wilderness of Baremar stretched out before them, where the barbarian hordes of the Kaidri held dominion.

It was a rock-strewn land, sunburned and bare. The barbarian presence was visible almost immediately. The land was charred and dry. There were remnants of places that used to be an encampment, or ruins of previous villages. Once a part of Arinon, it had long ago been overrun by the Kaidri.

The sun was hot and little shade was to be afforded. Very few trees grew in the wastes, no groupings large enough to be called a forest. It was said that the Kaidri feared woodlands, although the reasons were unknown. Some would argue that they considered forests to be indwelt with evil spirits, or that a curse would be laid on them upon entering. Whatever the cause, the Kaidri were superstitious and would never enter a patch of trees where the other side could not be seen.

Theadrin had learned a good deal about them during the great raids. He and the others hoped they would be able to pass through Baremar without interference from the Kaidri, but knew this was unlikely. Once, at midday, they saw smoke from a campfire a distance away but no barbarian ever came into sight.

They followed the river, which ran south through the heart of Baremar into the Aegris mountains, resting only a portion of that night before continuing on. Even then they did not risk a fire. Morning light found them moving once more at a quick yet cautious pace northward.

If any of them were dubious at first about Caed being with them, the feeling was soon diminished.

Caed was lighthearted and laughed often. In fact, when the others were of low spirits because of the hot, arid conditions, it was always Caed who lightened their moods. Yan was the last to succumb to his wit and charm, but it became apparent very quickly that Caed had won him over as well.

That afternoon, as they worked their way through an area strewn with large, sharp rocks, brown and split, they stumbled upon a small barbarian encampment. There was no time to hide or run, for they were seen immediately and the cry of alarm sounded.

Theadrin unsheathed his sword. The barbarians were rushing to weapons and were in temporary disarray. Theadrin saw this and called for a charge. "Behind me!"

Formed in a rough wedge shape, they managed to cut through the first foemen that they met. The barbarians fell with echoing cries as the horses rammed into them and trampled them underfoot.

Halfway through the camp, a more organized body of warriors surrounded them, and their advance was slowed. Theadrin parried, sliced, and thrusted as fast as he could. So long as he kept the horses moving they could keep from being overwhelmed. The

Kaidri did not like horses. Theadrin knew without the steeds the battles fought in Caledon would have had quite different outcomes.

Still the Kaidri would not break. The horses were slowed to a near halt. Theadrin called to the others, "Press on!"

A wild battle whoop sounded behind Theadrin, and Caed came surging past. One brawny warrior lurched a forked spear at him, but Caed was able to catch the handle and draw it away from himself. He wrenched it from the howling brute's hands and kicked him back. With two weapons now, Caed pressed into the barbarian wall. Two more fell before him, and he hurled the spear at the last one to block his way.

This opened up their escape and they broke free of the enemy ranks, bolting from the camp. One of the enraged foemen lofted a spear that sliced the air past Theadrin's ear. But they could not keep up with the five horses and were soon left far behind.

When they were far enough away to be safe, they reigned up. "Anyone hurt?" Theadrin asked.

They all reported no injuries save Mathwin. "Just a scratch on the leg," he assured. "Barely skin deep."

"That was well done," Theadrin commended Caed.

"It was nothing." Caed grinned and turned his horse north.

With that they continued the journey. Word had spread throughout the Kaidri of the presence of strangers from the south, but they did not encounter any more barbarians.

Night fell once more, and they camped amongst a clustered patch of gray trees beside the murky river. Before sunrise they forded the water and set out on the other side. Another hot day assailed them, but they made good progress.

As the sun vanished and a warm evening broke, they mounted a brown ridge that was vacant of trees and scattered with sharp twisted rocks. On the far side they beheld the northern lands of legend.

"I heard tell lots'a strange tales a that place," Yan scratched his bristled double chin. "Monsters, dragons…"

The others were silent, studying the vast country unfolding before them in evening's haze. There, its blue foggy crown barely visible on the horizon, was the Tor.

Twenty-Eight

The lands of the north were densely forested. Two rivers ran from the thick tree line. They later connected and ran south, cutting through Baremar, dispersing into the Aergis mountains. Forested hills shaped the landscape. West of the Tor, dim mountain peaks broke the skyline. It was a vast country, all unknown to them.

The ground between the brown knoll on which they sat and the tree line was covered in fresh green grass. It was clear that the Kaidri barbarian tribes did not go further north, although they used the hill quite often. Fire rings were scattered about. The darkling forest was an imposing sight.

Eager to be gone from the dry, hot Baremar they descended the ridge and camped at the forest edge for the night. The sun was gone and twilight rested over the lawn. Still wary of a barbarian attack, they only allowed for a small fire. They spoke little, spending the night in the shadow of the foreboding forest, and the next morning entered with caution.

It was dense and overgrown, and the going was much slower from thereon. They were forced to travel by foot much of the way.

The sun was warm but the forest shade was cool and refreshing. They stayed as steady a course north as they could, but many of the hills were too steep to climb and they were forced to find other ways around. Aside from the two great rivers, there were many other streams and winding brooks. Countless waterfalls spilled over moss-draped rocks from unseen heights.

As the day wore on, toward evening there was a light rain that fell and lasted far into the night. They camped near the easternmost river under the shelter of a huge twisted oak tree and took turns keeping watch through the night hours.

It was during Theadrin's watch that the rain let up and gave way to a heavy fog. As he sat against the cold, wet, gnarled tree trunk, he heard something by the river. It was the sound of something in the water. Not a splash, but indistinct and muted. He walked down to the edge and peered out across the waters.

The pallid fog veiled anything that might be there. But he heard the sound again; and although he could not place it directly, it strangely brought him back to Faranor. Even stranger, he thought of Peran when he heard it. He heard it many more times but could not find its source.

When the time came for him to wake Myran for the last watch, the sound had stopped. He crept silently back up into the woods and shook Myran gently by the shoulder.

"Your watch," he whispered so as not to wake the others. He also told him of what he had heard. Myran took it into account as he stood and stretched. Small beads of rain that had clung to him now cast off and plunged to the spongy ground.

Theadrin settled himself down and Myran began to walk about to throw off the cloak of sleepiness still clinging to him. The forest was heavy with the scent of wet bark and damp soil. Myran breathed in the fragrance and continued to walk about, keeping to the outskirts of the camp.

He remembered the first time he had taken a night watch. It was when Ao-idh was still alive and had taken his two young pupils to northern Arinon. That night they had spent in Percel's lands, and the nobleman kept his estates well surveyed. They took shifts watching throughout the dark of the night, and Myran realized then more than ever what a precious blessing sleep was.

Now, years later, he had kept watch many times and had grown used to little sleep. That first night was a good experience, however, and had done much to prepare him for the nights he would face alone.

His footfall made little sound on the wet forest floor. Even twigs and leaves were too water logged to crunch or crack. He stopped and gazed up through the high tree branches to where the moon was just becoming unveiled from behind the clouds. Its soft white light seeped into the fog, making it glow like ghostly vapors. He could just make out two stars burning in the dark heavens.

Standing there in the quiet of the night, his thoughts turned to Theadrin's account of seeing the Highest of Kings. He had grown up with a firm belief in the Highest King, but now he hungered for more. He desired to know him personally. Ao-idh had that relationship but Myran had never made it his, for Ao-idh's death had ripped the desire away from him. It had disillusioned him and doused the fire that had begun to burn within.

Meeting Caithal had helped somewhat, but even the words of the good hermit had not restored that fire completely. It had perhaps scraped together the right kindling, but nothing more. He needed a spark to ignite it.

There was still a burden that remained; there was still anger. But it was not anger at the Highest King. Instead he was angry with himself. He had put the blame upon his own shoulders. Until it was removed, he knew he could not find peace.

He lowered his head and looked eastward, where the forest grew over a hill that was a stone throw away. The illuminated fog was bright, and Myran could see the dark silhouettes of the trees within. Something moved at the base of one of them. It was quick and was gone immediately.

Cautiously, but with curiosity, Myran advanced toward the spot. Nothing was there save the trees and some green underbrush. He stood a moment longer before turning around to go back to camp. But he halted at once, noticing a branch nodding quickly up and down. There was only the slightest breeze, not enough to move the bush. Yet there was nothing there when Myran made an inspection, so he returned to camp.

The remainder of the night watch was uneventful and passed slowly. Myran woke the rest and they broke fast on biscuits and sausages fried over the fire by Yan. Their double-chinned friend had proven himself an excellent cook on the journey.

Caed chewed a mouthful of the crisp sausage and said, "It is delicious, Yan." He leaned back against an arched log that had dark moss cushioning it. "Ah, yes. It is much better than Myran's cooking." This comment drew laughter from the others.

Myran smirked and glanced at Caed. Theadrin said, smiling, "I don't believe I've ever tasted your cooking, Myran."

"And I wouldn't ever wish that torture laid upon you." Caed laughed out loud.

Myran's smile widened and he chuckled, shaking his head.

The gentle chorus of waterfalls was constantly at play in the background, and the fresh scent of the river's sandy bed drifted on the currents of the wind about them. Circling their camp on the bank of the river were walls of layered, gray rock speckled with white lichen. The sloping ground was coated with red leaves and bright, vibrant moss.

"I've had plenty of practice since the last time you tasted it, Caed." Myran asserted.

"Poor Myran; nothing to eat but your own cooking for two years. How did you survive?" Caed tossed his head back and laughed heartily.

Theadrin laughed to himself and took up the map that he had brought from Caithal's hut in Caledon. "It looks as though this river runs right by the Tor," he observed aloud. "So if we follow it, we should have no trouble finding our destination."

"Aye. That'll be the least of our troubles fer sure." Yan took a mouthful of sausage. Theadrin knew what he was implying.

Indeed, he was forced to admit to himself that not a day had passed on this journey that he had not thought of the stories and myths of the northern lands.

"Are you saying you believe those stories about trolls and goblins?" Mathwin scoffed at his friend. He was reclining on his bedroll and holding a golden biscuit in his big fingers.

"They had ta start from somethin' true!" Yan argued. "Why jes last night I was a hearin' and seein' strange things, was I not?"

"We should have known better than to put you up for the first watch my friend." Mathwin laughed loudly and tore off half of the biscuit in one bite. Myran chuckled at Yan but knew what he had meant. Yan had probably seen things like the ones he had.

"I'm more'n certain there was somethin' watchin' us," Yan persisted. Mathwin continued to laugh jestingly.

"I thought I heard some things moving around last night." Caed spoke up, seeming serious for the first time that morning. He chewed on a biscuit and continued, "I happened to wake while Theadrin was rousing Myran and stayed awake for some time. I thought I heard something like footfall. It was faint but definite. I turned as slowly as I could in the direction I heard it, but whatever was there was gone."

"Have none of you heard forest creatures before?" Mathwin would still hear none of it.

"That is just the point, my friend." Caed looked sincerely at him. "I can tell the sounds of the forest very well, and what I heard last night was not a curious raccoon or skunk."

Myran listened to the banter but did not join in. It seemed they all had some kind of encounter last night. Could it only be that they were on edge? Or was there something out there, watching them?

Continuing on their journey, the banks of the river soon grew too steep to travel on. Farther along, the sides became a gorge of sheer rock faces on either side of the river. The five companions were forced to take to the cover of the forest once again. Another day passed with no great gain in distance.

They camped by a stream with a swift waterfall. This place they had stumbled upon quite by accident, for it was well hidden. It fell in a cascade that spilled over large slabs of rock like giant steps. Its light azure color bled into the deeper bluish green of the pool. All along the bottom there were rounded white pebbles flecked with black.

They chose a portion of the ground that was coated in thick, soft moss to sleep that night. The green moss had the depth of Mathwin's finger and made for a comfortable wilderness bed.

That night about the fire, Theadrin asked, "What is your background, Caed? How did you come to know Myran?"

Myran looked at Caed silently. Caed sat hunched in his cloak and stared at the fire. "My father was a noble under Valdithin. We enjoyed an easy, happy life."

His eyes brightened. "I remember how adventurous I was. Every day I would go out to explore the surrounding hills and glens of my father's land, and each night would return home to the call of my mother and the evening meal. When Gurn gained the throne things became hard for us, for my father was loyal to King Valdithin and did not approve of Gurn's crowning. My mother died"—Caed swallowed hard and blinked; the light had disappeared from his face—"died from an unknown and sudden illness. For a summer I watched as my father crumbled within under the weight of his grief. Then he was mortally wounded in a duel."

Caed glanced around at the faces of those with him and then back to the fire. "He lingered for several days before he, too, died. My father's lands were given to another. I was left alone..." he paused, staring into the yellow flames as if he could see the happy life he once had through a dim window. For a long time he was silent, and Theadrin thought he would not continue.

His eyes were filled with pain. They gleamed unshed tears. Emotions were churning inside of him like a roiling sea. Myran had been watching his friend's face and now sadly turned his eyes toward the ground.

Then Caed seemed to swallow his grief and looked up at Theadrin. "One day Ao-idh, a noble of your father's who was outlawed by Gurn, found me and took me in. That is where I met Myran. We lived in the forest together for several years."

Myran nodded slowly. His gaze became far off.

After Caed's story there was little talk about the fire.

The following morning, as the new light beamed hazily through the high green trees, Yan's shocked voice split the calm.

"What is it this time, Yan?" Caed asked with a quiet laugh.

"It's gone!" He was exasperated. "The bag'a food!" He tossed aside his blanket with a look of bewilderment.

"Perhaps you misplaced it." Caed sat up from where he had been resting against a rock.

"Prepost'rous!" Yan continued to fumble through things. "I had a snack durin' m'watch. An it was right here!"

"If you allowed an animal to make off with our food, Yan..." Caed quipped.

"I would have heard it," Myran spoke up. He had taken the watch after Yan.

Theadrin stood and began to pack his horse. "We are in a foreign place that we know little of. I have no doubt that there are things here we have never encountered before."

"Ya sure are right 'bout that," Yan muttered, giving up his search. "I jes hope it don't get a bigger appetite than that bag'a food!"

"Let's move out." Theadrin tightened the girth on his horse. "We will have to do some hunting along the way to replenish our rations."

Yan went to where Mathwin still lay sleeping and shook his shoulder. A soft moan escaped the man's lips and Yan shook him again. Still Mathwin did not move. Yan placed a hand on his friend's forehead and suddenly called, "Ya best come 'ere, Theadrin."

Noting the worried tone of Yan's voice, Theadrin hurried over and felt Mathwin's brow. It was hot to the touch. "Wet a rag in the stream and bring it here," he ordered Yan quickly.

The errand was promptly accomplished and after some time they managed to revive their friend.

"My leg," Mathwin winced.

After an inspection they found the wound he had received from the barbarian fight had become infected, festering for more than a day. "It has been hard to keep clean in this damp forest," Mathwin said.

Myran filled his water skin in the stream and brought it to Mathwin who drank it down. It seemed to revive him and bring some strength back. The skin around his wound was red and puckered and had become feverish.

Myran looked at Caed, who only stared in silence. He knew the situation was bad.

"Can you travel?" Theadrin crouched down in front of Mathwin.

"Don't worry about that. I won't slow you down." Mathwin rose slowly and swayed unsteadily on his feet. "Help me to my horse."

After wrapping a clean bandage over the wound, they moved on, finding the way as difficult as it was before. They climbed over moss-coated logs, squeezed through the openings between the trees, and cut their way through the clawing underbrush.

Mathwin did not have the strength to walk and remained on his horse. They moved at an even slower pace. By the next night they were weary, cut up, and sore, with little progress to show for it.

The darkness enfolded them on all sides as they searched for a good place to make camp. Where they were was much too overgrown. They pressed on through the dark shadows of the forest walking their horses behind them, Mathwin sitting silently in the saddle with his head down and his chin bobbing slowly on his chest.

All at once the forest broke and they were standing at the edge of a large field. It was surrounded on all sides by the forest, but it was a good distance to the other side.

The field was alive with the dancing light of fireflies. There were thousands of them covering the entire field. They were blinking continuously; flashing high and low. It was like looking over a dark, blue-green lake that sparkled and glimmered in the full moon. Theadrin and his four companions stood looking on in silent wonder at the fantastic display.

It was there they made camp, staying at the edge of the field. They slumped wearily down, each with his back against a tree trunk, and continued to watch the tiny lights dance and blink through the dark waving grass. They did not have the strength and energy to do much else.

They propped Mathwin against the tree with the most moss around the base. He said nothing and fell asleep quickly.

All knew that his condition would only grow worse and that he could not survive much longer at this pace. Yan was too troubled to speak and sat staring across the field. Theadrin sat beside him and spoke softly. "Yan, fret not over our friend. The King is able to keep him."

Yan could not even force a smile and he only nodded once. Theadrin leaned back and prayed silently for their friend.

A sweet summer breeze leaned gently on the long grass, rustling through their hair and brushing against their clothes. The stars in the heavens came out in force to beat the performance of the fireflies. The tree branches overhead whispered softly as they shifted in the cool gust.

Caed and Myran leaned against a tree with a wide girth, neither of them saying a word. It seemed a lifetime had passed since that fateful day in the forest. They had both changed— became older—and life experiences had hardened them. But being together once again showed that they still owned familiar characteristics.

"We will have to reopen the wound," Caed said quietly without turning his head. "He will not survive otherwise." Myran nodded quietly.

He was thinking about Caed's story the night before. Caed had never talked about it before. Myran had heard some of it from Ao-idh but had never dared to bring it up in his friend's presence. Caed hid well whatever sadness he had about his past. There had been many times before when Myran wondered whether he held grief over it or not, for he masked it well. But when Caed told them his tale the night before, Myran saw that the heartache still festered painfully inside. Caed had not forgotten nor forgiven.

Suddenly Myran leaned forward. He looked at his friends and Caed responded in a low voice, "I heard it too." Something had moved in the forest to their backs. It was not the wind this time.

Myran stood slowly and turned toward the trees.

No sooner had he turned than a spear sank into the ground in front of him. Startled, he jumped back and drew his sword.

The others' swords were instantly out as they leapt to their feet. All faced the trees, ready for a wave of enemy to come flooding out. Then, at the same time, they each felt a spear point to their back.

They knew they were beaten. If they made a move now it would be fatal. "Throw down your weapons," Theadrin said, tossing his to the ground. The others followed his example.

Slowly, materializing from the dark folds of the forest, the foemen emerged. But it was not the barbarian warriors they were expecting. From the trees stepped a handful of, among all things, children.

Most held spears, and several carried bows with arrows notched and ready. The one closest to Theadrin spoke, but his words were in an unfamiliar language. It was his voice that betrayed them. Although no taller than children, they were indeed adult men.

Seeing they did not understand, the short man decided to use his weapon as his voice. He stalked fearlessly toward Theadrin and prodded him with his spear toward the woods.

Theadrin looked at his companions. "It seems we have no choice." He stepped forward and followed the lead captor into the forest. Reluctantly the rest followed. Two of the small warriors took hold of the unconscious Mathwin and dragged him along behind.

Twenty-Nine

King Brudwyn sat in his camp chair gripping a jar half full of ale. The day was hot but the shade from the canopy was somewhat cooling. All around, the tents of his army were temporarily erected. Many of the men were occupying themselves with various sports and games, but the king took no part in any of them.

His mood was unpleasant and his brooding eyes showed it. Before his march to Arinon, news had come to him of the lady Merion's disappearing. The time had arrived for her to marry Sir Dathin, but she did not show up. An immediate search had played out, but to no avail. Lady Merion was gone and everyone suspected she was with Ruadhan in hiding somewhere, whether it was against her will or not.

Now he had met with lord Anromir, and the news the noble brought served to sink his glowering mood all the more.

"Tell me again why Theadrin has left?" He sipped the contents of the jar. Brudwyn was confused and distraught at the leaving of his nephew. What was it that had driven him away? Had he made Brudwyn assemble his army and come to Arinon for nothing? The Caledonian King stared at Anromir in frustration.

"He has undertaken an important mission, lord king," Anromir informed him, doing his best to explain what he had enough trouble understanding himself. "One that brings him to the far north, and to the Tor."

"The Tor," Brudwyn repeated. "What is the urgency that drew him there?" The Tor was famous in legend, and there were many dark stories about it. Centuries before, the tribes dwelt there before fleeing to establish the southern kingdoms. That was what all the stories were born out of. No one knew the reason why they had fled, only that they had.

"I must confess I know not, King Brudwyn," Anromir admitted.

"And am I then to return to Monivea?" Brudwyn scowled over his cup.

"No, my lord. My orders are to meet with you and proceed with the war," Anromir stated.

"Proceed without Arinon's future king?" Brudwyn roared, giving vent to his anger. "What is Theadrin doing? Is he mad? His duty is to protect his people, not go skipping off merrily on some fool's errand!"

"Indeed, King Brudwyn, that is what he is about; defending the people, I mean." Anromir defended Theadrin.

"What do you mean?"

A stiff, warm wind blew through the camp. "That is all I know. If Theadrin does not go to the Tor and do what it is he must do, this war will not matter. That is what he told me, and I must believe him."

Brudwyn sat quietly and contemplated what Anromir told him without taking his stern gaze away. Was it folly to start a war at this point? It was one thing to aid his kindred against a murdering tyrant, but now that his nephew had run off chasing something that was probably not there, it was another matter.

Anromir studied the king's eyes. They did not appear convinced. The king's general, Aedrius, stood solemnly behind the king's camp chair with his arms crossed over his chest.

"King Brudwyn, Theadrin will return," Anromir stated confidently.

"Indeed," the king answered dubiously.

Anromir nodded.

Brudwyn put his chin in his hand, stroking his dark mustache with his finger. He was weighing the situation in his mind. Anromir waited, taking a slow sip of his ale as another gust of wind ruffled his clothing.

General Aedrius watched his king in silence. Whatever decision was made, he would stand by it. He feared no fight and would gladly die doing his king's will.

At last the king drew a breath and decided. "I will stay. I gave my word to Theadrin that I would give aid, and I will not go back on it. Though it seems a foolish errand he is on, I will trust him."

"Thank you, lord king." Anromir was relieved.

"Now then, what is our plan of action?" Brudwyn drained what was left of his drink and they began to plan. They viewed all options possible and decided which ones were best. By evening, as the sun slipped below the western hills, they were agreed.

The following afternoon as they began to assemble the troops, a messenger arrived on horseback. He had ridden hard and far through the hours of the night. "My lords!" He jumped from his horse. Anromir, Brudwyn, and Aedrius stood at an outside table looking over a map.

"My lords, I bring dreadful news." He raced up to them, panting.

"Take a slow breath, man. Then tell us your news," Brudwyn said.

"No time for that," he stammered. "My Lord Rhyd is besieged in Averby. He calls for aid."

Anromir started forward. "Averby is across the kingdom. We would not be able to see its borders before sunset tomorrow even if we march through the night at our fastest pace," he told Brudwyn.

The king of Caledon squared his broad shoulders. "Then we can waste no time. We must march at once."

"My army is still at Caulguard," Anromir said. "I will ride immediately and gather them."

"We can meet at the ford of shallows on the Wetrim River," Brudwyn declared.

Anromir agreed. He mounted his horse and sped off to his keep as Brudwyn and his general ordered the men to march into Arinon.

"Break camp!" The king's sergeants called to their units. "We march through the night!"

They traveled at a pace that was not quick enough for Brudwyn, although he knew they could go no faster. All throughout the dark hours of night they did not let up their march, and by late morning of the following day they arrived at the waters of the Wetrim River. Halting at the ford of shallows, it was clear that Anromir had not yet arrived. A shout of alarm rose in the ranks.

Brudwyn, riding at the head of his army, saw the enemy warriors mount the northern ridge and rain arrows into his lines. Many of his men fell in that volley never to rise again.

"Sound the alarm!" He called to his trumpeter. The mounted warriors quickly formed in five ranks behind him.

"Aedrius, form the men for a defense!" the king called as his horsemen spurred their mounts toward the archers on the ridge.

When they had gained the halfway mark, more enemy warriors poured forth from the other side of his men. Brudwyn's footmen, under command of Aedrius, formed a wall and met the onrushing attackers with shields up. The clash was loud and the hated din of battle instantly filled the air.

Brudwyn and his mounted warriors gained the crown of the ridge, and the archers fell away to be replaced by a score of footmen. The king's riders clashed into their ranks and cut down the first two rows of men. The enemy held fast for a time before turning and retreating.

The king of Caledon chose not to pursue and risk another ambush away from his main body of troops, but instead turned to aid Aedrius below. He wheeled about in a wide sweep of his men and around into the side of the enemy force. Gurn's army held fast and gave no ground. Once again the archers mounted the ridge and rained down swift death upon the backs of Brudwyn's army.

But Caledon's archers had assembled by Aedrius's quick sense and returned fire on the hill. Still the enemy kept coming, pouring into the small valley by the ford. For every man they killed, three more would replace him. Brudwyn fought to keep his men in a defensive formation, but they were spread out in marching lines and this proved a difficult task. His powerful, booming voice called orders wherever he was; the lines slowly and painstakingly drew together. Yet they could not gain any advantage against their foe. More and more emptied into the battleground.

Brudwyn's horse suddenly went down, casting the king into the midst of the enemy warriors. With shouts they descended on him as he hit the hard ground. His breath left him and he struggled to regain it as well as his footing. The first sword thrust clipped his shoulder, the second his chest. But the blow was weak and the sword point merely glanced off his breastplate.

He parried another cut, but his breath had not returned and he stumbled and fell forward expecting to feel the hot sting of cold steel in his flesh. When the fatal strike did not come, the king rolled over to see his faithful general standing over him.

Aedrius fought with achieved strength and skill. No blade was able to get near the king. The general pushed the enemy warriors back away from Brudwyn who rolled up to his hands and knees, finally finding his breath. Then he was up again and the two stood in the front of their men, all fighting for their lives.

The king's heart sank when he saw the huge force of armored horsemen bearing down on them from the east. The footmen were falling back only to give the mounted warriors room to finish the Caledonians off.

Brudwyn struggled to line his spearmen to meet the charge, but there was no time, and there was too much confusion and chaos. He managed to gain the front of his men and lofted his crimson-stained sword high above his head. The hot afternoon sun glinted off the silver blade and gold handle. His men would see and rally toward it.

But before the fatal collision, the enemy horsemen swerved and followed the retreating footmen. It was then Caledon's king caught sight of the banner—the white rampant lion on a sky-blue background. Anromir's coat of arms!

The recognition of the allied warriors brought a resounding cheer throughout the Caledonian ranks. Anromir at the head, they drove back the enemy, cutting down much of their number in the frantic flight. Brudwyn met Anromir, when he returned, with a powerful handclasp. "Good timing, Lord Anromir. Although our numbers were surely greater, I am afraid we could not have prevailed. Our lines were sprawled in marching ranks when they hit us."

Brudwyn had scouts scan the road ahead as they reformed ranks and continued on to Averby. They arrived by nightfall.

After posting guards and seeing the setup of the camp, Anromir and Brudwyn crested the hill overlooking Averby. The land about was spotted with the campfires of the besieging army. There were also fires inside the walls of the Averby keep; most were the result of the relentless battering of the siege engines.

"They are in dire sorts," Anromir observed.

Brudwyn agreed, stating, "Their defenses are greatly weakened. They may gain the keep on their next assault. Thank the Highest King they have held thus far."

"If only we could keep our presence hidden until we attack."

"No doubt they know of us being here already," Brudwyn said. "They will be preparing for us."

"When shall we attack?" Anromir relinquished this decision to Brudwyn's greater experience.

"Our warriors must rest. We will make our move at dawn."

"I agree."

The two returned to camp to get what rest they could before the battle. The next day would be long and difficult, and they did not know when they would rest again.

Thirty

Sunrise brought a flood of golden light to the forest. The morning was alive with the merry chatter of songbirds, and the wood was bright and green with a warm, fragrant breeze wafting through the trees.

Theadrin and his companions awoke to find they were under quite intense observation. It was a child, small and wide eyed, watching the large visitors from behind the protection of a thorny gooseberry. His eyes were big and bright green, like the forest; his hair dark and curly. The lad studied them as though they were one of the world's strangest creatures; one of the greatest mysteries revealed before his wondering eyes.

When Theadrin moved, the boy was instantly running from the glen shouting at the top of his lungs in the strange language of the forest folk. Theadrin sat forward and studied his surroundings. It all looked much different in the light of morning.

The short warriors had led them on a long walk to this small glen and, using some simple hand gestures and strange words, implied they were to remain there. They left, taking Mathwin with them. Theadrin made to protest but was given a sharp command, and the leader pointed his spear at him. So they sat down and eventually drifted off to a light sleep.

The light of morning transformed the forest. All about them were massive trees, wide enough to fit a horse inside if hollowed out. They grew scattered amidst other regular-sized trees. Many had roots that coiled up from the rich soil and were clothed with light-green moss.

Plants grew lush and full. Ferns, black raspberries, jewelweed, and countless others were in abundance. There were wood sorrels, toadstools, and wildflowers. In and amongst these buzzed honey-bees and humming birds. Large, multicolored butterflies fluttered calmly about the green glen.

There resided a feel of peacefulness on the sunbright woodland that gave Theadrin a lackadaisical mood. He nearly forgot they might be in danger, or that Mathwin had to be found.

One of the forest folk, a man whom they had seen the night prior, entered the glen from behind a tree. He had the same green eyes as the little boy and dark hair. He wore a green shirt with an animal skin vest and dark leather trousers. On his feet were well-made boar-leather moccasins.

The little boy was right behind him, staring at the strangers with wide eyes.

Yan was the last to wake up. He rolled over, and his eyes flashed open. His hand darted up to his neck to reassure himself it was not slashed open.

Theadrin stood and lifted his hand in a peaceful greeting to the man. It was returned and he came closer.

"Ri es chiv." The man spoke after taking several steps. He looked for an answer but realized he was not understood. He cocked his head slightly to the right.

Theadrin decided to speak even though he would not be understood. "Where is our friend? The bearded one." He made a motion with his hand around his chin.

After hearing this, the man's eyes brightened. "Ah, you know southern tongue."

They were nearly knocked backward when the man said this. "You can speak our language?" Theadrin asked.

"Not well, but enough. You are from south?"

"Yes. We come from Arinon," Theadrin answered, but the name meant nothing to the man. "What have you done with our friend?" he asked again.

The man ignored the question and said instead, "What are you called?"

Theadrin was a little taken off guard at the question. "Ah… Theadrin."

"I am called Tagin," the man said simply and with a friendly demeanor very unlike the night before. "You follow me, then you will see bearded friend."

Tagin led them through the wood to another glen rimmed with more of the huge trees. Theadrin realized as they moved out of the glen that they had not gone unwatched during the night. Two other men appeared from the other side of the glen and followed along.

To Theadrin and the others' surprise, the huge trees were homes and the area they now entered was a small village. In each of the massive trees was an arched door. There were windows in several of them at a higher level than the door. Theadrin figured there must have been several levels inside. The bark was pale yellow in color, its leaves a faded red that contrasted beautifully against the green of other trees.

People no taller than Theadrin's waist milled about at different tasks. Most of them stopped their work to stare at the tall folk in curiosity.

In the center of the elongated glen was a large fire pit over which assortments of foods were cooking: greens, mushrooms, and meat. Theadrin thought from the aroma the meat was boar, but from the mixture of other smells it was difficult to tell. A pot hung over a portion of the flames heating up a dark, golden liquid.

On the far end of the village glen the ground rose above Theadrin's height as a small hill. A tree, much larger than the rest in the glen, grew up from the top. Half of its thick roots were visible, curling out of the dirt slope. In the midst of the entanglement a way was cleared, and a deer-hide door was barely visible.

They stopped near the entrance and Tagin entered alone.

There was much murmuring among the little folk looking on, and Theadrin and his friends endured the speculation with friendly countenance, for they did not want to seem at all aggressive or hostile to these people. Although small and lanky and seemingly primitive, these forest people would have no trouble disposing of them if they felt threatened.

All of them wore clothing that had the colors of the forest expertly woven in. Facial hair was rare. On those men who did have any, it was no more than short whiskers on the chin. The women all wore their hair long and usually had a hat of some kind. Mostly it was a hoodlike piece that came down around the ears.

When Tagin reemerged, he beckoned them to enter the hill. Stooping low, they went in one by one. Inside the hill they found it surprisingly comfortable and well kept. Although they could not stand up to full height, it had a feeling of openness.

A bright fire burned in a small, arched hearth that was blackened from long years of use. There was a low, round table on which burned a candle, and in one of the walls a window looked out into the forest. Wooden steps led up to another room in a higher level, no doubt into the wide base of the tree that grew atop the mound.

All around thick tree roots coiled from the walls and were polished from years of wear. There were four places to sit, cushioned with animal hides. The place had been prepared for their coming.

Before the four sitting places was a wooden chair in which sat a squat, hunched old man. His hair was white and wispy, his nose large and his skin wrinkled. His eyes were dark and the firelight glinted hazel off them. He had a bushy brow that was sunburned and there was a wart beside his left eyebrow.

Tagin motioned them to sit on the hides as he took his place beside the old man. "Men of the south," Tagin introduced them.

"You don't have to tell me, I can see plain enough myself, young Tagin." The old one spoke excellently in their tongue, and his voice was strong, if somewhat raspy. He regarded the four young men before him as though he had been expecting them for a long time.

"Allow me to introduce myself and my companions," Theadrin offered amiably. "My name is Theadrin. This is Myran Cai, Caed, and Yan."

"I am known as Cormik." The small, old man returned and fidgeted in his seat. "As you have assuredly guessed, your presence here is very important to us. You must understand it has been quite a while since our last visitor from the south."

Theadrin took note of this. "Forgive my abruptness, but we are anxious to know what has become of our fifth companion," he said.

"Your friend is quite safe, I assure you. We have him in our house of healing. He will soon be in company with you again." Cormik promised them. The old fellow's southern speech was well practiced. "We must speak first of your coming here. Let us do so as we break fast." Without taking his hand from the arm of his chair, he lifted a bumpy, wrinkled finger and looked at Tagin.

This must have been an awaited sign for the man nodded and deftly left the room. Cormik cleared his throat and fell to scrutinizing them in awkward silence.

Theadrin and his friends did not know if he was waiting for them to speak or not. They glanced at one another but decided to keep quiet.

In a moment Tagin returned followed by several women of the village, each clutching a plate of food. Most were placed on the floor before the tall visitors while one was set on a small round table beside Cormik's chair. Lastly a tall mug was set before each of them with white curls of steam wafting up from within. The drink was dark, golden brown, and hot—the same liquid they had seen heating over the fire outside.

Theadrin lifted his mug to his lips and sipped its contents. It was familiar to him, but he could not remember where he'd had it before. The food, though it appeared at first only slightly unattractive, was exquisite in taste. All four ate heartily of the freshly made bread that they dipped in warm stewed gravy, greens that were glazed in a delicious sweet sauce, and juicy woodland fruit.

Theadrin took the time to study the dwelling. He noticed that there were no books, only scrolls.

They talked with Cormik and Tagin, telling only reservedly of their quest, and they did not reveal that Theadrin was the heir to the kingship of Arinon. When they reached the part of their tale about going to the Tor, Tagin set his mug down abruptly and Cormik stopped eating and regarded them placidly. Theadrin wondered if they should not have let that slip.

"What makes you want to visit that place?" Cormik asked in a suddenly cold manner. Tagin, sitting cross-legged beside Cormik, watched them ambiguously. The mood had taken a sudden and drastic turn.

"We are searching for something," Theadrin told them. "To save our kingdom from the darkness."

"You must not go there. No one lives who goes near Rut Wen," Tagin blurted.

"What lives there?" Yan asked. He had forgotten about his food and now stared intently at the old man.

"Evil itself," Cormik answered darkly, to which Yan's eyes widened. "It is a place of darkness. As Tagin says, you must not go there."

Yan gave a pleading glance to Theadrin. Myran and Caed exchanged wondering glances as well.

Theadrin put aside any trepidation he may have felt. He swallowed a mouthful of the hot drink and said, "Thank you for the warning, but we must go all the same."

After another moment of analyzing them, Cormik shrugged it off and continued on with another subject as though the Tor had never been mentioned.

"How did you come to learn the southern tongue?" Theadrin asked Cormik after he had finished every scrap of food on his wooden plate, regretting there was no more.

"Many summers ago a wise man came here from the south. He stayed with us for a time and taught us his language. He too wanted to visit Rut Wen."

Theadrin grew interested in this news but could learn nothing more about it.

When they finished their meal and talk, Tagin took them to Mathwin. They left the glen and went through the trees to a cave. Inside was lit by openings in the ceiling where streamed sunlight. Forest folk bustled here and there from shelves and tables, about their work.

Their friend lay sleeping on a bed of moss beneath a bearskin covering. When they drew near his eyes slowly opened and fell on the newcomers.

"Hectur!" Yan ran to his side. "Are ya well, man?"

"Yan," he said and lifted his head.

Myran bent down on one knee and laid a hand on his forehead. "How are you, Mathwin?"

"Fine," the bearded man answered somewhat tiredly.

"You don't feel warm at all," Myran said, surprised, and withdrew his hand.

The corner of Mathwin's mouth rose in a smile and he said, "These forest dwellers are good with medicine."

"What about yer leg?" Yan asked.

"It is on the mend."

"He must stay off it," Tagin said, standing beside Theadrin. "Two days." Mathwin grunted his disapproval when he heard this.

"I'll be up before that," he assured. "We can't wait that long."

"We will see." Theadrin said, crossing his arms.

"His fever left quickly. We did little for it." Tagin added, looking at them. "Did he drink Yusin Abwi?"

"Drink what?" Theadrin asked bewilderedly.

Tagin looked down and frowned as he attempted to find an adequate translation. He glanced up and offered, "Life water."

Theadrin was about to answer no when Myran stood and looked at him. "The hidden waterfall where we camped—I gave Mathwin a drink from its pool."

"Do you think it possible?" Theadrin wondered.

"He did seem to revive quickly."

Tagin watched them as they conversed, then stated, "Infection gone too. It would have been very bad," he told them. "He drank Yusin Abwi. Still, he must rest."

So they were forced to wait for their friend's recovery. They bid their time in the village where they made many friends and learned much about the forest folk culture. These woodland folk were called the Avyrian, which meant People of Song—and they were just that.

Every night they played, and with such skill. Never before had any of them heard music of equal beauty. The songs touched deep within the heart of the listener. They were captivated; the songs bringing to mind memories or locations that held a place in their heart, or sights they had dreamed of seeing. It lifted them up making them feel stronger.

They played the harp, pipes, violin, whistle, drums of many deep tones, and more.

The main instrument they used was one of special making—a craft only the Avyrian knew. It was, by appearance, a flute, but could reach three different octaves very easily and clearly.

It was crafted from the wood of the Falon, the large trees that the forest folk lived in. But the instrument could only be made from the sapling and was harvested at a certain width. The inside was coated with pure silver hammered so thin that it became almost transparent. When Theadrin saw it he wondered how it did not tear.

The holes for the fingers were carved out larger and then a ring of ivory was fixed inside each. There were intricate carvings around its length inlaid with gold.

Myran took great interest in the instrument and Tagin, who was among the most skilled players, taught him the proper way to position his fingers, blow air into the mouthpiece, and other techniques.

During their sojourning in the Avyrian village, they also picked up a saying or two of the peculiar language. Most of the Avyrian did not know the southern tongue. Tagin had studied it, he told them, in hopes that one day more visitors would come and he could speak with them.

"Ri es chiv" in the Avyrian language, which was the first thing Tagin had said to them, they learned, was a common saying. It meant, literally translated, "be it well," which was used as a universal greeting or farewell in any circumstance.

Although they very much enjoyed abiding with the Avyrian, in a few days' time Mathwin was ready to travel, and they became restless to finish their task.

Thirty-One

Lianna dug deep into the soft black dirt and inhaled the rich, sweet scent of the blossoming garden. Tenderly, with careful fingers, she lowered the small flower into the hole she had dug. It was a small plant now, but with great care it would grow to be one of the tallest flowers in Caulguard's gardens.

Patting the soil around the base, Lianna then leaned back on her heels, took up the water flask, and emptied it around the new plant. Then she backed away to admire her handiwork.

"I confess I never thought of placing this plant here," the older man beside her said. He was the garden overseer and had been so for many years. His hair had long since turned gray and his skin was dark from the long days spent in the sun. "It is a brilliant idea."

"Thank you, Gadden. This tiny plant will soon be reaching the railing of the terrace above." Lianna wiped her dirt-smeared hands together and placed them on her hips.

The garden terrace connected to the hall at the back of the keep. She spent most of her time in the gardens since her brother and the others had left to go north and Anromir had gone to war. She and Ellia spent the long days awaiting any news of them.

As Lianna stood looking up at the stone railing, a face peered over the top adorned with a smile as bright as the sun. "Hello, Cadi. Come down and see what I have done." Lianna called up to her.

The face disappeared and soon the girl came dancing around the base of the balcony, golden hair flowing behind. "It is so small," she said after stopping and briefly observing the blue flower. "Why did you put it there?"

Lianna laughed quietly and answered, "It is a type of delphinium, and it will soon be far above your head." She lightly stroked the flaxen strands that curled happily down Cadi's head.

Cadi looked down at the small flower in doubt. Then her eyes brightened. "I forgot, Ellia is looking for you. Anromir is back."

At last some news had come. "Tell them I will join them as soon as I have changed into something clean."

Without another word, Cadi was darting away again. Lianna looked at Gadden and said, "I'll be back down here in the morning."

"As you are every morning." The older man smiled and bowed his head. "Good day, my lady."

Lianna found Anromir and Ellia waiting in the hall a while later, arm in arm. "Welcome back, my lord Anromir," she smiled nicely. "What news do you bring?"

Anromir stepped forward and kissed her hand. "My lady Lianna, things go as well as we could hope for the time being."

"Let us sit and we can talk," Lianna offered, and he agreed, calling for his steward.

The man bustled in with a tall jar of ice-cold water and several cups.

"I met king Brudwyn at the ford as planned only to find he had been ambushed and was surrounded." Anromir sat beside his wife and took a draught of the cool water that the steward had finished pouring him.

"The Caledonian lines were spread abroad in marching order and were in a losing situation because of it. We arrived just in time and were able to rout the enemy," Anromir said before taking another drink.

"I am relieved to hear my uncle is all right," Lianna said, sitting with her hands folded around the cup in her lap.

"We continued on to Averby to find it nearly fallen." The nobleman set aside his empty cup. "We made the attack at first light. It was not an easy fight, but in the end we sent the enemy running and rescued Averby." He stopped to take another guzzle from his refilled cup. After draining the contents, Anromir wiped his mouth.

"We ride now to Avross," he said. "I have returned here to pick up what provisions are needed."

"Surely you will need more troops as well," Ellia said, clinging to his left arm. "Why not take the rest that are here?"

"That is impossible, my love. They will remain here to protect you. Gurn's lords may sweep around and lay siege here. There must be plenty of men to defend."

He smiled at his wife and glanced Lianna's way. "No word from Theadrin?"

She looked down. "Nothing." Anromir noted the concern in her voice and across her face.

"They would have reached the Tor by now, if they kept a steady pace and met no trouble. No doubt they have found what they seek and are on their way home." He looked back at his wife. "Everything will come out aright in the end. But now I must be about my task so I can rejoin Brudwyn." He stood slowly, stretching his sore muscles.

"Can you not stay and rest for a day?" his wife pleaded.

"I cannot. War does not give a commander the luxury of a reprieve at home while his men fight. But walk with me as I make the preparations."

The two walked off arm in arm, leaving Lianna alone in thought. She hoped what Anromir said was true, that Theadrin and Myran and the others were already on their way home.

A cold storm wind screeched outside the ancient tower. Lightning flared in the windows and thunder boomed, resounding like a battle clash around the ruined castle. The old man remained unmoving in his chair. It was more often than not that storm clouds hung over the Tor.

His eyes were closed, but the man was very much awake and alert. Soon his pupil, his apprentice, a young man filled with vigor and ambition, would arrive with the news that he already knew. Then he would commence with his plan; his dark deception. The kingdoms of Arinon and Caledon would soon fall under his rule, then following, the lands beyond the sea.

How long he had waited; how long he had hidden away patiently for the right moment. He had worked long and hard against Valdithin before finally succeeding. He had seen how Valdithin's noble, Gurn, lusted for the throne and used it to his will. Gurn, unknowingly, had played his part very well in the dark scheme. Everything had come together as he wanted. But then, his entire plan was thrown into jeopardy when Valdithin's heir was taken away and hidden. However, it may have turned out for the better in the end. Forced to wait these long years for the appearing of Valdithin's son, he had molded a new plan.

He had perfected it once, twice, a hundred times over; yes, it was sure to succeed. Now the waiting game was at long last over. His deception had worked beautifully up to this point. Sure, he had lost a few battles here and there, but they were unimportant when it was said and done, and did nothing to harm his plan.

After these blights, he realized it was better that Theadrin was alive. Another plan began to take shape. It would strengthen his claim in the end.

He had, through crafty and cunning deception, transformed the church in Avross into a temple dedicated to another god; a god named Amlek. It had been a slow process; getting the people familiar with another god. But all deception begins with the sowing of one small seed of compromise.

The door opened to his tower chamber and his long expected second-in-command entered. A very handsome man, tall and strong in build, stepped into the dark interior of the room and bowed at the waist. "I have returned."

The old man's eyes opened and his head came forward. "Welcome back, Vithimere." He gazed at the younger man and brought his hands together. A low growl emanated from the dark curtains behind his chair. "Easy, Ciarcu. You know young Vithimere."

Turning his attention back to the young man, he checked, "I trust Rhodgrim is brought safely back."

"He is. It was as easy as you said," Vithimere returned.

The older man nodded with approbation and said, "Now, recite to me the news that I already know."

Vithimere stood square shouldered and asserted with a staid expression, "Avross is surrounded by the armies of Caledon and Theadrin. Gurn is surrounded, and victory is in the eyes of his enemies."

The older man cackled happily when he heard this and rubbed the tips of his long fingers together. "Do you know how long I have waited for this?"

"Too long," Vithimere's reply came readily.

The man in the chair rested his hands on the arms of his seat. "You are right. But I have not waited in vain; indeed, the wait was necessary. Arinon and Caledon will be under my rule before the next winter. Then, aside from the lands across the sea, I will hold all under my control." He gleefully crowed and repeated the word.

"Control. Do you understand the power of that word, Vithimere?" Vithimere looked on but did not answer.

"Perhaps you do not yet, but one day you will. For one day you will hold it." He sighed. "Ah, I remember when I won the lands of the north; ages ago it is now. It was then I began to understand how wonderful control is, and I hungered for more. Now see where it has gotten me?"

"Yes," Vithimere answered simply. The older man stopped and looked at him, marking his sober disposition.

Vithimere watched him quietly. The older man furnished a grimace. "What is it, Vithimere? You have other news for me?"

The young man looked back at him. His gaze held no indication of trepidation, neither did his posture or movements. He was a confident man and did not show fear when in the presence of the older man.

"Theadrin has left Arinon," he said. "He is heading north."

"He is coming here," the older man informed him. "Already he has made it through Baremar."

Vithimere was not surprised that his master already knew.

"What are we going to do?" he asked.

"Keep to the plan. You know what happens next?"

Vithimere nodded.

"Then be off with you."

Vithimere gave another bow. Straightening once more, he turned on his heel and was gone from the room.

Thirty-Two

It was a wet day when they finally left the village of the Avyrian. The rain had started early morning before first light and had progressed to a steady downpour. The forest was dark and gray beneath a canopy of shadowy green leaves.

Theadrin tightened the last pack on the back of the horse and turned to the others. Cormik stood wrapped tightly in a green cloak with a wide hood. Steady drips of water that ran down from the top fell from the brim. Tagin had volunteered to guide them part of the way and stood ready beside Myran.

They were prepared to leave now except that Caed was not with them. He was gone when the rest had awoken, leaving no clue as to where he went. Even Myran could not think of why he had left. They waited for his return most of the morning until deciding to set out. Myran knew Caed could easily catch up with them upon his return and assured the others of it.

After Theadrin and the others thanked the Avyrians for their help and hospitality, Cormik said, "Before you depart, accept these gifts."

Several of the forest folk stood behind Cormik and now stepped forward. Each bore a gift wrapped in the large leaves of the Falon tree.

"We know that whatever quest you have undertaken is of great importance. We also hope a lasting friendship may be weaved between our peoples, as there once was of old," Cormik said as each man was handed one of the small bundles.

Once unwrapped, each held two different rocks in their hands. Theadrin recognized them immediately. One was a milky white and the other a grayish blue.

"Minaw and illmal. Strike them together and light will illuminate your surroundings." Cormik explained what Theadrin and Myran already knew about the stones. "When you face the darkness, use these gifts. The shadows will flee from the light."

"Thank you, my friend," Theadrin said. "Know that I will do all in my power to see that our peoples may own friendship."

With that they took their leave. Tagin led them along a well-hidden path that took them northeast.

As they moved along in silence, Theadrin thought again of the golden drink served to them by the Avyrian. He hadn't guessed it until the day before but it was the same Caithal had made the first night they met. After having it many more times, he became certain of it. Then, when they were given the stones of light; it was the same stones Caithal had used against the Cruthene.

"*Caithal must have been the one of whom Cormik spoke,*" Theadrin thought to himself. "*But why did he not tell me he had come here, and why did he go to the Tor?*"

He cast a slow glance at the forest around as he turned the matter over in his mind. The tree bark had darkened and water streamed down their rough surfaces. Ferns sagged from the continual battering of the rain, and leaves now and again bobbed up and down. All about the steady sound of rainfall played upon their ears, and in the distance was the deep rumble of thunder.

The morning trudged on with the relentless pelting rain. Their guide continued to lead them on the paths only the Avyrian knew. He moved easily along, a master of the wood, his fine leather shoes making no sound and leaving no track.

They were a curious people, the Avyrian. None grew taller than Theadrin's waistband, yet they were not lacking in strength because of it. They were a lanky people, most having dark hair and eyes the color of the forest. As Theadrin and his friends had experienced, they were friendly, but Theadrin knew they would be a formidable enemy if provoked.

He had watched some of the men practice spear throwing while waiting for Mathwin's recovery, and was amazed at the skill and accuracy they owned. They could move through the forest without being seen or heard.

At last the trees parted and they found themselves on a hillside looking north. And there, looming like a crouching giant was the Tor, rising from the mist and haze. The description given by Cormik fit the place too well.

It was dark and foreboding, encased in shadow and darkness. High on its summit, like the crown on the giant, rested the ruins of a stone castle. It could barely be made out through the mantle of rain. Just standing at a distance and looking at it brought a feeling of dread to the travelers.

Myran leaned over to Theadrin and stated grimly, "The highest height."

Theadrin nodded. Even in the rain it was easy to see that the Tor dwarfed any other rise in the area.

Tagin stared long at the Tor, pulling his hood lower on his face. There was no misreading the mixed expressions of fear and hate of the place in his leaf-green eyes. After a long moment of silence between them, Tagin spoke. But it was without taking his eyes from the Tor, as if he expected the giant to rise and attack when his back was turned.

"I take you no farther," he told them.

"Thank you for guiding us this far. We can make our way without getting lost from here," Theadrin answered gratefully. He knew it had taken much courage for the man to come even this close.

Tagin put a hand to the pouch strap around his shoulder.

"Why do you go there?" he asked them. It was a question that had been turned over in his mind since he first learned of it being their destination. To him, no sane person would go to that dark place.

Myran looked at the short fellow and answered, "It is to protect our country." Tagin looked at Theadrin to further explain.

Theadrin caught the glance and said, "Tagin, I didn't tell you before because I did not know your intentions toward us. But I will tell you now. I am… the prince of Arinon."

Tagin looked up at Theadrin in surprise at the revelation.

"We have to go to the Tor because our home is in danger," he explained further.

Tagin nodded but his eyes betrayed that he still did not understand. How could he when Theadrin didn't understand himself?

Tagin did not say anything but turned to Myran and lifted the strap from his shoulder, handing the pouch to him. Myran accepted it and asked, "What's this?"

"A gift," he answered simply.

Lifting the cover, Myran held it so the rain would not get in. When he found what it contained, he looked at Tagin in wonder. "An Avyrian flute?"

"You practice." Tagin said, wearing a smile. "When I see you, you show me how you improve."

"Thank you, my friend." Myran returned and slung the bag around his neck and under his arm.

Tagin looked once more at each of them and said, "Bunichiv," their word for farewell, and then disappeared into the forest.

The rest looked toward the Tor once again. There was not much forest left between it and the hill they stood upon. About halfway it ended, and a river cut through the flatland below the Tor. They stood there for a long time, dreading to continue.

"May God go with us." Theadrin breathed in and let out slowly. "I wish Caed had not gone off."

"But I am not far away." The voice from behind startled them. Caed stepped from the tree line with a wide grin on his face.

"Where have you been, Caed?" Myran looked relieved.

"Where else?" His smile took on a joking curve. "Hunting."

"Hunting? Didn't you know we were planning on leaving?" Myran asked incredulously.

Caed chuckled. Ignoring the question, he said, "You should have seen the size of my stag." He shook his head and let out a breathy whistle. "I finally got him."

The mirth that had begun to play in Myran's eyes died suddenly and he did not speak. Caed's smile slowly faded and the sound of rain took dominance once more. The two looked at the ground, recalling a day and time long ago.

Theadrin studied them before speaking. He saw genuine sadness in Myran. In Caed it was hard, was it also sadness, or could it be regret, or shame?

"Let's be off." He said, gripping the wet leather reins. Slowly the five companions descended the grassy slope into the remainder of the forest.

"Where is your stag then?" Myran asked as he pushed aside a wet branch.

"I gave it as a parting gift to the Avyrian. I knew there was no time to skin it and I certainly couldn't carry it along with me. They were glad to have it."

Yan's feet suddenly flew out from under him after he stepped on a patch of mud and he landed on his back. Theadrin was there to help him up.

"This confounded rain." Yan growled. "It'd have to start rainin' agin just as we're leave'n."

"Cheer up, Yan," Mathwin muttered, not at all cheery himself. "At least you didn't injure your leg, put a halt to the journey, and jeopardize the fate of Arinon."

"I may yet git injured…a broken leg if I slip again!" Yan retorted.

"Take heart, my friends." Theadrin perceived the attitude of despair beginning to clutch them. It had been growing with every passing day since setting foot out of Arinon. Now, being in the shadow of the looming Tor, the feeling was heightened.

"Do not let the darkness grip your minds and hearts. When things seem helpless, dwell on the memory of better times. Remember the deeds of our great King; remember his mighty works," he encouraged.

"Yan, do you remember the war against the Kaidri; when you and I were riding alone and were ambushed."

"Yup. I thought it was our last day alive fer sure."

"And what happened?"

Yan took in a breath as he recalled the incident. "Ya said to me, 'Blow the horn, Yan. Let's show 'em what a real fight is.'" The corner of his mouth lifted as he remembered. "So I sounded our battle call."

"And then?"

Yan chuckled. "An' then those barbarian's panicked an' we chased 'em over the hill."

"Why did they suddenly run?" Caed asked who had grown interested in the tale.

Yan laughed. "We figured that hearin' the battle horn made 'em think we had all our men nearby, ready fer a fight. They weren't ready fer an all-out battle, I guess. Whatever the reason bein', those barbarians ran like a firestorm was at their heels."

Caed laughed at it. "Amazing."

"It was the great and mighty King of Heaven who put the fear and panic in their hearts. We have nothing to fear with him to fight for us," Theadrin said.

The mood began to lighten as other memories sprang forth to be told.

The unremitting downpour did not let up as they approached the river that hugged the base of the Tor. Its waters surged past in a swift torrent, swelled above its banks as the clouds emptied into it. There was no possible way to ford it.

The five stood in silent contemplation over the dilemma. Now that they were at the very base of the Tor, they did not want to stop again. They wanted to be done with their mission so they could return home.

Theadrin, wet to the bone, looked up at the Tor. Its top was no longer visible since the rainfall had thickened and veiled everything a stone toss away. No one spoke. There was a heavy, menacing darkness hanging over the area. Theadrin could feel it well and shivered from the combined lack of warmth and sense of danger.

It felt like he was being stalked by one of the lions in the Ambered hills in southern Caledon. He had heard too many stories and accounts of people who had been hunted and killed by the vicious beasts.

"Theadrin, look!" Myran shouted over the drum of rain. Theadrin followed Myran's pointing finger and made out an object farther up the river.

When they made their way closer they found an old bridge, which was cracked and broken in the middle. It was as old as the ruined castle on top of the Tor. And tied to it on the opposite side of the river was a small boat. There was no way they could get the horses over the bridge, but it was quite possible they could jump the gap in the middle.

It was their best chance of getting across. Theadrin called out to the rest. "Let us tether the horses in the shelter of those trees over there." They did so quickly and returned to the tattered bridge.

"We will have to jump," Theadrin said, observing the split in the middle.

"I will go first," Myran offered.

"It's all right. I will," Theadrin stated and walked out on the once-sturdy stone-and-wooden-beam bridge. He reached the middle and the gap was wider than he had first anticipated. He halted a step back from the edge. The bulging waves of the river flew by below him, calling out threats in liquid voice.

Focusing on the other side of the bridge, Theadrin gathered his strength and courage. His heart quickened as the adrenaline pulsed through his veins. He back up several steps and then was off running. His feet left the rubble and he was flying over the raging water.

An instant later his feet touched the other side, landing on the slick stone and flying out from under him. He sprawled out and landed on his shoulder, obtaining a bruise, but was otherwise unharmed. Slowly he rose on shaky legs and waved to the others.

Myran was coming next. While waiting, Theadrin glanced around and saw a large, detached wooden beam. If he could move it, it would serve as a good bridge replacement for the broken part. He took hold of it and pulled, budging it, but realizing he could not get it across alone.

Myran took a running jump and landed near him. Theadrin put out his hand to steady him. "Help me with this." They both strained and managed with great effort to get one end across.

Caed was next and tested the new bridge with his foot. It was a wide, flat-edged beam but would require steady footing to cross, especially with the torrent of rain and gusts of wind. Caed, satisfied that the beam would hold well, stepped up onto it. Both of his arms stretched out straight, he moved across quickly and with ease.

During Caed's crossing, Mathwin had retreated to the horses and returned quickly with a coil of rope in hand. Yan had not crossed over yet but stood staring down at the wet beam and taunting waves.

"I got terrible balance," Yan duly admitted.

"I know that all too well," Mathwin chuckled. "Why do you think I brought this rope?"

"So ya kin tie it around my waist and pull me out'a the river when I fall in?" Yan guessed.

"Watch." Mathwin climbed to the edge of the gap and tossed one end of the rope to Myran. "We will hold each end and you can use it to steady yourself." So Yan, still apprehensive, took firm hold of the rope and began to cross. The idea served to be well thought out, yet even so Yan nearly pitched off once. But he continued on and made it safely across.

Mathwin came last, still gripping the end of the rope with Myran keeping it taut, and they left the bridge to observe the boat. It was solid and could fit three grown men inside.

"Someone is here," Theadrin stated the obvious. He looked at his friends through the torrential rain. "Take courage, my friends. We will need all of it to face what lies at the top of this Tor."

In silence, they turned and began the slow, wary climb up the incline. The grass was slick and it took all their skill not to slip and slide all the way back to the bottom. Gradually the ruins of the castle became visible. The sight of its black silhouette towering darkly above them set Theadrin's heart racing. *Great King, give me courage,* he prayed silently.

All that was running through his head was the tale of The Seven, a favorite legend of his childhood, where a beast was waiting there at the top to devour them.

They reached the face of a crumbling wall and crouched behind it half expecting some great terror to come flying over in a bloodthirsty rage. Waiting a moment longer, Theadrin peeked over the edge. The yard was empty save piles of stone and crumbled debris scattered abroad. The castle keep rested across the yard. It was squarely made with one long tower rising from its side.

Facing the broken wall and standing full height, Theadrin placed both his palms on the lowest part and pulled himself up. The others watched as he disappeared over the top and Myran was promptly at his heels. When the others were all over, Theadrin and Myran were across the courtyard and observing a rotting wooden door. They tried it, but the bolt was long rusted and unusable.

Myran took a step back and gave the door a firm kick. The sound of splintering wood and grating metal followed as the door easily gave in.

"The place is deserted," Caed stated. Inside it was dark, dank, and dust-coated. Spider webs were in abundance. It had been uninhabited for centuries.

They entered, glad to be out of the rain at last, and walked cautiously through the smaller room to another door. This one opened no easier, and when they were finally through they found themselves in an old hallway. There was an awful odor wafting through like the smell of rotting flesh. Theadrin gave a low cough and looked right and left down the hall.

"I don't know what it is we need to find, but I believe we will know it when we see it," he said to the others. "Myran and I will go right and Mathwin, you, Yan, and Caed explore the left. Use your heads; watch each other's backs."

Theadrin and Myran's path took them through several smaller rooms, much like the first one they had entered by, and ended up in the great hall. They came in by a side door to a raised platform that followed a flight of stairs to the lower floor. The style and structure was very much similar to Monivea and Avross, though much smaller scale. At one end was the raised dais where the king and his queen would sit. On the far end was a huge stone hearth.

It was there Theadrin inspected first. He knelt down and put his fingers to the ashes. They were warm, confirming that someone else was present in the ruin. He rose and told Myran what he discovered. The deep rumble of thunder echoed around the ruined fortress and Myran looked to the dais.

There was a door behind it. "If my bearings are correct," Theadrin began, following his friend's eyes, "that door would lead to the tower we saw from outside."

"Where the king's quarters would have been," Myran concluded. Theadrin nodded. They both knew that if someone was in that place, the tower was the most likely spot he would be.

The two were across the hall quickly and Myran cautiously opened the door. This time the latch opened with ease and the hinges did not grind. They found the beginning steps of a long winding stairwell. A blazing torch, fastened to a black iron sconce, lit the passageway. Theadrin and Myran glanced at each other before advancing further. They followed the stairs for a long way and came to the end where another door rested open on its hinges.

The crowning stone in the frame of the doorway was nearly circular in shape and Theadrin noticed an odd carving in its center. He had seen it before. Quickly, he took out the object that Caithal had given him and found the same marking on it.

Myran noticed it too. It was carved long ago, but he guessed it had been done long after the castle was actually built.

They both slowly drew out their swords and gazed into the dark room. It seemed empty. But before they could advance, a crowlike voice suddenly stopped them.

"Theadrin, come in, lad. And young Myran, do both of you come in. I have been awaiting you."

Thirty-Three

"Come, come; there is no need for drawn swords." The voice came from the deepest shadows of the room. But the two friends did not put down their weapons, although the benevolence of the voice caught them off guard.

"Set them aside," the voice continued. "There is no cause for violence here." Despite their best efforts, Theadrin and Myran were put at ease by the lilting voice, and the sense of imminent danger started to melt away. Theadrin relaxed his sword arm and took a step inside the doorframe.

"Easy, Theadrin." Myran cautioned. But the mysterious voice was quick to counteract his warning.

"There is no danger. I mean no harm toward you."

Theadrin's grip tightened on the handle of his sword and he demanded, "Who are you?"

There was silence for a time and they heard the creak of a chair somewhere in the darkness. "Will you not come in?" The voice floated out once more.

"It is a trap." Myran whispered. He had moved in as much as he could beside Theadrin, facing the dark interior of the room readily.

"No trap," the voice contradicted. "Myran, your caution is clever but, I assure you, pointless. There is no danger that awaits you here."

"Why should we believe you?" Theadrin shot back "How do we know you don't mean us harm?"

"Because, Theadrin, son of Valdithin, I wish to talk with you. We cannot talk if you are lying on the floor dead. Besides, if I had desired, I could have killed you by now." At that moment a brilliant flash of lightning lit up the room, and Theadrin brought up his sword, for directly in front of him stood a tall man dressed in a black cloak.

His hair was as black as his clothing and his face was worn and colorless. From the corner of his thin mouth to his long chin was a jagged scar that oddly twisted his mouth when he spoke. His eyes were deep and piercing, devoid of any warmth.

Theadrin was surprised that he had not seen the man, because he was so close; within arm's reach. Myran was at his side ready to strike when the man let out a cackling laugh. Although the room had gone dark again he was still visible.

"You see? I could have killed you before your sword was drawn. Now I insist; come in." He backed away and walked to an old, high-backed chair. As he did, suddenly there was light again in the room. But this time it was not lightning but firelight. There were torches on either side of the room, but there was no one there to light them. They had simply sparked to life seemingly out of nothing.

Theadrin and Myran entered the room cautiously, still baring drawn swords.

"That is better." The man took his seat. "Please, have a seat yourselves." His voice was once more benign, wearing further at Theadrin and Myran's distrust. Against their better judgment, they sheathed their swords and took the chairs before the old table, behind which sat the old man. Myran, however, kept a firm grasp on the handle of his dagger.

"Let us share a drink as we talk," he continued amiably. At once there was another flash of lightning, and the two blinked because it was so close and bright. The boom of thunder was earth shattering in their ears and shook the frail wooden chairs they sat on. Looking back at their host, they saw him indicate with his thin left hand the goblets in front of them.

Theadrin nearly rose from his seat, for the cups had not been there before, he was certain. "Forgive me for declining your generosity, but I will not drink it," he stated resolutely.

"You don't trust my hospitality? Have I not proven to you already that I mean no harm?" he asked Theadrin with an edge of hurt in his voice.

Theadrin felt his resolve begin to ebb as the man's deception took hold. He took hold of the cup and lifted it to his nose. It was wine, well aged. Its delicious scent played well on his nostrils and he began to put the cup to his lips. Suddenly something smashed against his hand causing him to lose his grip on it. The cup clattered to the floor and all its contents spilled out. Myran withdrew his hand and turned on the man.

"I don't know what trick you are playing, but we will not fall for it."

For an instant a hot fire leapt up in the magician's eyes, but it faded as quickly as it came and he smoothly spoke once again. "Myran, Myran; always the untrusting one. Caution can protect you from many dangers but can also withhold you from hidden blessings. No, young Myran Cai, your wariness and caution are wasted here and are keeping you from the blessing of refreshment after a long, hard journey." His reasoning words, at first, seemed to have little effect on Myran, whose bronze eyes stared hard into the black eyes of the man across the table. But inside, Myran was already giving in. He felt at once ridiculous and silly for being so suspicious.

"I know how your throat is already parched and calls out for drink," their cunning host continued after a short time.

Myran glanced at the cup. He suddenly realized how thirsty he was. His mouth and throat became uncomfortably dry. He tried to swallow, but his efforts produced little effect because no saliva would form in his mouth. The dryness and thirst began to grow so intense that he reached out and took a firm hold of the goblet. The deep, alluring red of the sweet liquid glimmered and sparkled in the torchlight.

Slowly he brought it toward his mouth. The cool, gold metal of the cup rested on his bottom lip and the first liquid trickled over his tongue. His dry thirst was instantly quenched.

As Myran sat once more, the man's teeth showed in a reassuring smile. "Let us talk now. Enough suspicions and arguing."

"You know who *we* are," Theadrin stopped him. "But we do not know you. Let us start there."

The man accepted the interruption by lifting his eyebrows and inclining his head forward. "That is a fair question." His eyes glanced from one to the other of the two as he took in a slow breath and pondered his answer. "Alas, I wished to tell you when more was said," he began. "But very well." Here he paused and fixed his eyes on Theadrin. "I am the wind that fills the sail, the unseen hand. I am the current beneath the surface."

"That is not a sufficient answer," Theadrin retorted.

"It will be after you hear what I have to say." He leaned forward. "I offer a proposition for your considering; and please, consider wisely. You know that the people of Arinon have left the one they called the Highest King. Gurn has seen to that. But what he does not realize is, I will soon be the ruler of Arinon and Caledon. I would have you there to give me the throne of Arinon in the sight of all the people. Your loyalty to me is what I ask."

Theadrin leapt up in sudden rage. "Never!" He slammed his palms on the table. "I would never sell away the people of Arinon! Not even for my own life!"

The man remained calm at the outburst. "Theadrin, do you really think you are capable of leading a whole kingdom? You are too young and inept."

These words pierced Theadrin like an invisible knife blade, but he could not say anything in his defense.

The man continued. "I offer you, however, the chance to be everything that you can for the people as my appointed regent over the kingdom of Arinon. You will defer to me in all matters. Hear my reasoning. If you truly wanted the best for Arinon's people, you would realize your leadership would plummet the kingdom into ruin. Arinon needs a leader who has the power to rule them."

Theadrin was silent as the older man smiled and pressed the matter. "You will have the authority over Arinon that you truly desire, and yet you will not have to worry about the weight of responsibility and fear of failure. That will be in the hands of one who has the ability and maturity for it."

Myran shot out of his chair and was at Theadrin's side. "And what makes you think you are that man?" he yelled. "You are a sorcerer and a servant of the darkness! Not while we draw breath will you sit on the throne."

"You, Myran, are trying to be to Theadrin what you could not be to Ao-idh." The man laughed mockingly, and Myran grew suddenly stiff. Theadrin was puzzled at the man's words. What did he know of Ao-idh?

"Theadrin, your trust in Myran would not be so high if you only knew." The dark man said, keeping his fierce gaze on Myran Cai. "Someone once trusted in Myran as you do now"—his eyes narrowed in accusation—"and that man is dead because of it."

Theadrin looked at Myran who stood unmoving. As much as Theadrin did not want to believe it, he saw guilt on Myran's face.

The black-haired man sneered. "If you cannot make a wise decision in who you have as your right-hand man, Theadrin, then you cannot make wise decisions for Arinon. I will be the sovereign that the people of Arinon need."

Theadrin's jaw muscle flexed as he stood in momentary conflict. He blinked and his eyes seemed to clear as a spark was kindled. "On my life, you will not!" Theadrin stated through gritted teeth.

"Then you will not take my offer?"

Theadrin straightened. In a cool voice he stated, "I will not."

"That is the gravest mistake you will ever make. This runs deeper than you know, boy. What you have seen here, tonight"—he waved his spidery hands around the room as if the undeniable proof was all around them—"is nothing. I hold a power far greater than anything you could ever imagine." He stood, a head taller than the two young men before him. "You will understand, young Theadrin, that my plans were set into action long before you made your first appearance upon this earth."

Here he stopped and let out another soft chuckle. "Long ago I saw the lust for power in Gurn's heart. He was a perfect candidate—handsome, charismatic, someone the people could easily fall for. An easy pawn. Quietly he gained the support of most of the nobles through promise of high position and increase in wealth. He then turned his attention to winning over the people. What is it that really gets people's interest? Gifts. He held festivals and gave away many little treasures. Word spread throughout the kingdom among the poor folk; how wonderful was this young, handsome noble. I myself roamed the land disguised as a tinker and spoke to many. 'How good would it be for us if he were king?' I would ask them."

Theadrin listened in stunned silence. The realization of all the years and deception that had been laid into his dark plot made him feel overwhelmed.

The man continued. "Now that I had my pawn in place, all that remained was the removal of Valdithin. I am the cause of your father's death."

This declaration hit Theadrin like a slap in the face. "What did you say?"

"Do you not remember the document signed by royal huntsman, Begron, on his deathbed? The one who testifies your father murdered his brother who was the oldest son and rightful heir?"

"That document is a lie!" Myran declared angrily.

"Of course it is," the man cackled. "Begron thought, in his sickened stupor, he was signing his last will and testament. I poisoned him."

"The King Sword is proof of the true line of Arnoni kings!" Myran shot back.

"Well, the sword is gone forever, and with it the line of Arnoni kings!" the older man yelled, and then his demeanor cooled again. "I have seen to that. I took it the night Valdithin stood in defense of his line's claim to the throne. An arrow struck him and he was dragged into a room. Balthor and Dolemar could do nothing to protect their king."

Theadrin stood stock-still in disbelief and rage. As he spoke his voice was a low quiver. "You killed my father then; stabbed him in the back as he lay injured?"

"Your father would be disappointed, Theadrin. It took you this long to figure things out." The man's white teeth flashed in a taunting sneer. "I did him a favor by killing him so he would not have to see the failure his son would become."

Theadrin's hand went to his sword, but before allowing him to speak or act, the sorcerer said, "At this moment your army and the army of your uncle surround the walls of Avross. This is well according to my plan. What I have waited for is finally coming to pass. They have the fox cornered, but their backs are turned to the lion in the thicket." He bent and opened an elongated chest next to his chair. "With this I shall rule all kingdoms," he said grandly as he drew out an object nearly as long as the chest.

Theadrin saw the sword that the sorcerer held and had to marvel at its beautiful crafting. It was made of shadow iron, much stronger than regular iron, and something Theadrin had only heard of. Also known as black metal, its color was dark silver.

"The King Sword is gone forever, and this will take its place in a new era. I leave this night for Arinon." The sorcerer paused and snickered. "How will it be, do you think, when Amlek appears in the flesh; visible before the eyes of the people? They will have a new god, I think." His eyes were fierce and he gave a hideous laugh. Amlek: the name was a shocking blow to Theadrin. But he realized then what it all meant. How subtly this sorcerer's deception had been laid out. Amlek would use his sword of shadow iron to forge a new age, where all kingdoms were under his dominion.

Theadrin drew his sword. Myran unsheathed his in turn and they rushed at Amlek, who did not flinch but stood rigid and watched them come, evil mirth playing in his black eyes. Suddenly, he called a name, "Ciarcu!"

From behind a curtain leapt a huge black wolflike creature. Theadrin recognized its kind; he had fought them before. The Ustvil leapt toward him with a fierce growl. Theadrin saw Myran, out of the corner of his eye, suddenly crumple to the floor. Myran gave a sharp cry and gripped the front of his torso in agony.

Theadrin swung toward Ciarcu's head, but the hound darted out of reach. Then it lunged at him and he was sent sprawling to the floor. The impact of its massive head shattered Theadrin's breath.

Myran struggled up on hands and knees. He made to stand but once again doubled over in pain.

The beast spun itself back around and dove in for the kill with deathly quick speed. Theadrin could not move aside quick enough, for his breath had not returned.

Myran had risen up on his knees again and drew his knife. As the beast reached the right distance, he sent the short blade spinning toward its mark. The point sank into the hump on the back of its shoulders. It halted and snapped its head around in an effort to rip the knife out.

Theadrin took the opportunity and jumped on its back. The Ustvil took off at a run around the edge of the room. Theadrin plunged his sword into the side of its neck, and with a whining yelp the Ustvil crashed to the floor. It thrashed for a moment before giving in to death.

Then Theadrin was at Myran's side. Myran had his arms about his stomach and was groaning in pain.

Theadrin bent over Myran desperately searching for a wound of some kind, but to no avail. In a rage he stood and whirled about to face Amlek, but the man was gone, though the echo of his haunting laughter still resounded through the room and in his mind. Through the window lightning blinked brightly followed by an echo of thunder.

"He has gone to Arinon." Myran spoke through clenched teeth. Theadrin knelt down again beside his friend.

"Where are you hurt, Myran?"

"There is no wound," was the pain-filled answer. "It is the wine…it was poisoned. I am a fool."

Theadrin's stomach knotted. He knew nothing of a cure for poison. At least if there was a wound he could clean and dress it, but poisoning killed from within. A desperate fear he had never felt before overcame him. He was helpless.

"We must get out of this tower." He laid a firm grasp on Myran's arm and helped him up.

Myran put his arm around Theadrin's neck and they stumbled from the room. Going down the long stairway was very difficult. Every few steps Myran would halt and grip his stomach as waves of sharp, intense pain washed over him.

"It is my fault," Theadrin muttered, despair enfolding his heart like a heavy cloak. "I made the decision to come here."

Myran looked over at him through pain-squinted eyes. "I was the one who decided to drink the wine, Theadrin. No fault is yours."

Theadrin kept looking ahead. "It is too late," he mumbled again. At last they gained the bottom and made their way through the ruined great hall.

Reaching the door they met Yan. "There ya are," he said panting. "We found…" He stopped in midbreath realizing something was wrong.

"Yan, where are the others?" Theadrin asked quickly.

"Back that way." He indicated the hallway behind him; but his eyes never left Myran, who was gripped with another surge of pain and groaned. "What happened?"

"Myran has been poisoned!" Theadrin told him. "You must get the others at once!" Yan darted away without hesitation as Theadrin and Myran continued on the way they had come, reaching the broken door before they heard the running footsteps of their friends.

"Over here!" Theadrin called them over.

Yan and Mathwin came into the room just as Theadrin was helping Myran to sit against the wall. The storm raged outside the shattered door. The wind howled, thunder boomed, and the rain pounded heavily down.

"You must get back to Arinon," Myran told Theadrin, gripping his abdomen tightly with both arms. "Take the boat at the bottom of the Tor. Leave me behind."

"Throw away that notion, Myran Cai. We will all leave this place together." Theadrin told him confidently, though he felt little of it. Fear and panic were battling against what courage still remained.

He looked at Yan and Mathwin. "Where is Caed?"

"We split ways briefly," Mathwin answered.

"Yan, show me where you last saw him. Mathwin, stay with Myran." The tall man nodded, and Theadrin followed Yan back into the deeper interior of the castle in desperate search of Caed.

Thirty-Four

The siege of Avross was well underway when the messenger from Caledon sped into their camp. He had ridden long and very hard, having two horses drop out from under him during the way. But at last the exhausted man reached his destination and was brought directly to the battle line where King Brudwyn was with Lord Anromir.

It was a humid day and the armies were tired, making work on the siege engines slothful. The sun beat mercilessly down on their camps. The messenger found them observing the construction of a wooden tower. Despite the heat of the day all wore breastplates and cloaks over their regular garb.

"My Lord!" the messenger shouted between gasps for breath to the Caledonian king. "Make haste!"

Brudwyn whirled about to see who it was that addressed him with such urgency. His eyes landed on the man coming toward him as recognition dawned.

"Slow yourself, Maric. What urgency has brought you from Caledon?"

Maric collapsed exhausted onto one knee and began to speak, but he was so out of breath the words came hard. "Caledon… needs you…it is…"

"Take a breath, man. What has happened?" The king's heart began to pound for worry of what the man was saying.

"The barbarian war host, sire…It is the largest ever seen, and Hrodgrim leads them." He gulped another breath of air and continued. "Northern Caledon is in flames as they pillage town after town."

Brudwyn's heart fell. For a time he could not speak and he looked at general Aedrius who was just arriving from another section of the battlefield. "My king, what has happened?" Aedrius asked, noting the drained expression on his lord's face.

The messenger named Maric spoke up once again. "I have not told the whole of it, my lord king. Your trusted advisor and friend is a traitor."

"What? Who?"

"Sir Dathin, my lord. He leads the barbarian hosts as his own."

The feeling of a heavy stone settled in the King's stomach. Ruadhan had tried to warn him of this. His son was right, but Dathin had been his most faithful noble, or so he had believed. How could it have happened?

"Your son, Prince Ruadhan, is the only resistance against this evil," Maric informed him. "But he is sorely outnumbered and I fear will not hold out much longer."

This brought the king from his stunned daze. He was moving away instantly, calling to his general. "Aedrius, prepare the army to return home with all speed." Without further urging needed, the general saluted and attacked his mission with ardor.

Anromir was at a loss for words. If Caledon's army withdrew, he and Rhyd alone could not continue the siege. He opened his mouth to say something but no words came. Brudwyn looked back at him in lament.

"I am deeply sorry. I must lead my army home," he said.

Anromir nodded and swallowed, "As you must, King Brudwyn."

Brudwyn looked at him a moment longer in sympathy and then turned quickly to see to his leaving preparations. Anromir remained rooted where he stood. His arms hung in despair at his sides as he stared after the withdrawing man.

When Caledon's army had assembled in traveling ranks, Anromir came to stand beside the mounted king. He looked up without a word. The look was returned as Brudwyn adjusted himself in the saddle.

"You are a worthy commander and ally, my friend." Brudwyn said to the forlorn commander. "Do not give up this fight."

"I will never do so, my lord," Anromir answered. "I only wish I could aid you now as you have done so for me and my country."

"But not enough I fear. I meant to see this through. Alas, this is the one thing that could have torn me away. The Highest King be with you, Lord Anromir."

Anromir bowed his head once and stepped back. "Farewell, my lord. Godspeed."

Brudwyn stood up in the stirrups, twisting his upper body to look back at his men. "Warriors of Caledon! March away! To the defense of our home and loved ones!" And then the Caledonians were away. Anromir and his men watched despairingly until they disappeared.

"There fades our last hope," one of the men brooded.

Anromir turned on him quickly. He had to take action before hopelessness spread through his men, drawing away their courage like poison. "Brond! Hope is far from gone. Theadrin will soon return."

"And what if he does not come back? He has been gone long already. What if he is gone forever?"

"Take heart, man! Be courageous!" Anromir gripped Sergeant Brond's breastplate with both hands. "I do not know where Theadrin is, nor whether he will return, but hope still remains so long as the Highest King is at our side."

Brond glared back, not defiantly but more in resignation. "And what do we do in the meantime? We no longer possess the strength to besiege this mighty city."

"We will hold here yet a little longer," Anromir decided. "Send word to Lord Rhyd on the other side of the city of what has taken place."

They did so. The sun rose and fell three times with no progress on the building of the siege engines. Anromir wore himself ragged trying to keep up the spirits of his men. All day he moved through the camp, and into the night he sat by their fires, always offering encouragement.

All the while he prayed ceaselessly for Theadrin's return. He also hoped word would come from Caledon bringing encouraging news. But he hoped in vain. The days wore slowly past, and on the fifth day, as the sun sank low, he felt as though it was dragging his last string of courage and endurance down with it.

The following morning light revealed a new sight to the army of Arinon. The camp awoke with the shout of alarm from the sentries. Anromir rushed from his tent after getting hastily dressed and armored and found one of the lookouts.

"What is it?"

The man answered by lifting a finger to the northern horizon. Along the top of the distant ridge was another army.

"Who is it?" he asked the man.

"My lord, that rider knows." The warrior indicated one of the sentries galloping in on horseback.

Anromir waited impatiently for the rider to reach them. The man rode through camp ignoring the questioning shouts of his comrades to bring his news to Anromir.

"Lord Anromir!" He hailed as he approached and swung down deftly from the saddle.

"Who stands atop that ridge?" Anromir asked immediately.

"The armies of both Lord Percel and Lord Taromar." Anromir put a bold face on as the men around him mumbled to each other.

He stared back at the man and ordered. "Ride as swiftly as you can to where Lord Rhyd is encamped to the west. Inform him of this new threat and bid him collect his forces and come immediately."

"As you command, my lord." The man put his forearm across his chest in salute and remounted.

Anromir felt all the hope he had barely been holding on to begin to slip away. He looked around at the warriors' faces staring back, and their eyes crying out for some encouragement from him.

"Brave men of Arinon." He called them together, fearing his voice was too weak. "This fight can turn the course of the war. Here formed against us are Arinon's two most powerful lords under Gurn. If we defeat them here, the war is ours! So bestow yourselves with courage and valor. Today—today the world will see that the Highest King fights for his people! We will form ranks along the low ridge there." He made a sweep with his drawn blade. "And then we will meet them. May God be with us all!"

With an encouraged shout, the army moved into position. Anromir rode up and down the lines directing the formations, all the while keeping a wary eye on the amassed enemy. But Percel and Taromar remained in position. Anromir's battle lines were long drawn and ready, yet the impending attack did not come. Minutes turned to hours and the sun started the snail-paced plummet.

Just before sunset, Rhyd arrived with his men. Anromir sat in the saddle gazing across the green expanse between them and the enemy when Rhyd joined his side. The dying sun cast a rich, incandescent light across wavy grass making it as burnished gold ripples in an emerald sea.

"Hail, Anromir." Rhyd called as he neared and reigned up. He rode a sleek black steed with large flecks of white.

"Rhyd, I am glad to see you." Anromir cast a glance back at the enemy lines as a cool wind rustled his hair. "They have not made a move since we first saw them."

Rhyd's leather saddle creaked as he leaned on the pommel and observed the enemy with a keen eye. "No doubt they wanted us together so they could finish us in one battle. Very well. We are together; let them come. They will soon learn what a battle truly is."

Anromir looked at his fair-haired friend. There was no fear in Rhyd's eyes as he beheld the enemy, only confidence. Neither was there weakness in his voice; instead it sounded bold and more than ready for the challenge.

"Rhyd," he began, and his friend turned his bright-blue eyes back to him. "Does it not seem hopeless to you?"

Rhyd drew a slow breath as he thought of his answer. "Yes. I suppose it does look so."

"Yet you seem eager for the fight."

Rhyd's answer was not slow in coming this time. "Why be otherwise when the fight is unavoidable? Besides, after making such a terrible mistake at the counsel, I intend to, if I can, redeem myself and repay Theadrin's mercy with my loyalty."

Anromir felt foolish for his next question. "Do you think that Theadrin will come back?"

"There is no way of knowing that. But I believe that the Highest King has raised him up to rule and rebuild this kingdom under his authority. So I believe Theadrin will return. And I, for one, want to be standing against the enemy when he comes."

Anromir took heart at the faith of his friend. Rhyd looked back at the enemy, blue eyes clear and sparkling. A cool breeze blew past, one fresh and clean. Rhyd drew it into his lungs and let it out once more.

"Now look there, they are on the move. Let's give them a fight they shall never forget should they live to tell of it."

"I will see you in the fray," Anromir said as he raised his helm above his head.

"Indeed, my friend. God go with you," Rhyd replied.

"And with you."

Thirty-Five

Theadrin and Yan worked their way as fast as they could through the halls and rooms to the place Mathwin had talked about. But when they reached the spot there was no sight of Caed. The room was small and square, and in the far corner gaped a dark passage blacker than night.

Yan was all for returning to the others but Theadrin hesitated. "Perhaps Caed went in," he guessed.

"He wouldn't go down 'n there without a light." Yan wanted badly to leave. The foul feeling and stale air that rose from the dark tunnel was daunting to say the least.

"How would we know?" He glanced at Yan with a determined look. "I'm going to check it out."

Theadrin took three long strides and was at the spot. "Yan, there is a staircase here."

"Are ya goin' in?"

"I must. You go back to the others, Yan, just in case Caed returned to them."

"Oh no, beggin' yer pardon, but I'm not gonna leave ya 'lone. We don't know what might be lyin' down there."

"I just thought you would want to go back," Theadrin replied.

"Yer right, but I ain't goin' back without ya."

Theadrin smiled. "All right then. Let us be about it quickly."

"Only thing is, how are we gonna see in that darkness?" Yan looked into the blackness of the stairway uncertainly.

"Don't worry about that," Theadrin declared. He reached down into the leather pouch at his side and withdrew the two stones that the Avyrian had gifted to him. "Come on, Yan. Let's get Caed and leave this evil place."

They descended into the blackness, and when it was too dark Theadrin struck the illmal and minaw stones together. The result worked better than he hoped. The white light flashed and the passage remained lit for a good while as the light bounced and illuminated off the chiseled stone of the passage.

Theadrin went to the wall and ran his fingers along the hewn surface. It appeared to be ordinary rock. Then his eye caught a discoloration in the stone face. There was a streak of a different substance. It looked strikingly like silver yet dimmer. The light danced through it like the glowing red embers of a fire. Ember iron—Caithal had told him about it once. It caught and held the light within it for some time before dying out.

They proceeded down the long stairway, only needing to strike the minaw and illmal once more. At the bottom they found a tunnel that snaked and curved in a gentle slope downward. With the light from the stones, the going was easy.

The tunnel opened up to one large cave. There was a short flight of stone-chiseled steps that brought them to the floor of the cavern.

Theadrin gave the two light stones one last strike. This time they were both taken back at the result. The light reverberated off the walls of the massive cave and off the many stalagmites and boulders. The dazzling light filled the whole of the cavern making it as bright as daylight inside.

The metal that he had seen in veins earlier was everywhere in the cavern. No doubt, in ages past before the tribes had left the Tor, they had discovered this metal inside it and mined it.

Theadrin watched in awe and thought he caught a glimpse of movement across the cavern, but it was gone as quick as it had been there. There was a deep rumble, like a growl, and yet as the light began to die away, Theadrin saw a large shadow move in the rocks and was sure they were not alone.

As the interior dimmed the sound came again. This time Theadrin knew it was not thunder.

When the light was gone, Theadrin found he could still see somewhat. The metal in the cavern seemed to have soaked in the white light and now held it within. It was a strange type of glow, not in the leastways bright. It was as if the moonlight had pierced through the Tor and the last dim remnant filled the cave.

In this dim lighting Theadrin could just make out the huge form of something mounting itself on top of a large boulder. The black shape lifted itself on dark wings and took flight. It combed the edge of the cavern, drawing swiftly nearer to them. Theadrin and Yan unsheathed their swords just as the beast whipped past them letting loose an ear-shattering shriek.

A blast of air from its wings hit Theadrin and Yan but the black beast turned away from them and flew across the cavern once again. Theadrin quickly sheathed his sword and struck his stones together again. The light found every corner of the huge cave.

They saw the massive beast flying low on the far side. Its wings were broad and leathery, its tail long and forked. A long muscled neck connected its snakelike head to the rest of its sleek, scaly body. On the back of its shoulders there was a small bulky object that seemed to be clinging to the beast.

But the winged beast was gone in a heartbeat as it shot upward and through a shaft in the roof of the cavern.

Theadrin and Yan stood in silence while the light began to diminish once again. The black beast did not return after long moments of waiting, and Theadrin could see there was no one else in the cave.

He turned to Yan. "Come. Caed is not here."

Yan was all too ready to leave and so they departed from the cavern the way they had come.

Back where Mathwin and Myran waited, they found conditions had worsened. Myran's eyes were closed and Mathwin was bent over him, trying to keep him from falling asleep. Myran's eyes flashed open when they entered, but Theadrin saw they were weighted down and weary.

"Caed?" Myran's voice had become weaker.

Theadrin shook his head. "We could not find him, but we can waste no more time. Let's be gone from here."

With Myran supported between Mathwin and Theadrin, they left the castle and made their way down the side of the Tor. The rain had reduced to a light sprinkle, and already the eastern sky was growing light.

At the bottom, they found the boat was still there and they helped Myran into it. On closer inspection they found it was not large enough to hold all of them at once, and they stood pondering what to do.

"Leave me behind," Myran said.

"I will not," Theadrin avowed. His mind was sprinting faster than a racehorse to find a solution. "We will all go home together," he said, but not with the confidence he needed.

"Theadrin, I would not last the journey." Myran's voice was weak, and Theadrin knew he was right. "The Avyrian village," Myran managed. "They may be able to help."

Theadrin did not say anything as the decision warred in his mind.

"I will take him," Mathwin offered. "We can come behind you when Myran is well again."

"All right." Theadrin hated the idea but was forced to realize that there was no other alternative if Myran was to have any chance at all. So he conceded. "Go with him, Mathwin. See that he is well looked after."

Theadrin ferried the two across the river with the boat and they helped Myran out onto the bank.

Theadrin hesitated. "I hate to go without you."

"You must!" When Myran said this, another seizure of pain gripped him and Theadrin watched helplessly as Myran winced and groaned.

"This is my fault," Theadrin said. "I am sorry."

Myran opened his eyes. "Theadrin, you must not believe so. It is a greater weight than you know." He blinked away the stinging sweat and looked deep in Theadrin's eyes. "Do you remember what Amlek said…back at the Tor?"

Theadrin knew what he was talking about. He crouched down before Myran and said, "There is no end to Amlek's lies."

"But he was right, Theadrin. Ao-idh's death was my fault." Myran blinked painfully up at him. "Before the fight began, I saw the sun glint off something metal behind me. I should have known it was enemy warriors…I should have told Ao-idh…but I did not. He died that day…because of me."

Myran's breath came in draws, but he continued, "Knowing it was my fault wounded me greater than any weapon could. It is such a heavy weight to carry…such a heavy weight."

He winced and a tear rolled down the side of his face. "I will understand if you do not want me at your side anymore, should I recover."

Theadrin looked at Myran with hard eyes and swallowed. Then his jaw set and he placed a firm hand on the side of Myran's head. Looking directly into his bronze eyes, Theadrin promised with great assurance, "There is no man that I trust more than you, Myran Cai. You have proven your quality many times over."

Myran looked back at him as rainwater, mixed with sweat, ran over his brow. His eyes were weary. Theadrin's words visibly gave him reassurance but still did not break the weight of guilt over him. "Farewell, Theadrin. Don't look back."

Theadrin had to fight back a surge of anguish from taking over him. "Until we meet again, brother."

The rain was gone and the sun erupted over the eastern hills. The storm clouds sailed away like giant ship sails of fiery gold, orange, and red. As the beautiful morning light reclaimed the land out of darkness, Theadrin paddled the boat back to where Yan still waited on the other side of the river. He did not feel in himself the peace that the new light might have brought. Grief greater than anything he ever knew before overwhelmed everything else.

He glanced up at the Tor, resting quietly in the soft light of morning. Green, rolling hills surrounded the mount and the river sparkled in the rising sun. For a brief moment, Theadrin felt a yearning deep inside him. This place was once the center of his people's kingdom; long ago when the seven tribes had lived in peace here. What a beautiful sight that castle would have been in the day it was clean and unbroken. *How long had evil resided there, twisting what was once good and pure into ugly darkness?* He wondered to himself. Would that same evil now take dominion over Arinon and Caledon?

Yan boarded the small vessel and the two started away, following the river south. The last view they saw of their friends was the two walking toward the forest, Myran's arm slung about Mathwin's neck.

As the morning grew late, thick fog settled over the river and forest. By midday they knew they would have to put ashore to find food, for their supply was greatly depleted. They ran the small boat up onto the pebbly shore and jumped out. Both knew it could take all day to hunt game and thus bring a long delay to their return journey, but they had to have food.

The gray-pebbled bank rolled out to the forest edge where green pines were only half visible in the white fog. Their bushy boughs materialized out of the gray haze and hung motionless and silent.

As they neared the tree line, a small man stepped out from among the fir branches. It was Tagin. He gripped a leather strap over his shoulder that connected to a large bundle. The fog swirled about his feet as he moved forward and slung the package from his back, landing it at Theadrin's feet.

"Bearded one says you have no food," he said simply. "This will last you many days."

Theadrin stooped to pick up the small, brown bundle. He would ask how Tagin had found them but knew such a thing was not difficult for the forest folk.

"How is Myran?" Theadrin asked. He was greatly encouraged to hear that he and Mathwin had made it to the village. Tagin did not answer right away, and his voice took on an edge of solemnity.

"There is black poison inside him. No herb or medicine we have can stop it."

Theadrin felt the words like a blow from a battle-ax. "You must do all you can."

Tagin looked sadly back at him before turning and disappearing into the misty forest again. An evergreen limb wagged up and down, dropping beads of rainwater to mark where he vanished.

Back on the water again, Theadrin tried to put Myran's bleak condition from his mind. "He is in your hands, mighty Healer," Theadrin prayed. He listened to the swirl of the oar in the water and closed his eyes. Things were becoming very dark and seemingly hopeless. He didn't know how things stood back in Arinon. Was Caithal still alive? Were *any* of his friends who went to war alive? Did the war go ill for them?

Amlek's plan was well thought out, but Theadrin could not imagine why he had waited all those years until now. What held him from taking control until this point?

Once again the oar dug deep into the water. Theadrin opened his eyes. Something in the sound of the paddling seemed to be nagging at him. He looked out over the fog-covered river and his heart froze.

That first night in these forests, he had heard something out on the water that he could not place, but now he knew. It was the sound of paddle in water, only there had been a lot of them. Who could it have been?

He remembered something Amlek had told him, "Their backs are turned to the stalking lion." Then it hit him. It was Amlek's army leaving the Tor: the barbarians of the north.

Thirty-Six

Thunder rolled over the plain as a thousand horsemen charged to battle. In the west the sky was bright crimson penetrated with spears of rusty gold. The towers of Avross gleamed in the dying light and its lofty banners streamed in the cooling wind. In the long stretching shadow of the great city, the armies clashed.

Instantly the battle clamor rose in a deafening roar. Anromir and Rhyd, at the head of their mounted warriors, drove fearlessly into the lines of Percel and Taromar. Anromir thrust as fast as he could with his spear, and when it snapped in two, he drew his sword and pressed on. The fighting was thick, and the charge had penetrated deep into the ranks of footmen.

When the advance had considerably slowed, Anromir and Rhyd turned their men around and fell back to re-form. The enemy footmen took this to be a retreat and pursued, but they were met with a deadly volley from Rhyd's longbowmen.

The horsemen formed and charged again. Although the odds were against Rhyd and Anromir five to one, the clash served to be devastating for Percel and Taromar's troops. The footmen stood against it only for a short time before turning and retreating toward the ridge. Anromir and Rhyd pursued and greatly cut down the number of foemen.

But when the tide seemed to be turning in their favor, the mounted enemy hit them in the side. Suddenly they were outnumbered again.

The clash of steel and the shouts and cries of men and horses filled Anromir's ears in the familiar but hated scream of battle. His muscles and joints ached and sweat streamed over his eyes. He swept aside a quick thrust of a foeman's sword and swiftly cut the enemy warrior from the saddle. Another struck his left, but his shield was there and ready. He lifted the battle-ax upward with his shield and stabbed underneath into the ribs of the man.

The next thing he knew, Rhyd was beside him. He parried a blow with his sword and hammered the assailant in the head with the rim of his shield, sending him from the saddle. Anromir looked back and realized that the rest of his men had been separated and the two lords were alone. Rhyd had seen what was happening and fought to his side.

Anromir saw their footmen had been engaged as well, but were quickly becoming outnumbered as more enemy warriors joined the fray. There were so many of them, Anromir wondered how he could have misjudged their numbers to begin.

Rhyd shouted something but his voice was drowned in the noisome din. He pointed with his red-stained sword, and Anromir saw that fresh troops were joining the battle under a different banner. It was another one of Gurn's nobles.

They could not fight so many, especially now that it was almost nightfall. Anromir signaled for Rhyd to fall back. Rhyd was already of the same mind, and together they carved a swath to rejoin their men. Side by side they charged through, protecting each other's backs, and the enemy could not bring them down.

When they were among their men once more, Anromir had his trumpeter signal to withdraw.

"I will cover the retreat!" Anromir yelled, and Rhyd rode off to direct the footmen.

Anromir rallied the horsemen and together they slowed the rush of the enemy army so Rhyd and the footmen could get away. Men were falling on all sides of him and soon he ordered the retreat for his mounted warriors. They fled exhausted up a ridge and Anromir halted to assess the situation.

He saw the enemy roiling below them like an angry, dark sea, and made out the banner of Lord Belrant. Once the two nobles had been friends and hunted together in summer's green forests. There had been a day when Anromir looked forward to and enjoyed the young lord's company. How dark was this day that saw them on opposing sides of the battlefield.

Anromir fought back the remorse of such a travesty and spurred his horse away.

They retreated through the night and managed to get to Caulguard and regroup behind the safety of its walls. It was then they realized how devastating the battle had been for them. Their numbers had been cut in half.

News flew throughout the keep of their coming and it was not long before Lianna was there with Ellia. The two women stood atop the flight of stairs that led up to the main door of the keep and scanned the tired and battle-grim faces.

Anromir emerged from the throng of warriors with Rhyd at his side and wearily climbed the stairs. Ellia was in his arms in an instant, ignoring the dirt and grime of battle.

"What has happened?" she asked.

"The war has gone ill," he answered. "But let me see the men are given places to rest and then we will talk." So saying, he called to Brond to set a guard on the walls and ordered his chamberlain to bring food and drink for the men.

Then they went inside the keep, and Anromir briefly told of all that had taken place—how Caledon had been invaded, forcing King Brudwyn to withdraw his men from Arinon. He expected that an attack on Caulguard was imminent. As he finished speaking through exhausted breaths, Anromir unbuckled the straps of his breastplate and let it clatter to the floor. Already he had cast aside his helmet. Then he slumped wearily into a chair.

"And still no sign of Theadrin." Lianna's worried tone did not go unnoticed.

"That is no cause to lose hope, my lady," Rhyd encouraged as he took a seat beside Anromir.

"Indeed," Anromir agreed. "We will continue to fight; and though we may be outmanned, courage will make up the difference." As he spoke, however, the exhaustion and despair was clear in his voice. He wiped a tired hand over his eyes.

After several moments of regaining an easy flow of breath, he inquired, "How is Caithal? Is there any improvement?"

"None, my lord," Lianna answered sadly.

Anromir accepted the report with a slow, grim nod. Ellia, resting on a stool beside him, urged her husband to get some sleep. He brushed aside her attempts and rose slowly, straightening his back. "I must check on my men first, and the watch."

The expected siege did not come directly. Instead, a different sort of army set upon them. Beginning the following day, in late afternoon, the first trickle began. Over the country came farmers, and men of other trades. There were blacksmiths, merchants, innkeepers, tanners, potters, and more. All of these, families along with them, came to be sheltered in Caulguard.

The stories of all were one and the same. Gurn's army had turned to pillaging the countryside. All who were suspected of treason against Gurn had been attacked, and that number was rising every day. They heard that Caulguard was the only safe house left for them.

But Anromir's keep was not big enough to hold so many people.

"We cannot stay hidden behind these walls," Anromir insisted, and Rhyd agreed readily.

"We will ride out," he declared. The young nobleman was never one to cringe.

"But we have so few men," Ellia fretted. "How can you stop them?"

"Arinon's people are under attack. Who is there but us to defend them?" Anromir said. "And how selfish would we be to hide behind these walls when they have nowhere to run to? Caulguard can hold no more. We must go."

Rhyd stood, his eagerness getting the better of him. "I will form the units."

The men seemed just as eager to go. They also had seen how many were being put out of their homes and heard the stories they brought of how they had barely escaped, or how their loved ones had been cruelly put to the sword. They heard of the burning of villages and homes, and now were more than ready to fight once again.

Before the sun was yet in mid sky, the two rode out of the keep as a strong western breeze rolled across the green fields. Lianna stood on the wall above the gatehouse and watched as they crossed the river and joined the main road to the capitol city.

She hated all this waiting, and felt completely helpless sitting there in the keep. She wanted to do something, but realized with dismay that there was nothing she could do.

The road took the two men behind the hills and Lianna sighed.

"It is hard." The soft voice beside her drew Lianna away from her thoughts. She looked over to see that Ellia had joined her. The woman watched the road bend where her husband had disappeared from view and shook her head slowly.

"The men like to think that they have the hardest job; riding off to their battles and wars. But they do not know what it is to have to wait for so long, hoping and praying that their loved ones will come back." Ellia gazed at the distant road. She knew what Lianna was feeling and tried her best to help.

Lianna looked at her dear friend and could only nod her agreement. Ellia gazed sadly after her husband and then wrapped her in an affectionate embrace.

"Dearest Lianna, one day it will all be worth it."

⧗

Gurn knelt, bound in heavy chains, before the dark-haired Vithimere. He glowered up into the younger man's face and spat.

"Curse you, Vithimere!" He raged. "You are a traitor!"

Vithimere's eyes gloated and he allowed a jeering chuckle. "You are an ignorant fool, Gurn! How could you be so blind? Amlek set you up for this before the night of Valdithin's death. Your usefulness has come to an end."

"I still have an army," Gurn snarled.

"You had an army. Yet what is left of them is now against you; they never were truly for you."

"What do you mean?"

"He means, Lord Gurn, me." A tall figure stepped from the shadows.

Gurn's eyes widened. "Percel! But we were as brothers!"

Vithimere's eyes flashed with sudden fury at Gurn's words. He swung his arm sharply and slapped Gurn across the temple with the back of his hand. "Do not speak of brothers, Gurn! You who had a brother, a true brother, but killed him! You betrayed him as you betray anyone when it is in your best interest. Well, now, how does it feel to be on the other side of things?"

Gurn looked at Vithimere with narrowed eyes. Then slowly they widened as the realization hit him. "Is it…but it can't be." Fear drained the color in his face.

Vithimere straightened and glanced at Lord Percel. "Leave us."

The man bowed and left the room. Vithimere watched the doorway by which he left for a time and then turned to Gurn once again, drawing his dagger.

Thirty-Seven

Anromir sent scouts to discover where the nearest enemy troops were located. It was a humid day—gray clouds scraped the sky and what breeze there was provided no relief from the heat.

Anromir and Rhyd rode at the head of the long column of warriors listening silently to the knock and clink of the men's armor as they moved. Their enthusiasm began to disappear as the heat wore at them unrelentingly.

"Hard weather for a battle," Rhyd observed after a time.

"Aye. Days like this were meant to enjoy in the cool of one's own home," Anromir agreed, wiping sweat from the side of his face.

"I shall look forward to doing so with you when things are aright once more," Rhyd told his friend. "With cool drinks in hand, we will look back on this and talk of what brave feats of heroism were accomplished."

One of the scouts returned and reported seeing a small configuration of enemy troops pillaging some small farms to the west. Directly after, another scout came back and told of a larger force amassing outside the town of Lundel.

It was quickly agreed that Anromir would lead sixty of his mounted warriors to save the farms and then rejoin Rhyd and the main body of warriors who would march to the defense of Lundel.

It didn't take Anromir long to reach the farms, and he caught the enemy by surprise. He and his men made quick work of them and when the short fight was over, one of the farmers spoke with Anromir. He was an older man, white haired but strong.

"We are indebted to ye, my lord," he said gratefully in a rough voice.

"We are only doing what is required of us," he replied. Another farmer was not as friendly.

"Indebted indeed! We were foolish to trust in these men." He glared up at Anromir. "Where is Theadrin? Eh? Run away just as the fighting starts? A coward I say. We need someone else to lead us!"

"Peace, Jaimus! Do not rant so! Ye disgrace yerself," the other farmer chastised.

"The only way I have disgraced myself is trusting that cowardly son of Valdithin!"

"Where is your faith, man?" the raspy voiced farmer rebuked. It was clear he was completely incensed, but not altogether surprised, at his friend's disposition. "I talk of faith in the Highest King. He will fulfill his purpose through this son of Valdithin or another."

"The Highest King," the farmer growled in disgust. "I say he is just like Theadrin, a coward who hides away and cares nothing for anyone."

"I have heard enough, Jaimus! Be ye gone off my property. I will not have it soiled by the feet of a blasphemer!"

"Ha! You are deceived if you think any one of us owns anything. Gurn has it all. But I will go all the same." The impudent man began to walk away.

Anromir had remained silent in the saddle, allowing the argument to take its course. He was discouraged by what Jaimus had said.

He addressed the other man. "You show yourself to be a good man. What is your name?"

"Call me Beorn, sire."

"Has your friend always been so?" Anromir asked, glancing at the direction Jaimus had gone.

"Not always, milord. But the pain of such devastation and hate has driven all sense from him. There are many others like him, I am afraid. Since Theadrin disappeared, there have been many unkind and disloyal murmurings. I do not take part in them," Beorn assured him.

"Your brave and faithful loyalty will not go unnoticed, my friend," Anromir smiled.

"Thank ye very kindly, milord. But my reward will be to see peace in this fair land once again. I have no use for riches or powerful position. I would be discontent with anything more than my place here. My heart's desire for the rest of my life is to live free to serve the Highest King with my wife at my side, and to watch my children and grandchildren grow to work the land in my place. All I want is freedom."

Anromir was amazed and refreshed at this man's easy sincerity and simple desire. "If only every man had your heart."

With that, Anromir bid him farewell and took the road to Lundel where Rhyd was undoubtedly already engaged. Riding silent at the head of his mounted warriors, he could not get his conversation with the farmer from his mind. What could he do to persuade the people that Theadrin had not abandoned them? Alas, only Theadrin's return would. But could that, even now, change the people's hearts?

Thirty-Eight

The small, brown vessel floated gently down the middle of the river under a sweltering sun. Yan, in the back of the boat, dug the oar into the muddy water every now and again to keep them going at a fine pace, though the river current did most of the work.

Theadrin was at the prow, staring southward with an anxious gaze. Nothing could make the time speed up or make them go any slower. Amlek was surely already at Avross putting his plan to work. What Theadrin would do once he arrived there, however, he did not know. He did not have the King Sword. What could he do to stop Amlek?

If only I had gone north sooner, he thought to himself, shaking his head slowly in despair. Perhaps if he had listened to Caithal right away he would have had more time; perhaps he could have stopped Amlek from going to Arinon. Maybe Myran wouldn't have been poisoned. These thoughts weighed heavily on him.

Afternoon turned to evening, and the sun disappeared in a brilliant blue and gold display behind a wall of clouds on the western horizon. The moon was full and shone a pallid yellow in the east. The brown and barren landscape of Baremar gave way to the green grass and flourishing forests of Arinon. In the dwindling light of the evening, the land took on a fresh and serene atmosphere.

The silent hills were multishaded with deep, undulating tones; they faded from emerald into a bluer hue like the deep of the sea. The trees were of the darkest shade, almost black, and the moon highlighted their branching arms silvery green.

A light evening breeze filled Theadrin's lungs with a familiar smell, and it occurred to him how much he had missed that land. He realized how badly he wanted to see his sister again. Lianna's smiling face would be a warm welcome that he looked forward to. But then, Theadrin's shoulders slumped. He would have to tell her what happened to Myran. He had not failed to notice the way she was around him; unusually silent, and acting more grown up than when he wasn't around.

At least he could bring the hope that he was with the Avyrian, who were masters of medicine. But Tagin had not given him hope. Would it be better to just tell her that he wasn't coming back? Would false hope, in the end, be worse?

The dark folds of night came on quickly once the sun was gone and Theadrin turned to spell Yan at the oar. He stepped to the back of the boat, and the craft swayed from side to side with each stride. Yan had fallen asleep. At the rocking of the boat he came awake with a jerk, and his hands flew straight out as though he was falling.

Coming to his senses, he looked about irritably before noticing Theadrin standing before him.

"I will take over, Yan," he said.

Yan protested Theadrin's offer. "Ya need rest more'n I." But he could not hold back the yawn.

"I could not sleep if I tried," Theadrin insisted. "My mind has too much to contemplate." Yan relented and settled himself in the bow of the boat.

Theadrin worked at his task of rowing with vigor through the night. The full moon was bright on the land and gleamed pearly white off the gentle ripples of the river water. The peaceful serenity calmed Theadrin's disgruntled spirit. On such a beautiful night, not even Yan's loud snores and snorts did much to ruin it.

However, morning light found him no more ready for rest. Yan woke to find the boat had been beached and Theadrin was unloading what few supplies they had onto the wet sandy stretch.

"I was just going to wake you," he said. "We have a long day before us."

They had reached the foothills of the Aegris mountains and would have to continue on foot the rest of the way, for the river from there entered the mountain range and either emptied into lakes or dissipated into smaller streams.

"Will we be goin' ta Caulguard first?" Yan asked in a gruff morning voice as he stepped unsteadily from the boat.

"I think it would be wise," Theadrin replied.

"That's a fair journey t'make on foot," Yan observed wryly, rubbing the sleep from his eyes.

"We will barter along the way for some horses," Theadrin promised his reluctant friend.

"I s'pose we don't have ta worry bout money. When we say it is Theadrin who's needin' the horse it'll be given freely." Yan smiled.

"That we cannot do," Theadrin suddenly warned. Yan looked at him questioningly. Theadrin began to explain, "We have no idea what has taken place here since our departure, and thus we do not know how the people's loyalties rest. I think it best not to mention who I am just yet."

The first farm that they came to had no horses. And what was more, there was no cattle, sheep, or pigs. They wondered at this but did not stop. For the first several that they passed it was the same story. At last, by midday, they came across one that humbly boasted two scraggly looking horses in its pasture.

They both agreed it was worth an attempt and so came to the house and knocked.

"What do you want?" a challenging voice called out. "Answer me quick!" the voice came again, this time more agitated.

"We have come to barter for your horses," Theadrin called back.

"They are not for sale!" The voice became louder as the door opened enough to reveal a gray, bearded face.

"We have a long journey before us," Theadrin started the process for bartering.

"I know where you are going," the farmer interrupted, indignant that they should think him slow witted. They were taken off guard at this.

"How can you?" Theadrin wondered. "We have not met before."

"Because everyone in the kingdom is going to Avross," the farmer retaliated, still incensed, like they thought him dumb.

"But we're not bound fer Avross," Yan blurted out.

"Ye think telling a lie will make me more apt to sell ye my only horses?" the farmer threw back.

"But it's the very truth, we here'r bound fer Caulguard." This quieted the farmer.

"Had ye said any other place, I would not have believed ye," he said in a more mysterious manner. "Jest who are ye fella's?"

Yan looked at Theadrin and knew that he had said too much already. Theadrin confirmed it with a chastising glance. Then he said, "We are friends of Lord Anromir's. It has been long since we have seen one another."

"What about Theadrin," the farmer's words came unexpectedly, "are you friends of his too?"

Theadrin thought a moment. "We feel no ill will toward him."

The farmer studied them. After a few tense moments, he said, "I can see ye hold no lie. I don't mind sayin' I'm loyal to Theadrin as good King Valdithin's son and heir. That's why I'm here and not in Avross."

"What is going on that so many go to the great city?" Theadrin wondered.

"Too much, an I don't rightly understand it all. All I can say is everyone is talkin' of some newcomer who has saved Arinon from Gurn. We all know it is not Theadrin, the fella's too old."

Theadrin swallowed. "What do you mean by being saved from Gurn?"

"Ye really have been away for a long time. Gurn went insane, it's the very truth. After Caledon's army left he jest tore into the kingdom in a fit. Killed many, destroyed even more. Then this new fella arrives"—the man scratched his bearded chin—"I don't know much about him but that many people are ready to follow him. Not me though; I am loyal to Theadrin, and to the Highest King. This newcomer doesn't sound right in any way. There are tales of him possessing powerful sorcery."

A rock seemed to have settled in Theadrin's stomach. He knew whom the farmer was talking about. He realized then that Amlek had been waiting for the time when Gurn had so enslaved and terrorized the people that he could come as their savior. With the name of Amlek already introduced to most of Arinon, Theadrin feared the people would readily accept him.

"Thank you for the news," he said and stepped closer to the man. "We also are humble servants of the Lord and have pressing business in Caulguard that pertains to your story."

"If I knew it would help ye get there faster, I would lend ye my horses, but I am afraid they would slow ye down rather than speed yer course. They're both lame and weak."

"Thank you," Theadrin smiled. "You are a good man, my friend. The Highest King sees your loyalty, and may he reward it."

The farmer wasn't sure what to say at Theadrin's words. He studied Theadrin as though he saw something familiar in his face. "I do have a friend who lives down the road a ways. He owns two good horses." He frowned quizzically. "Where'd ye say ye was from?"

Theadrin smiled and looked him in the eye. "Arinon is my home, as it was the home of my father."

Then the farmer realized with whom he was speaking. He personally brought them to the farm of his friend and got horses for them. Theadrin thanked the man, and he and Yan left.

Later they came across a barn that had been burnt to the ground; only a charred, broken skeleton remained of the structure. The marks of what the farmer told them about was evident everywhere. Gurn had raged against them and, whether he knew it or not, had set up Amlek's plan perfectly. Theadrin's mind went back to the vision of the dark storm. The darkness had descended on Arinon already. It came with Amlek, and it was engulfing Avross. Soon there would be nowhere in all Arinon that it did not cover.

He knew he had to get to Caulguard with all haste, and from there on he would trust in the great and mighty King for further guidance. Still, fear tugged at his heart. What could he use to rally the people without the King Sword?

Thirty-Nine

Anromir met Rhyd outside of Lundel. Rhyd and his companies had routed Gurn's warriors, led by Lord Belrant. In the shade of a wooded hillside, they conferred on what action to take next.

"My scouts report enemy movements everywhere. We will spread ourselves too thin trying to combat all of them at once," Rhyd stated grimly.

Anromir stood in silent contemplation, stroking his dark beard and frowning. Above them the bows of a great maple sighed gently in a breeze rich with the smells of midsummer.

"What say you, Anromir?" Rhyd asked.

"What area occupies the largest force of Gurn's men?"

Rhyd scanned the map in his hand. "They are hitting the hardest here; mostly Taromar's warriors."

Anromir leaned in to look. "Manivry. Let us first go there then."

Rhyd agreed and gave the call to mount up. The village of Manivry was north of Lundel. When they arrived in the region, Anromir reined his horse to a stop at the crest of a ridge and put up a fist to halt his men. Rhyd joined him and together they considered the mass of enemy assembled for battle on the next hill.

"Scouts must have warned them of our approach," Anromir gathered and squinted at the banner displayed among them. "Taromar."

"I wish I could see what was beyond that dell," Rhyd indicated a niche between the opposite ridge where Taromar was and another tree-capped knoll. "I would feel better to know what kind of animal is lurking there."

Anromir nodded and swept his gaze over the scene before them. "I will take care of Taromar. If there is an army hidden in the dell, you wait until they show…"

"On the contrary, Anromir," Rhyd interrupted, "I will take the front. You, meanwhile, circle around to the dell and smoke out any skunk that is slinking there."

"You have the best bowmen in the entire kingdom, but my men are trained for the frontline," Anromir argued.

Rhyd would not hear of it. "Do not doubt our capability with the sword. Every man of Averby is trained with the sword as equally as the bow."

"I do not doubt that, my brave friend," Anromir insisted. "I do not speak against your skill in hand-to-hand, for I have seen it proven many times. But my men are certainly not the archers that yours are. *You* could better accomplish the task of varmint hunting than I."

Rhyd finally agreed reluctantly to Anromir's plan. "Assemble your men across the crown of this hill then. I will move behind you and out of Taromar's sight."

They did so, Rhyd leaving behind one company of bowmen. Anromir formed his warriors in ranks and unsheathed his sword at their head. "Mounted warriors first, then footmen! Archers advance!" Rhyd's longbow men moved forward and knocked arrows to their strings.

"Ready! Release arrows!" Instantly one hundred oak shafts sailed into the sky, hanging for a brief instant before falling in a rain of death upon their foes. Taromar retaliated with a volley of his own, but his bowmen could not shoot the distance that Rhyd's could. His line began to move back to avoid the missiles of the longbow men.

Satisfied, Anromir ordered the horsemen to charge. The longbow men covered them with three more volleys. Anromir followed behind his mounted warriors in front of his footmen. They gained the crest of the hill just as the horsemen pulled back after engaging the enemy. Anromir and his men slammed into Taromar's lines with a mighty shout.

Meanwhile, Rhyd led the rest of his archers on foot through the valleys and out of sight of Taromar on the hill. Before reaching the hidden dell, he sent his two most stealthy warriors to scout ahead. They returned to confirm Rhyd's suspicions of an ambush.

Rhyd and his warriors crept cautiously toward the place, stopping to hide in the trees when the enemy came into view. Quietly, each man set an arrow to the string. The enemy warriors were forming to move against Anromir.

Leaning against the rough bark of a red oak, Rhyd clicked the knock of his arrow onto the flax bowstring. He wrapped three fingertips around it and pulled. Bows groaned quietly as three hundred men took aim. Breath released slowly, and then the dell was alive with the terrifying whistle. The enemy was clearly startled and panic settled over them as another volley of death showered down.

Back on the ridgetop, Anromir's horsemen circled back and hit Taromar's ranks in the side. Anromir pressed deep to reach Taromar, surrounded by his best warriors. He cut through the first two in one fast maneuver and bored through two more before facing Taromar.

They clashed blades, and Taromar looked in the direction of the dell. He saw that no help was coming. He turned his roan and fled, escaping into the press of his men. Anromir and his warriors surged against Taromar's quickly routing army. It was not long before it was an all-out retreat. Anromir paused and spotted Taromar fleeing down the slope then gave chase.

No enemy warrior turned aside to hinder him. The horse soared over a rock protruding from the grass and closed the gap on the fleeing noble. Anromir stood in the stirrups and launched himself off onto the back of Taromar, pulling him from his horse. They both hit the ground hard and rolled. Anromir was up first. Taromar clumsily parried the first few attacks but was no match in skill to the younger lord. One quick thrust ended his traitorous life.

After the battle Anromir and Rhyd moved their beleaguered army westward. The sun was almost beneath the horizon as the pale glow of evening began to settle over the hills. They were making their way through a forest when Rhyd came to a stop. Anromir turned about and questioned, "What is it?"

Rhyd's head was cocked to the side, attempting to draw out any sound in the forest. His eyes turned to Anromir and then to the tree branch above. "Look out!" Rhyd cried with alarm as he threw a hand to his sword.

Anromir was hit off his saddle from behind. With a short struggle, he threw the enemy warrior off and wrestled his sword from its scabbard. From the trees and bushes instantly swarmed a great number of warriors with the crest of Lord Percel. They surrounded them in a heartbeat. They fought the swarms of Percel's troops but as many as they slew, it seemed two more sprang up in their place. They fought valiantly and dropped a score but there were just too many, and soon the fight was finished.

Forty

Theadrin and Yan rode over the green hills of Arinon on the horses that the farmer had lent them. Trying to keep their presence as unknown as possible, they had ridden south for Caulguard. It was late morning now, and they mounted a grassy, bare-topped hill and saw the gleaming towers of Avross to the west. They stopped and observed it for a while.

"He is there," Theadrin said, leaning on the saddle horn and half squinting against the sun.

Yan looked at him in question. Theadrin explained. "Amlek is in that city, preparing for his final move. The time is short."

After several moments more, they started on their way again. By midday they were in sight of Anromir's keep. As they were crossing the river, Theadrin suddenly reigned up. He surveyed Caulguard's walls with a frown.

"Is somethin' wrong?" Yan asked, halting his mount alongside Theadrin's and peering at the stone keep.

"I'm not sure," Theadrin answered. "There seem to be a lot of guards atop the walls." He shrugged. "Come on."

They left the bridge and covered the rest of the distance to the main gate at a trot. A guard addressed them from above, questioning who they were.

"Theadrin's returned!" Yan shouted back up. "Open the blasted gates, man!"

"Can it be?" The guard disappeared from view. His voice carried over the wall as he shouted orders to the other men.

Theadrin could hear as the call was sent across the yard of the keep about his arrival. He studied the abandoned buildings outside the walls while he waited, wondering what had caused them to hide behind locked gates.

Presently, the thick wooden doors began to groan and creak as they opened. Theadrin led the way through and was met by a massive rush of warriors and others joining the throng. All wanted to see for themselves if it was really true that Theadrin had returned. Brond, who had spoken to them from the walls, led the mass of men. "Praise the High King! It really is you!" he exclaimed happily. Joyful cheers rose from the warriors when they saw him. Theadrin was taken aback at the moving welcome.

Inside the walls he noted how crowded the place was. There were makeshift dwellings and tents erected everywhere to shelter the people who were occupying every space about. Men and women, dirty and haggard, were grouped around cooking fires and children ran here and there, smeared with mud.

The crowd press thickened as people saw and came eagerly to see Theadrin. He could see in their eyes the destruction that had taken place in Arinon. They were a people who had suffered much—enduring torture, loss of loved ones, the burning of their homes. Theadrin's heart grieved deeply to see them.

He dismounted and was nearly carried along to the front door of the keep. When it opened, his sister's face was the first that appeared. She seemed hesitant at first, as though she did not recognize him, but it was gone in an instant.

"Lianna!" Theadrin exclaimed as she rushed into his brotherly embrace. "How I have missed you, my dear sister," he said happily as he held her for a moment.

"And I you." She squeezed him tightly. "So much has happened, and it seems you have been gone for years." Theadrin noticed her eyes stray behind him for a brief instant when she backed away.

"I want to hear it all," he said and began to step into the hall of the keep. "Where is Anromir?"

"He rode out yesterday; he and lord Rhyd," Lianna answered, glancing behind her brother again.

"On what business?"

Lianna seemed not to hear him at first. "To... to free the people from Gurn's men. That is why there are so many seeking shelter behind Caulguard's walls. Their homes have been burned, many of their loved ones killed."

"I must learn what has happened in my absence here. Will you tell me?"

"Of course. I will do my best to remember everything." The glance behind him was lingering this time and Theadrin knew who she was looking for.

"I must tell you something, Lianna," he began. "But let us get away so we can be alone." So saying he turned to the crowd gathered behind him, eager to hear of his journey, and dismissed them with the promise to recount it over supper that evening.

Many protested, not wanting to wait. Brond stepped forward and stated, "Theadrin is weary after his journey. You will learn all you want tonight, but for now we must let him get his well-deserved rest."

He and Lianna then made their way out to the garden. They strolled among the colorful flowers and fragrant bushes in silence until Theadrin was sure they were alone. He stopped and faced his younger sister. She looked back at him with worried eyes, knowing he bore terrible news.

Theadrin drew a breath and began. "Lianna, in the north we faced many dangers, but there was one we could not overcome." Lianna's eyes were already brimming with unshed tears; she knew what he was trying to say.

"Myran was poisoned, in the ruins atop the Tor." Theadrin said, and the first single tear broke out and rolled down his sister's cheek.

Theadrin forced himself to continue. "I hate to be the one to bring you such pain. I know that you loved him. And he was a true brother to me."

Lianna, unable to speak, went to a white, stone-carved bench. She sat down, dropping her head down to rest in her hand. Theadrin stood for a moment before joining her. He put his arm about her shoulders.

"I am sorry, Lianna."

With only a brief hesitation, she gave into his consoling and buried her head in his chest. Gentle, silent sobs shook her shoulders. Theadrin could think of nothing more to say. He could only be there with her.

That evening, after washing and dressing in new clothes, Theadrin fulfilled his promise and told the people of his journey. They listened in eager silence. When he re-counted the part of going to the Tor and meeting Amlek, he told the people that Amlek was behind Gurn's evil and had come to Avross.

One man seated at a table close to Theadrin's spoke up. "There are two! Two men have come!"

Theadrin frowned at this. Amlek was alone when Theadrin saw him. "Can you describe them to me?"

"One I have not seen," the man answered. "But the second is young and acts as the other's voice. He is called Vithimere."

"That's right!" another man called from the assembly. "He says that this other man, whom we have not seen, is the one who has saved us from Gurn!"

Theadrin told them he knew nothing of Vithimere, but that the other was surely Amlek.

Then one of the soldiers stood and asked. "What did you find at the Tor? Do you have the King Sword?"

What did you find? Theadrin swallowed. He had not found the King Sword as he hoped he would. What could he tell these people now?

It was then he heard a silent voice deep within him. It was not audible, but spoke to his heart, and he knew it was the Highest King. He stood slowly.

Readjusting his composure, Theadrin said, "I have found that which will conquer. Is it a physical item? No. However, it took me going to the Tor to discover it. There I learned the identity of our true enemy. He uses well-crafted deception. He comes in the guise of a hero and a savior, but behind it he is a raging lion ready to devour us all."

Theadrin was at first speaking uncertainly, for he didn't know exactly where he was going. Still he found that he was never at a loss for words. As he spoke the words came to him clearly, and he began to warm to his speech and delivered it with increasing vigor.

"It is not the King Sword that will save us from this darkness. For that is only an object. My friends, Arinon has lost its course. It was founded upon a solid rock. The Highest King is the foundation of all that this fair kingdom has ever before held dear and true. But then we slipped. It was a slow, gradual fall and it is just now coming to a collision.

"Can we stop this plummet? No, we cannot. The crash is inevitable now. There are jagged rocks below us that will shatter us without mercy, and without hope. But"—he gazed with confidence over the fearful but hopeful faces—"there are everlasting arms that wait to catch us. They have always been there, waiting, hoping that we will open our eyes and call for help. Our King has never abandoned us. He alone is the One who can save Arinon. Does this mean that we don't have to do anything? By all means, no! Our weapon is the sword of truth! It is sharper than any sword we can craft. Only truth is sharp enough to penetrate the deception, like rays of light on an overcast day. And in the end… we will have victory."

"What do we have to do?" a woman asked.

"We must take a stand. When the time comes to go to Avross, we will set ourselves apart from those who would follow Amlek. We will declare the truth. But"—Theadrin paused to gather himself for what he knew he had to say—"I cannot guarantee that we will return. It is likely that no one else will stand with us, and we may lose our lives."

Every face was alarmed at this. One man said, "What do you mean? I thought you said we would have victory."

"Victory is certain for the faithful," Theadrin told them. "Even in death. If we stand to the end for our King, we've already won—even before the fight."

With that, Theadrin ended his speech and sat down.

The evening progressed with a more serious tone and Theadrin learned, from Brond, of the departure of King Brudwyn and the Caledonians and of Sir Dathin's betrayal. He should have seen it before.

Lianna had not attended the meal, and Theadrin did not blame her. But he did grow worried for Anromir and Rhyd. There was no word from them, and he asked Ellia if she knew when they were to return.

"I cannot say," she told him, worry marking her tone. "Oh, Theadrin, you don't think something has happened to them, do you?"

"Don't fear for them, Ellia. It is the enemy that should have cause to fear when Anromir and Rhyd ride together." Theadrin spoke to encourage her and keep her from worrying, but he did not throw aside the matter himself.

After dinner he went to see Caithal. His friend appeared the same as Theadrin had left him. He lay on the bed, resting quietly. Theadrin did not stay long and walked out onto the stone-paved dais overlooking the keep's garden when he came upon Cadi. She was just coming up the stairs from playing in the garden with some other children, but their mothers had called them to bed.

"It is getting late, Cadi," he said with a smile. "You should be in bed."

"I was waiting for Lianna to get back," she said with a yawn.

"Oh? Where has she gone to?" Theadrin asked.

Cadi shrugged and brushed aside a lock of golden hair from her sleepy eyes. "She went riding before dinner."

"She didn't say where she was going?" Theadrin suddenly became alarmed that she was not back yet at this hour.

"No. She said she wanted to be alone but would be back soon." The young girl was about to continue but a heavy yawn took over.

"Go to bed now, Cadi. I'll find Lianna and send her to kiss you goodnight." Theadrin saw her to her room, then made his way to the gatehouse. The guard there saluted him and asked if he might be of assistance.

"Has my sister gone out riding today?"

"Yes, indeed, my lord," the guard answered, happy to be of assistance. "The lady Lianna left a little before sundown."

"Has she returned yet?" Theadrin asked.

The guard's face grew serious. "No, my Lord. Not through this gate; but I'm sure she must have at the postern gate, sir."

Theadrin thanked the man and went directly there, but the guard at that gate had not seen Lianna. Theadrin waited until the sun sank into the western horizon. Something had happened to her. There was no other excuse for her to be gone past dark. So Theadrin rode out with Yan to search. After first talking with the gateman they learned that she had gone north. Joining the main road they followed it for a fair distance. Then they left it and mounted a nearby hill to survey the surrounding country.

"She coulda gone anywhere," Yan said. "If we only had a' idea where ta look."

Theadrin turned his face north. Over the hills, just out of sight, the city of Avross rested. Could she have gone there? But why would she? It made no sense. Yet something deep inside told him to go there.

"I must go to Avross," Theadrin finally said, and after thinking a moment longer, told Yan, "I want you to return to Caulguard."

"What?!" Yan was incredulous.

"Let me finish. Anromir and Rhyd have not returned and now Lianna is missing. It is time to finish this; whether we win or lose. You must go to Caulguard and muster the army. Tell the people that, if they will stand, the time is now. I must ride on to Avross." Theadrin looked back at Yan and knew his friend did not like the idea of leaving his side.

Yan nodded and reluctantly turned his horse around. "I'll meet ya there as soon as I can." He saluted, spurred his horse, and galloped back down the slope.

Theadrin rejoined the road and made his way to Arinon's capitol. He set a swift pace and was soon in sight of the walls. The plains surrounding the mighty fortress were covered with the camps of thousands of people.

⧖

Lianna left Caulguard just before the sun touched the west. She rode her gray mare across the river and into the countryside off the road. All she wanted was to disappear and never be heard from again.

The sun washed amber over the green, grazed turf. Already the chorus of frogs chanted from the marshy lowland below the knoll she stopped on. Hills smoked golden mist until the sun slipped at last under the western ridge. In the immense expanse of sky, purple and orange clouds pulled into the radiant, blazing orb. Their rich colors painted the surface of the puddle mire below. A cool evening breeze pushed the wet boggy scent up the slope toward her.

Lianna dismounted and ambled several paces aimlessly before collapsing to her knees as she gave in to the weight of her grief.

"Why?" she cried out loud to the Highest King. "Why did you take him now? Why now?"

Her tear-streamed face turned upward to the painted sky. She could make no sense as to why. It seemed to her now that her whole life had died with Myran.

With her anguish mounting she again cried aloud. "If he must be taken, then take me as well! There is no purpose for me! Take me too…" her voice trailed off to be replaced with sobs.

"I have a purpose for you." The whisper seemed to blow past her on the gust of wind. Lianna was a bit startled by it and quickly looked about to see who was on the hill with her. She was alone.

Wiping her eyes, the memory came of when Theadrin told her about his vision of the Highest King. Was this voice the voice of the Highest King?

The words brought a bittersweet feeling; bitter, for they implied she would not get her request; sweet, for she now felt a new touch. The touch gave the feeling of a love she had never truly known before. This Great King cared for her. Although she had heard this many times, she had never really known it, until now.

Still mourning and with tear-filled eyes, she whispered, "Your will…I will abide by your will."

A horse nickered down the hill and she turned sharply toward it. Three riders were mounting the slope and coming directly at her.

Acting quickly, she grabbed the reigns of her mare and swung up into the saddle. She turned its head and set it to running, but by then they were already upon her.

Forty-One

Myran's eyes fluttered open. Above him the oak boughs shifted in the soft, sighing wind, and the leaves voiced their rustling refrain back. It was a familiar sound, calming and peaceful to him. He felt, in the forest-scented breeze, a small remnant of familiarity that he once knew when living with Ao-idh and Caed in Arinon's green forests. He closed his eyes, oblivious to anything else around him. He did not know where he was, nor did he care.

His mind drifted as a sweet sleep overcame him. The next thing he knew he was standing at the edge of a green forest glade. Large, gray rocks clothed in moss of the richest green were strewn about a brook of liquid crystal. The stream sang a pleasing melody. In the glade a light that was of the purest gold shone down into the emerald haze that hung about the glen.

Myran looked toward the stream, and it took several moments before it dawned on him that there was someone at the water's edge. A man stood there on the opposite side. Myran thought he should know the man but could not make out the face from the distance between them.

The man turned and strode across the green glen and disappeared amidst the trees. Myran followed. He splashed across the stream and ran through the forest glade.

Moving deftly in and among the trees Myran soon found himself looking out across a vast green country. He stood on a high hill with a trim, grassy slope. At the edge was formed a jagged rock outcropping. There was a large river that snaked between the hill he was on and the country beyond.

That land, set vastly before him like the most beautiful picture, rose and fell in hills, bluffs, and mountains. Waterfalls abounded, and he could see their soft, white showers in roaring plummet and the mist that was spewed from them. Fruit trees in eternal blossom of white, pink, and a host of other colors swayed in the scented breeze among varied other trees of the most vivid hues of green.

But the thing that arrested his attention was far out on the horizon. There, rising from the haze, was a large mountain crowned by a white, jeweled city. The city was wrapped in golden light and was larger than any he had seen—even Avross—and much more beautiful. Towers rose from within, and from their peeks fluttered colorful banners on a sweet, steady breeze.

Music emanated from it; the clear ringing of silver trumpets. It was, without comparison, the most beautiful sound that had ever reached his ears. The music caused sweet tears to well up in his eyes. Although he was sure he had never seen such a place, he became aware of a strong sense of belonging. This was home. The city, or something within, cast a beautiful light over the country. The river caught the light and glinted like liquid bronze entwined with molten gold.

There was a fragrance on the breeze that carried with it complete familiarity. The scent was fresh and clean, like the first warm thaw of spring, mixed with the flowering perfume of budding fruit trees. It bore the aroma of a warm summer night when the fireflies dance and light up the forests and fields. There was also the crispness of a cool autumn day when the leaves are all colored like fire, and a hint of the bright winter night when the full moon illumines off the fresh fallen snow.

Myran's heart was filled with a joy that he had not felt since his boyhood.

He had made up his mind to start running toward the river when he realized that the man he had seen in the glen was standing beside him. The man was gazing over the fresh land with satisfied eyes, deep and confident. A moment later they looked toward Myran. Myran gazed into them and was overcome with a powerful sense of lowliness within. This man was so noble, and his presence so commanding and awesome. He was taller than Myran and wore a purely white robe of a fabric he had never seen before.

Myran recognized him. He felt he should fall down at the King's feet but could not move. So he remained, gazing into the strongest yet tenderest gaze he had ever beheld.

"Welcome, Myran Cai." The beautiful voice seemed to usher forth a wave of love and warmth. "You have journeyed far, but the journey is not yet ended; it has only just begun."

"I am tired." Myran's weary voice sounded puny compared to that of the Great King's. He had been through so many trials, through pain and tears. "Can I stay?"

"You must return to Avross. Theadrin will need you." The compassionate eyes remained on him.

Myran felt again the weight of his guilt. "I am afraid I would fail again. He would be better off without me."

The King's expression was full of understanding. "I know what it is to carry such weight, Myran Cai. I have borne the sin of the world on my shoulders."

Myran looked at him. Unshed tears rose in his eyes and he cried out, "I cannot carry it any longer; it is too much!"

"Then let it go." The simple answer surprised Myran. "Give it to me." The King told him and extended a hand.

"I…I can't." Myran stammered, gazing down at the well-muscled hand. "It is my burden. I deserve it, for Ao-idh's death was my fault."

"Ao-idh is home." The King smiled and indicated the direction across the river.

Myran's heart lifted suddenly. "I must see him! I have to tell him how sorry I am!"

"It is not your time. You are chosen for a task that is not yet completed." Then the King stepped closer, inclining his hand further. With eyes so deep and forgiving he said, "Ao-idh's task was finished. I called him home."

These words hit Myran like a blow from a battle shield. He looked once more at the hand of the King and slowly reached out and took hold of it. Something snapped, like an invisible rope that bound him. Myran fell to his knees before the Mighty One in sweet release. Instantly waves of peace followed, crashing over him. With unspeakable joy he realized that the burden of guilt had fallen off. He didn't know how long he knelt there, thanking the Holy One and worshiping, but he felt a gentle touch on his shoulder.

"You must return now," said the Great King.

Myran did not want to leave. The world from which he had come seemed a dim shadow compared to this. It was fallen and corrupt. He did not want to go back to the painful and lonely life where people were greedy, selfish, and ignorant. "I want to go home," he pleaded. "I don't want to go back."

"The time will come, Myran Cai, when you shall be called home to rest in the country of My Father; but now you have a task at hand. Go." The King watched him and allowed a reaffirming smile. Then he added, "You must return to the Tor. *In the deepest dark of the highest height*, there was cast the kingly light. Then return to Avross by way of Monivea."

Myran looked down, and then his eyes strayed again to the green land across the river. His heart ached to cross its waters and forever be home. The King stepped closer to him and laid a firm hand on Myran's shoulder.

"Rejoice, you are not alone; I am with you always. I know what is in the darkness; the light dwells with me."

The touch placed in Myran a strange sensation, something that could not be explained through mere words. He looked into the eyes of the One before him again and the feeling intensified. The King held the gaze for a time and then stepped past him. Myran again saw the great mountain city towering higher than any other object.

Then, from somewhere, a thick fog began to appear and obscure the shining city from his view. He tried to run toward it, so not to be taken from it, but he could not force his legs to move.

Then it was completely taken from his sight, and he began to weep; for he realized then that all his life he had been searching for that place. Now when it was in his grasp, it was whisked away again, as though he had been trying to grasp dust on the wind.

The King was no longer there, but he heard his last words echo through his mind, *The light dwells with me.*

Then all was gray. He closed his eyes, put his head down, and gripped it with his hands in sorrow of losing sight of that blessed place. He suddenly felt lightheaded and took a steadying step to the side. His vision dimmed as he felt himself begin to fall. All became black.

When he came to once again, the sound of rushing water filled his ears. He was on his back and staring up into the high-swaying branches of aged oaks. His right hand felt the ground beneath him and he discovered he was lying on thick moss.

Myran slowly raised his head and glanced about. The place seemed familiar. There was a waterfall that spilled over rock steps of brown and gray into a deep azure pool. After rubbing his eyes, he looked up to the top of the waterfall where there was a rock outcropping surrounded by bright-green foliage. He must have fallen from up there, and it must be there that he had seen the land of the Highest King.

If he could climb back up, perhaps he would still be there. Then, to his right, he heard a light footstep and turned. His eyes landed on a man no taller than his waist, and memory suddenly flooded his head. He remembered how he had drank the wine and been poisoned. It was Tagin who stood there, a leather bag slung over his shoulder.

"Ri es chiv!" He exclaimed exuberantly when he saw Myran up on his elbows.

"Where am I, Tagin?" Myran asked, greatly confused.

"Yusin Abwi." Tagin allowed a relieved smile and came forward.

Myran blinked and looked at the waterfall again. He realized now it was the same place they had camped when Mathwin had become feverish. This thought brought remembrance that Mathwin was the one who brought him to the Avyrian.

That was the last thing he recalled, however, before he had lost all consciousness.

Myran recollected all of this as he and Mathwin left the forest and came once again to the base of the Tor.

Tagin told him that the Avyrian were doubtful that the healing water could make him well. They thought him too far gone, but Tagin and Mathwin had brought him there anyway.

Mathwin had been asleep behind Myran against a tree. He had stayed with Myran at the pool, but Myran's breathing had become so faint that Mathwin thought life had left him.

Indeed, Myran wondered if he had in fact truly died, or at least stood on the extreme brink. He realized with certainty that the shining city he had beheld was the city of the Highest King. Ao-idh had told him of the place once; that all the true and faithful who died went to live with the King there forevermore.

Tagin provided Myran and Mathwin with a bag containing food enough to see them to Arinon, and the two said farewell. Before setting out, he filled his water skin with water from the pool. Tagin and Mathwin watched him curiously but did not question him.

When he returned and tied it to his belt, he asked Tagin, "Has there been any word from Caed since Mathwin and I arrived? He went missing at the Tor."

Tagin frowned. "We not see him after you left. Did he find you?"

Myran froze and looked at Tagin. "Caed did not come back here with a stag?" Tagin shook his head. "We must hurry, Mathwin, time does not wait for us."

Myran was truly sorry to have to say good-bye, for Tagin had become a good friend to him. But he knew he had to get back with all haste. He had to help Theadrin, who was going to face the hardest battle he had yet known. And he wanted to see Lianna again...more than ever.

The Avyrian provided them with a boat of special craft, one that was built for speed. With it they could get through Baremar in a long day.

They crossed the river and climbed the grassy slope of the Tor in the light of a late morning. It did not appear nearly as foreboding with the sun shining upon it. Perhaps, since Amlek had left the darkness had gone with him. In golden shower of the rising sun, the Tor's appearance was magnificent. Beads of dew gleamed upon green carpet that rolled over the Tor. At the top Myran momentarily paused to look out at the surrounding country, trying to imagine it as it might have been in the day when the seven tribes lived there.

Inside Myran told Mathwin the words of the Highest King; the ancient prophesy of the King Sword. "In the deepest dark of the highest height. The Tor is the highest ground," Myran glanced around them. "There has to be a passage of some kind that leads down into its heart."

They searched through the halls and chambers until finding a room with a gaping black hole in the back corner. They inspected it and discovered chiseled steps fading into the darkness.

Mathwin looked at Myran who nodded once, indicating that they had found the place they were looking for. Mathwin went first, holding a torch, but the deeper they went it grew more apparent that its light did them little good. The blackness of the passage seemed to swallow the dull flickering torchlight as though it were a living thing.

The lighting grew so poor that Mathwin stumbled and the torch went out. They stood in total darkness, thick and oppressive.

Myran fumbled around and found his pouch and pulled out his two stones of light. With a quick strike they flashed brightly and filled the entire tunnel. Mathwin gazed about in wonder and slowly stood back up. Myran took note of the veins of metal in the chiseled wall that glowed from the light of the minaw and illmal.

After following the long tunnel leading ever downward, they came at last to a huge cavern. "The heart of the Tor." Myran whispered. "The deepest dark."

"What are we looking for?" Mathwin asked.

"We will know it when we see it." Myran returned confidently.

They combed the bottom of the cave, using the stones of light when they were needed, searching through the rocks and boulders. When a lengthy search had turned up nothing, Mathwin spoke first, "There is nothing here."

Myran rubbed a hand over his mouth and swept the cavern with his eyes. Was he missing something in the words of the prophecy? The deepest dark...*Deep and hidden things will be revealed*...Hidden.

Still scanning the room, he asked Mathwin, "If you were to hide something of great value down here, where would you do so?"

Mathwin scratched his beard. "It would have to be covered and out of sight."

Myran nodded.

"The only thing in this blasted cave are boulders," Mathwin observed. Their eyes connected momentarily and then went to the pile of heavy boulders in the middle of the cavern.

They went to it and began hauling off the heavy rocks. With a groan they together rolled out one of the bottom rocks and half of the pile toppled away. Clearing it out a little more they found a crevice in the floor.

Myran struck the light stones together above the opening. It wasn't very deep, but it was narrow. So Myran put his arm in as deep as he could reach. He rummaged through smaller stones and finally his hand grasped a long, wrapped bundle. He carefully pulled it up and out of the cleft. Upon drawing it out of its leather wrapping, both men caught their breath. In his hand Myran held a magnificent, beautiful sword. Its blade was made of the same metal they had seen in the tunnel, ember iron, but it did not glow. The handle was gold and it was well weighted.

"Mathwin," Myran breathed in awe, "this is the King Sword."

Forty-Two

As Theadrin neared the gate, he heard the blast of a trumpet from the top of the wall. At its sound the people rose as one and began to leave their tents and camps to stream through the huge gates. Many had come to see the new man who had saved them from Gurn.

Theadrin dismounted and continued to the open gates on foot. The crowd press soon enveloped him and he was pulled along inside but came to a halt in the large square before the cathedral. The crowd filled the entire area.

The sky was clouded over, and there was a chilly breeze wafting through the streets. People murmured to each other, excited to see the man. They took no notice of Theadrin standing in their midst, though if they truly looked some might have recognized him.

Nothing happened directly. Morning dwindled on until at last the cathedral doors swung slowly open and a column of priests strode out. It was the same scene Theadrin had seen more than a year before when he first came to the city.

The high priest was in the front, striding erect and pompous. He halted on the stone platform. The look in his eyes was that of arrogance and pride, and it made Theadrin's blood boil. It was as if he had just won a great victory and had come out to gloat.

"Today you will know who is God in heaven," Theadrin whispered under his breath.

When their observation of the swelling crowd seemed to have been satisfied, the high priest motioned to one of the lower priests who held tightly to a small horn. At the signal, the priest, a long faced man with a bent nose, brought the horn to his lips and blew several high-keyed blasts. Theadrin recognized him as well, the one he had struck in the nose when he was rescuing Cadi. He smiled, remembering how good it had felt.

The horn blasts were meant to silence the people and gain their attention, but it was hardly needed. After the long wait the crowd had endured, just their approach served to gather attention. Satisfied with the result, the high priest began to speak.

"Arinon!" He called grandly as he addressed them. "You all know me. I am the high priest of this glorious temple. But there is one who you do not know, and yet he has saved you from certain death. I know there is not a man, woman, or child among you that does not wish to know this great one." His words drew some murmured agreement.

"Indeed," he continued, "today he shall be revealed to you. Knowing well your eagerness, I will not needlessly detain you from this desire." So saying, he turned about and, facing upward toward the temple doors, raised both of his hands and went down on his knees.

All of the lesser priests mimicked his actions. Theadrin saw and recognized what was about to happen. This was the point of no return, and he had to act now or it would be too late.

So, heart racing and palms sweating, Theadrin shoved his way through the crowd calling out, "Stop! Wait!"

He gained the steps and mounted them in several long bounds before reaching the platform. The high priest was instantly on his feet. "What are you doing? Who..."

Theadrin looked at him and the high priest's angered expression fell away. "Theadrin. Where have you been, boy? You were expected to come sooner." A wicked smile curved his lips showing his white teeth.

Theadrin glared at him. "No more shall you defile this place with your heinous acts. It shall once again be holy."

The high priest chuckled mockingly. "You have no authority here. If you think you can do anything about it, go ahead and try," he challenged. "You will find you are too late. The people do not want you anymore. Go ahead, speak to them."

Theadrin stared at him with a fierce gaze before facing the crowds. "My people!" he called. It was then that the people began to recognize him.

"Theadrin has returned!" "It is Theadrin!" "Look!" "He has come back!" some said excitedly. Others grumbled and uttered unkindly words. The majority, however, watched him with lifeless eyes in silence.

Theadrin put up his hand to quiet and gather their attention. "Hear me! Good people of Arinon, listen! This place was once the house of the Living God, the Highest King. Who among you holds grievance against our great King, that you would look to another? How has it come to this?" He looked at them, hoping that his words would spark them to life or at least make them start to think, but the people only stared at him with mute expressions.

Swallowing his mounting apprehension, Theadrin continued. "You are about to witness the revealing of none other than Amlek!" This surely would shock them out of their lifeless daze. But they remained as before.

Theadrin's eyes swept the sea of faces sorrowfully. It was then he noticed the lone rider approaching the city on the road. The man dismounted and began to push his way through the throng toward Theadrin. It was Yan. Yan had come, but unaccompanied. No one else from Caulguard was with him.

Heavy hearted, he cried out to the people, willing them to see. "Open your eyes to the truth, people of Arinon! Amlek is he who required the sacrifices of your children!

"Though I am still young, all of my days I have never seen the true servants of the Highest King lack for anything; especially protection. Here in this dark hour he has not abandoned us."

Someone from the throng called back. "Then where is he? I have not seen him! Where was his protecting hand when hundreds were slain and thousands put out of their homes? Why would he allow such to happen? Answer me that!"

Theadrin found the man and locked eyes with him. "Many afflictions come to those who hold on to the truth, but their King will deliver them from all of it."

"Well, he is too late, I say!" The farmer shouted. A few others voiced agreement.

Yan finally succeeded in digging his way through the crowd and climbed the steps to join Theadrin.

Theadrin looked at him sadly. "You did not have to come, Yan," he said quietly.

Yan did not answer but remained rooted where he stood.

Faithful Yan, Theadrin thought, and allowed his friend a half-hearted smile.

The high priest was enjoying Theadrin's predicament immensely. "Go on," he goaded, "keep trying."

Theadrin implored to the people once again. "It is not too late, people of Arinon. Turn aside from your course. Do not be deceived."

"You are the deceived one!" The farmer, who had spoken before, accused back. "You cannot see that the Highest King has abandoned Arinon! Amlek has just saved us! We know that we can trust him!"

"I cannot make you see." Theadrin told the man directly. "If you do not love the truth, you cannot understand." So saying he turned his speaking to the whole of the crowd. "Amlek is not for you! Do not believe the lie! You will all die under him! The truth…"

"Truth!" the farmer mocked loudly. "We do not want truth! We choose security under Amlek! Away with the Highest King!"

At that moment another voice called out. It was weak but most everyone heard it. "I choose Truth! The Highest King!" Theadrin found the owner, slumped against the wall of a building not far away. He recognized the blind beggar whom he had helped on his first time coming to Avross.

No one else took up the call, and Theadrin grieved. Of all the people amassed, only a blind old beggar could see the truth. Then, a moment later, a farmer shoved his way from the crowd and said in a raspy voice, "I too stand for the Highest King!" He was a shorter man with white hair, and carried a stout oak staff. He came up the stairs and stood before Theadrin.

"I am Aethelbeorn. I stand with ye, my king," he said, placing a fist to his chest.

Theadrin put a hand on the man's shoulder. "Thank you, my friend. We stand alone, so be it."

"More are comin', m'lord." Yan informed him. "I came ahead, but the people a' Caulguard'll be here."

"They are coming?" Theadrin felt relief.

Yan nodded. "I apol'gize. Thought ya knew."

The high priest came forward with a jeering laugh.

"You say you serve this Highest King; you follow truth. Ha!" He seemed giddy, drunk almost. "Listen to me Arinon! This little king does not know what truth is! He does not know the Highest King!"

The crowds looked on and Beorn's eyes darted toward him. The high priest kept on. "I asked him once, but he had no answer! He was speechless!" He laughed again. Directing his attention to the three before him, he spat. "Your God is not real!"

Theadrin faced him as a hot fire leapt up in his eyes.

"Who is he? Can't you tell us?" The high priest defied Theadrin and swept his hand toward the people. "Tell everyone if you can!"

"He is God in heaven. He is the Strong and Mighty, and has already won the victory." Theadrin began to move toward the high priest, his voice building in intensity. "He is the Purifier and Refiner and will purify and refine his house."

The high priest started backing away as Theadrin advanced, a look of growing fear mounting in his eyes.

"He is the Almighty. He is the Light of the Morning. He is the Truth! And the light of Truth dwells with him!"

Theadrin halted, towering over the cringing man whose eyes were wide. "Every knee must bow before his awesome might! Even those who blaspheme his holy name!"

Suddenly the high priest seemed to be struck by an invisible force and fell on his face, screaming loudly, "No! No!"

The people started to murmur to one another and the other priests could only watch with mouths agape.

True to Yan's assurance the people from Caulguard, led by Brond, had arrived at the gate and seen the spectacle. Theadrin was encouraged at the sight for all had come.

His attention was drawn away when a voice boomed from the top of the stairs. "Enough!" All eyes looked to see the tall, dark-haired young man standing rigid with arms raised. Vithimere took a step down and halted, gazing over the scene with a burning fire in his eyes. Theadrin saw him and his fast beating heart seemed to stop cold.

It was Caed! Caed looked at him and started to come forward. "Theadrin, you should not have come back."

"Caed!" Theadrin realized the betrayal.

"Step down, Theadrin. This is a fight you cannot win." Caed descended several steps and stopped again. "I am sorry, Theadrin. It is over for you. You never did have a chance from the beginning." He paused. "Stand down, and your life may be spared."

Theadrin became enraged. "Traitor!"

Caed's smile was sinister. "My men came across a dark-haired young woman riding alone and brought her back here to Avross. You should have told me your sister was so beautiful." His eyes carried a darkness that Theadrin had never noticed before.

"I will be sure to tell your sister that you died bravely when this day is over." Caed put a hand on his sword handle.

Theadrin took an angry step forward. Caed stepped aside and looked up at the doors of the cathedral. Theadrin looked and beheld another figure stepping from the shadows within, and he froze. Ushered forth by a burst of hot flames before the doorway, the one called Amlek emerged. The people gasped and cringed at the magnificent display.

The clouds seemed to darken in the late afternoon sky. A chill fell over the city and silence descended upon the gray square.

The priest with the bent nose called out. "Behold! Amlek in the flesh! There is no further evidence needed! Amlek is god!"

The one farmer who had spoken against Theadrin rose up. "You see? He comes forth with signs and wonders! Why serve one we cannot see? Bow before Amlek!"

Then, to their everlasting shame, the people knelt. Theadrin looked on them with grief. Only a handful stood, aside from the people from Caulguard.

Theadrin called to them. "Stand with me! Now is the time!"

"Look!" someone standing cried. He turned and his heart sank.

Forty-Three

They came from the eastern hills where they had hidden themselves. The hordes of barbarians were approaching the gates to join the battle against Theadrin. There were so many of them, Theadrin was stunned and couldn't speak. They were outnumbered beyond hope. It was not long before the barbarians flooded through the open gates and into the city.

The square grew quiet as Theadrin looked at the new host of enemy warriors surrounding them. Their appearance was fierce. They were painted with blue designs over most of their bodies, and wore necklaces and armbands strung with the sharp teeth of animals. Their hair was wild and their weapons sharp and ugly.

Theadrin turned and fixed his eyes on Amlek. The old sorcerer called out, "I give you one chance to live. Throw down your weapons and bow to me, or be killed." If he did not heed his words, Theadrin and those who stood with him would surely die.

"Amlek, you know I will never bow to you!" Theadrin answered at last.

"Then you choose death." Amlek said coldly. "And what about the rest of you? Who will bow and live?"

The people looked at one another. They glanced at Theadrin, and at the savage looking warriors ready to kill them in an instant. No one made a move to take Amlek's offer.

The sorcerer realized this and said, "You are all afraid. I can see it in your eyes. Know that if you obey me, you will have no more cause to fear. Arinon's kingship is finished. The King Sword has been lost for too long." Then Amlek put a hand into a fold of his black robes and drew out the blade he had forged.

"With this, a new sword, I will unite all lands!" As the people watched in fearful wonder, Amlek pointed the gleaming, shadow iron blade skyward. Immediately the clouds began to darken. They began to churn and boil like the fiercest of storms. The wind began to pick up and the clouds started to swirl. The swirling clouds came down in a funnel of black smoke engulfing the sword blade.

The people gasped as the smoke vanished, the clouds lightened and settled, and Amlek's blade was wreathed in flame. Theadrin was amazed at the dark power that Amlek possessed. He had not imagined such evil was obtainable.

Frowning up at the sorcerer, Theadrin shouted, "We serve the Highest King. He is God, not you, Amlek!"

Amlek's eyes grew fiery. "My power is greater! You will all see! You have seen nothing yet!"

At that moment, a score of men, all on horseback, mounted the nearest ridge outside the city. Theadrin looked through the open gates as they descended the slope quickly and closed the gap between themselves and the back of the barbarian horde, whose main body was still outside the walls. The sun at that moment split the veil of clouds and its brilliant rays alighted on the streaming banners of Caledon. The mighty force of horsemen swept like a wave into the barbarians.

They all but ran over the top of the surprised enemy, who had no defense against the charge of the mighty warhorses.

Theadrin's men gave a glad cheer for their allied warriors. But the shout died when the enemy warriors within the city walls charged them. Theadrin and his men set to fending off the onslaught.

From where he fought, Theadrin saw Caed running down the stairs calling orders to Percel. The nobleman drew his sword and rushed off into the swarms. Weapon drawn, Caed lurched into the mass of fighting and disappeared.

It was then Theadrin saw the doors swinging to a close. Percel was shutting the gates to keep out the Caledonians. Before he could act against it, Theadrin found himself face to face with Caed.

Angry and desperate, Theadrin thrust his sword at Caed's chest. The strike was easily averted and Caed went on the offensive. With one fluid motion he hooked crossbars with Theadrin and twisted the sword from his grip. Stunned, Theadrin watched his weapon clatter away and found himself guarded by Caed's sharp sword point.

All in the square heard Amlek's loud command, though the battle din was ear shattering. "Enough!"

Caed shouted to Theadrin's remaining warriors, "Cast down your weapons, or I will kill him!"

Yan and the other warriors saw with bewilderment Caed ready to run Theadrin through, and immediately dropped their weapons.

With despair Theadrin watched the huge, impenetrable gates shut. The Caledonians were cut off, and Theadrin's men were outnumbered greatly. Two enemy warriors instantly guarded each one of them.

Amlek descended the steps of the cathedral and walked gloatingly through their midst. He went to the gate and climbed the steps to the stone ramparts above to view the battle still raging outside.

"Bring him up here!" He ordered, pointing at Theadrin. Caed motioned a handful of warriors forward who grabbed Theadrin and pulled him away from the rest of the group. He was hauled roughly up the steps and halted before Amlek.

The man's eyes blazed with anger and malice. Theadrin had expected to see victory gleaming in his eyes, and wondered at it. What did he have to be angry about? He had won.

"Shall I kill him?" Caed's cold voice stung Theadrin's ears.

Amlek's answer surprised him. "No." The dark man took a step forward; his long fingers seized Theadrin's jaw in an icy grip. The strength of it astonished Theadrin.

"Deny your God!" Amlek hissed in his face.

Theadrin then realized why Amlek was angry. Just killing him outright was not enough. He wanted to break him in front of the people to prove that he was indeed more powerful than the Highest King.

"I will die first." Theadrin answered back.

Amlek appeared like he would burst with anger. He looked at Caed and said, "Fetch the prisoners."

Caed left quickly, a look of wicked glee in his eyes. They had not long to wait before he returned. Theadrin saw two men, bound in chains brought forward below with a guard on each arm. They were Anromir and Rhyd. Anromir's chin was split and there was an ugly gash over Rhyd's right eyebrow.

Caed forced them to their knees. He drew his sword. Theadrin attempted to free himself, but one of the enemy warriors struck him hard in the stomach and once in the face. Yan saw this and began to fight back himself. There was a warrior on each arm, however, and they halted his attempts with a rain of blows. Yan dropped to his knees, struggling to keep from losing consciousness.

As Caed made ready to execute the captives, Amlek stopped him. "Not yet! I want them to watch. I want all to see."

The Caledonians still outside the city had reached the gates. Theadrin looked down over them. His eyes searched the foremost horsemen. One seemed familiar the way he sat in the saddle. Squinting through the stinging sweat to see clearer, Theadrin recognized him. Myran!

Amlek stood tall so all could see him and spoke. "I am Amlek, lord of this earth! You will all see how my power is superior to this Highest King you thought to follow. Then you will know how foolish you are."

With these words Amlek struck Theadrin across the face. The warriors about him amply followed his example and began to lay hard blows at Theadrin; beating him to the ground.

"Amlek!" Myran shouted in rage from below the wall.

Rhyd flew into action. He vaulted himself into the stomach of the nearest warrior, sending the man tumbling into two others. The first warrior who tried to restrain him collected an elbow to the nose and stumbled back with a cry.

Anromir took his chance as well, but both were overwhelmed by enemy warriors and pummeled to submission once again. Rhyd was beaten down, and the warriors would have continued on pounding him, but Amlek stopped them.

"I want them alive to see this, you fools!"

So Rhyd was hauled back with the others, bruised and bleeding.

"You have no power greater than my King." Theadrin glared in defiance at Amlek.

The dark sorcerer spoke so all could hear him, repeating his first words. "I am Amlek! Watch as my power overcomes Theadrin and his little God!" Saying this, Amlek lifted his hand in the direction of a burning torch lit on the wall. He cried out a word in a different tongue. The flame on the torch began to shift violently as though a fierce wind was blowing. Amlek began to chant more words in the dark language and the fire suddenly grew. It expanded and heightened, all the while contorting and writhing as though a living thing, until it became a huge, dancing ball of fire.

"No!" Rhyd yelled, struggling again. He was weaker now, and the warriors held him back.

Myran unstrapped the long bundle at his side and swiftly began unwrapping it.

As Theadrin regained his feet, swaying weakly from his injuries, Amlek sent the ball of flame toward him. It moved so quickly he had no reaction time. Theadrin's hand went up in front of his face before the fire struck him, consuming his body from view.

"Theadrin!" Yan yelled in horror. The rest of Theadrin's men stood in mute disbelief and rage.

The huge tongues of hungry flame remained in the place Theadrin stood. Caed laughed out loud and Amlek smiled, lifting his thin hand in triumph. His power was greater, and everyone was there to see it.

"Behold the power of the Highest King!" Amlek mocked.

"Amlek!" Anromir thundered in fury. "I will kill you!"

Suddenly a woman gasped. Something was happening within the heart of the flame.

Myran looked at the ball of fire. He saw, deep within the heart of it, a white light. It started small, like the most distant star, yet grew in intensity and brilliance. With one mighty flash, the ball of flame vanished. Everyone blinked for the forceful brightness of the white flare.

"What is this?" Amlek shrieked.

The light dimmed quickly and took the form of a man. The people gasped anew to see Theadrin standing whole and unharmed. Not a single hair had been scorched. Instead of destruction, the opposite was evident. His dirty, battle stained clothes were gone, and he was dressed in a suit of beautiful new armor, polished and shining. A deep red cloak draped neatly down his back clasped at his shoulder with a golden brooch that was set with a large emerald gem. He appeared taller and his shoulders broader.

To Myran, it seemed even his countenance was altered. Theadrin looked as if the last impressions of uncertainty and insignificance, fearfulness and insecurity were washed away like dirt to reveal the true man hidden underneath.

"No!" Amlek shrieked again and drew out his shadow iron sword. Myran heard him spit out a mouthful of words in the dark tongue, and the sword blade was instantly flaming. He came at Theadrin, lifting it to strike.

"Theadrin!" Myran yelled as he pulled back a sword with all his might and threw the naked blade up into the air. It spun and landed perfectly in Theadrin's extended hand. Bright light flashed as Theadrin's grip closed over it and swung around to block Amlek's attack.

A great, metallic crack resounded, and Amlek's shadow iron blade shattered. Amlek stumbled back and gazed in utter fear at the white glowing sword in Theadrin's hand.

"The King Sword!" a voice cried from the crowd of people. "He holds the King Sword! The sword of Arinon!"

Myran saw Theadrin turn his face from the sword toward Amlek, who frantically raised his hands and began to call out a strain of words in the dark tongue. Theadrin drew back the sword and hurled it at the sorcerer. The gleaming blade burned brilliantly as it sang through the air and pierced Amlek in the heart.

Amlek bent from the force of it and flew against the breastwork of the wall. Caed stared blankly as Amlek attempted to rise, gripping at the shining blade. A moment passed and then Amlek sank back in death.

The enemy and false priests watched in horror and then began to flee as one from the city. Their leader, revered as a god among them, was dead. They frantically unlocked and opened the gate, only to be met by the Caledonian army still outside.

Caed took his opportunity in the mass confusion to slip away.

Theadrin retrieved the King Sword and ran to Anromir and Rhyd. Seeing he could not unlock the chains that bound their wrists, the two lords held the chains against the stone pavement and Theadrin, with a mighty swing, hacked through the iron links. Then he did the same to those around their ankles, and the two were free. The shining blade seared through the chains effortlessly.

Suddenly Percel was there with several of his men. Theadrin ducked swiftly beneath a swing and rammed shoulder first into the chest of the foremost attacker. Anromir was quick to retrieve the fallen man's sword and he flew at Percel. The two fought furiously and Anromir was pushed to the steps. His foot hit the first ledge and he went down. Percel saw his opportunity and swung toward Anromir's head.

But Anromir deflected the blow with the shackle that was still locked on his wrist and thrust upward. Percel cried out and stumbled backward, and then fell to never rise again.

Anromir got up and he and Rhyd stood before Theadrin, who put a hand on each one's shoulder. "My faithful friends." He smiled. "Let us finish this."

"We are with you." Rhyd thumped a hand to his chest. His blue eyes gleamed through the blood and grime over his face.

Theadrin saw Caed running in the direction of the palace and took after him, but it was Beorn who reached him first. Theadrin watched as Caed ducked below a quick swing and parried two other stout raps. Theadrin didn't see the blow, but Beorn stiffened. His staff clattered to the ground and he fell. Caed disappeared amidst the confusion.

Theadrin charged the spot. Myran appeared a second later and saw Beorn. He knelt and bent over the old man. "You fought a good fight, my friend. Rest now. Be at peace." Myran's eyes were hard as Beorn's body relaxed in death. He stood and looked Theadrin's way.

An enemy warrior, running from the Caledonian horsemen, assailed Theadrin in his flight, wielding an ax and a short sword. He attacked furiously and quickly, and Theadrin met each strike.

"Caed!" Theadrin shouted to Myran. "He has my sister in the palace!"

"Leave him to me!" Myran called back as he turned in a run toward the palace.

Theadrin finished off his opponent as two Caledonians approached on horseback. Theadrin recognized the one and greeted him by lifting his sword. "Hail, prince Ruadhan."

The Caledonian prince put a fist to his chest and inclined his head. The man beside him did the same and Theadrin smiled, "Peran!"

"Hail, King Theadrin!" Peran called. His face held an expression of wonder.

Theadrin called to all his men, "Come! The work is not finished!"

He ran inside the cathedral and was followed closely by the two lords and the others. Many warriors and people flocked behind. They went through the building and out to where the sacrificing altar sat. Theadrin mounted the stone dais and began to push. The ugly altar creaked and slowly began to slide. Rhyd reached the spot and aided in pushing it. Anromir was next and then Mathwin. They pushed with all their might.

The heavy stone altar slid across the dais and to the edge. They mustered for one last shove, with Peran joining them, and the altar went over the side. It crashed to the ground far below and shattered to pieces. Everyone cheered greatly at the sight. Theadrin stood in the middle of the platform and, raising his sword, proclaimed, "This place is claimed for the Lord our God. May His name reign forever and may His presence dwell here once more!"

All cheered loudly once again.

Forty-Four

Myran trailed Caed, picking his way through the scattering enemy. He saw him enter the palace and pursued until coming to where the king's chambers were. Running down the hall, he heard a woman's scream come from the room and he quickened his pace. Myran reached the door and rushed inside ready for a fight, but the room was empty. He spun about, searching frantically, but Caed was not there.

Another scream sounded, more distant this time. It came from the direction of the west wall where there hung a heavy crimson curtain. Myran stepped quickly up to it and tore it aside to reveal a hidden passage. Spiraling steps led downward. In a heartbeat he was speeding down them and was brought into the great hall. He paused to scan the huge room.

Caed, accompanied by two strong warriors, was pulling the struggling Lianna through a side door. Myran leapt from the dais and all but flew across the hall. He went through the door that opened up to a long, drawn-out hallway.

He would have caught up to them had not several enemy warriors blocked the way. Myran met them without a single moment's hesitation, plowing through the first two and easily dropping the third with a quick maneuver. Then he was sprinting down the hall which led through another smaller room and then finally outside.

Caed was hauling Lianna, her hands bound, onto the back of a horse when Myran emerged from inside. Lianna saw Myran right away and called out a warning to him. He saw the brawny warrior just in time and caught the man's spear with his sword. Then he spun and hauled the man over his shoulder with mustered strength, the warrior's spear clattered across the paved yard.

The second one came at him, a big man with huge arms, hefting a two handed sword. Myran clashed blades with him. He used the big man's strength against him by guiding a heavy swing to the side. This allowed him plenty of time to bring his hilt up into the face of his enemy. The big man fell unconscious as the first rose for another attack.

Myran finished him off just as easily. "Caed!" he roared. "Release her!"

Caed turned sharply and let go of Lianna. "Myran…" he took two steps away from the horse.

Myran Cai advanced several paces and halted. "It is over, Caed. Leave her and surrender…" Caed's sharp laugh cut him off.

"Only one battle in the midst of many is over," Caed told him.

The anger in Myran's eyes dwindled to remorse. "How long have you been Amlek's man, Caed?"

Caed stared back at him with a scornful frown. "But I have never been his man, Myran," he insisted. "I was using Amlek. I wanted to get closer to Gurn so that I could have my revenge. Gurn was my uncle, Myran." Caed's hard eyes betrayed him for a moment.

"My mother's sudden and strange illness was because Gurn had her poisoned. He was in love with her but she would not return his affection. If he couldn't have her, neither would my father. He ruined my life."

Anger suddenly burned away the sadness that had been in his eyes. "I vowed that I would do the same to him." Caed moved to ready his horse. "I've had my revenge."

Myran looked sadly at Caed. "What about all that Ao-idh taught us?"

"Ao-idh." The name seemed a bitter taste on Caed's tongue. "Ao-idh was too restricting. He would have had us slaves to the

Highest King, with no lives at all. I learned that power and control create a much more satisfying life," Caed answered. He took a step in Myran's direction. "You would find this is true, Myran. Come with me, and we can gain anything. We would be unstoppable. We are brothers, you and I."

"Come out of it, Caed! I cannot do as you ask." He lifted a hand to his old friend imploringly and said, "Come back to the light."

Myran looked in Caed's eyes, but saw no give. Caed sneered back, "Light! Ha! Very well, you have chosen. I care not. Farewell, old friend." Caed turned and started toward his horse.

"I will not let you leave, Caed." Myran's words halted him in his tracks.

There was silence for a moment and then Caed applied a grip on the handle of his sword. He drew it out slowly and faced Myran.

Lianna watched as both men advanced slowly, step-by-step, toward each other. It was Caed who struck first; with such speed that Lianna was surprised Myran was able to parry it. The fight erupted full force as each cut and thrust, every parry and counterstrike, came with swift accuracy.

Sweat poured down each man's brow. They moved about the paved yard. Caed was the quickest on his feet. One moment he was attacking the right and the very next he was on the left. But Myran was ready each time.

The yard rang with the sharp clang of steel. Suddenly Myran moved to the offensive. He accurately hooked swords with Caed at the crossbars and twisted Caed's sword from his grip. Shocked, Caed could only stare at Myran's blade now guarding him as his own clattered away. Heartbeats passed by in stunned silence.

Lianna's scream drew away Myran's attention. An enemy warrior had pulled her off the horse and now held his sword point across her throat. Instantaneously, Myran's hand went to his knife. He pulled the small dagger back behind his ear and, blade straight, sent it spinning. The knife flew perfectly, piercing the man in the head. He fell to the ground not to rise again.

Myran turned just as Caed thrust his dragonhead knife toward his heart. The blade pierced him deep in the shoulder. He cried out in pain.

"Myran!" Lianna screamed.

Caed stepped back as Myran gripped the knife handle in agony. Myran's sword clattered to the ground and he collapsed to his knees.

Caed bent and picked up his own sword and began to pace victoriously around him. "Did it ever occur to you, Myran, how strange it was that Gurn's men were able to find our hidden passage that day? It had never happened before." Caed's words drew Myran's painful gaze.

Caed halted in front of him and spoke in a cold voice, "Ao-idh was restraining me from what I desired. I dealt with him as I will all who try to do the same."

"You, Caed?" Myran's expression was incredulous. "That…that was your doing?"

"Blind as ever, Myran," Caed snarled. He straightened, bringing back his sword arm. Myran held his eyes.

Before Caed could make the finishing strike, something struck him hard in the back. He doubled over. Myran saw the sword sticking out of his back.

Lianna stepped away. Caed rose weakly, gulped air and tried to pull the sword from his back. The pain of this brought a cry from his lungs. He stumbled toward his horse, falling twice.

Myran watched as Caed's foot gained the stirrup. He pulled his torso slowly over the saddle, shaking with pain. Then his body went limp as the horse suddenly took off.

Myran stood up weakly. He took hold of the dagger and, looking away wrenched it from his shoulder. The hurt was excruciating and he fell back to his knees, unable to hold back a groan.

Lianna was at his side, and though her wrists were still bound by cords of thick leather, she helped keep him up. Myran put a hand to his wounded shoulder and looked up to see Caed and his horse disappearing down a side street.

Myran held up the dragon knife and Lianna cut off her bonds with it. Then she laid him back on the stone pavement.

"Lianna…" Myran started to speak but she stopped him.

"Rest, and let me see to your wound," she directed.

Myran protested, but his voice was tired and displayed little strength.

"Shh." Lianna placed a smooth finger on his lips and Myran relented. Then she sat down, folding her legs beneath her, and rested his head gently on her lap.

She bit her lip and tenderly moved away the ripped cloth from around the wound. Blood streamed from it cleanly, and she pressed her kerchief on it. Then, tearing another piece of cloth from the hem of her dress, Lianna made to grab his water skin so that she could soak it.

Myran stopped her. "Wait. Don't use that."

"Why not?"

"It's for another purpose," he told her. "For Caithal."

"There is plenty of water for him." Lianna did not understand.

"Please, Lianna. Trust me. My wound is not fatal, I don't need it." Myran did not know how to explain.

"If you insist." She gave in, still not understanding. So she cleaned the wound as best as she could and he lay exhausted in her lap but unable to take his eyes from her face.

Myran studied the curves of her cheeks and the delicate line of her jaw. He watched her expressions as she worked and saw that she wanted to ask something, but looked as though she was deciding against it.

"What is it?" he asked her.

Her mouth opened a little, but she closed it again.

"You want to know how I am alive." Myran smiled a little and was surprised to see a glint of tears begin to well up in her eyes.

She nodded.

"I promise to tell you everything. For now, all I can say is I have not completed my task; what I was created for."

Lianna blinked to clear her eyes and sniffed. "And what is that?"

"I think I know at least part of it." Myran smiled more broadly. He slowly reached up and took hold of her hand. His was so large compared to Lianna's; and where hers was smooth and untainted, his was rough and battle-scarred.

She stopped her work and their eyes connected. Myran gazed deep into hers and was, for the first time, happy that the Highest King had sent him back. More tears rose unshed in her eyes and she offered a delicate smile.

Myran lost himself in her beauty, oblivious to whatever pain might still be in his shoulder. After a time Lianna shook herself and said, "Here I'm letting you bleed all over yourself." She sniffed, resuming her work once more as Myran rested on her lap.

It was in this way that Theadrin and the others found them.

"I never thought to see you again," Theadrin told Myran. His eyes were still burning with energy.

"Nor I you," Myran answered with a half-smile. "I was sure I was finished."

"I cannot tell you how good it is to see you alive. You will have to tell me everything."

"I will," Myran promised as the corner of his mouth lifted in a smile.

"I am gathering the warriors who can still fight and riding with Ruadhan to chase the remains of the barbarians from our lands," Theadrin said.

"I will get ready." Myran moved to get up, but Lianna pressed him back down.

"You are not going," she told him, and looked at Theadrin with sharp warning in her eyes.

"I am afraid my sister is right," Theadrin said, glancing at her and holding back a smile. "You are not in any way conditioned for any more fighting for a good while. You will have to stay behind while your wound heals. Rest." He placed a reaffirming hand on Myran's good shoulder.

Myran looked from one to the other of them and knew they would have their way. So he gave in and let Lianna finish with the bandage.

Forty-Five

While Theadrin was gone, Myran, under the watchful eye of Lianna, was well on the mend. He did, however, insist on riding to Caulguard to give Caithal the water that he had taken from the pool.

When Theadrin returned, Caithal was already able to stand and walk about the room. The color was back in his face and the old familiar twinkle back in his eyes.

They sat about the hearth in the great hall of the palace late one evening and Myran told Theadrin of his vision of the Highest King, his return to the Tor to find the King Sword, and his detour into Caledon. He told of fighting with Ruadhan and King Brudwyn in a battle to defeat the traitor Dathin. Afterward, they had ridden immediately for Avross, arriving just in time.

Theadrin looked contentedly around at his friends. They had endured much together and a deep fellowship had grown between them all.

"You went to the Tor, Caithal." Theadrin leaned on the arm of his chair and asked, "Why did you never tell me?"

The old man returned his look and said, "I journeyed north when your father was king. Valdithin and I studied the mystery of our heritage, but I never actually made it to the Tor itself. I met and stayed with the Avyrian." He then looked at Myran, "And the relic you gave me, Myran—the Dorrani chieftan's knife handle—it contained a written copy of the complete prophesy."

"You sent me to the Tor to find the King Sword," Theadrin added as he sipped a hot drink.

Caithal continued, "When I discovered that copy in the broken knife handle, everything I had studied before came together. I knew if you went it would be found. It accorded with the prophecy." Caithal's eyes glimmered with wisdom as he continued, "I told you once that we must learn to hear and to heed." He leaned toward Theadrin as he spoke in a voice full of passion. "The Highest King speaks to his people, Theadrin. As a king and a leader it is vital that you draw close enough to hear his voice; and not just to hear, but to heed and obey that which you are told."

Theadrin nodded. He felt a quickening in his spirit at the words of his friend. He felt as though some form of energy coursed through him, and it left him with a feeling of excitement. In that moment, he felt a burning desire to speak to the Highest King and hear him speak.

Theadrin smiled. "It is good to see you well and back to yourself again, my friend." He rose from his seat. "Please excuse me, friends," he said and then retired to his room.

Several days later, after much preparation and planning, Theadrin's coronation was held. The interior of the great hall was decorated beautifully. King Brudwyn came, and Ruadhan and Merion with him.

Roryn the hunter also came along with his wife and Peran. All of Theadrin's good friends were there, and the hall was filled to bursting with people. As Theadrin drew and held the King Sword, the light began to dance in its blade, and Caithal crowned him with a blessing:

> May your reign be long and prosperous. May the sun shine down upon you, and may the rain always water your lands. May the Almighty regard you with favor. May he grant you your heart's desire and fulfill all of his plans for you. May he answer you when you call. May you always look

to the Great Light to guide you, and may the joy of his name be your strength. May you fear the Lord, and forever look to the Strong Tower to defend you. May you lead the people in wisdom under the sovereign authority of the Highest King. And may you always love his Truth.

After his crowning, the people cheered greatly. He stood from the throne and quieted them.

"It would be wrong to accept the honor and glory of this day for myself. Let us remember those who gave their lives so that we could see this day." He paused and looked over the faces, finally resting on Myran.

He then continued, saying, "Let us also remember those who have fought for truth and are still with us. Lord Anromir of Caulguard, come forward."

Anromir sat beside his wife, Ellia, and stood when he was called. He looked back down at her and she nodded, smiling. Then he moved slowly up to the dais where Theadrin waited. The people cheered him as he came to stand in front of the newly crowned king.

Theadrin smiled and placed a hand on his shoulder. Then he called out again. "Rhyd of Averby."

Hesitantly, Rhyd came forward. He ascended the dais rigidly. Theadrin put his other hand on Rhyd's shoulder. "Faithful Rhyd. Anromir has not failed in telling me of your devotion while I was away. Well done, my friends. As your reward for your faithfulness and bravery, your lands will be increased."

Another cheer resounded. "And," Theadrin continued, "you will be the first two in my new order of mighty men, for such you are. May you be blessed."

As they moved to stand beside him, Theadrin called out again. "Yan and Mathwin, come forward."

The two men lumbered up to the front and stood before him. "Both of you, who like myself were only simple peasants, will also be accounted among my mighty men. Well done, both of you. May the Great Light always shine upon you with favor."

The two could hardly believe it. Theadrin smiled widely at their reaction and motioned them to stand beside Anromir and Rhyd. Then he called Caithal to him.

"I do not know what to give you, Caithal. Anything you ask and I shall do it. But one thing I shall offer, that you become bishop of Penred's Cathedral. And also that you live here in the palace."

Caithal bowed his head in acceptance. "Thank you. I will accept it, but nothing more."

Theadrin smiled, then turned to the people once again. "Myran Cai."

The tall young man, with his arm in a sling, walked rigidly up to the dais. Theadrin put both of his hands gently on Myran's shoulders and gazed into his eyes. "Most courageous of men. No one among us has given more than you."

"That is not true, my lord."

"Theadrin. Never shall you have to call me anything but by name in any circumstance. To you I give the position of third highest in the kingdom, answerable only to myself and the Highest King. You also shall be among my mighty men and shall be given lands of your own.

Myran looked at Theadrin speechless. Theadrin beamed. "What do you say to that, brother?"

Myran did not know how to answer. He did not want such position. He did not want the restrictions of it upon him. "I…I cannot take it," he told Theadrin.

"Nothing would please me more than to have you accept, Myran; to have your wisdom and judgment for all of my days as king."

Myran did not answer at first. He looked down for a moment and then up at Theadrin again. "Then I will accept, Theadrin."

The smile broadened across Theadrin's face, mostly out of relief. He continued to reward others, giving out gifts to all of the warriors who had fought for him.

As a victory feast was being set up, many of the people danced on the large veranda outside the great hall to music. Theadrin came up to stand beside his sister and watched his people.

"This is a good day, Lianna," he beamed happily.

Lianna nodded, but her attention was occupied elsewhere. Theadrin followed her gaze and saw Myran making his way through the people. He came to stand before Cadi, and Theadrin saw him bow and offer his hand to her. Little Cadi smiled shyly and glanced at Lianna. Then she lightly took his hand and Myran led her to where the dancers were.

Theadrin laughed out loud. "That is a sight I never imagined I would see!"

Lianna was smiling as she appraised Myran's performance. "He is too stiff," she critiqued.

Theadrin looked at his young sister. "Perhaps you should go show him how it is properly done."

Lianna shook her head. "I would not interrupt Cadi's dream."

Theadrin leaned close. "I think you would actually be saving her; Myran is no dancer."

The feast was announced ready and the people came inside. The trays and platters, overflowing with delicacies, and the jars and pitchers of drinks came endlessly. And after that, everyone went to the cathedral where Caithal led a rededication of the building to the Highest King.

Hundreds of candles had been lit and the place glowed red-gold. The booths were filled and extra chairs brought, and still everyone could not fit inside. All wanted to be there.

Theadrin stood with Lianna, Cadi, and Myran in the front row. The peace that filled that place was unlike what anyone there had ever experienced.

Caithal stood before the people and prayed. His words reached the innermost parts of the people and many wept for the beauty of the awesome presence filling the huge room.

"Abide with us," he prayed, his face lifted heavenward. "This eventide and always, gracious King. Even when days of darkness deepen about us and we lose all comforts, remain always with us."

Theadrin listened to the words and prayed them in his heart. With each one he felt more peace and joy than the word before. He felt his heart would burst within him. The presence of the Most High was so powerful that night that Theadrin felt if he opened his eyes he would see his King standing bodily in their midst.

They remained there hours into the night. There was not one person there who was not touched deeply and amazingly by the Master.

Myran and Lianna were wed several weeks later. Under the shading oak boughs of Arinon's green summer forest, the marriage was held. It was a small gathering, only their closest friends attended, and Caithal was the one who wed them.

The previous night there had been a heavy rain which had lessened during the early morning hours, and now a silvery mist was forming over the waters of the small lake behind them. The scent of the forest was strong and refreshing.

Myran, standing a head taller than Lianna, could not help but gawk down at her. She was dressed in a long deep-green gown with pure white sleeves. A belt of braided gold was about her slender waist and a scarlet cloak was clasped at her neck. A golden brooch clasped it together with a design of interwoven flowers. Her long, dark hair curled down the back of her shoulders and was crowned by two delicate braids clasped around the back of her head. She had never appeared so elegant and beautiful, and Myran could not tear his eyes away from the sight of her.

Lianna gazed back up into Myran's bronze eyes and smiled. The light, which for so long had been absent and replaced with cold sorrow, once more burned bright and fierce. It was stronger than it had ever been before.

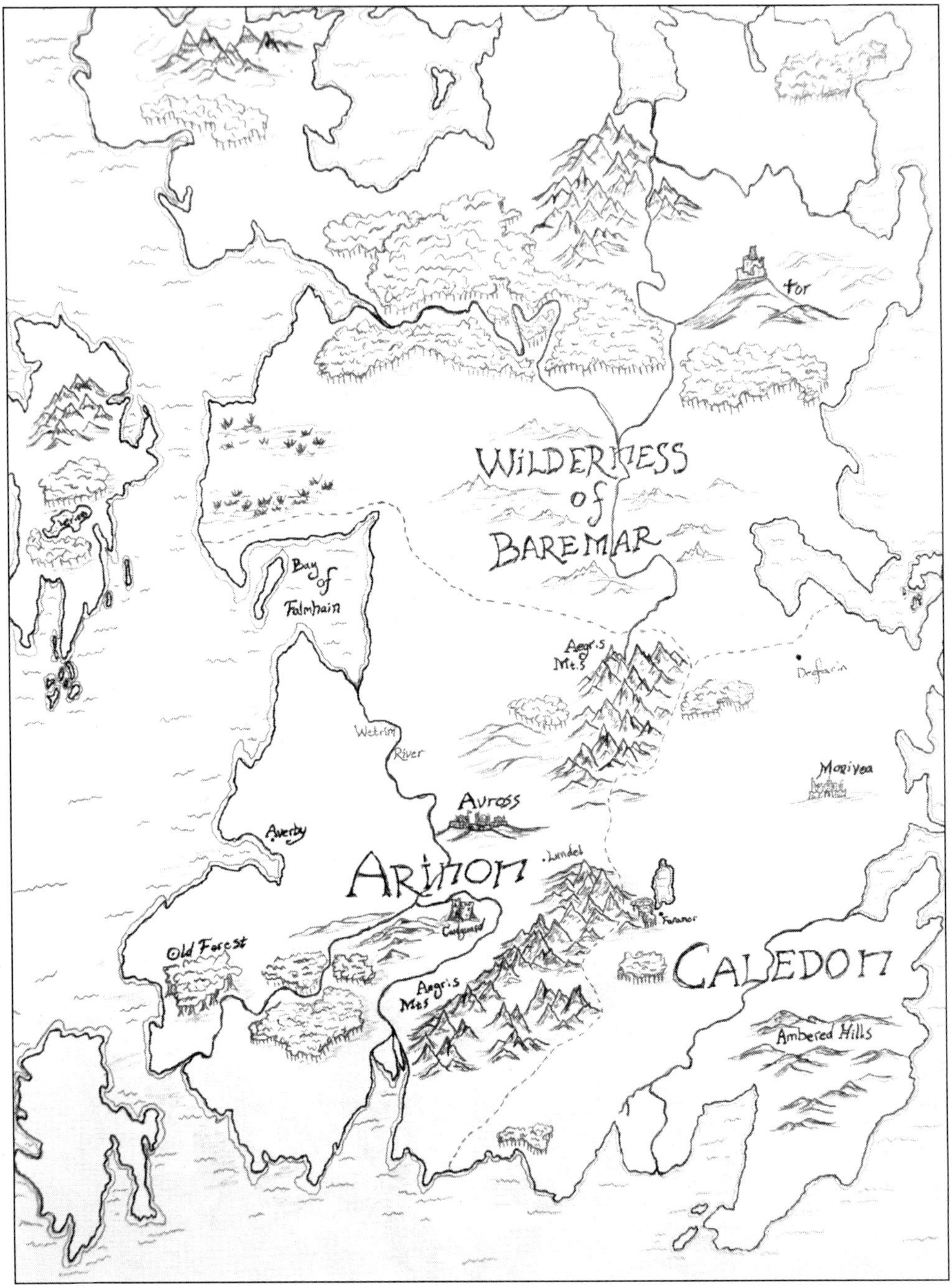

Tor
WILDERNESS
of
BAREMAR
Bay
of
Falmhain
Aegr.s
Mt.s
Wetrim
River
Moriyea
Auross
Averby
Arinon
Lundel
Old Forest
Aegris
Mts
CALEDON
Ambered Hills

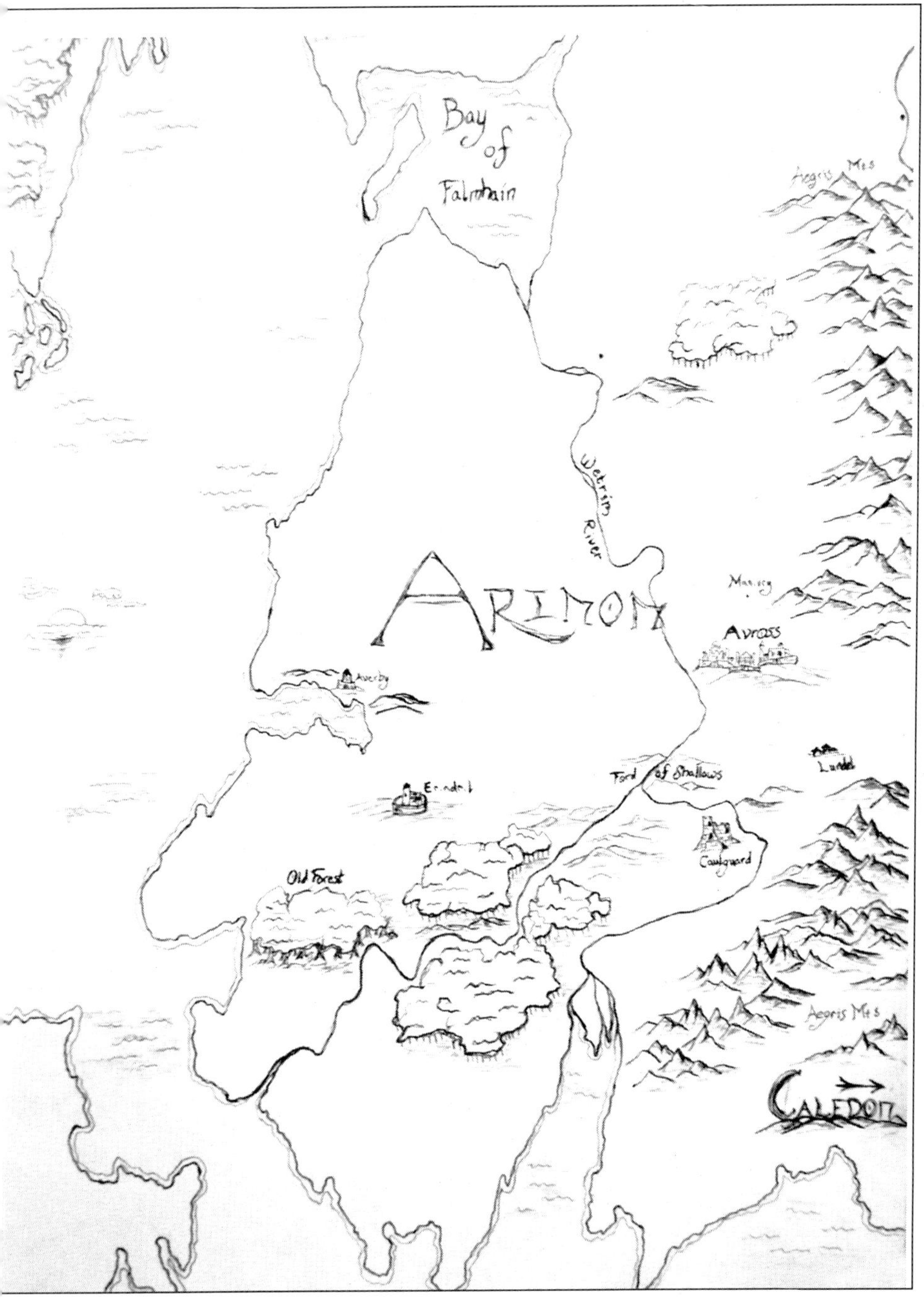
Bay of Falmhain
Aegris Mts
Webrin River
Arinon
Avross
Averby
Ford of Shallows
Caulguard
Old Forest
Aegris Mts
Caledon

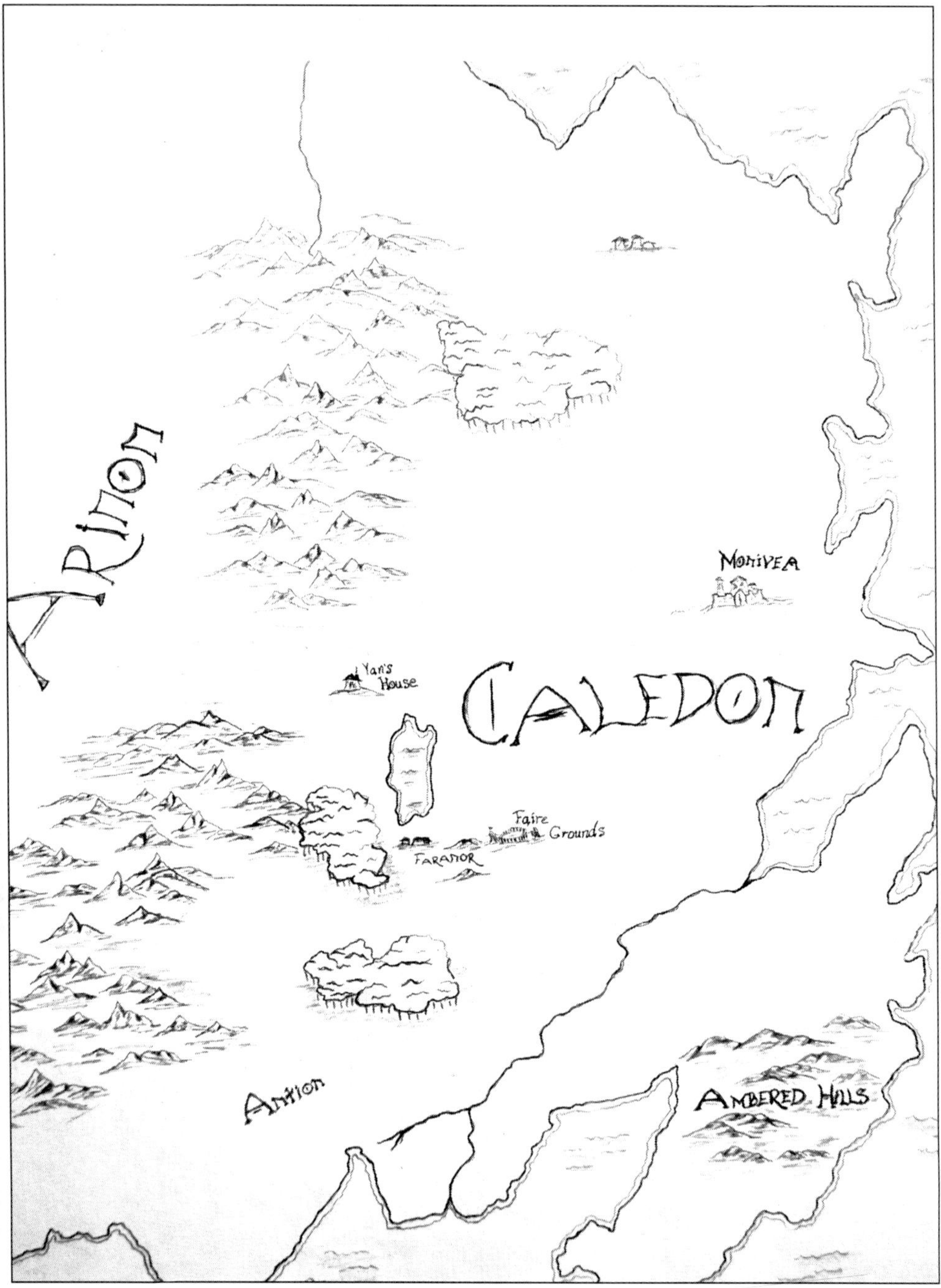